Pheidippides  very spot where he ~~~~~ ~~~~~~~~~~~ ~~~ pulling away from the shores of Marathon. Now, garbed only in a sleeveless white tunic of light muslin and green britches that came down just below his knees, the leather marching sandals on his feet, he stared out at the foggy waters. Through the glistening early afternoon haze, he made out the silhouetted shapes of enemy galleys reforming for a southward course.

He shivered despite the rising afternoon humidity and heat as he envisioned the absolute horror of those very warships beaching at the port of Phaleron, only a short march from Athens. He thought of the many inhabitants of that grand city as the massive Persian army descended on them. And he knew, in his heart, it was unlikely the Athenian army would have time to mobilize here in the wake of so violent a struggle and hasten homeward in time. The young foot courier trembled in the knowledge that he alone was the one hope for Athens to muster a standing force that might yet hold Darius' savage hordes at bay till Milteades and his militia arrived to mete out Greek justice once more.

Perhaps.

Praise for *THE SAGA OF MARATHON*

"Nicholas Checker's *The Saga of Marathon* combines all the best elements of the Pheidippides story with overtones of modern political drama. His youthful hero has mom and dad issues, troubling friends, and no shortage of self-doubt. Yet he's compelled to complete his quest by a deep commitment to the Athenian ideals, under threat from a totalitarian outsider. The hills are long and hard, and the stumbles many, but Pheidippides refuses to give up. The first marathoner is born, and democracy survives."

~Amby Burfoot, Winner, 1968 Boston Marathon
Longtime editor of Runner's World Magazine

The Saga
of
Marathon

by

Nicholas Checker

Historical Fable Checker

Nicholas

The Saga of Marathon

Cover Art by *Jennifer Greeff*

The Wild Rose Press, Inc.
PO Box 708
Adams Basin, NY 14410-0708
Visit us at www.thewildrosepress.com

Publishing History
First Mainstream Historical Edition, 2020
Trade Paperback ISBN 978-1-5092-3180-5
Digital ISBN 978-1-5092-3181-2
Historical Fable
based on the author's stage play *Run to Elysia*
Published in the United States of America

Dedication

To family members, my parents especially,
and friends who have long encouraged
my writing pursuits;
to everyone ever involved with
my musical stage version of this story, *Run to Elysia*—
the premise from which I adapted my novel;
to the memory of
the angelic Samantha Deglin (an original cast member)
who runs forever in the Fields of Elysia;
to the late John J. Kelley,
in whom the spirit of Pheidippides dwelled…
and still does;
and to everyone who still believes
that a promise is sacred.

Acknowledgments

In acknowledgment, I would like to thank Rick Spencer for the beautiful music and lyrics he composed for *Run to Elysia*; cast member Valerie Azlynn for the gift of the "Greek Treasure Chest" that inspired me to keep writing about Ancient Greece; my two test readers and dear friends, Steve Loyd and Tim Valliere, for always believing and always helping, and to Steve's family—Cheryl, Katie, and Matt; Eileen Morehouse and Jack Morehouse for a lifetime of support in my arts endeavors; my older sister Verna for her contribution to this work; the memory of my two other older sisters, Carole and Rene; my twin nephews, Harold and Bobby Joyce, for believing; Mitch Cote, Carin Estey, Noah Todd, and Erin Sousa Stanley for helping resurrect this tale; the late Billie Johnson (publisher of former Oak Tree Press) for bringing my first two novels, *Druids* and *Scratch*, into publication; Amby Burfoot for urging me to put my *Saga of Marathon* project ahead of all the others; Jeanne & Steve Sigel of the Garde Arts Center; Lee Howard and Rick Koster of The Day newspaper; Bank Square Books; Kato McNickle, Michael Bradford, Linda MacCluggage, Peter Marcus, David Tetzlaff, Nancy Hoffman; screenwriters Peter and Jason Filardi; and Nan Swanson - Historical Editor, Jennifer Greeff - Cover Artist, Dianne Rich - Copy Editor, and the entire company of The Wild Rose Press, Inc. (especially co-founders Rhonda Penders and RJ Morris) for believing in my work.

Chapter One

A Courier Yearns...A Tyrant Plots

The slender teenage boy sucked in another breath and pressed on over the narrow marshland path, imagining he was en route to Athens for a good deal more than delivering a sack of herbs to the city's healers. He imagined he was on an important trek from perhaps the Oracle at Delphi, or from Athens' rival Greek city-state, Sparta—not merely returning on a three-mile run from the tiny village of Penthes where marsh herbs grew abundantly. The boy glanced warily at the trailside brush, his mind picturing dangerous bandits or beasts of prey lurking there, not simply harmless rodents and birds. He imagined so much more...that he was one of the elite runners on a mission of import to the city's leaders, perhaps even to the High Archon himself. But he wasn't. He was Pheidippides, a poor, simple foot courier, hired to run errands from Athens to its local villages and back. Nothing more. He ran on.

****

In faraway Persia—out of sight and mind of young Pheidippides running his mundane deliveries—the undisputed power of early fifth century BC, Great King Darius, had plotted a course that would intersect not only with the young lad's routine treks...but with a culture that would soon be forever changed. Darius, a ruler more like a god to those of his own lands and beyond, seethed and plotted coldly: for it was Greece, a land known as the Hellespont, and its squabbling city-states lying at the center of his scheme.

Persia had long held dominion over a fair number of vassal Greek colonies, those along its own coast on the Ionian Sea. The colonies had been subservient...until rebellion had germinated quietly. And, far away on the Hellespont mainland along the Aegean Sea, Athens alone—among all the other bickering city-states of Greece—had helped foster that rebellion brewing against Persia's mighty Lord Darius. Stately Athens, the hub of culture, arts, and science throughout the Hellespont, had offered its support to the tiny colony of Ionia in casting off the yoke of Persian rule. Not even the crème of mainland Greece's military might, Sparta, had offered help to the Ionians. Nor had a single other Greek city-state. Only a distant kindred folk, the Eretrians from the tiny northern isle of Euboia, had set sail with the Athenians to free fellow Greeks in Ionia.

This rebellion had thus set in motion a chain of events that would one day shake the very core of both civilizations. It had all begun several years earlier.

****

The palace of King Darius was the pride of the Persian capital, Persepolis. Tall, majestic, impenetrable, it was said the mere sight of its towering walls and thick turrets was enough to impose an instant retreat on any invading force. And for those who had never laid eyes upon it, the legends of the fabled fortress were sufficient enough to discourage resistance or opposition of any sort. Yet there were always those who scoffed at legends and dared even to challenge them—as had the Ionians and Eretrians, with Athenian help. Those actions would not go without consequence.

Darius I sat on his throne as two of his Persian *satraps*—province governors—bowed low before him, mindful not to gaze directly into the steely eyes of their liege, as was the custom. No Persian (or any other, for that matter) held the right to meet eyes with a god. Both men appeared more ill at ease before their king than seemed natural this day.

Darius waited impatiently, as neither satrap seemed eager to speak first. Finally, the shorter—a plump fellow named Artaphernes—spoke up after clearing his throat nervously. He put a hand to his mouth, knowing that those subservient to a god dare not taint the air he breathes.

"Eh, Lord Darius, it is our pleasure to report that the Greek revolt in Ionia has been suppressed."

Darius stifled a yawn, as though expecting such a report, letting but a wisp of a smile slip over his bearded face, not wanting to give hint there had been even the slightest doubt of this outcome. "And our city of Sardis that they burned?" he queried somewhat casually.

"Retaken," the plump governor responded with a nod and an eager smile.

"Then why bear such welcome news with the look of oracles about to pronounce doom?" Darius quipped. The gaggle of courtiers lining the hall grinned accordingly, as though an unspoken command had been uttered and granted permission for them to do so. The two satraps, however, exchanged glances—Artaphernes giving the other, Datis, a look that read, "Your turn."

"Eh, sire," the taller and thinner governor, Datis, posed squeamishly, "it is reported that a distant Hellespont city-state, Athens, sent an army from its mainland to assist their Ionian cousins."

"What!" Darius' eyes widened and took on the look of blistering bolts of fire.

The court fell instantly silent as the two satraps eyed each other. Plump Artaphernes shook his head in response to the taller governor wanting him to take over. Datis glowered down at his fellow satrap, then covered his own mouth again, cleared his throat, and stared deliberately to one side of King Darius.

"They sailed there along with a people known as Eretrians—from an isle called Euboia, north of the Hellespont mainland, sire." The man's eyes shot downward again.

"Those pitiful cities dare send their puny armies to challenge the world's greatest empire?" roared Darius, half rising from his cushioned throne. The hall of courtiers stared at one another in fright—anywhere but at their suddenly aroused liege and master.

Satrap Datis lifted his lean head just high enough to signal to Artaphernes that it was all his now. The chunkier man glared back at him, then summoned his rapidly ebbing nerve.

"When they burned Sardis, my lord, the Greeks were heard proclaiming, 'No Persian tyrant shall ever rule over our colonies again!' " The portly governor slinked back a step, lowering his gaze once more and muttering a silent curse that he should be placed in so dread a position.

Darius took a long moment to draw a breath and

regain his composure, embarrassed by his initial burst of rage. He eased back down onto his throne, once more the cool and collected Lord of Earth. "First…we quell this rebellion happening on *our own soil*." He fixed his gaze solemnly on both governors, the mud-brown eyes smoldering into a slow burn of ruddy sparks and roaming finally over the entire hall of courtiers and warriors. "Then, by Mithra, a day shall come when we visit these bold mainland Greeks from Athens—but not before meting out justice to their upstart allies."

****

Four years later, while a sixteen-year-old foot courier named Pheidippides ran on toward his home city of Athens, daydreaming, a sack of medicinal herbs strapped to his side, King Darius of Persia paced arrogantly at the prow of a massive war galley, its ultimate destination the Hellespont mainland. For now it entertained a brief detour as the fleet bore down on the isle of Euboia.

On board the huge flagship that was decorated with symbols and sculptures of demonic sea beasts, Darius conferred with a husky man dressed in the flamboyant, colorful attire of a Persian sea captain. They were flanked by the very pair of satraps who had first reported the Ionian rebellion.

"The isle of Euboia, My Lord," said the ship's captain from under his moustache. "Home of the Eretrians."

Darius stared coldly at the island. He nodded with reptilian calm.

Satrap Datis waited, making sure that his lord did not opt to follow with some comment. Both satraps and the ship's captain all exchanged a look. "Then on to

Athens, Great King?" said Datis, one hand to his mouth as his eyes gazed to one side.

King Darius' mouth curled into a barely perceptible smile. "Aye…then on to Athens."

Chapter Two

While Gods Watch

"Darius shows his usual mercy," quipped a male voice that contained a curious mix of disgust and mirth. The remark referred to a brutal massacre followed by flames that soared skyward from the ruins of Euboia, rising high and nearly touching the very clouds. A solitary craft, bearing the scant few Eretrian survivors from the Persian assault, sailed away from what was left of their homeland.

"Greek or Persian, they are all barbarians, Lord Pan," retorted a melodious feminine voice.

The small sailcraft fluttered on across the rolling blue-green waves of the Aegean, its crew casting furtive glances back toward the smoking isle that was once their home. And from within a misty fissure, emerging seemingly out of the sky itself, two unworldly figures peered down…and frowned.

"Why, Keres dear, I'm surprised to hear you speak so of fellow Greeks," chided the male figure playfully, his face a bizarre blend of man and beast, his trunk, arms, and legs also bearing features that seemed to combine both human and animal traits. It was none other than Pan, God of the Nightly Wood and Lord of the Elysian Fields. He regarded his companion, a winged fairy-like creature of exquisite feminine beauty,

7

with a face that bore a mix of mischief and charm.

"I am an *Elysian* now," Keres responded curtly, the charming aspect of her face diminishing with the tone of her retort. Pan sighed, his sad smile containing yet a shade of dark amusement.

"It seems to me some of your old Spartan blood has been roused again," he quipped.

Keres shot him a cross look, and Pan acquiesced with a mock surrender gesture of his hands, knowing a bit more than blood had just been stirred. The winged beauty shook her head in a flash of despair and fluttered away in a quiet rush. Pan stared solemnly after her, then followed.

Below, the Eretrian craft had reached the relative safety of a mainland jetty, where a tall young man, sturdy and lean, hailed them ashore. He was garbed in white, tight-fitting breeches, a sleeveless *chiton* shirt of muslin, and light durable sandals on his feet...a foot courier's garb. Bronze-skinned from the sun, the courier waited eagerly for the craft to beach. His posture changed as he beheld the haggard look of the men on board. A pall of defeat hovered over every one of them. The courier read the truth before a single person spoke, his shoulders slumping and his face clouding as he listened to the grim account of the massacre. Turning, he waved a perfunctory farewell as the sailcraft put back out to sea, then forced himself into a steady trot down the jetty, knowing the run ahead of him would be as grueling as the news he bore.

****

Keres zipped through the wispy air of a lush woodland filled with pines, firs, oaks, maples, poplars...an array of every imaginable tree species that

8

could spring from a god's mind and will. Exquisite rock formations decorated a terrain that boasted rolling hillocks and trails where graceful felines romped side by side with canines that might normally have been their mortal enemies…where bovine herds grazed in nearby grassy fields, unfazed by creatures they would have feared as predators in a more earthly realm. Pan tagged along behind her as colorful birds whizzed past both Elysians, regarding the two humanoid beings as nothing more than fellow creatures of the air.

Keres finally turned and shot a haughty look back toward the Lord of the Elysian Fields, then glided down into a small glen where an oval cave lay notched into a knoll surrounded by weeping willows. A narrow stream snaked along by the knoll. Pan swooped down—not as gracefully as his beloved nymph queen—still ready to follow with a bit of light haranguing, till recognizing that her taste for playful banter had evaporated. He eyed her sympathetically as she sat curled up on a narrow rock, wings folded, knees tucked in together, her slender arms gripping them tightly. She bore the look of a teenage girl dismayed by life's ordeals.

"What is it, Keres?" Pan prodded with the gentle air of a father straining to know his daughter's pain. Keres held her silence and her confined posture, not looking back to him when she finally spoke.

"There is no *Greece*. You know that, my lord."

Pan nodded, bowing his head in a gentle melancholy. He knew now the source of her dismay.

"There is Sparta and there is Athens…and there are all the rest of those foolish *poleis*—those cities that favor either one or the other. And they will die by that," she proclaimed almost matter-of-factly, as one who knows there is no answer.

Pan forced a smile and slipped in closer. "Such is the way of mortals who worship the gods of Olympus…Ay?" His hands gestured wide, punctuating his words. Keres turned her head slightly and stared at him as a teenager might acknowledge an adult. "And no longer the concern of those who are now Elysian immortals. Mmm…?" he added.

Keres pondered that a moment, then rose, fluttered her filmy wings, and swooped down to the narrow stream, gazing into it and eying her own beautiful reflection. She nodded, a pert smile forming reluctantly on her youthful face. "True enough, my dear lord. Let the Spartans and Athenians have at each other…and let the Persians have at all the Greeks, while they all have at one another!" She giggled in forced defiance of her earlier mood.

Pan grinned, satisfied with her saucy rally. He glided down to join her. "Agreed."

Keres rose to her feet in a further display of resolution. "The Persians can all pray to Mithra…the Greeks can pray to Zeus…"

"And the lost and the hopeless have only we Elysians. Ay?" Pan chimed in.

Keres gave a snappy nod of her head and uttered a laugh that was yet soaked in sorrow.

"So why let dim spirits dampen ours because mortals are such fools?" Pan followed up, wanting to fend off the cloudy murk slipping back over her again. "Shall we wager on their pitiful antics?"

She eyed him with a playful suspicion. "I've little ambrosia or nectar left after our last wagering."

"Too great a challenge to match wits with Pan?"

And that had Pan's desired effect as she smirked back in mischievous defiance. "A full cup of nectar says Darius has dealt the Greeks enough lesson and returns to Persia."

Pan shook his head woefully, his tone still playful, but his heart knowing her hopes were too real.

"Ooo…Keres dear. That is a free cup of nectar you offer me here. I may as well drink it now."

"We'll see," she replied kittenishly.

"No, no, no. You bet with your heart, not with your mind," he protested genuinely. "This is a wager I'd gladly lose if there were any chance of—"

"Perhaps a strong heart might wager away such ugliness as these mortals make?" Her golden eyes pleaded with the dark gray of his own, hoping, wanting yet to believe…

Pan put a cloven hand to her shoulder, his face radiating pride and undisguised love. "It has always been clear to me why I once brought a young Spartan girl here to Elysia…but even a heart like yours cannot weave enough gentle magic into so foul a web."

She stared longingly back at him, knowing her Lord Pan would never deceive her, though wishing he might this one time. She held her smile steadfastly, a last strain of hope that he could yet be wrong.

Chapter Three

A Boy's Fragile Hopes

And while the city of Eretria smoldered in ashy ruins, and a lanky courier sped nobly over the northern Hellespont terrain, bearing gruesome news he would pass on to the next courier-herald of a massacre about to spread to the mainland, while two Elysian gods wagered on the consequences of an advancing Persian war fleet—young Pheidippides loped his way over a widening path of cinder and dirt that led to the walled city of Athens looming ahead. No heralds or pennants signaled the approach of this sixteen-year-old village courier carrying his parcel of healing marsh herbs. There was, after all, nothing of extraordinary significance that a slim boy should make a routine foot trek of six miles, bearing worthy items any reliable courier could have delivered had he not been available. Pheidippides knew this as he passed unnoticed through the city's wooden gates.

Within the walls of the magnificent Greek *polis*, throngs of Athenian citizens—and those of lower caste as well—bustled about the *agora,* the public square that marked the hive of all city activity.

Vendors barked out praise for samples of their wares and held them high to attract attention—clothing, pottery, jewelry, and the like—while men gathered under roofed colonnades, drinking wine and talking politics and business; acrobats and dancers tumbled, turned and leaped with the grace of dolphins romping in the surf; women hoisted jars—*amphoras* filled with water from beautiful public fountains; stately Athens in her afternoon glory celebrated life itself...unaware of the predatory force en route.

Along a narrow side street, Pheidippides picked up his pace on the dirt city road, aware he would soon round a corner that led smack dab into the midst of the agora's activities. He tugged the parcel of medicinal herbs out from the sash at his waistline and clutched it prominently in one hand, trying to lend it an air of greater importance. Pheidippides turned another corner and gazed ahead through a tunnel of stone and mud-brick homes, squinting as he eyed the magnificent columned structures at its end—structures that constituted the architectural wonder of Athens' fabled agora.

But a moment more...

He entered the public square and, knowing it was indeed that right time of day when the agora was filled with nearly every walk of Athenian life, Pheidippides put on an added burst of speed, pumping his arms earnestly and making sure that the one clutching the parcel of herbs rose higher than the other. Some of those working at their stalls nodded an acknowledgment—more as though a fellow vendor displayed an item of sale. One or two watching the acrobats shifted an eye his way, noting his pickup in speed, and either smiled or gave a perfunctory wave, though when he passed by the roofed colonnades where the men debated politics and business, none bothered looking his way.

Pheidippides ran on, comforted by the few morsels of acknowledgment given his work, smiling as two middle-aged women scooping water into their pottery jars from a public fountain waved warmly to him. His efforts were appreciated by some at least, he mused.

The healer's stone-and-brick shop lay at the end of this crowded stretch, and he would soar his way there, past the sacred *temenos*—the temple grounds—and on to his destination, perhaps impressing the master healer with the speedy time he had made to complete the two-league journey to Penthes and back...possibly even commanding a bit more coin of service from him, maybe even a *half-obol*.

Then Pheidippides spotted the man he had hoped but not expected to see at this time.

Garbed in full military attire, a brightly plumed helmet in one hand, the burly warrior of some forty years, powerfully chiseled and handsome, strode confidently in Pheidippides' direction. The boy nearly gasped at the notion that this man was headed practically right at him. He knew it was Captain Boros, Commander of the Elite Athenian Guard. And they were now on course to meet? Not once had they ever spoken, nor had this decorated warrior of Athens' boldest ranks even acknowledged him.

Pheidippides drew a tired breath and unleashed a display of his finest running technique. For a moment there was the briefest flicker of eye contact. And then the man looked away. The esteemed captain of the Athenian Guard fixed his gaze directly ahead instead, as though the boy striving for his attention had not even been there. Pheidippides glanced back weakly, seeing only the back of Captain Boros striding off. His eyes shifted from the military man, back in the direction of the healer's shop, just some fifty strides away. The arm clutching the tiny sack of herbs dropped to one side, loose in his grasp now, and he jogged the rest of the way to the healer's in barely more than a walk.

Chapter Four

A Hidden Truth

From the outside it was clear that the stately stone-and-marble structure was a dwelling belonging to someone of above-average status. It was spacious and walled in where a garden of exquisite plants decorated a beautiful yard, and a small fountain there indicated a home whose residents had no need to visit the agora's public square for water. Sturdy marble columns rose at each corner of the sparkling white dwelling with its pitched, tiled roof, and it appeared without question as one that housed comfort, status, and a degree of wealth.

A trim figure, whose garb did not match the look of one associated with the elegant home, slipped through a rear gate that led into the neatly kept yard. The figure, a woman, paused by the garden and stroked some of the flowers affectionately, as though they were her own. A plain muslin bundle slung over her back indicated that this lithe young woman was an honest visitor, though if not for her cheap working smock of cotton, she might well have been mistaken for an intruder. But she did belong there—as the materials for housecleaning and gardening hoisted over her shoulder gave her right of passage. Yet, the added nature of her visit could not keep her from glancing about furtively before slipping discreetly through the unbolted back door and into the graceful-looking home.

****

The bedroom wall boasted fine tapestries and portraits that hung in proud display of military campaigns, coats-of-arms, Athenian landscapes—all of it overlooking a large bed strewn with a rumpled layer of woolen covers and linens where Captain Boros Constantis and the woman seen outside had shared intimacy. The woman, now dressing herself, was in her thirties; tanned, lithe, and of a sleek beauty her common clothing could not contain. Dressed differently—or even remaining naked—she might well have been mistaken for an Athenian aristocrat…at the least, a consort to some wealthy merchant, statesman, or military official. In truth, it is precisely what she was…a *hetaera*, one of the Greek "women of pleasure." Often they made their subtle entries into the homes or stations of the men they serviced as maids and gardeners and the like. Such was the case here, though tension now ruled the room as she dressed in haste, her finely proportioned arms rippling with angst.

Boros, garbed only in a sleeveless samite chiton and cut-down woolen breeches, stood apart from her, uttering words he knew were the wrong ones. "Symethra, must we quarrel forever over this?" He sighed, exasperated. She did not respond nor even look at him, but merely continued dressing. Boros shook his head. "What you ask of me is not possible—ever. You know that."

"It is beyond a soldier's courage then?" she replied without turning to him. The tall captain bit his lip, rose from the bed, and paced. They had played this out far more times than either could count. His absence of a

17

response caused her to turn her head toward him as she tugged on her cleaning smock. "And would it soil your rank so much to admit—"

Boros cut her off with a dismissive wave of his hand. "An Athenian officer cannot make public his affairs with the hetaera."

Symethra slipped on her sandals. "No…but he can make his woman slink about her entire life like a common thief, pretending to be—"

"Has it made my love for you any the less?" he countered, sliding on over and sitting beside her on the edge of the bed. He put a hand to her shoulder. Symethra pursed her lips but did not move away. Boros drew a breath. "You are not required to be in service to any other men," he murmured gently.

Symethra flinched at that. "What more could a woman of pleasure expect?" she responded, making no effort to disguise the sarcasm in her voice. She rose from the bed and began gathering up the cleaning items she had used earlier while awaiting his arrival.

Boros stared down at the floor. "I'll not be drawn into this today, Symethra. I've an important military council to attend soon, and—"

She whirled round and eyed him hard. "More important than what is to become of your son?"

Boros shut his eyes, simmering softly to himself. "Symethra, please…"

"Of course. Why speak of your son when you will not even look at him when he passes you by in the street?"

Now their eyes met, and after a moment Boros shook his head. "You understood our ways once," he said quietly, an undisguised plea in his tone.

"And I've seen what sixteen years of understanding our ways has done to my boy." Her words slipped under his guard, as she knew they would. Symethra followed up, hoping maybe this time she might finally break through. She sat down next to him again. "Especially now that he's discovered *who* his father is."

Boros glanced around the room, anywhere but into her eyes. "That doesn't allow me to change the way Athenians live. He...he will be fine. He runs well enough on those errands."

"It will not be enough to support him when he is a man," she urged. "You cannot provide for him always, Boros," she pleaded gently, mustering every bit of rationale she had left. This was the time and she knew it. But still he failed to meet her eyes.

"He'll find work in the marketplace...or some other worthy trade."

"With no father to guide him?" she snapped, her patience ebbing.

Boros faced her finally, putting his hands on her shoulders. "He has the most gentle and caring of mothers to guide him." Wrong response and he knew it no sooner than it had left his mouth.

Symethra was up off the bed and away from him instantly. "Whom every well-bred Athenian still looks upon as just another 'pleasure dainty' for sweating, hungry officers!"

Boros rose, again at a loss for words. Symethra struggled to control the heaving sobs she did not want him to hear coming forth. It was an honest decision she wanted from him, not his pity or guilt.

He slipped up behind her and hugged her gently. She did not turn back to face him.

"And had I dared refuse your needs when you—*or any other of your sort*—first called upon me, I'd have been locked away or sent to live in the Kaboni as a beggar or thief."

Boros turned her gently to face him. "I have no power over our city's unwritten laws." His voice broke slightly, and Symethra heard it. "And I'd never have had you sent to…"

She reached up and put a single finger to his lips. "I know…I know." They hugged.

"It's not good for us to quarrel this way," he said, holding the embrace.

"No. It's not," she said patiently. "It's not good for Pheidippides either." She eased slowly from the embrace. "And it's not good that your concern is for *us* and not him too."

"I do have concern for him," Boros protested. "But…"

"You think he is weak."

Boros stepped back, not expecting that, trying to hide his guilt.

"Boros… What of all the learned men of Athens whose love of music and verse and nature's mysteries is the same as your own son enjoys? Our goddesses, the Muses, are revered for it."

"Symethra…he is hardly one to have caught the eyes of our revered Muses; nor is he a 'young Pythagoras' by any means. I doubt we will see him sitting at the agora exchanging philosophies with the stoics." He smiled softly, hoping his lighthearted comment might quell the mood of their dispute. But again he had failed. She pulled back from him, glaring.

"No…He is *Pheidippides*. And I've not heard you

ever call him by name." Eyes watering, Symethra turned and finished gathering up her items. She eyed him politely, formally.

"Will I be needed for any other services this day…Captain?"

Boros stared blankly at her, his silence containing a myriad of emotions. The beautiful young hetaera turned and left him standing there alone, frustrated.

Chapter Five

Disruption!

Pheidippides sat cross-legged by a large outdoor stone pool—one of many public square attractions amidst the grand temples, tall columns, beautiful amphitheaters, and brimming market stalls. He loved the agora, not only for its bustle of activity and throngs of Athenians that ranged from the wealthy highborn, the *eupatridae,* to the rest of the city's proud citizenry that was recognized as *ecclesia*—those who boasted of voting rights; but the grand public square also welcomed the poorest of people too, thus allowing *demos* of all castes that lived inside Athens' walls to visit there. Young and old ranged through on a given day...including masterful artists and craftsmen, agile athletes, wistful stoics, cunning merchants. Here was the absolute pulse of Greece's most blessed city!

Not that Athens had ever treated his mother and him with blessed kindness. It hadn't. They were *not* citizens, and therefore of a caste that was not afforded privileges of voting, nor any say at all in a culture that boasted of equality. "Equal for the *chosen*," his mother had often quipped, especially when unfair struggles and disappointment fell upon them. No, that was not the Athens he cherished. Rather, it was the spark of life and hope the city generated in the hearts of those who dwelled there—or at least that's the way Pheidippides Deglos saw it, though his mother did not embrace Athens in the same light. And since there were so few he could honestly regard as friends—none who likely would have agreed or understood, anyway—the boy was prone to keeping his dreamy thoughts to himself.

So, other than when he ran, making deliveries between Athens and its surrounding villages and hamlets of the Attica region, it was the agora that brought out the depth of his thoughts...and his dreams. It was here, in this very hub of the city, where he became absorbed in its magnificence and truly believed it was the place that might one day effect the sort of change in his life he yearned for so desperately. Yes...here was where he might one day approach those who could help deliver such dreams—perhaps even commanding the attention of the Athenians he admired most: the stoics, great teachers and philosophers who gathered under the roofed colonnades daily and taught wondrous lessons to their students, all of whom were Athenian citizens. Pheidippides dreamed of being included, some day, in that circle of knowledge reserved only for those born to the eupatridae and the ecclesia.

The young courier now sat, using a sharp pointed *stylus* to write on a wax-covered clay tablet. He glanced up occasionally to smile at the antics of turtles, birds, and fish that populated the small manmade pool area that had been designed and sculpted by the city's gifted architects. He scribbled a bit more, then paused to look over the pond's creatures again, regarding a nearby turtle crawling through the mud toward the water.

"And how long have you been alive, my little

friend?" he murmured quietly, his chestnut-brown eyes studying every movement of the turtle's thick, slow-moving legs. "What stories you'd tell if only you could speak, eh?" Pheidippides smiled as the turtle seemed to eye him curiously, then slid off into the pond water and disappeared. He turned back to his writing, but a hand reached down and snatched the tablet from him! Pheidippides jerked his head up to see the mocking face of another teenage boy, bigger, perhaps a year older. The boy's face was dirty and rough, a wide leer etched on it.

"Talking to the little pond creatures again, eh, Pheidippides?" the gangly lad snickered. He danced backward, holding the writing tablet just out of reach. Pheidippides stretched out an arm, trying to snatch it back, but the boy leapt back a couple steps, causing him to miss it and stumble forward. The intruder laughed again and glanced at the tablet. "Or are we drawing more pictures of silly Elysian gods again?"

"Give it back, Barthus!"

"Ooo…Pheidippides gives commands now. I best beware."

"You have no need of it," Pheidippides said in a vain attempt at trying to reason with the older boy, a seasoned street rogue he wished he'd never met. "It's just…"

His voice trailed off; he knew better than trying to explain what was on the tablet. Besides, Barthus, too, had been taught how to read writing symbols, though not formally—not the way privileged family members of the ecclesia's citizen class learned.

Dancing farther out of Pheidippides' range, Barthus held up the tablet and studied it a moment.

"Why it's—a poem!" Another grin curled over the young rogue's face, and Pheidippides lunged toward him, trying again to seize it back. But Barthus dodged smoothly and stuck out a foot to trip him. Pheidippides fell flat on his face. Barthus leapt atop the low circular wall surrounding the agora pond and started to read the contents of the tablet in a mock oratory. "My Athens…my home. She stands here before me, sparkling in the sun." The older lad rolled his eyes and giggled. "Ooh…very good, Pheidippides. Very good."

Pheidippides drew himself to his feet and moved toward Barthus prancing around on the wall.

"Barthus…please."

Seeing how much it bothered him, Barthus pressed on: "Glorious city, place of my birth!" He paused, laughing again. "Perhaps you can read this aloud before the High Archon himself. He might let you pretend you're a real citizen for a day."

"I *am* a real citizen of Athens!" Pheidippides exclaimed, fists clenched. He took an angry step toward Barthus, who leered down at him from atop the wall. The older lad raised an eyebrow and slid a step to one side. His dark eyes narrowed and bore down on Pheidippides.

"You're a poor little messenger boy with stupid dreams." He held the tablet up, displaying it as a visual aid. "And 'your Athens' cares only for those well-born, the eupatridae—not fatherless rogues like us. When will you—"

"Give him back the tablet, Barthus," an older man's voice commanded firmly, coolly. Barthus' head snapped at the sound of the voice. He knew it well. So did Pheidippides.

Standing not ten feet away was a gaunt, wiry man, middle-aged, perhaps older, and garbed somewhat shabbily in a loose-fitting tunic and long, gray *himation* robe. But he wore his ragged attire with the flair of a wily buccaneer. From Barthus' obvious regard for the man, it was clear this was no one to trifle with.

Barthus forced a sheepish laugh. "Oh, but I was just having a bit of fun here, Garathi."

"Give it back. We have work to do," the man Barthus called Garathi said flatly.

Barthus acknowledged with a reluctant though dutiful nod. He held the tablet aloft and eyed Pheidippides, who had remained frozen in the presence of the older rogue.

"Read your soft, loving words of 'sweet Athens' to the turtles and the fishes and the birds you like speaking to so much." Barthus stepped down from the wall and offered the tablet back. "They're the only ones who care what thoughts are in your head."

Pheidippides reached for it...and at that same moment, Barthus let the tablet fall from his grasp. It landed hard on the ground and cracked, the sound causing Pheidippides to wince. The tablet did not break, though, and Pheidippides bent down and scooped it up, giving Barthus a dirty look as he rose back to his feet.

Barthus sneered, seeking to save face in the wake of Garathi's reprimand. "Or you can always come to the Kaboni and learn something more *profitable* from Garathi here."

"I'm not interested," Pheidippides uttered quietly, not wanting to offend Garathi, just the same.

Barthus laughed and swaggered off, leaving with a parting dart. "Then learn for yourself that a thief's life is the only one for sons of the hetaera…eh, Garathi?"

Garathi responded by ushering Barthus away roughly. "Save your advice for the new apprentices, Barthus."

Barthus shrugged and stalked off, trying to maintain his smug air.

Garathi turned to face Pheidippides, who drew back from him a bit, clearly uneasy around the man. Garathi noticed and spoke gently to him. "Eh…Pheidippides. I've always room for you, should you…" The older man punctuated his words with a nod, then turned and walked off.

Pheidippides remained, gazing down at his cracked tablet, then back up at the tall, lanky form of Garathi striding off. His thoughts were interrupted by a sudden cry.

"A courier comes! It is…Zagorus!"

Pheidippides turned sharply and peered in the direction of the city walls. A moment later, a tall, lean runner came striding rapidly out from the same tunnel of houses the boy himself had passed through, virtually unnoticed, days earlier.

"Zagorus! What news of the North?" someone yelled out.

"Is there cause for alarm?" another yelled—for the chain of courier-heralds stationed along the routes north, south, east, and west did not send in their runners nearest the city—earlier than scheduled—unless something of urgency was upon them.

Zagorus simply ran by the entire crowd without answering. As he passed by the two departing Kaboni rogues, Barthus yelled back to Pheidippides: "There, noble Pheidippides!" he chortled. "Run well enough on your little errands and the Archon might let you join the ranks of Hermes' Messengers like Zagorus there! Hah! Then you too can run those great distances as a brave herald and tell us news of the world beyond!" Barthus laughed on heartily at his own joke, but his laughter was squelched by Garathi shoving him roughly along his way.

Still standing at the pool area, Pheidippides watched, mesmerized, as Zagorus approached and passed by while everyone cheered and some continued calling out the same questions of alarm. Zagorus acknowledged with a polite wave and a single comment: "The Archon…I must see the Archon immediately!" he gasped hoarsely.

Soldiers in military garb rushed out to greet and escort Zagorus off to the *Bouleuterion*, the great Council House. Pheidippides stared in awe, smiling at the reverent treatment given this elite courier…and noticed the Captain of the Athenian Guard stepping forth to also escort Zagorus off to the Archon. Pheidippides' smile disappeared as Captain Boros passed him by with hardly a glance.

More well-dressed citizens rushed by as the teenage boy lingered near the pool, watching them all pass. His face sank as he gazed at everyone disappearing in the direction of Zagorus, the soldiers…and Captain Boros.

Pheidippides stared down at his tablet, then went over to sit against the stone wall encircling most of the pool. Dejected, he watched the same turtle trudging along one of the large surface rocks inside. He glanced back down at his cracked tablet, then over at the turtle, and quietly spoke the first lines of his poem toward the pool.

"My Athens…my home. She stands here before me, sparkling in the sun…"

Chapter Six

An Alert...As Gods Still Watch

A magnificent-looking man, mid-forties, stood tall upon a high dais in the elegant marble hall. He stared out from a tanned handsome face, his long brown locks combed neatly down to the base of his neck, where they hung aesthetically perfect. The expression he wore as he surveyed the Bouleuterion, the Athenian Council Hall, betrayed the deep concern, the worry lurking in his ruddy eyes. This was the High Archon of Athens, the most powerful and influential of those charged with the splendid city's direction and well-being.

Where Persia had imposed its longtime tradition of no underlings daring to look directly at its deified ruler, Athenians, quite the contrary, all gazed openly at their own lordly leader—and did so with great affection and warmth. And though the distinction between the Athenian elite and the city's secondary and lower caste was of a clearly defined nature, no lesser noble or recognized citizen, nor even those of humbler sects— not even servants or slaves—had cause to fear reprisal for meeting eyes with the city's most revered leader or for drawing breath from the same air. Prominent Athenians believed theirs was the city-state—the polis—of mainland Greece chosen by the gods to set a path for others to follow...where people had the freedom to roam and think and speak openly, though it could easily have been argued some were granted more room to do so than others.

So now, Archon Kallimachos gazed thoughtfully over the beautifully columned hall, studying the flock of important dignitaries and military leaders gathered before him, including the robust and rugged General Milteades—a huge man of muscular girth and of a stature not unlike the Archon himself. Captain Boros of the Elite Athenian Guard was there too, among the rest of the state's governing hierarchy and military leadership. The Archon surveyed the plush gathering.

"Fellow citizens!" he proclaimed loudly as his eyes scanned the hall, holding at times on a specific group, occasionally locking onto the attentive stare of various individuals. "The tales of evil doings in our northern lands are all true. The gallant foot courier Zagorus of our brave Hermes' Messengers, our *hemerodrome*, has learned from fellow route runners that a vast Persian force has invaded and destroyed our island kin of Eretria…and may soon be advancing on Athens!"

A respectful hush had already enveloped the room the moment Archon Kallimachos had started to speak. Now a deathly pall fell over the vast gathering. Some exchanged fearful glances, some nudged one another uncomfortably, while others, Milteades in particular, wore frowns that twisted into scowls. The Archon allowed a moment more for his words to penetrate fully, then followed up:

"Shall we tolerate this cruelty by the tyrant Darius, all because we once thought to help free fellow Greeks? Shall we send word to this self-proclaimed 'God of All the Known World' that we here in the Hellespont now make a plea for his mercy and hope he will grant it?"

As if on cue, General Milteades responded in the way a grizzled bear might rumble a warning prior to attacking. "No...*Never!*" It was all that seemed necessary to ignite the rest, as a veritable chorus echoed the general's bold reply—though not everyone responded in kind.

The Archon's eyes roamed the crowd, most of the faces there assuring him of the support needed to muster together a unified stance against a likely invasion. But Kallimachos also knew there would be dissenters—even here within this very gathering—and in various quarters of the renowned city-state. A solid resistance to such a choice might well be expected. And he knew why.

There were still partisans of Athens' onetime tyrant, Hippias, lurking within its walls. The man's deplorable past treatment of the city's demos had resulted in those very people rebelling and ousting him nearly two decades past. But another would-be Athenian dictator had usurped control of Athens two years later, in 508 BC, with the aid of rogue hoplite soldiers from the rival military state of Sparta. They had surprised the citizenry and seized control of the city...but only briefly. Having already expelled one dictator, these were a people who were not shy of defending what was theirs: a rising polis that was growing in every way, both in culture and in might. So once again, tyranny was overthrown by Athens' demos...citizens who valued freedom and the right to forge their own way of life.

With Hippias and those who followed him deposed, a revolutionary new "Rule of the People"—

democratia—had been instituted instead by a onetime aristocrat, Kleisthenes. The hated tyrant Hippias had fled the Hellespont lands, making his way to faraway Persia...where his alarming tale of a rapidly growing city-state across the sea permitting its *people* to rule, instead of an all-powerful king, had raised concern throughout the foreign empire, but to no great alarm. That is, until stray Greek colonies along the Persian Coast, previously annexed by Great King Darius, had rebelled—and with aid from those intrepid Athenians who deigned to interfere, and who apparently also sought to spread their fledgling "Rule of the People" to where it did not belong.

That, at least, is what Hippias had coyly suggested, stoking the suspicions of Lord Darius and currying the Persian King's favor enough to earn himself a position as guide along the rough Hellespont coast to this precocious Greek city-state called Athens. In doing his part, Hippias would then be assured of reclaiming his former stature as tyrant of that troublesome state—all in accordance with the Persian King's design. For there were those who still quietly preferred the notion of rule by the few and who yet lurked in the city's underground, waiting...

Such were the thoughts that passed through the mind of High Archon Kallimachos as he surveyed the throng gathered inside the Bouleuterion. He knew there were covert dissidents roaming within the shadows, always plotting, always paying heed to rumors from near and afar that might lead to a resurgence of opposition to the new Athens that had only recently emerged.

One particular troublemaker of whom he was

aware—a fervent supporter of the deposed Hippias—was an abrasive fellow named Hahnitos. How anyone of good sense might be hoodwinked by so serpent-tongued a demagogue as this man had always baffled and disturbed the Archon, but Hahnitos had followers amongst the city's demos—people deeply committed to whatever he spouted during underground gatherings in Athens' more remote quarters.

For another moment the Archon's eyes scanned the hall with greater scrutiny, searching for signs of the portly, pink-faced dissident, catching no sign of him yet knowing that Hahnitos may well have slipped inside here. He was a crafty scoundrel, and the Archon knew better than to underestimate him. It was time, however, to follow up on the bold proclamation made moments ago by General Milteades. So Kallimachos raised a robed arm to quiet the crowd. He spoke in a soft tone...one that bore the strength of liquid iron being poured into a casting for armor and weapons:

"We shall meet any challenge thrown down to us by these Persian beasts," he said, an assuring calm in his voice that carried the same strength as the general's booming call to arms. Again the great hall erupted in cheers.

"But not before sending forth our bold courier Zagorus again—to Sparta—to end the feuding with our Greek kin, so we might join together against this enemy from afar who would seek to destroy us!"

There was a moment's prolonged silence at this unexpected premise of seeking Spartan aid...of placing trust in their arch-rivals who themselves might have welcomed an opportunity to bring mighty Athens to its knees. But the Archon had already made it clear this was to be a struggle between Persians and Greeks, and that rivalries now needed to be set aside for the sake of the entire Hellespont lands. So another cheer went up, tentative at first, but in deference to the city's trusted leaders.

From within the shadowy cover of one of the hall's marble archways, a portly, pink-faced man of middle-aged stature glowered beneath a pair of thick, graying eyebrows—one of few people in attendance who had not joined in support of the Archon's proclamations. Several others flanked the surly fellow, henchmen of his, clearly, and they all exchanged looks expressing their discontent.

****

Sitting by the agora's manmade pool, still reading aloud the poem about "his cherished Athens," Pheidippides paused momentarily as the cheers of a distant crowd approaching distracted him. His chestnut eyes searched the cobbled footpath, but thus far he could only hear what sounded to be an approaching throng clearly excited about something. The boy shrugged, puzzled, then gripped the wax-covered clay tablet more tightly with his thin fingers and continued reading to his comforting audience of pool inhabitants. "Full of the sounds of the passion of life…"

And then the noisy throng from the distance grew louder, distracting him again and causing a frown to furrow his young brow. What could there possibly be today to create such added commotion? Athens' most distinguished foot courier had only recently appeared with such urgency and alarm that it commanded the mustering of the city's most prominent leaders. Why such undisciplined revelry now in the wake of that?

Pheidippides' mouth turned down in the remembrance that his own father—unable to even grant recognition to his illegitimate son (unworthy of the man anyway)—bore status enough to be among those distinguished figures heading his way, yet he himself…

His head bowed, he lifted his cracked tablet again. But now the raucous procession was not only visible as it approached on the agora's main street-path, the clamor from it was in full force. Pheidippides lowered the tablet and squinted to better view what was taking place. Voices were oddly jubilant as the parade of revelers drew ever closer to where he sat. And as they did, he finally made out the unmistakable form of Zagorus himself at the very head of it, still looking weary from his recent trek. The famed courier was hemmed in by the city's staunchest military figures— the grand general of the Athenian army, Milteades, and some prominent officers, including Boros. Sturdy arms were clasped round the taut young runner, who smiled thinly in polite appreciation as they all but hoisted him into the air and fairly carried him. Zagorus raised a hand humbly and waved politely to the accompanying crowd and those gathering along the sides of the stony path. A good many chanted, "Run well, Zagorus…Alert our Spartan kin and bring us their aid!" Others raised clenched fists and hollered, "Death to the devils of Darius!"

Pheidippides gaped at the extraordinary sights and sounds of the militant revelers erupting before his very eyes. Hearing these proclamations as the mob passed no more than a few strides away, he pieced together what must have taken place earlier in the great meeting, not far from where he had sat reading his simple verse to the turtles and frogs and fish in the agora pond. Perhaps the rascally Barthus had been right in his parting shot earlier: "They're the only ones who care what thoughts are in *your* head."

As he watched the raucous procession pass by, it seemed Zagorus appeared to glance his way, knowing not the name or the face of the teenage boy standing by the pond but offering a courteous smile and a nod of the head. For that flicker of an instant, sixteen-year-old Pheidippides, pauper and son to a hetaera woman, met the gaze of one he had so often dreamt of becoming. A surge of warmth washed through the callow youth, then cooled and chilled in the very next instant as his eyes also caught those of Captain Boros, who barely held his gaze and turned away as if ordered to do so. Pheidippides sank slump-shouldered and sat on the pond's low wall. He stared down pointlessly at his cracked clay tablet, the sharp writing stylus dropping from his hand.

The noisy procession passed him by. Moments later, the sector of the square in which he sat was silent and deserted again, but for the soft ripples of the gentle creatures flitting about in the pond waters. He caught sight of one of the larger turtles resting on a rock and eying him curiously. Pheidippides could not suppress the sliver of a smile that fought its way back onto his face, despite the gloom that had draped over him a moment earlier. He pressed his eyes shut tightly, then opened them again, never breaking his gaze from the turtle's, and held his tablet back up…to resume reading: "Glorious city, place of my birth, still standing here unharmed. My Athens, my home."

****

Along the southern Athenian coastline, a lone figure ran over a sandy stretch of beach as waves crashed and sometimes seeped up far enough along the grainy turf to moisten and tickle his sandaled feet. Zagorus, garbed only in a breech cloth and sleeveless tunic—a dagger and a slingshot tucked round his waist, along with two pouches, one filled with water, the other with olives and fruits—kept up a steady loping stride. His sharp eyes were ever fixed on the horizon of beach and hills—a trek of a good hundred and fifty miles to Sparta before him, and no knowledge whether their longtime rival polis would respond in kind to the urgent need for unity against a pending Persian onslaught. Like all Athenians, young Zagorus knew these two most powerful city-states of the Hellespont lands could not have been more different: Athens with its revolutionary democracy; Sparta with its traditional oligarchy, touting two kings and a small council lording over a supremely militant culture.

The war-minded Spartans viewed salvation in the form of an army that raised and trained recruits from the time they were children; the more refined Athenians boasted an impressive navy and a solid army as well, but built its culture and its future more in line with being the hub of Greek arts and sciences and the philosophical teachings of educated stoics. Two great poleis at perpetual odds...and with no sign of ever alleviating longtime tensions born of their differences. Now, with both city-states imperiled by a monstrous foreign power, a lone foot courier ran on to plead they do just that.

****

High above the world of squabbling city-states and

their impending plight, two other-worldly beings again gazed down...perplexed by the ongoing antics below and disdainful of the futility of it all.

"How gallant are these Greeks, eh?" chirped Keres in melodious sarcasm, her long, flowing hair flipping side to side and seeming to change from a brown hue to a sunshine golden-red. But her tone lacked its usual sparkle of bright mischief. Pan eyed her curiously, his human features showing concern, while the mix of him that appeared bestial showed more a look of mirth as he too peered downward at the earthly realm—and Zagorus toiling along the lonely southern Hellespont coast.

"Amusing, were it not so tragic," the Elysian lord mused.

"Always tragic where Greeks are concerned," Keres quipped with an uncharacteristic edge to her voice. Her lovely young face clouded with undisguised sorrow.

Pan nodded thoughtfully, knowing his spritely nymph queen and sensing the brewing gloom about to usurp her usual cheer. Like a father addressing a petulant teen who struggles to make sense out of sorrow, Pan sought to deflect her moody descent.

"Eh, we stray from the subject, dear Keres," he said.

"My Lord...?" she said as if tugged back from a daydream.

"Darius readies his move for Athens now," he answered flatly, a lighthearted 'I-told-you-so' smirk on his rough face.

"Indeed he does," Keres retorted at being told the obvious. She frowned, as though chiding him for so simple an observation.

"There was a cup of nectar, I believe…?" His coy smirk widened as he held out one cloven hand. Keres sighed, then shot him a playful dirty look in response. Pan smiled, pleased to have lifted her mood slightly. A golden goblet of foaming nectar drink appeared between her smooth, perfect fingers. Pan reached over for it, then paused, his thick eyebrows lifting in a gesture of suggestion. "That is, unless you'd care to wager a bit more…That Sparta chooses to aid Athens?"

Keres smirked impishly in response. "No. I know my Spartans all too well."

"Then we wait for a better wager, eh?" Pan said, draining the goblet of nectar with an air of great satisfaction and smacking his lips to emphasize the sweetness of its taste. Keres laughed in spite of his triumphant glee, and Pan smiled back at her resurgent humor. Both flitted off into their godly realm, taking no further notice, for the time being, of Zagorus striding on below along the earthly shores.

Chapter Seven

A Boy's Faint Dreams

In a more humble quarter of Athens, a neighborhood of tiny mud-brick, stone, and wooden hovels, connected by nothing more than dirt footpaths, Pheidippides ran earnestly, his feet negotiating the pebbly, rutted turf with an impressive ease. He mounted his pace down the longer stretches of small dwellings and rounded the bends and twists in the paths dramatically, as though some dire urgency was upon him. He cut the tangents of these narrow strips so closely, his pivoting foot sometimes scraped the thorny weeds of yards as he swept by them, and even grazed the edges of hovels hugging the thin street corners. The slender boy's mind, as usual, played out a far greater scenario than another mere romp to the village of Penthes and back, delivering the usual medicinal herbs for the city's healers.

No, he envisioned these looping twists and turns and open stretches of Athens' lower-caste suburb to be a maze of vast boulders and hillocks—where wild-land bandits and other perils lurked, all seeking to impede his progress, perhaps even laying an ambush for him as he hustled along. So, with one dramatic dash down a final stretch of the narrow path, flanked by bushes and skimpy willows, Pheidippides put on a final burst and sprinted up victoriously before a simple, well-kept little dwelling made of sturdy ash and pine wood. A modest garden bordered the property.

An abode lacking in the finery, stature and wealth of those more fortunate, it was, nonetheless, clean and prideful—like people who never stop trying for something better. The handsome lean boy caught his breath, glancing behind him as though having thwarted imaginary pursuers. He wiped the dust from his muslin chiton and gray breeches before entering the little house.

Pheidippides stepped inside to a rustic, neatly kept interior of the remote little dwelling. It was swept clean of dust and debris and flaunted a charming fireplace and hearth on one side, a small kitchenette and dining area in the center where an attractive oak table had three wooden chairs tucked under it. This small section, a number of steps from the entryway, looked to be a modest space for guests as well; the other end was partitioned off by woolen throws decorated simply with soft animal and nature images sketched over them. They separated two obvious sleeping areas. One throw was tugged back, revealing a simple trundle bed with plain cotton and wool blankets and a pillow. Resting on top was Pheidippides' cracked tablet and his stylus writing instrument.

A beautiful brown-haired woman, Symethra Deglos, was dressed in an attractive cotton smock as she laid out a delightful-smelling serving of vegetables, fish, and cider on the table. Her gray eyes lit up with joy and warmth as her son entered the *andron*, the main room of their tiny dwelling. She smiled, noting he was short of breath. She knew of his daydreams and enhanced versions of his courier errands and how they spurred him into running home with greater earnest. In spite of the toil of their lives and their socially pre-cast status, the woman's love for her boy was akin to a morning sunrise.

"You're early," Symethra said softly, smiling again at the comfort of just seeing him. "Was it a short errand?"

Pheidippides shook his head no. "Three miles out to the village of Penthes again for more marsh herbs and olives for healing oils, then back here right away."

"With no rest?" She frowned gently at him.

Pheidippides walked over and hugged her in greeting, then turned to the wash basin and dipped his hands inside. "The acolytes at the Hall of Healing wanted more herbs immediately, and they were much in need of more olive oil too."

"And done so soon," she said in a tone of being most impressed.

Pheidippides sat at the table, affecting the air of one who is containing his bravado in order to appear deliberately modest. "Six miles is a trifle compared to what Zagorus is doing."

Symethra placed rice, eggs, and bread in front of him and poured some of the brown cider juice into his mug. "Well…the Hermes' Messengers are well trained for that sort of grueling task," she replied soothingly, sensing the direction the conversation was likely to take.

Pheidippides stared down at his food, nudging it with his wooden spoon but not lifting it off the plate. "As a *worthy* courier is trained…when his father is one who can request such a status for him."

43

Symethra sighed uncomfortably. "Pheidippides, there are terrible dangers the hemerodrome messengers like Zagorus face on those journeys," she said, her gray eyes clouding.

"And there are great rewards given for such tasks—far greater than those given mere village couriers." He picked at his food again, chewing it slowly and silently, still looking down.

"You're too young to be thinking so seriously on such matters, my son."

Pheidippides finished chewing and looked up. "Zagorus began his training for it at sixteen."

"But I'm sure he did not run missions over eight and ten leagues until he was old enough," she said of the twenty-five and thirty miles often done by the hemerodrome.

"But—"

"And Zagorus was not asked to risk his life running over many times such distances until now." She reached a slender arm across the table and tilted his chin up gently so his eyes met hers. "Pheidippides…"

"I know, Mother…I know. It's just that someday I will need more than the few obol coins and favors they give me for these short errands." He shook his head in frustration, the long, brown locks waving back and forth as though with a sentient angst of their own. "Any beggar off the streets or clever thief from the Kaboni has more to show."

Symethra's eyes flashed with sudden alarm. "My son, please do not say such things!"

He lowered his head and slipped in a couple morsels more, which he gulped down in a twinkling, then rose dejectedly. "Is my father so ashamed of me,

Mother, that I am not even permitted to try?" He pushed his chair politely from the round table and gazed directly at her. "At least my mother feels no shame in calling me 'son.' But when has bold Captain Boros ever looked at either of us in public as though even knowing us?"

Pheidippides and Symethra eyed one another in a prolonged silence, both knowing she suffered the same silent sorrow as he over this. Finally he turned and walked over to his bedding area and picked up the clay tablet, staring at it as though it might offer an answer.

Symethra began clearing the table of the plates and utensils, wiping a tear from one eye once she saw her son was no longer looking her way.

Chapter Eight

The Eyes of a King

Far north of Athens, along the coast of the isle of Euboia, King Darius stared out at the smoke-infested ruins of what had been the grand city of Eretria— onetime home to the Greeks who, along with the Athenians four years earlier, had aided their Ionian kin across the sea in a struggle for liberation from the Persian tyrant. But that Greek triumph had been short-lived. Now, four years later, Great King Darius had made good on the first of his vows to "mete out justice to the upstarts."

Raging flames still licked at the remnants of the former Eretrian palace, and the smoke from those fires streaked higher than the knoll upon which Darius stood gloating. The Persian king gestured down the knoll, not bothering to look at the man next to him.

"You are certain of these two, Captain Kazek?"

"Aye, sire," replied the flamboyantly garbed Persian captain, his cold eyes nearly as frosty as those decorating the reptilian helm covering most of his forehead. "They represent the finest of assassins who serve Persia's cause."

Walking toward the knoll was a pair of tall, burly men, both garbed in thick metal armor—one bearing a huge broadsword at his side, the other toting a massive war axe. Beautifully shaped, savage-looking daggers were also sheathed at their hips. Each wore heavy leather leggings tucked into thick boots designed for either marching or travel on horseback, though neither was decked out in the outlandish Persian war attire that reflected the demonic faces or bestial heads flaunted by the captain and others. These two husky rogues seemed more of the mercenary lot that armies were wont to employ at times for tasks outside the range of traditional soldiers. Neither was of Persian descent.

The ruddy-skinned, bearded giant flaunting the war axe was actually from a land north of the Hellespont—a tribal folk known as Macedonians—and somewhat bound to Persia since Darius had annexed their scattered territories but a few years earlier; the tall black warrior bearing the broadsword was a Nubian from the southlands across the Mediterranean, whose bold clans were now deemed in servitude to King Darius and his ever-expanding empire. Different as the pair was in lineage, they appeared curiously akin to one another.

"Rojese—or 'The Bull' as he has oft been called—was taken to our Persepolis Palace after being captured by a squadron of archers in the hills of Macedonia. He, eh, slew a goodly number of our finest footmen when they tried seizing him, and only the throng of arrows aimed at him made his capture possible," said Captain Kazek as the two assassins continued in their approach. "But he has taken supremely to the well-paid task of hunting down enemies of our empire."

Darius nodded in grim approval. His appraising gaze shifted and fixed on Rojese's black-skinned comrade. "And the Nubian? What do we know of him?"

"Ah…Jamjon," said the captain, a narrow smile curling over his lips. "His tribe has long been under Persian rule…since before he was born. He is well trained and bears the seasoned skills of a wild jungle cat. Our own great General Mardonius has sung this man's praises along with those of Rojese."

"Good," said Darius, his mud-brown eyes still fixed on the fierce-looking pair approaching. "For I am told of hardy couriers who speed across the Hellespont territories—reporting all that they see and hear. I want no Greek spies or fleet-of-foot messengers roaming between where we will put ashore on their mainland and Athens. None must know of our forthcoming march over their lands."

The tall, stocky king continued studying the two assassins, a suspicious scrutiny yet in his gaze as they neared the foot of the ash-dirt knoll. He blinked suddenly as it appeared to him that the husky Nubian had caught his gaze and *held it*. Darius stared hard at the man that Captain Kazek had called Jamjon. The Nubian's dark eyes did not drop until his Persian comrade induced him, with a subtle nudge, into breaking it off.

Darius' chest expanded and heaved, a cloud of disquiet crossing his bearded face as he wondered if he had been mistaken in what had seemed a flicker of a brash gesture on the Nubian's part. He noted that this Jamjon now seemed to focus his gaze on the surrounding landscape instead—the same as Rojese—and that his eyes, perhaps, had only caught and held his own by mere chance. That could be the only explanation for any subordinate having foolishly locked eyes with the Supreme Ruler on Earth. So the Persian King turned his thoughts, instead, to the more pressing matter of meting out justice to a brash state filled with arrogant Athenians, whose indiscretions could not be overlooked.

Chapter Nine

Sparta

Pan and Keres peered down from their godly perch in the Upper Worlds and regarded Athens' vaunted courier Zagorus still striding on through the moonlight along a lonely beach area. Keres shook her lovely head, her bright amber eyes twinkling in a dark mirth.

"Fortunately for this gallant messenger, those Persian riders Darius is sending forth will be prowling far north of here," she mused.

"Aye," said Pan with a frown of his horned forehead. "Else Sparta would never learn of the pending danger to them all."

"It matters not, dear Pan. Sparta will give no aid to Athens."

Pan's dark eyes twinkled with a sudden new merriment. "Ah…and since you think not, my sweet Keres, I'll then wager one small bite of ambrosia that Sparta says, 'Yes.' "

"Ooh, but my dearest Pan is indeed a fitting 'Lord to The Lost.' Our precious ambrosia takes so much longer to replenish than even does our nectar. Are you certain of this wager? For you know I shall gladly seize it from you and savor each morsel before your own eyes, while you yearn for your own store of it to replenish…ever so slowly."

Pan winked in a taunting fashion, the mere look of him doing so as unattractive as his wager. Keres giggled with a renewed confidence in her own playful bet, her mind drifting away from the gravity of the earthly drama playing out below…as Pan had hoped it would.

****

Zagorus forced his lean runner's frame into a stronger-looking posture as he approached the sturdy walls of militant Sparta. But he could not hide the strain of well over a hundred-mile trek—nearly fifty leagues—a daunting run even for the most gifted and durable of elite couriers. (With good cause, Symethra had been leery of encouraging such a future for her teenage son, glory or not.) Depleted from his grueling trek over the Peloponnese to the rugged Spartan coastline, Zagorus eyed the sentries on the fabled war city's stone walls. Conveying to this longtime rival the urgency of Athens' plight would be as difficult as his run had been.

Sparta was *not* Athens, not in any fashion. Neither shared much in common with the other, except for a mutual distrust and resentment that was born of differences in governing and cultural mores going back to mainland Greece's notorious Dark Ages. As both staunch city-states had emerged from those dread war-scarred times—several hundred years before the start of more cultured achievements, those Archaic Ages of 750 BC-500 BC—the world of Greeks had long been one where individual poleis fell under the rule of the few: oligarchies, where several prominent overlords dictated a city-state's laws and military and social standards. The alternative had been tyrannies, where kings (and perhaps close advisors) ruled without opposition or question. This had been the norm.

But the dawn of an emerging New Age had brought on the advent of another line of thinking...where past beliefs of rule by the few had simply meant rule by the *aristeia*...only the best. This was now being challenged by the stealthily growing new conviction brewing in Athens—rule of the people. The controversial democratic form of governing— where the *many* evaluated, determined, and approved the manner in which their lives would be lived—had risen from within the minds of those who dared challenge longtime mores. Athens was where the likes of Solon, and later Kleisthenes, had rescued the lower class of a state's citizenry from harsh overlords like its onetime notorious Draco. Now a more egalitarian, more equitable treatment of polis residents was on the rise...one striving on behalf of *all* its citizens. Striving...

Sparta, however, was unyielding in its adherence to traditions that left governance in the hands of the "capable few": a hierarchy of two kings and five *ephors*—overseers; and a council of elders—the *gerousia*. The ephors and gerousia were empowered to prevent total control by the duo of kings, who yet maintained their "kingsmanship"—one wielding more on the military front, the other concerned primarily with domestic matters. Sparta felt fully inclined to maintain this status; but Athens saw its rising new democratic structure as the rule of the future. And in this matter, the two most powerful and influential city-states of the Hellespont sowed seeds of discontent between one another, thus laying the groundwork for a brewing conflict…and the turmoil that would follow.

It was under these conditions that Zagorus, elite courier of Athens, now knelt before both kings and their council, urging Sparta to aid Athens.

"And you are quite certain these riled Persians are now marching on our mainland?" asked the elegantly robed man. He sported on his head a gold crown that glittered in the sunlight pouring in through the airy window space of the Spartan palace. His face and physique indicated a man in his fifties, though hale and hardy as one much younger and built just as sturdily. For this was Sparta's military king, Kleomenes, whose duty was to rule over the most potent aspect of Spartan society: its army, where boys were taken at a young age from their families and homes and raised into a life as the finest fighting men in all of Greece (or in all the world, as many would come to say). Kleomenes had spent a lifetime in those ranks—a veritable fiend on the battlefield and a cunning older bull who knew how to govern and how to lead a storming herd of warriors into emerging victorious time after time. The dusty-eyed king studied the scant-of-breath Athenian courier somewhat skeptically.

Sitting close by on a similar throne was a shorter, stockier man, also elegantly robed and flaunting a gold crown upon his head. This stout fellow was younger by some ten years than his royal counterpart and also of a most durable look—though not so formidable as the towering elder. Where Kleomenes was more of the battlefield lot, the shorter Demaratus was the designated overlord of the city-state's religious and civic affairs. His rounder, wistful-looking face virtually marked him so. And the air of scrutiny with which Demaratus examined the spent Athenian courier was of a far more thoughtful nature than the intense stare leveled at Zagorus by Kleomenes—who fairly measured the courier as he would a foe on the battlefield.

Zagorus knew something of Kleomenes' reputation and also the older king's volatile temperament (according to Athenian officials). Both of Sparta's current kings had had past "business" with Athens and her own civic struggles less than two decades earlier— and Sparta had played no small role in it, Kleomenes more directly. Memories of this past enmity clouded the faces and eyes of both Spartan rulers. Zagorus knew he would have to choose his words carefully, as the Archon and *Prytany* council members of Athens had advised him. He nodded formally, meeting their gaze, knowing that would draw some portion of respect from these two lords of military might.

"Yes, sires. I was among the field of couriers who first delivered word of the vast Persian fleet preparing to sail off from the flaming ruins of Eretria."

King Demaratus raised an eyebrow and turned his head slightly toward his kingly counterpart. They exchanged a subtle glance of silent concern.

"Mmm...the Eretrians," murmured Kleomenes somewhat insidiously. "The very city from Euboia Isle whose soldiers set sail with Athenians for Ionia...on a voyage that drew much attention from this Great King Darius?"

Zagorus again nodded his head tiredly, sensing the direction of the questioning to follow.

"As I recall," added Demaratus, "we did caution Athens against meddling in the affairs of so powerful and aggressive a *distant* foreign power..."

Kleomenes nodded in solemn agreement.

Zagorus felt a knot of impatience and resentment forming in his stomach. If this was to be their decision already, why not say so openly and immediately so he might hasten back to Athens and alert the city of Sparta's rejection. He was coming to resent these disagreeable Spartans all the more.

An aged voice croaked out from behind Zagorus, sounding like old bones being rolled over parched paper—a voice that was coarse and edgy. "And is this not the very Athens that openly condemned Sparta for failing to embrace its 'Rule of the People' as your own Kleisthenes and all of your archons tried spreading it throughout the Hellespont?"

Zagorus turned wearily as he wondered who this new adversary might be. He beheld, over his right shoulder, a robed elder, hunched, yet bearing himself with a pride born of self-importance.

"Ah…Councilor Trimos, we hoped you might have time to visit here and listen to the words of this Athenian courier," said King Demaratus. From the civic king's tone, Zagorus gathered this wiry elder was a figure of no minor stature. The lanky Athenian courier forced a congenial nod toward the haughty Spartan elder as the man passed arrogantly by him, one bushy brow raised suspiciously as a bleached old eye scrutinized him. The elder stepped slowly up to stand between the twin thrones where both kings rose to greet him.

Trimos acknowledged them both graciously, then turned back to face a now disheartened Zagorus. "Odd how Athens—with her 'wondrous democratia' should now be seeking the aid of 'tyrants' in fighting a tyrant…mmm?" the elder quipped, one side of his wrinkled mouth turned down into a sardonic half-smile.

Zagorus had had enough. He had run earnestly and with little rest, nearly a hundred and fifty miles, on a mission of dire need. Yet these Spartans, who always laid claim to valor and honor, were treating him with disdain for all his efforts. He tired of this useless charade and now only wanted to return to his own people and at least inform them of Sparta's rude dismissal of their need.

"Very well…sires," the proud young messenger responded tersely (though mindful not to sound disrespectful), "I…thank you for the courtesy of your audience. I must now make haste and return to tell our Archon of your decision."

The two Spartan kings exchanged a look, then regarded the courier politely. Kleomenes stared down from the dais at Zagorus and spoke firmly. "Eh…'Zagorus' is it…?"

Zagorus nodded, even more annoyed that they could barely recall his name. "Yes," he answered coolly.

"We've not yet given you our decision," said King Kleomenes.

Zagorus' head lifted as though jerked up, and his eyes widened in a flicker of unexpected hope.

Kleomenes and Demaratus exchanged another look, and Demaratus nodded in agreement for his fellow ruler to speak for them both.

"The Hellespont mainland shall *not* become the next host of colonies to the Persian Empire," Kleomenes said with conviction. "We will discuss this with our gerousia, of which Trimos here is a prominent council member—and then with the ephors, our Council of Overseers—regarding an armed force we most certainly will send to Athens in this important defense of our homelands."

The two Spartan kings offered reassuring smiles of acknowledgment, and Zagorus felt his heart leap so eagerly in his chest he nearly cried out for joy.

"*If* both councils concur," added Trimos stolidly and with an air of self-importance.

Zagorus barely heard or heeded the old geriousa councilor's words, so thrilled was he already with the decision of the two Spartan kings, and could not refrain from an eager response.

"Why, yes, of course," said Zagorus. "It is only fitting that you inform them of this gracious choice you have made here to aid us!"

"And to determine *when* our soldiery force is to come aid you," said Trimos.

Zagorus stared at him, then at the two kings, puzzled by the elder's statement.

Kleomenes appeared a trifle embarrassed now and gestured for Demaratus to explain. Demaratus leaned forward. "Eh, as the King of Sparta who presides over all religious and civic matters, I believe we must first consider the matter of our current festival that pays homage to our patron gods."

The Athenian courier gaped in undisguised disbelief. "A...*festival?*"

"Yes...and one that our people take most seriously," Trimos said solemnly, as though Zagorus' response was out of line.

"But our need is most urgent, sires," Zagorus persisted, mindless now of their stature. "The Persians likely move against us even now!"

"And homage to our gods is most urgent too...my dear courier," said Demaratus, clearly already having forgotten the young man's name. "Sparta shall lend aid to Athens, but in a timely manner that permits our religious festivities to be completed over the next few days."

"And upon conference with both councils," Trimos added importantly.

Zagorus stiffened, controlling himself admirably. "Have I leave to go then?" he asked politely.

Kleomenes regarded the worn young courier sympathetically, almost apologetically. "Yes, good Zagorus. And I will see that you have water and fruits for your return run."

Zagorus held King Kleomenes' gaze a moment, his own eyes softening in meeting the elder king's stare. He nodded respectfully—then gave the other two a perfunctory bow.

Chapter Ten

Gods Watch As a Courier Runs Again…
and Leaders Plot

Zagorus trod down the stone steps of the Spartan palace, two armored hoplites watching like trained guard dogs as he departed—while other eyes also followed and watched from far, far above.

Lord Pan wore a wry smirk that was more an expression of knowing sadness than one of triumph. He eyed his beautiful nymph-queen Keres with an "I-told-you-so" look that contained more a reluctant irony than a sense of genuine satisfaction. And in the filmy ethereal plains over which they hovered—a setting that fairly mimicked the harsh turf over which Zagorus would soon be running again, Pan held out one cloven-shaped hand in a "gimme" sort of gesture.

Keres' amber eyes caught the gesture. A frown crossed her smooth brow.

Pan lifted one thick eyebrow expectantly. "The ambrosia, dear Keres…"

She blinked in disbelief.

"A wager is a wager."

"They denied him!" she snapped.

"Eh…no," said Pan. "Our wager was whether Sparta would fail to offer *any* aid to Athens at all. And you too most certainly heard, that upon conclusion of their sacred festival—"

She waved her arms furiously, wanting to hear no more of his twisted rationale. A tiny glut of ambrosia food appeared magically between Pan's very lips, sealing off any further explanation.

"You'd have made a fitting Spartan lord yourself, oh Pan," she added sarcastically—then vanished into thin air, leaving the Lord of the Elysian Fields alone, the tasty ambrosia dangling from his lips. Pan smiled with an air of irony that held only a tinge of true humor, gobbled up the delightful morsel, and vanished in a twinkling.

Far below, Zagorus was already jogging away from Sparta on his long journey back.

****

Standing atop the beautifully designed outdoor marble hall with its thick classic columns and arched roof, Archon Kallimachos surveyed the throng of concerned Athenians gathered at the foot of its stone steps and spreading throughout the agora streets. Flanking him and decked out martially were General Milteades, Captain Boros, and other high-ranking Athenian commanders, along with elaborately dressed members of the great city's Prytany democratic council.

On this fittingly gray overcast day, the normally bustling agora—usually teeming with the exchange of goods, potent discussions on philosophy, commerce, and politics, dashing displays of arts and athletics, or with the tasting of delicious foods and refreshing wines—now harbored an air of gloom amidst the crowd of Athenians and outer villagers all crammed together for as far as one could see. There was but a single topic prevalent and on their minds this day: an announcement anticipated from Athens' most prominent leader whether an invasion was imminent or not.

Archon Kallimachos took a moment to confer with the city leaders gathered under the roofed outdoor dais, then strode over to the glossy podium erected before the steps that led down to the vast assemblage waiting anxiously below. As one, the entire mixed crowd consisting of Athens' citizens and its lower caste fell into a hush. Among them were Pheidippides and Symethra. Both took furtive note of Captain Boros standing among the city's vaunted elite.

Finally the High Archon prepared to address the gathering. Earlier that day, the recognized citizenry of Athens had cast its vote in the form of more white pebbles than black ones being placed in the huge vases on display, validating the choice for war. Once announced, nowhere—except in the shadows—was the presence of dissenters like Hahnitos and his ilk any longer evident; they surfaced only when the trauma of *eris*—strife—was overwhelming. But with the will of Athens' demos, its people, having declared strongly for resistance should Darius come, the dissidents had apparently withdrawn.

"Fellow Athenians," Kallimachos' rich voice boomed out firmly, confidently, "while we await the return of our bold messenger Zagorus—and what will surely be the welcome news that Sparta marches to join us in the need of defense—as High Archon, I am pleased to inform you that a chain of our elite couriers, the hemeredrome, roam from here to Plataia also seeking aid from our cousins there, and from our other northern kin. Our gallant runners also watch for movements of the enemy. These Persian marauders who slay innocent people shall never come close enough to taint our blessed city!"

A hearty cheer went up from the military and governmental personnel flanking the archon, and it caught on, rippling through the crowd below like a powerful wave and spreading among those crammed along the surrounding stone-and-dirt streets of the agora region. Archon Kallimachos reached upward and outward as though not only gesturing to his citizenry and village outliers, but also to the very heavens and to the gods themselves. If his intent was that such a gesture would help reassure the masses, it had the desired effect.

Pheidippides himself stared up at the archon as though the man himself were a god—and in the eyes of many gathered there he was exactly that. But standing next to the wide-eyed young boy, looking shaky and pale, Symethra's thin youthful face was suddenly drawn and filled with worry and fear. She allowed her gaze to drift over to the stolid form of Boros, who was applauding heartily along with everyone else. But his face did not match his bodily gestures. The tall captain could not mask entirely a look of unmistakable consternation.

Chapter Eleven

Athenian Equality…?

Pheidippides and his mother walked slowly away
with the rest of the dispersing crowd from the mass
gathering outside the great Bouleuterion hall.
Symethra's soft gray eyes were dappled with worry as
she cast a glance back toward her son. She noticed that
his head, too, was turned back toward the dais area atop
the marble stairs, the boy's neck craning, his gaze fixed
upward in a clear attempt to catch sight of Captain
Boros. She sighed and urged gently, with a touch of a
hand upon his shoulder, for him to face her as they
slipped off through the crowd. He met her eyes, the
turned-down smile on his face conveying the obvious
thoughts clouding his young mind.

"Will you come home with me now?" she asked
simply.

Pheidippides paused, then shook his head no, just
as simply. They walked a few more steps in silence,
easing their way carefully from the main crunch of the
crowd which, in itself, constituted a bizarre mosaic of
those dwelling in Athens: the eupatridae—the elites
whose wealth and status granted them far more say and
clout in the city's affairs; the workers and craftsmen
and artisans who also commanded a degree of prestige
and priority, along with the highly respected soldiery

caste—hoplites garbed today for the occasion in their
stock bronze armor (leather for those of lesser status);
and the *perioki*, the lower class of the city that dwelled
in its outer reaches (like Pheidippides and his mother);
and even a notable turnout of rogues from the notorious
Kaboni quarters, where the likes of the rangy elder
Garathi dwelled with his followers and younger
denizens like Barthus.

All had attended the widely announced gathering,
knowing now that the vague reports of an advancing
Persian horde had grown beyond mere rumor. Even
those who had wandered in from the vast surrounding
Attica region that lay outside the walls of Athens,
seeking sanctuary within the great city-state's
borders—the *metics,* those considered foreigners—had
journeyed there to hear the archon. Metics who had
found productive work were granted rights a notch
above the public slaves—who were known more widely
as the *demesioi* and *doulas*—"living possessions" as
many citizens regarded them. They and a fair number of
others who comprised Athens' underbelly had all been
present this day to learn what was to become of their
homeland; for, in spite of such disparity in class, all
bore the right to assemble before the High Archon of
Athens and hear, firsthand, the plight of their state. All
faced the same peril now...one that held little or no
regard for status or rank. And as everyone departed the
agora, they knew that this time they all shared a
common concern.

Breaking finally from the main body of the
dispersing throng, Pheidippides nudged his mother and
gestured with his head toward another roofed, much
smaller pavilion-type structure. A robed, white-haired

elder sat under it in an ornately decorated chair, addressing a group of teenage boys and girls gathering there. All were dressed in smart, clean chiton tunics and fine himation robes. In spite of the brewing threat, Kallimachos and the Prytany council had deemed it wise for people to continue with their daily lives, even as the hoplites and citizens' militia mobilized for pending deployment.

The air of strife that had fallen over the city from the time Zagorus had burst into the agora with word of danger massing in the north had seized everyone. And a population falling victim to eris was one already in the throes of defeat. The archon understood that an air of normality might fend off such strife and all but ordered that Athenians behave as they would on any other day in their city. This was how a demos living under the freedom of democratia would resist the brutal ways of the *tyrannos*—and how they would remain a free people.

Pheidippides was among those who believed and cherished every word a man such as Archon Kallimachos uttered, and so he made his way eagerly toward the roofed, columned structure.

"Oh, Pheidippides," Symethra said, a tiny tremor in her now lilting voice, "you know you are not allowed to sit among those students there."

Pheidippides bristled involuntarily at that, restraint in his response.

"I sit *away* from them, Mother. The stoic does not seem to mind as long as I listen from outside the columns of his *stoa*."

"Well if he does mind you being so close during his lessons, you must leave immediately."

He made to protest, but she pressed on. "I would not like to hear later that you were escorted away or even arrested for disturbing an important class for young Athenian citizens."

Pheidippides drew himself up proudly. "For all I have learned from listening to Stoic Rolios speaking of nature and the gods and…and everything else, it would be worth it to me. I feel as much an Athenian as any of them," he added, gesturing with one hand toward the well-dressed youths.

Symethra eyed him with a growing concern, but then felt her lips slipping into a soft smile in spite of herself. The boy laughed innocently at his mother's inability to truly be upset with him. She surrendered a hug, smiled warmly again, and stroked his cheek gently before turning and striding off like a delicate phantom slipping through the city's bustle and gloom. Nothing could ever wipe from her face the irrepressible smile of pride; or the powerful love she felt in knowing that this was *her* boy.

****

While Pheidippides and his mother parted near the outdoor classroom of one of the city's more renowned stoics and teachers of promising young Athenians, the man to whom neither Symethra Deglos nor her son might speak publicly stood within the hall of the Bouleuterion chambers, listening to the Archon of Athens and General Milteades—commander of that polis' entire military.

"We must yet be prepared should the Spartans choose to leave us to our own fate," said Milteades. "Given past aid by some of them to usurpers among us, I am not filled with confidence."

Boros and the other military leaders nodded in agreement with General Milteades, and it did not escape the eye of Kallimachos, who frowned with concern.

"But with or without Spartan aid," said the Archon. "I believe Athenians would rather face death than live as Persian vassals."

Agreement filled the hardened faces of every soldier in the room.

"And, as has been reported, that is not necessarily the way of it with other Greek poleis—some of those states, I'm told, have already said they will surrender to Darius. But we of Athens must stand firm! Thus, we will not rule out the rousting of an entire civilian militia if we are to meet this pending threat with any hope of resistance—futile as it may sound to others," the Archon added solemnly.

****

Captain Boros strode earnestly down the steps from the Bouleuterion, taking note of the dwindling number of Athenian citizens and other dwellers of the state still milling about in the area. Upon seeing the esteemed Captain of the Elite Guard, some called out eager questions concerning the city's plight. But Boros dismissed their inquiries with a polite wave of his hand, pressing on down the stone-cobbled street. So much was on the mind of the tall, uniformed man—his thoughts dominated by the mounting threat—that he hiked on pointedly, mindless of the exquisite craftsmanship of the city's artisans, or the business and recreation stalls where vendors still engaged both citizens and outer villagers to consider their various wares. Boros paid no heed at all to any of these resumed activities.

How in the name of Zeus himself were they to contend with the largest, most potent military force in the known world? And why had Athens been the one city-state in the Hellespont to provoke the ire of this seeming madman of a Persian tyrant...this Darius! And did these vendors and crafts people and all the others out here in the streets even wonder about that themselves...or had a mere speech from the Archon arrested their fears so easily?

Not his. Boros stared up to the heavens as he continued on through the agora strip, still acknowledging the occasional question from those he passed by, still dismissing each with a polite wave. Perhaps so cavalier a response to the premise of so imminent a storm would help in stemming the tide of panic that could easily grip these people. The disquieted captain hoped some attentive Olympus god might put into his head (or into the heads of those he served) the solution Athens dearly needed. But he knew no such answers were forthcoming. Boros Constantis was not a man to put faith in the aid of gods (as others were wont to do), but a man who believed more firmly in the hands of men's will.

Now, though, he might welcome such counsel or aid from whatever celestial spirits might happen to overhear their plight. Aid that would not now be necessary, he reflected bitterly, but for blunders made in these past few years by Athenian heads of state in aiding distant colonies, Greek or not. Had Athens not foolishly involved herself in struggles on a faraway, foreign shoreline—so close to a vast nest of hornets that reveled in its own rule over colonies of mosquitoes and gnats—they'd not have riled a temperamental tyrant so obsessed with his own image as a "god on earth."

Boros had heard horrid tales of how this "Great King Darius" would ridicule, chide, even punish severely his own subordinates and underlings for the slightest, barely perceivable break in the protocol for paying him proper reverence. There was no need, then, to ponder how he might mete out consequences to any who dared engage him in territorial defiance...as Athens had done. The Ionians and Eretrians served vividly enough as morose examples. How could Athens withstand an army which, in all estimations, was akin to a stampede of enraged oxen advancing on scattered colonies of fox dens?

A crisp, elderly voice that Boros recognized interrupted his gloomy thoughts.

"And with all that is happening now between Persia and our Hellespont states, I am not surprised that many of you are so curious of a distant people and their ways," the older voice proclaimed.

Boros turned his head in the direction of the speaker, an expression of pleasant familiarity already crossing his face. He knew the source of that voice and the strength behind it. Some fifteen strides away, he saw a small-columned pavilion, roofed for protection from the elements—a stoa—where a short, grizzled elder sat atop the stairs, a clay-and-wax tablet in one hand as he gestured to a half-dozen or so teenage Athenian citizens taking in every word, spellbound. This was Rolios, one of Athens' more renowned *stoics* who lectured not only the city's prominent youth but also advised Boule council members, prestigious businessmen, highly regarded military personnel...and was even said to have the archon's ear on certain civic matters. None was deemed more learned or versed in history, culture, or nature…as Stoic Rolios.

Boros could not help pausing to listen in a bit, as he was wont to do on occasion. He smiled as he also eyed the stoic's students staring up at the honored elder so reverently.

"Stoic Rolios, is it true that Darius believes it was the Persian god, Mithra, who chose him to be King?" asked an immaculately dressed boy of some seventeen years.

The stoic smiled congenially. "Not only of Persia, but of 'All The Known World,' yes," said the elder stoic. "According to *Persian* lore."

"But Zeus is the mightiest of all gods," countered another clean-faced lad, his beautifully tanned features and silver chiton and himation garment advertising privilege and wealth—the norm for those eupatridae awarded the status of a stoic's protégés. "And Zeus would never allow any Persian to rule this world," the self-assured youth added smoothly, confidently.

Stoic Rolios smiled with an air of warm amusement. "Zeus is the mightiest of *our* gods," he responded, amending the boy's pointed assertion.

The youth frowned. "But Stoic Rolios…he most certainly is stronger than those worshipped by Persians. Who but our own Olympians are great enough to be called gods?" he all but insisted.

"The Elysian gods," a softer young voice chimed in from beyond the grouping of students gathered on the steps below the stoic. In spite of its quieter nature, the voice behind those words was imbued with conviction.

Stoic Rolios' ash-gray eyebrows nudged closer

together in a half frown, a glimmer of recognition crossing his face, though not one of annoyance.

The same could not be said of the youths gathered below him on the stoa steps. Their heads had all turned as one, their probing eyes falling on none other than...Pheidippides, crouched beneath a small planted olive tree, some twenty strides away.

He had half-risen from the seated position he had taken at the trunk of the tree that was lush with green olives—the words of the students regarding the gods of Olympus having spurred on his involuntary response on behalf of the oft-neglected Elysians. Now his thin legs felt weak as he bore the stares and full attention of the distinguished Stoic Rolios and his young Athenian scholars.

Standing farther away from the group—and from Pheidippides too—near another columned pavilion that was empty of occupants, was Boros. The hoplite captain had not recognized the intruding young voice, for he had never so much as spoken a word with the child he and Symethra Deglos had conceived some sixteen years past. Nor had he ever been close enough physically to peer directly into young Pheidippides' eyes, though he did know his illegitimate son on sight and from passing glances exchanged between them on occasion. And Pheidippides had not seen Boros, who was still obscured by the thick marble columns of the nearby stoa pavilion; neither were Rolios or any of his students aware of the captain's presence. All eyes were now trained on the eavesdropper lurking under the nearby tree.

"It's that *ostraka* again, sir!" snapped one of the boys within the group, rising and pointing right at

Pheidippides. Some of the others in the group echoed the disdainful sentiment uttered by the first.

Standing yet within the shadows of the empty pavilion, Boros fairly flinched at the word "ostraka"—the hardy captain looked suddenly ill at ease and like a man who wished he might be whisked abruptly away to anywhere else.

"Only an ostraka would even think to speak of Elysians as gods," snickered a fair-skinned girl within the group, her near-angelic face made suddenly ugly by the sneer distorting her mouth. The rest of the youths giggled in agreement, causing Pheidippides to turn his head away in shame. Boros himself stared down at the ground in a rare moment of seeming hurt.

The tirade of taunts, though, was cut off no sooner than it began as the sharp, crackling voice of Rolios clipped through the humid afternoon air. "We shall not use such language in my classes..." His scolding old eyes turned from his rebuked students and back to Pheidippides, now standing and apparently readying himself to depart, the boy's embarrassment all but tangible. "There is no cause for any of you to call another Athenian 'outcast.' "

Surprised by the elder's firm but kindly defense of him, Pheidippides lifted his head and met Rolios' gaze directly...gratefully, as he fought off the mistiness mounting in his own eyes. Their momentary exchange was one the bronze-skinned lad would never forget. But it was broken by an insistent protest from the same feminine voice of a moment ago, the tone of it every bit as discordant.

"But our Olympian gods see the Elysians in that same way, Stoic Rolios."

Rolios frowned, a flicker of annoyance again crossing his brow as he turned his eyes reluctantly from the intelligent-looking youngster crouched under the olive tree's shelter…and back to the young woman who was too obtuse to recognize the stoic's slowly mounting ire.

"The Olympians are *gods*. They may act in such ways if they please," he responded, his thick gray brows furrowing.

"But—" she persisted in the manner of one accustomed to a flutter of her eyelashes assuring her of her own way.

"But young Athenians shall *not*," the elder commanded crisply, assuring the young beauty such was not to be the way of her behavior here and now…or ever.

The haughty youngster nodded in humbled acknowledgment of his chiding tone.

Near the bottom of the steps, one of the teenage boys whispered disdainfully to another of the group— discreetly but more audibly than intended—"So we welcome those whose parents are barely more than slaves?"

The stoic's eyes now flashed with unmistakable anger as he rose and stepped down to the base of the stairs and thumped a thorny old forefinger over the head of the callous young boy.

"Yes!" Rolios assured him in a voice resounding like the crack of a whip. "*We are all Athenians*." Not another of the city's future young elites offered a look or a word—not the faintest whisper or hint of a frown— that might even suggest rebuttal.

Rolios held his stern gaze on them all a moment

longer, then turned a softer eye back to Pheidippides, who also had heard the boy's cruel whisper, even from where he stood. His smooth young face was draped in humiliation and hurt. And though the old stoic raised his arm in a polite gesture for him to approach, Pheidippides had had enough. He gave a dejected look to the group of highbrowed young Athenians and shook his head with the knowledge of one who knew they would always regard his ilk that way, in spite of kindly stoics who would not always be there to scold them.

A somber Boros had not missed a moment of his undeclared son's torment, and stepped out involuntarily from the concealment of the empty pavilion—almost as though to intercede. At nearly the same moment, Pheidippides raised his head for one last glimpse of thanks at the distinguished elder who had taken his part...but his eyes met, instead, with those of the man who had denied public recognition of him since birth. The two held each other's gaze in a locked stare, longer than any that had marked such a moment in all the boy's sixteen years of life. And Captain Boros Constantis saw in that smooth tanned face the very look of his beloved Symethra...and he saw also, in the boy's deep chestnut eyes, the probing intensity of his own intelligent gaze.

"Captain...is there something we can do for you here?" the old stoic called out, aware now that a man of some military merit stood among them.

As though jolted from a trance, Boros broke off the visual exchange he had been holding with Pheidippides. He turned to regard the graceful elder whose aged eyes studied him curiously. The gaggle of teenagers looked on curiously at this respected captain of the Elite

Athenian Guard who had so abruptly advanced into their mix.

"Eh...no, good stoic. I merely happened by and heard the last of your...lecture."

Rolios nodded thoughtfully. "Then you doubtless heard some of the sentiments expressed here?"

"Yes," said Boros, nodding back to the stoic. "And...you speak true of what our great Kleisthenes most surely intended for all who dwell in Athens and in her villages...in all the *demoi* of the Attica regions where Greeks roam freely," he added, giving an assuring glance to the students.

He straightened himself and raised a hand in a parting wave to the group, followed by one last visual exchange with Rolios—who yet eyed him with extended curiosity—then turned to leave. Boros noticed, in the near distance, Pheidippides trodding slowly away down the narrow roadstrip, slump-shouldered, head hung low. The big man bit his own lip, his hazel eyes clouding momentarily; then he straightened up again, throwing his broad shoulders back in true officer's fashion, and strode off, never looking back at the stoic and his group of Athens' young finest.

****

Far north, King Darius stood facing several more of his legion chieftains who were garbed in the flamboyant, fearsome-looking armor that signified the Persian military—complete with headgear that flaunted bestial and demonic designs, crafted that way deliberately to strike hesitation, doubt, and even abject fear into an enemy. It was a tactic that had always worked all too well, most recently here in the smoldering ruins of Eretria on the northern isle of Euboia. Standing next to the Great King now was his vaunted general, Mardonius, a thick-bearded brute. Both surveyed Persia's newly won turf.

Flanking General Mardonius were Darius' two devoted satraps—Artaphernes and Datis—the governors who had first delivered to their liege and lord the unwelcome news of the Ionian revolt that had been augmented by Athens and ill-fated Eretria. They were joined by a wiry elder whose raw, unshaven look belied the rich robes and fine silver cap he wore. This was Hippias...deposed, banished tyrant of Athens who, in his bitter exile, had found a home among the Persians. Having paid all due homage to Darius—a ruler of limited tolerance for those who faltered in displaying the sense of reverence that suited his expectations— Hippias had not been remiss in his flattery and unquestioning acknowledgment of Persia's "Great King" as the rightful "Ruler of all Earth." Thus, he had earned his right to ascend, once more, to the status of Athens' overlord—where he would conduct all affairs there in accordance with Persian dictates.

Hippias' younger years were long past, but the bitterness and resentment over his defeat and exile had not waned. Though the year 510 BC was now two decades past, to the gnarly elder it had lingered as vividly as a fossil preserved in perfectly frozen soil. The one-time Athenian tyrant had clung to that memory the way a hungry tick might cling to a longtime host. He most certainly would abide by all directives given him by the temperamental King Darius of Persia. And upon being installed as Persia's satrap over Athens— and possibly over Sparta too—he would demonstrate to his onetime fellow Greeks a punishing justice befitting them all.

Darius eyed his entourage thoughtfully now, always suspicious of those around him, always wondering if (or when) any of them might harbor machinations to undermine or even to overthrow him. He knew well that the lot of those akin to himself—that rare breed born to rule—always lived in the shadow of perpetual treachery from lesser men (and women) who envied them. And though the ones standing reverently before him now, here on this very hilltop where he surveyed the scorched ruins of another telling Persian triumph, he yet felt a need to reaffirm his kinship with the Lords of the Higher Worlds. So Darius drew forth an arrow from the long quiver strapped to the back of General Mardonius and, beckoning for the bone bow slung over the man's shoulder, he nocked the arrow to it, then proclaimed up to the heavens:

"Oh Mighty Mithra, who did name me 'Ruler of all Earth'…grant me my vengeance now upon the vile Athenians who sought to disrupt my rightful rule over these lesser beings and all their lot!"

With that, he lit the arrow afire with a burning brand and drew back the bowstring, then sent the flaming missile high into the air. Darius turned back imperiously to his small gathering of regal and militant underlings and declared coldly, "At least thrice per day, till all justice has been meted out in full, let any one of you proclaim to me—'Oh Master, forgot not the fell deed of the Athenians!' "

The two satraps, his outlandishly garbed captains, and General Mardonius, all stared solemnly at their liege and master, howbeit with averted gaze, and nodded their heads in dutiful acquiescence…while Hippias contained a smirk of triumph as he, too, bowed his head politely.

Standing at the base of the knoll, the two assassins, Rojese of Macedonia and the Nubian Jamjon, eyed each other with a subtle unease; then they too gazed up toward the posturing king and nodded in solemn acknowledgment. The Persian Lord would be generous, as always, in rewarding their work.

Darius thrust back his broad shoulders, stretching his six-foot-two-inch frame to its fullest and allowing him the distinction of towering over his minions gathered lower on the knoll and below it.

"Once this broken isle is garrisoned against foolhardy enemies who might seek to seize it back, we will set sail for an isolated coastal plain called Marathon. From there we will disembark and march a distance of nearly nine leagues over the difficult Hellespont hills toward Athens; thus, our advance will not be sighted by the enemy." He paused and stared hard at them all, a grim smile marking his thickly bearded face. "Have one ship dispatched early, so our two bold assassins here might move quickly in hunting down any spies who happen along the way. And any troublesome Greek foot couriers, of which good Hippias has spoken, shall be flushed out in the same way…much like birds flushed out and dealt with by cunning cats."

Chapter Twelve

Troubled Minds

Boros sat up in the polished oaken bed, the light
satin covers draped over his waist and legs, his sturdy
chest, abdomen, and brawny arms exposed in the late
afternoon light. Symethra was nestled close to him,
most of her supple, tanned body still tucked under the
covers in spite of the late summer day's
warmth...typical of this *Hekatombion* season of year.
She stared up at him, unsettled by the frown crossing
his brow and the pursed lips—always a sign that her
man harbored some element of concern. He had greeted
her earlier with an air of distraction, but Symethra had
dismissed it as a mood born of the city's brewing
struggles. She would provide him with a more pleasant
distraction to help banish such forebodings, if only for
the briefest of whiles. But it had not been so, as his gray
mood darkened and now seemed to envelop him all the
more.

Symethra reached a hand up to his shoulder and
tapped gently with one finger.

"What is it?" she asked gently.

Boros shook his head, his eyes still distant and
indicating his thoughts yet roamed elsewhere. "It is
nothing," he answered absently, his tone every bit as
soft as hers.

"Yes, there is something. You know it is not possible to deny when such feelings are upon you, my loving lord." She had long been in the habit of addressing him in such a way—in one manner acknowledging their contrast in social status, in another (and more significantly), as a term of affection she was not permitted ever to display in public. But despite the angst she suffered from it all, Symethra knew how he truly felt for her and accepted it as graciously as her heart might permit.

Boros pursed his lips again and ran a strong hand gently through her long locks.

"It is just…" He seemed bent on saying one thing, but instead, different words poured out from his mouth. "It is just this war that appears most certain to be coming upon us. I am worried that our city's defenses…"

"You have said that already tonight." She smiled, sitting up more and allowing the silver satin covers to drop from her shoulders and chest, revealing her beautiful bronze-skinned breast. Boros took only partial notice of that, his face growing all the more distraught.

"Boros…please?" she cooed softly again, rubbing him about the shoulders and chest.

His strong hands closed gently on hers, and he hugged her ever so lightly, trembling as he did. "I was thinking…if it seems the fighting may come too close to the city itself…"

"Yes…?" she asked, her eyes finding his.

"I want to see that you and…the boy are sent somewhere safe. Away from here. I will make sure of it myself," he added. "I want you both to be…" Boros pressed to continue, but strained to draw his next breath; he choked, unable to form the words.

Symethra stared at him in a curious wonder. "Of course," she said soothingly. She waited as Boros worked up the next few words finally.

"He is a…good boy, yes?" He bit his lip, and she felt his hand trembling again in hers, the quiet choke in his voice so very clear. She hugged him round his thick neck, the quiet sobs in her own response a match for the ones he struggled to suppress.

"Yes, he is a very good boy," Symethra whispered as their moist eyes met tenderly.

****

In a rundown quarter of Athens—not refined enough to even rate on a scale with the city-state's lesser villages and outer settlements—Pheidippides skulked through what could only be termed an Athenian ghetto. It was more a polis-afterthought, where human (and animal) castoffs dwelled and where they also retreated when their time in the more prominent sectors of Athens had exceeded all tolerance by recognized citizens. Even captured slaves—those seized via city wars—who served their wealthy masters by doing menial chores, rated higher on the social scale than the residents here.

For this was the notorious Kaboni, where rogues of all ages—all from the same underclass—were permitted to dwell in their covert and slovenly existence; thus, it was a limited time granted any of them for roaming the agora and other byways of Athens, where the extent of their numbers in a single group was carefully regulated. And though Pheidippides was son to a hetaera woman and a mere sliver above the slave caste himself—given the humble neighborhood of lower class perioki he and his mother inhabited—the Kaboni itself was deemed such an underbelly of the great polis of fair Athens that the young courier might well have been accused of "slumming" simply by being there.

Rats scurried through the banked stone and dirt paths he now walked; stray dogs and feral cats roamed boldly by, ever on the prowl for scuttling rodents and other varmints, while now and then a skulking hooded figure darted by. On one occasion, two roguish-looking children flitted through the shadowy haunts—pausing to regard curiously the lean teenager whose demeanor and finer apparel did not identify him as a Kaboni resident. Pheidippides could not help wondering if this sense of quiet revulsion he felt here was akin to the way more highbrow citizens of Athens' main quarters eyed him. He did not have long to consider it further, as his way down the gloomy alley was abruptly blocked by a fierce-looking hound that loomed ahead in his direct path.

The dog had somewhat of an undersized wolfish look to it—the long, thick, pointed ears, already pricked high, and the shaggy black-gray fur over a lean body that was fairly muscled—but it was the shaggy fur and the soft gaze that identified this animal as a creature of domestic origins rather than one of the wild. Still, Pheidippides felt a tinge of unease as he beheld the dark canine that had emerged so suddenly from the shadows and eyed him now with an odd air of curiosity. Instinctively, the long-haired boy dropped to one knee, offering the furry interloper what might be taken as a sign of friendliness, followed with a soft unintelligible greeting he hoped was reassuring to the dog.

Recognizing no sense of menace or hostility from

the kneeling young human, the dog responded with a low whine and ventured a cautious step closer. Pheidippides smiled and offered the same cooing sounds again, reminiscent of his moments with the turtles at the agora pond weeks ago.

"And who are you, my wooly visitor from these unpleasant shadows?" he said with a smile that came naturally. The dog's amber eyes studied him more closely, and it crept nearer, haunches raised high, forepaws inching toward him. Another soft whine followed, and then the animal stopped mere feet away, its panting more like an audible "handshake" there in the mounting dusk.

"Atlas won't let many people that close to him right away," a lilting feminine voice declared from somewhere in the alley shadows.

Pheidippides sprang back to his feet, startled by the intruding voice and surprising the dog, as it jumped backward while rising again to its full stance on all fours. A slender, raggedly dressed teenage girl, with flowing black hair that hung down the length of her back, emerged from an alcove in one of the brick-walled buildings along the narrow strip. In spite of the tattered cotton *peplos* of a shawl draped over an equally tattered muslin blouse, and cut-down leggings of the same cloth, the girl's thin face bore a mischievous charm and a scampish beauty. She peered out at Pheidippides through a pair of sharp beige eyes that contained an obvious intelligence. He watched as she knelt down next to the wolfish-looking mongrel and rubbed it gingerly round the neck.

Embarrassed at having reacted so skittishly to her abrupt appearance, Pheidippides smiled, gesturing toward the dog. "This is your dog?" he asked, his eyes scanning the alley shadows to assure himself there were no others accompanying her. He had not forgotten the reputation of these haunts.

"You are in the Kaboni," she answered sharply, as though reading his thoughts. "No one owns anyone here." Their eyes met as they appraised each other. "Atlas is a friend," she said resolutely, stroking the animal round the neck once more. The dog licked her hand in response. "And you are not from the Kaboni," she added firmly.

Again his eyes roamed the shadows, squinting to see if any others lurked there.

The girl smirked sweetly. "We are alone," she assured him.

He nodded in acknowledgment, mildly guilty from his obvious air of suspicion. "I am Pheidippides...from the Athenian quarter of Kounaz."

She smiled ever so thinly. "I am Azelina," she said simply, and then her smile turned a little insidious. "You are looking for someone this eve?" she queried, as though already knowing who.

"I...yes," he answered with a nervousness he could not mask.

Azelina smiled slyly, her teeth white and clean in contrast to her shabby clothing. She gestured for him to follow, and Pheidippides did so, knowing there was no other choice now, here in the notorious Kaboni and in the company of one of its denizens.

****

Pheidippides had followed the sleek Azelina through a veritable maze of darkening alleys and side streets, wondering if the way to their destination was as complex as it appeared…or if this teenage vixen had only made it seem that way in order to ensure that he might not return again out of memory. He was certain he would barely be able to find his way back to where he had first met her and her dog, let alone negotiate his way again to this quarter of the Kaboni. On occasion, Azelina held back to reassure him, her eyes twinkling coyly, her lips offering a hint of a smile every bit as coy as the playful light in her gaze. Pheidippides wondered at those times if some deviltry lurked behind the seemingly angelic face of this lithe street urchin…and if that alluring smile was, in truth, a subtle smirk of triumph at having drawn him into a web from which he might not escape. But having allowed himself to be drawn in this far—and knowing the bitter reasoning he harbored for daring to trek the turf of the notorious Kaboni—he followed with a will that eclipsed any doubts that would previously have deterred him. Only when they rounded a bend of gloomy hovels and saw, finally, a large, dead-end dwelling, flat-roofed and made of thick stone boulders, did those fearful inklings slip back over him.

This structure was notably larger than the others that lined the brooding roadstrip, lit only by rush torches that revealed a narrow path to the front doorway. A pair of husky rogues, garbed in thick leather tunics and black muslin leggings tucked inside their high boots, stood ominously on either side—savage-looking curled scimitars strapped to their hips. Pheidippides froze, sure now that the raven-haired vixen had most definitely led him into a trap, delivering him practically into the waiting grasp of these swarthy henchmen. But her smile widened as, even from where she stood—a good ten steps away—his apprehension was as clear as the moonlight shining down on them.

"Atlas," she cooed gently to the huge dog waiting eagerly close by. The animal responded to her soft call by sauntering over to Pheidippides and nuzzling him round the thigh, then rolling its canine head back toward the dark, flat-roofed structure at the end of the lonely stretch of street.

Knowing there was no other safe choice now, the leery teenage boy followed Azelina and her wolfish sidekick right up to the doorstep, nodding back courteously to the two sentinels, who offered him a silent nod back of acknowledgment.

Azelina opened the door.

Chapter Thirteen

Old Acquaintances and New Ones

The stony room he beheld from the arched
doorway was well lit by rush torches and metal lamps
fueled by olive oil. It was stocked with thick oaken
tables and crudely built chairs. Rough-looking men and
women, mostly middle-aged, though some a good deal
older and a number of them younger—even teens and
wayward-looking children present—filled the room. A
number of the adults (and even some of the teens) drank
ale or wine from tankards and mugs, while nibbling on
chunks of meat or crusty bread. Pheidippides wondered
if he'd been lured insidiously to this seedy old café, for
it certainly did not bear any semblance to the kinds of
meeting halls he had seen in the agora.

His deep brown eyes scanned the large room of
Kaboni rogues and he was about to turn his gaze back
to Azelina when he caught a glimpse of a familiar
young face grinning slyly, though not with the air of
disdain he'd have expected of this rangy lad.

"Garathi…look who has come to see us!" crowed
Barthus, the mischievous teen who had cracked
Pheidippides' writing tablet that day at the agora
pond…a day that now seemed another lifetime ago. A
veritable phalanx of the hardcore rogues parted and,
sitting almost regally at a corner table, surrounded by

the fiercest-looking of the café crowd, was none other than Garathi himself, the gaunt elder who had come to Pheidippides' aid that day by the pond. Clearly the leader here, the man put down his tall tankard and raised a hand to his bony chin, eying the nervous youngster gaping at him from the doorway.

"Pheidippides," Garathi said with a dark air of affection. "Welcome."

****

While Pheidippides stood facing a room of rascals such as only the notorious Kaboni could house, high above the realm of those dwelling upon the secular Earth two ethereal beings gazed down at the world below. The object of their attention was a struggling lone figure in a more corporeal setting, straining to force one weary foot before the other in an utter parody of a run. The lanky elite courier of Athens, Zagorus, wiped back from his steaming brow the long, sweat-filled strands of hair as he plodded on. He panted like a stricken beast of prey worn to exhaustion by the chase. But Zagorus was not suffering the pursuit of predators...only the assurance that his beloved home city of Athens might surely perish if he failed to sustain a steady pace on his return trip.

"Will this gallant fellow even make it to Athens?" quipped the beautiful nymph queen, Keres.

"Mmm," murmured Pan wistfully. "It appears he now holds visions of *Erebus* instead of Athens." His wry smile turned down at his own words, the bestial, horned features bearing a frown.

"Indeed. The Lord Charon shall likely revel in another triumph as he claims one more bold Greek hero for his gloomy underworld," said Keres without hint of emotion.

And down below, Zagorus looked very much on the brink of soon mingling with the shade beings claimed by Charon, lord of those doomed to an eternity of flitting by as phantoms in a realm of oppressive mist and fog. Even now, the bold foot courier caught glimpses of erratically twisting figures darting before him on the dirt path, while others danced among the surrounding trees that suddenly appeared misshapen and hostile. He blinked and halted, unsure whether to press on or not.

From their glossy higher world, Pan and Keres both shook their heads sardonically, the two Elysian gods regarding the straining form of Zagorus with a mix of sorrow and dark amusement.

"It does indeed appear this gallant fellow will not see his beloved Athens again," said Pan. "Best not wager on *his* journey."

Keres, however, had shifted her attention elsewhere, her golden-hued eyes fixed on another haze of wispy images germinating off to one side—some distance from the plight of Zagorus running on below. She raised a slender arm and pointed at the other earthly image that had just distracted her.

"It seems the swift couriers that Athens sent north to spy upon the Persians will not see their fair city again either," she quipped softly, her lips pursed, though not harshly.

Pan took note of this parallel drama taking shape concurrently with the one below. And as he focused on it, the plight of Zagorus, struggling along, faded away into a flurry of shadows. The one on which Keres had fixed her gaze took on a more tangible appearance for both Elysians.

Another lean foot courier, bronze-skinned and sporting flowing black locks, ran through a stony passageway that led to a rocky overpass. The gray cliffs on either side climbed at least twenty feet, like great waves ready to crash down onto the narrow trail between them. The courier hastened his pace as he beheld the towering concave of rock and was virtually swallowed by it as he entered. Halfway through, he was met by another runner, garbed similarly in a sleeveless muslin chiton and white cut-down britches of the same fabric; tough leather sandals covered his feet. The Athenian symbol of the hemeredrome—a winged sandal—was woven beautifully onto an upper corner of each chiton, identifying and honoring them as their city's elite foot couriers, the Hermes' Messengers. After a brief verbal exchange, the courier who had been waiting in the pass for the first to arrive, turned and ran off—south toward Athens. The other sat down onto a large rock, utterly spent…unaware of his peril.

From roughly a quarter mile away, the two assassins, Rojese the Macedonian and Jamjon the Nubian, who had been let ashore earlier by an advance Persian sailcraft, sat upon their huge war steeds, perched high on a hillock where they had witnessed the exchange between the two Athenian couriers. The Nubian pointed a thick dark finger toward the first, who was still resting on a rock. Rojese nodded smugly at the sight of their quarry…the courier having absolutely no idea that Darius' hired assassins had been following him the whole time.

Pan frowned while Keres shook her head in a deliberate parody of despair as they both eyed the unsuspecting courier resting directly in the path of his own doom. "Sitting there plainly for Darius' henchmen to behold in all his fatigue...Hmmh!" mused Pan. "But if the ship putting Darius' two assassins ashore was seen by that first courier, the Persians' coming departure from Euboia might soon be known...*if* the message reaches Athens."

Keres yawned ostentatiously, wanting to convey a greater air of detachment than she actually felt. Pan caught her gesture, a look of mischief crossing his bovine lips. "I've a charming idea, sweet Keres!" he piped with dark merriment. "Let's look away from this sad dilemma and back to our daring messenger Zagorus instead. Perhaps we might yet witness dear Athens with a chance for salvation?"

Keres turned her gaze on him, one blonde eyebrow raised in a suggestion of her interest being piqued. She smiled sweetly, knowing well how to play at his never-ending games. "And a fair wager for nectar or ambrosia to go with it?"

Pan smirked knowingly and nodded as his nymph queen's eyes flashed in typical suspicion.

"And none of your tricks!" she cautioned.

"No tricks," Pan agreed innocently with a shrug of his knotty shoulders.

Keres nodded back, though skeptical as always, her face betraying a lingering sense that she might yet regret this new wager.

"Come then," said Pan, gesturing to her like a giddy child. "Let's go down and see to our noble Zagorus before the shade world of Erebus claims him on us."

"Very well," she said. "But only because I've even

less love for Erebus than for Athens or Sparta."

Chapter Fourteen

A Step in the Dark

Not far from the agora, in a plush neighborhood where regal dwellings of polished marble were bordered by decorative thickets and shrubs, several crouched figures lurked within the cover of woven branches and leaves. Tucked tightly within the dense shrubbery was Garathi, the rangy leader of the Kaboni rogues. He was flanked by two other men from their hideaway quarters. Lurking behind another cluster of brambles and brush were three more figures, younger; they were crouched low and out of view from anyone who might happen to pass by the strip of a road that ran alongside the stone wall with its peristyle of columns separating the beautiful marble home from the street.

The three younger members of the concealed group remained crouched, watching Garathi for the sign that would command them into action. One of the three was the ever impetuous Barthus, and on the far side of the heavy shrubberies was the saucy Azelina, her tanned features lit by a mischievous light in her sandy eyes. She seemed to hover almost protectively over the third youngster who was crouched between her and Barthus—Pheidippides, who appeared as pale and nervous as a house pet thrust into the company of fierce strays. His chestnut-hued eyes were wide and glossy as he stared across at the walled home of one of Athens' elite—knowing, for the first time in his life, he would be a part of the kind of act that would break his mother's heart if she were ever to find out. But it had been far too often that he and his mother had been treated as soot beneath the thongs of the eupatridae—those haughty well-born whom Garathi and his ragtag band sought to rob this night.

The boy had had enough of being made to feel like the ruck of Athenian society.

Garathi now stared steadfastly over at the innocent youngster he would convert this night—just as he had done with so many others of the ostraka lot: those whose lives were pre-cast into flawed molds well before birth, as his own had been long ago when heritage had dictated his destiny as a lifelong Kaboni resident. He thought grimly of a fair number of the young ones he had sometimes found abandoned on the sides of remote street-paths, left there by parents who had rejected them shortly after birth. Oh, Athens, thought Garathi, how much you have lost in all your foolish birthright arrogance.

He scrutinized the trembling teenager, knowing more of the boy's bloodline than any might have suspected—for the sharp-eyed rogue had watched and witnessed visual exchanges between Pheidippides and the high-ranking military officer who, by unspoken law, could never acknowledge his covert kinship with a lad who craved a caring father. How harsh, Garathi thought, that a loving mother's livelihood should cast a veil of shame over her boy, that a father's grandly respected role be so protected. For all of Athens' splendor and pride, he mused, this fabled polis yet lacked grace.

Garathi grimaced to himself, then peeked again over the edge of the thick bushes, seeing nothing to indicate their concealed presence had been detected. He sidled on over to the shrub patch where the three teens waited and looked Pheidippides straight in the eyes. "Young Pheidippides, tonight you serve as our sentry and merely watch," Garathi said softly.

Pheidippides all but sighed with relief at this lighter nature of his role. So, too, did Azelina—while Barthus nodded in silent understanding.

"This dwelling we are to…'visit,' " continued Garathi, "is home to some very wealthy citizens…much like the ones you say spurned you so harshly at the stoic's pavilion."

Barthus grinned. "Wealthy, yes…but careless too, eh, Garathi?" He gestured smugly at the apparent absence of any house guards.

"So it does seem, Barthus," said Garathi. "But our good Pheidippides shall lend a careful eye and see to it that we know for certain there are none about who might interrupt our doings."

Garathi and Pheidippides exchanged a long look—and in the gaze of the wily elder's sharp eyes, the youngster understood the trust being invested in him. He drew a long breath, then reached a thin-fingered hand over and squeezed the older man's hand, astounded by the iron grip he received in return. He felt Barthus touch him on one shoulder in assurance, Azelina doing the same on his other. Pheidippides gave a tiny smile, knowing acceptance—and liking it.

"Wait here until you see us scale the wall," Garathi said quietly to Pheidippides. "Then follow over to it after us and keep a watch from there."

Pheidippides swallowed nervously but nodded obediently, his eyes fixed on the man's steady gaze. He hoped he did not look as nervous as he felt, though he was sure he did. Garathi shot a darting glance at Barthus and Azelina, then turned and gave Pheidippides a reassuring nod and headed out from the bushy streetpath cover, motioning for the others to follow. Barthus added a playful pat on the shoulder to Pheidippides before slipping off with the others, smiling mischievously.

"Now, friend Pheidippides, you will see the way wealthy eupatridae repay those of us they call ostraka." The older lad winked in dark delight, and for some reason, Pheidippides found comfort in it. He certainly had not received any such gesture of camaraderie from the young people gathered round the stoic's pavilion that day at the agora. Ostraka…yes, indeed.

"And next time," Barthus continued, "perhaps you'll join in the raid too."

Pheidippides pursed his lips into a thin smile. Perhaps yes, he thought to himself. It seemed as if the older teen almost read his thoughts, for he squeezed Pheidippides' shoulder in acknowledgment, then gestured at the plush home they were about to rob.

"The rewards amount to more than running errands for the likes of their kind," Barthus added.

Pheidippides' soft brown eyes met the rangy lad's gaze and darkened to a muddier tint. He turned and stared now at the house as though it were an arrogant adversary that needed to be taught a sound lesson. He eyed its shuttered windows as though they were closed deliberately to him and to all ostraka who dared tread but a single foot in its privileged neighborhood. Pheidippides gripped Barthus by the arm and squeezed back with his own affirmation of understanding this night's work. Then his friend was gone, scampering off from the brush and crossing the stone road like a nightly shadow.

Pheidippides watched Barthus scaling the six-foot-high wall with a catlike grace, until feeling a nudge at his back. He whirled round in sudden alarm. It was Azelina. The pretty young street urchin looked especially alluring to him in the wispy moonlight. She smiled at him with a delicate warmth. "Do not be frightened, Pheidippides," she said soothingly. "You have made a right choice." She brushed his face lightly with two slender fingers…and then she too was gone in a twinkling.

Pheidippides stood there, staring solemnly at the stone wall as the lithe figure of Azelina slipped over it with a charming grace. Unsure whether he had indeed made the correct choice here, he skulked away from the cover of the gnarly brush, crossed the narrow strip, and then hoisted himself up onto the wall, hauling himself awkwardly to its top, ready to serve as sentry for a home about to be robbed.

****

While Pheidippides took the first steps that would alter the manner in which he might live out his life thereafter, Zagorus struggled through a coastal woodland mist somewhere between Athens and Sparta. He, too, was on the verge of taking steps that would alter the course of his life…and his death. For, the Athenian foot courier now saw, more vividly, the misshapen shadows drifting toward him from within the twisted trees and warped shrubs that comprised the ghostly spinney of woods he had entered. From somewhere, a discordant voice moaned softly, rising menacingly in pitch. Others joined in till a cacophony of equally discordant croaks and moans surrounded Zagorus, as though beckoning him. He halted, glancing at the brooding trees on either side of the path.

"Who's there?" he called out, though not with a great deal of challenge. A hollow snigger responded from the woody shadows, causing the young man to shiver. He peered into a misty gloom.

A lapping of water sounded from within the eerie mist, out of place here in this tiny wood. Zagorus shook his head and blinked, wondering if he hallucinated. The low splash and tinkle of water now mixed with a steady creaking, like heavy oars being dipped and sculled through a current. Sweat that had nothing to do with the hot August temperatures trickled down his cheeks. He found himself staring through a veritable portal, filmy and light, as though it had morphed all at once out of the trees.

Images formed inside the portal—a foggy lake banked by a muddy shore…and a large raft advancing toward him from out of the gloom. A solitary robed figure, hooded and bent, paddled the raft, dipping a long, crooked staff into the pitch-black water. Zagorus could only gawk. He wanted to flee this queer woodland he had somehow entered, but his feet were planted in place, unable to budge.

The robed figure raised its hooded head, and a pair of moon-white orbs peered out from inside it. The creaking raft beached on the misty shore and on the very edge of the filmy portal through which Zagorus watched. The ghoulish spectre extended a bony hand riddled with rotting flesh; a single finger pointed at the tall courier. Zagorus stared wide-eyed at the apparition…and from within the recesses of the hood, a bony face locked eyes with his own. Zagorus staggered back—but then a fair light shone suddenly in front of him, blotting out the robed boatman and the entire shade world.

Pan and Keres now hovered majestically before Zagorus. "Greetings to you, Zagorus of Athens…and our compliments to your heroics," Keres said.

"Yes indeed," crooned Pan. "But, eh, we see your journey brings you closer to Erebus than to Athens."

Zagorus gaped at them both, astonishment that bordered on fear etched over his face.

"Erebus…?" he said, barely audible.

"Why, yes," Pan answered flatly.

The spectre of the gruesome boatman reappeared behind the two Elysians, vague, yet still discernible through the softly glowing fog.

"Even now, Charon the Boatman looks to claim you as one stranded on the Shores of Death," the Elysian god added with a mock shiver. "Not a very pleasant reward for your dauntless efforts, eh?"

Zagorus gaped at the two Elysians, the reality of his peril sinking in.

"Odd, though, to see Charon in this form," Pan mused. "Usually when he claims souls from the woodlands, he slinks up next to them like an armored shadow." Zagorus gazed up at Pan, horrified.

"Oh, but do not be alarmed, brave courier," Keres chimed in. "There is a chance here you may deal with Elysia rather than with Erebus." She smiled sweetly at the bewildered courier.

"The Elysian Fields?" He stared in wonder at the horned figure before him. "Then you must be...Lord Pan himself!"

Pan nodded smugly.

"And Queen Keres of the wood nymphs," Keres said pertly, annoyed at being overlooked.

Even in his dazed state, Zagorus caught the cross look on the nymph's beautiful face and promptly bowed apologetically. Keres acknowledged with a curt smile, then turned and regarded the nearby spectre of Charon unpleasantly. With an insolent wave of one smooth hand, she dispersed the menacing boatman and his shade world, too, as though nothing more than pesky gnats and harmless smoke. Pan smiled approvingly at her deft display, then turned his attention back to Zagorus.

"We're here to see that you remain healthy enough to complete your journey back to Athens, bold runner."

"For the sake of our blessed city?" the gasping courier asked eagerly.

Keres giggled at that, and Pan shot her a silencing look. "Mmm...well, no. Not exactly. But if you agree to inform your Archon and his noble council that the Lord Pan—Master of the Revel and the Din—requests a temple be built in his honor—eh, not unlike those magnificent shrines Athens has built honoring her Olympus gods—well, I might then feel compelled to offer some aid in your struggles."

The horned god smiled impishly, pleased with own little oratory.

Zagorus was stunned. He glanced about, wondering if this was all truly happening, or whether he now suffered the fabled delusions he knew distance couriers to endure at times. He finally nodded, hoping this was not some cruel hoax of the mind. "I will do as you bid, Lord Pan."

"Why, then…run on!" the Elysian god proclaimed with a wave of one cloven hand. Then he and Keres vanished in a twinkling, leaving Zagorus standing there alone—all signs of Erebus also gone.

Zagorus stood up straight, feeling remarkably stronger all of a sudden as he stared around at the surrounding spinney of trees. He blinked, then smiled triumphantly and ran on. When he was gone, Pan and Keres reappeared.

"Oh…and we can be most sure that he will succeed," she quipped sardonically.

"He will," said Pan, all mischief gone from his eyes now as he stared on with a solemn pride.

****

Pheidippides crouched just below the wall of the plush dwelling Garathi and his band were raiding. He poked his head up occasionally to glance out toward the street, then ducked down again, waiting. A moment later the rogues reappeared, wriggling out from windows and climbing downward silently like human spiders. They dropped back onto the ground and skulked over toward Pheidippides. He noticed each had full pockets, along with trinkets and other baubles draped round their necks. He had heard stories of burglars known as the *toichorychoi*, who could scale walls like cats and even dig through them in some cases, but until now he had never truly believed it—and never expected to know any.

Garathi and two others approached Pheidippides,

the rangy leader making a sign with his fingers for silence. Farther down the wall, another sentry—unseen earlier by Pheidippides—popped her head up and signaled to Garathi that all was clear. Stunned to see there was someone else on watch the whole time, Pheidippides pursed his lips, wondering how much trust these thieves really had placed in him. But he had no time to sit and ponder it further, as Garathi made another signal with his hands and the band of thieves began scaling the wall out of the yard and scurrying off. Pheidippides followed glumly.

****

Candles glowed from within the round windows of the stone building. Voices were raised high in celebration as the ragtag men and women of the coarse group congratulated one another. Pheidippides stayed close by Azelina, seemingly more at ease now as many of the group seemed acceptant of him in the wake of the raid, his limited participation in it apparently deemed a successful initiation. The novelty of being readily accepted by this group of closely knit strangers was not a sensation familiar to him. Garathi strode across the room toward him, grinning broadly. The rogue leader proffered him a small sack of coins. "Take it. It's yours, my boy. You've earned it," said Garathi, nodding in approval.

Pheidippides gawked at him, stunned by the offering. "But…but I did nothing. And there was another sentry posted there the whole time. I saw her. You did not need me."

"No matter, lad. You did not shirk the duty we gave you," said Garathi.

Barthus appeared out of the crowd, nodding his

head in agreement. "You showed we could trust you," the taller youth added, extending his hand. A strange surge of comfort passed through him as he took Barthus' hand, shaking it and understanding the test he had passed. Azelina slinked over and hugged Pheidippides, drawing a wry grin from Barthus that fairly said, "See...there are many rewards for joining us."

Garathi held out the sack of coins to him once more. "Think what fine gifts you can buy your mother with coins of this sort." The older man followed up by nudging the boy's hands with the sack that jingled loudly. "You will find more than mere obols in there." Pheidippides bit his lip, thinking how a long village-delivery run might earn him two obols at best. He turned and glanced at Azelina, who nodded reassuringly. He paused again, then took the sack. "There's a good lad," said Garathi.

Azelina and Barthus and a number of rascals laughed in approval, while others slapped him on the back in welcome. Pheidippides surveyed the group of his fellow ostraka gathered in the fire-lit room, feeling more at home than he had in quite some time.

Chapter Fifteen

Advancing Consequences

A runner emerged from a patch of tall weeds and hustled toward the steep hills looming in the near distance. He raced on frantically while shooting furtive glances back. He had maintained a rigorous pace over the ten miles he had run since relieving the first Athenian courier. His chest heaved as he gasped for precious intakes of air, knowing he had pushed himself well beyond the usual pace he kept for this leg of the journey, but knowing also the stakes at hand. Once inside the narrow passes of the hills he would be hidden from the view of his unseen pursuers. The clop and clatter earlier of horse hooves had made it clear that riders had been trailing him and likely had followed the first courier too.

Farther back, Darius' two assassins, Rojese and Jamjon, guided their huge steeds along the stony trail, both mindful of the awkward ground that might hamper their mounts. They peered ahead for any fleeting signs of their quarry. The first courier had fallen victim to them earlier while he sat resting foolishly on a large boulder in the path of their pursuit. Rojese smirked in recalling the young man's face as they had ridden down on him, dashing from around a rocky bend and surprising him after a quiet and stealthy approach. They had left the ill-fated messenger's head in the middle of the path where Rojese's war axe had separated it from the body that now lay sprawled over the boulder. Both knew the Persian King oft made a great fuss over leaving "signs for other would-be dissidents to behold." The duty of assassins, Rojese and Jamjon both understood, was to execute the King's Will, not to question whether they agreed or disagreed with it. Both were noted for their efficiency.

Deeper into the hilly passes, which stretched for several miles, the fleeing courier pressed on, shuddering at the speculation whether his predecessor had been found by whoever now followed him, and fretting whether his own relief, Ginakos, was in place and ready for the next trek.

"Up here!" a young man's voice called out eagerly.

The courier nearly stumbled at the sound of the voice cutting through the steamy evening air. He peered up and saw a figure perched in the rocks overhead. "Ginakos...?" he called up in a voice desperate with hope.

The slim figure stepped out more openly from his rocky cover, waving an arm in friendly greeting. "Aye, Koulio!" Ginakos shouted down to him. "I've been waiting to take the message you bear back to Athens." He started to make his way down, but Koulio froze him with a word.

"No!" shouted the weary courier. "Stay there and hide...I am being chased! Riders pursue me," he gasped. "Wait until you see them pass by. Then fly like the Lord Hermes himself to Athens and warn them that the Persians sail soon for the shores of Marathon...So say the surviving Eretrians!" With that, Koulio waved a hand fiercely for him to retreat back into the rocks. Ginakos hesitated, unsure, and Koulio again waved him off. A thunderous pounding of approaching horse hooves made the point more clear. Ginakos ducked back into the cover of the rocks, and none too soon.

Rojese and Jamjon came bursting furiously into the ravine, urging their horses into a fierce gallop toward the tired runner in their path. Sweating, Ginakos poked his head back up and peered down the ravine trail…in time to see Darius' two assassins riding down the hapless Koulio and trampling him. Leaving the young foot courier lying wretchedly in the middle of the winding trail, the two paused to scan the surrounding area, Jamjon riding ahead for a bit while Rojese's cold eyes searched the cliffs above for anyone lurking up in the rocks there. Ginakos ducked his head barely in time to avoid detection by the bearded giant and stayed crouched as he heard the clop of horse hooves with Jamjon's return to the pass. Satisfied, the assassins turned back to rendezvous with their ship.

****

Ginakos waited a very long time before slipping back out from the safety of his hilly cover. He paused another few moments, making sure the pair of brutal assassins were truly gone, then picked his way carefully down the hillock. He drew a long breath and then jogged cautiously in the direction of Athens, pausing only briefly near the tangled, limp form of his slain comrade, long enough to drag his corpse off into the tall trailside weeds and to utter a soft prayer. The young courier's movements resembled more those of a burglar as he glanced about and then slinked down the path.

Chapter Sixteen

Changing Attitudes

Morning beamed down on the Athenian agora with vendors and other merchants already in the process of setting up their stalls and wares. Despite the pending invasion, the lure of the agora and its vital essence in the lives of all Athenians had not diminished. And with that came the sense of normality every citizen, occupant, servant, and city outlier needed, as if the very act of executing daily activities might somehow mystically ward off—or at least deflect—the evil brewing in the distant north. But the uncharacteristic presence of hoplite soldiers patrolling the agora and other quarters of the city was a grim reminder that the brewing menace was, in fact, no myth.

It was the very next morning after Pheidippides' baptism into the ranks of Garathi's Kaboni clan. Symethra already had felt pangs of suspicion when her otherwise innocent young son had come home uncharacteristically late. She had felt an immediate urge to question his unprecedented tardiness, but had stymied the impulse in the wake of their previous exchanges that had left both of them uncomfortable. So she had let it pass, but knowing it would not ease her growing sense of discomfort.

Pheidippides had been surprised, relieved that he

had not been made to answer for his whereabouts in the wake of his late arrival home. It had also spared him the lie he would have been forced to tell. So he had simply slipped into his trundle bed in the corner, grateful that his mother had not queried him. Yet her unexpected silence had also caused him some disquiet, as it was unlike her to say absolutely nothing. Breakfast had also passed with no mention of his late night return, so Pheidippides merely accepted his good fortune and left for the agora. Now he stood before a vendor stall he would never have approached or examined in the past. He eyed some exquisite-looking pottery as the vendor, a thick-browed middle-aged fellow, watched him suspiciously. The man edged closer to the intricately designed vase the boy in the cheap muslin chiton and britches clearly fancied.

Pheidippides ignored the man's prejudicial glare and continued examining the items.

"Is there something I can do for you…young man?" the vendor asked curtly.

"Perhaps," Pheidippides answered without looking up at him.

"You're looking for work?" the vendor pressed. "The pot makers don't perform their tasks here, but out in the—"

"I am not looking for work as a potter," Pheidippides replied flatly, knowing how lowly potters were regarded in spite of their exceptional skills as artisans. He had surprised himself with his tone.

The portly man tried containing a sarcastic smirk, his bushy brows widening. "Well, then, why stand here eying my wares with such interest?"

"I thought to purchase one," said Pheidippides.

At that, the vendor could not contain a chuckle. "These vases are most expensive, and…"

Pheidippides had already reached into the leather sack fastened round his waist and produced several *drachma* coins—each the equivalent of six obols—causing the vendor's eyes to bulge as he stopped in mid-sentence. Pheidippides' usually tender face shifted into a cool smirk.

"I am sure there must be someone in the agora who will permit me a purchase," he said in the same curt tone the man had used. He made to depart.

The vendor gestured awkwardly for him to stay. "Eh, now, uh…wait, good lad," the plump fellow fumbled. "Let's not forgo a purchase here simply because of a moment's haste on my part…" He stopped as he caught the smug look on the boy's face over this abrupt turnaround. They stared at one another a moment more, and then the vendor turned his eyes away and went back to tending his wares.

Content with his triumph, Pheidippides turned and marched off smartly.

No sooner had he rounded the road's bend than Barthus and another of Garathi's younger denizens, who had been on the raid the previous night, appeared out of the bustle of crowd activity. The two had witnessed his terse exchange with the pottery merchant and clapped him on the shoulders and back for his coy handling of it. Barthus took a moment to whisper hoarsely that if the bowl was still to Pheidippides' liking, it could "yet be his." The lanky Kaboni youngster and the other lad laughed slyly while Pheidippides responded with a bashful smile and shook his head "no." The two rascals then slipped away like shadows back into the agora crowd.

Pheidippides stood there a moment, reflecting on the morning's encounters. He looked up finally...and froze as he beheld a woman standing not ten feet away, directly in his path and staring at him sharply. "Who were those boys?" Symethra demanded in a tone he had rarely, if ever, heard her use.

Though the strip of dirt road where they faced each other was filled with people passing by and others talking with one another by the stalls, it was as if the two of them were quite alone now. Symethra's eyes were a cloudy gray, and her normally smooth features were taut and filled with angst. She stepped in closer to him.

"They are just friends," he finally answered, unable to muster anything more. How long had she been here? Had his mother actually followed him out the door this morning?

"Friends?" she asked sharply. "I have not seen you with such 'friends' before, Pheidippides."

"Can a young man not choose his own friends, Mother?" he answered, a strain of resentment in his voice. Symethra caught it and did not like the sound of it.

"A young man should choose his friends wisely," she said.

"You do not even know them," Pheidippides said defensively.

Symethra glanced about to see if any others were listening or overhearing their conversation, then motioned him over to a less crowded section of the road. He followed, wishing he were elsewhere, but determined to stand his ground here willfully.

"Pheidippides, do not play the innocent," she all but scolded. "Those two serve that thief Garathi from the Kaboni!"

He stiffened. "You mean they are ostraka like us."

"Pheidippides!"

"They treat me better than my father does."

Symethra's eyes flashed with sudden anger. She made to respond, but he persisted.

"Ask my father how proud he was of the son he saw made into a fool near the stoic's class."

Her eyes moistened with that, and she shut them tightly, not wanting him to notice. "Pheid—"

"*Ask him, Mother.*"

"Pheidippides," she pleaded softly, putting a hand to his shoulder.

"At least Garathi has a use for me, and..." He caught himself, knowing his frustration had got the better of him, so that he had already said too much. The look of sudden alarm on his mother's face was telling enough.

"What did you mean by that?" she demanded.

"Nothing," Pheidippides mumbled.

She eyed him hard, her maternal instincts afire now. "Pheidippides, where did you get all those coins you offered that wealthy merchant?"

Pheidippides flushed with indignation suddenly. "Do you follow me everywhere I go, and watch all that I do, Mother?"

"Perhaps I should," she snapped, her face tightening again.

Pheidippides puffed up righteously. "It is a young man's right to choose—"

He was cut off by a sudden commotion as

111

practically the entire agora exploded with cheers and cries: "A courier…It is Ginakos!"

Pheidippides and Symethra stared at one another, their heated dispute fizzling in the frenzy of the elite courier's unexpected early return from the Northern Attica region. The exhausted runner had clearly driven himself beyond his routine pace and could barely gasp out his fearful message.

"Marathon!" he cried out. "The Persians sail for Marathon!" Several hoplite soldiers rushed over to assist him and help him along.

Pheidippides and his mother exchanged looks of foreboding and dread as Ginakos and the hoplites disappeared off into the direction of the Bouleuterion.

Chapter Seventeen

Decisions

In the great meeting hall of the Bouleuterion, the Archon stood tall and alert, facing his magistrates and elite military personnel—General Milteades and Captain Boros among them. The air was thick with worry, and the faces of council leaders, military officials, and men of the city's highest status and accord reflected the impact of the reality Ginakos had just delivered. Archon Kallimachos took it all in, then drew a long breath, knowing the city's morale was now entirely at stake. It was no longer a matter of conjecture...the Persian hordes were definitely en route for Athens!

"I beseech all of you to take heart in the mettle and daring of our one surviving courier, brave Ginakos, who has overcome enemy pursuit, fatigue, and the limits of human endurance in hastening here, bearing this grave warning. That in itself demands of us the same in our resolve to withstand whatever this tyrant of Persia seeks to impose upon us!" Kallimachos boomed, his arms stretched high and outward, one arm gesturing in the direction of the courier himself, held aloft by two hoplites.

Applause and hearty cheers answered the Archon's proclamation, and men throughout the vast hall already looked less disquieted. After all, had Athens not always prevailed in times of crises?

"It is also the report of our gallant Ginakos that the northern city of Plataia has offered to help…for are we all not Greeks, however separate our borders and our customs may be?" His piercing dark eyes scanned the hall as though daring any man there to question his state of confidence.

The effect was as Kallimachos had desired—the spirit of Athenian pride long implanted in the hearts of all its citizens. He let his gaze come to rest on General Milteades, and the husky commander nodded in subtle understanding, then turned and faced the entire gathering himself.

"One bold courier has returned in true Athenian fashion, and our most powerful runner of all, Zagorus, must surely be returning soon with words that our Spartan cousins shall come and lend aid in turning back this Persian tyrant and his barbaric horde!" Milteades thundered. "By the grace of Zeus, with Sparta's help, there is no army in the world mighty enough to break us!"

Not a man in the hall failed to relish the power of the great general's assurances. Faces that had been grim and even downcast only moments earlier now beamed with a confident raucous war fever. All that was needed to complete the mood set by Kallimachos and Milteades was Zagorus himself and his word of a Spartan promise to put aside old rivalries for the good of all.

****

A lone sentry garbed in hoplite's armor, helmet, and cloak, a sword strapped to his hip—and a bone bow slung over one shoulder—gazed out into the nightly shadows that danced erratically in the early Athenian eve. Torches lining the high city walls added to the ghostly look of the moonlit turf. Normally he might have foregone the full military apparel, but with Ginakos' return from the northern couriers' route, anything looming out from the dark now might prove to be Persian reconnaissance scouts or, worse, even a vanguard attack unit.

So the sentry abided by his duty, blinking when suddenly a lean figure swaying side to side as though wounded, broke through the ashy twilight in a veritable parody of a run toward the city walls. Unsure what this interloper of the dusk surging toward his post might be, the gate guard unslung the long bow from his shoulder and nocked an arrow from his quiver to it, aiming it down at the approaching shape. But then the pale sheen of the full moon revealed a familiar figure dressed only in a sleeveless chiton, cut-down britches, and worn-down sandals.

"Dear Zeus…" the sentry breathed out in a mix of surprise and relief. He called out lustily to his fellow guards inside the walls, "Part the gates…*Zagorus returns*!"

****

Archon Kallimachos stared out grimly at the crowd gathered at the foot of the Bouleuterion steps, the gray of his troubled face matching that of the stone steps where anxious people awaited words that might assure them. He was flanked by several hoplite guards, including Captain Boros. Not a one bore the look of imposed confidence that had pervaded prior to Zagorus' dramatic arrival on the previous eve. The Archon drew himself up, knowing well his next words would make the difference toward reinforcing the morale of an entire city that was now but a thread away from panic.

"And so, my fellow Athenians..." he began, measuring each moment with a practiced calculation, "while we wait for our Spartan cousins to complete their religions obligations and then make preparations to join in our resistance to tyranny, it is the sacred duty of all male citizens of age to come forth and march for Marathon with our brave hoplites. For it is our citizen's militia that has long been the spine of our military custom!" He boomed clearly and with the confidence of a seasoned overlord in measuring the mood of his people. "It is in this very way that Athens twice gained her freedom from tyranny on those heralded nights when even the Acropolis could not protect the traitorous likes of men such as Hippias...who is now in the service of Darius!"

The crowd, gathered at the foot of the steps and beyond—rows upon rows of Athenians as far as any standing on the Bouleuterion plateau could see—erupted in hoarse cheers of agreement.

Most.

Among those gathered outside the revered council hall were Pheidippides and Symethra, both harkening to the powerful words spoken by Archon Kallimachos, both also casting an eye toward Captain Boros as well—whose stolid demeanor did not indicate he was even aware of his longtime mistress and illegitimate son standing among the throng of Athenians.

The ones who filled the agora streets and open spaces were a vastly scattered mix...all sandwiched together now: citizens and non-citizens, including lower caste workers—the perioki; along with servants and slaves—the demesioi and doula; and the metics who dwelled in outlying villages; and even those from darker city quarters like the Kaboni—the ostraka. Gathered also within that throng of bodies were the lingering covert supporters of Hippias—those whom the rule of a single dictator would benefit. Men like Hahnitos, who would seize any opportunity to disrupt the fledgling governance of democratia—a system yet with flaws, but one that still held in check those who reveled in the idea of absolute power in the hands of a solitary ruler.

All were amassed in a knot of tightly crunched bodies, and most with a single tie in common: the only home they had ever known might soon be trampled into ruin and burnt to ashes by Darius and his legions. Hahnitos and his ilk might well seek to persuade people that surrender at least meant survival.

The Archon waited for the initial clamor to die down, surveying the throng he knew was counting not only on his judgment but on how assured he sounded in this telling moment of crisis. He thrust back his shoulders once more and raised a single arm in a beckoning gesture. "So, once again in the true Athenian way, those with the voting privilege shall do their duty this day. Now that we know an attack on our freedom, our blessed city, our very lives, is indeed forthcoming and no longer in question, it is the right of all citizens of this democratia to decide, once more, whether Athens submits to tyranny—or defies it! As you all know, a white stone will show your favor for standing against Darius…while a black stone cast in any of the vases will indicate your desire that we submit without struggle."

117

A predominant murmur of discordant voices indicated there would be few black stones cast into any of the voting vases. If Hahnitos and his lot had words for the crowd, they were wisely withheld.

"I am of age, Mother," Pheidippides uttered softly. "Though I cannot vote, I am old enough and should serve in defense of Athens."

Symethra eyed him solemnly. "I am not sure what is worse: my son dead by a Persian spear or alive as a common thief of the Kaboni." Her eyes moistened as they probed his. Pheidippides looked away, put off by her words and the pain in her stare. "But perhaps neither fate need fall upon you."

Pheidippides turned back curiously, but activity on the Bouleuterion plateau interrupted them.

Zagorus, accompanied by two healers from the renowned Athenian Hall of Healing, had emerged from the Bouleuterion and approached the podium where the Archon and his entourage stood. A hush fell over the crowd. Kallimachos gestured grandly toward the tall courier in a manner that indicated this moment had been a planned part of the proceedings.

"Fellow Athenians," proclaimed the Archon while extending an arm out to Zagorus. "Our most vaunted of all Athens' superb Hemeredrome...*Zagorus*. Hero for his bold run to Sparta and back!"

Cheers erupted instantly from the crowd as many followed up with the chanting of the elite foot courier's name in a raucous rhythmical beat. But Zagorus merely stood stock still and stared out almost blankly at the cheering throng. He finally turned to face the Archon. The crowd quieted.

"Great Archon..." the young man said hoarsely,

his voice matching the worn and weary look of his supple frame. "What of Pan's Temple?"

The Archon's eyes widened involuntarily, and the great Athenian overlord was hard put to contain his shock at so unanticipated a query on the part of this renowned courier whose status had risen even more significantly in the wake of his unparalleled exploit. True, Zagorus had uttered strange rantings of having seen the infamous Elysian Lord of the Woodland Realms, but everyone had dismissed those reports as delirium suffered from the oppressive heat and the unimaginable rigors of his brutal trek. And though Zagorus had strained just to put forth those words here on the outdoor dais of the council hall plateau, they had poured out clearly enough for those gathered closest to the steps.

A flurry of reactions followed, spreading throughout the vast crowd like a gust of wind. Tales of disdain and mockery had long been the trademark of the more prestigious city-states in regarding the mysterious Elysian gods, Pan himself held in contempt as an impish pretender who simply envied the traditional Lords of Olympus, to whom all Greek states afforded full homage. These so-called Elysians were alternative deities for the downcast, for those dwelling in the underbelly of lesser lands claiming to be of Hellespont heritage...figments of minds "more fitting to the ostraka lot." And to now have Zagorus make so bold a remark before the Archon himself...? Madness it surely had to be. The journey of some fifty leagues and back again—a good three hundred miles—had ruined this fine young man forever. The crowd's murmuring and kibitzing rose higher in its mournful crowing.

Zagorus heard it too. He pleaded with the Archon, then turned to face the massive crowd. "But I saw the Lord of Elysia himself...and...and his beautiful Queen of the Wood Nymphs too!" His voice was swallowed up in further reactive chatter from the crowd, and Kallimachos took this opportunity to arrest the embarrassment of the moment. He hustled over and placed a warm arm around the lean courier, whose frail appearance alone was confirmation of his hallucinatory state.

"Why, yes, of course," proclaimed Kallimachos in a gentle but consoling tone that was clearly one of humoring the young man. The High Archon turned to the healers, flashing them a potent look that said, "Get this poor delusional lad away from here while he still has a reputation to preserve."

The healers, looking grim and heartbroken, gently tugged Zagorus free of the Archon and guided him off as the crowd murmured, argued, and debated what they all had just witnessed.

Pheidippides put one hand to his mother's shoulder for support as he watched his ruined idol being taken away. He felt both wounded and confused by it all. Symethra wept quietly.

Chapter Eighteen

Lords of Fate

Far above the grand city-state of Athens—in a realm yet questioned by skeptics who so willfully paid all due homage to the Gods of Olympus—the Lord Pan stared downward, his horned head dipped in an air of resignation, the hurt spilling over his craggy features impossible to mask. The fairy-like Keres reached a soft hand to his cheek in a futile attempt to console him. Nonetheless, he raised a cloven hand to hers, stroking it in gentle appreciation. He loved his dear young queen as a father so utterly loves a daughter who brightens his heart regardless the depths of despair.

"Did you not tell me, dear Keres, that Athens would scoff at my request?" he said softly.

Keres merely stared at him through moistened eyes that still shone with a golden light. Pan sighed, then slowly turned away, slump-shouldered. "Well, it matters not," he uttered more to himself. Pan, proud and witty Lord of the Elysian Fields, then slunk off, disappearing into the rich misty air.

His beautiful young Queen of Wood Nymphs watched him go, knowing well it mattered very much to him. She shook her lovely head covered with the long, flowing blonde locks and stared downward toward the world below, her golden gaze sharpened with silent anger now. "And when will you finally honor my Lord Pan, Athens? Only when Zeus and his fickle Olympians are too busy for you?" Keres shook her head again in a mix of disdain and disgust and fluttered off.

****

Symethra scraped some fish and vegetables in a metal pan atop a clay stove fire pit. She was distracted from the otherwise soothing aroma of the frying meal as it popped and sizzled in a way that usually would have tantalized both her and her son, who sat at the round dining table. Pheidippides appeared forlorn and not in the least aware of the delicious meal being prepared by his mother, whose tanned brow was furrowed with worry.

"He said *male citizens of age,* Mother."

"So now you are a citizen?" The soft, almost playful tinge of sarcasm in her tone caused him to bristle slightly, though she had meant no offense. "Pheidippides, not everyone is meant to be a soldier," she added softly. "Not all young men are—"

"Fit? Able?" he interrupted.

"I did not mean it in that way, my son," she responded apologetically, feeling a losing struggle here. "There are just some who may not...be expected to serve at Marathon."

There was a long, uncomfortable silence. Then Pheidippides rose and strode over to the fireplace, his head as much afire as the sparks crackling in its midst. "Like the people from the Kaboni?" he all but muttered.

Symethra eyed him darkly, her irises clouding. "The Archon and the Ecclesia Assembly want honest citizens to help our hoplites soldiers fight. Not scoundrels and thieves."

Pheidippides' eyes narrowed and his mouth tightened, the tension in the room pervading. "I do not care what the Archon or any of our grand Prytany councilors think of my friends. Look how they all treated Zagorus today."

"Zagorus is another matter," Symethra snapped sharply, something more pressing building in her. Her eyes met his and the cloudy gray of her own grew stormier. "There is that robbery of two nights ago where many jewels and gems and coins of great value were taken."

"Yes," said Pheidippides, his voice lacking any semblance of remorse, "such a loss for those who own plush homes where magistrates and wealthy Ecclesia and highbrow merchants dwell."

Symethra's mouth dropped.

Pheidippides noticed, but did not relent. "Perhaps a loss by those who never have to suffer anything teaches them something even the stoics cannot."

"And who taught you to speak in such ways, my son? Not me...and certainly not Stoic Rolios!"

"And not my own father, who never speaks to me at all!"

Symethra shook her head, stunned by the icy anger in his tone, more so than she had ever heard in the past. She was certain where much of this had come from, now. Yet she was also stung by an underlying truth she herself could not deny. She calmed herself, raising both hands chest high, and glided closer to her boy, touching him lightly on the shoulders with both hands. "There will be questions about this later that will have to be answered," she said softly. "That is, if our hoplites and citizen's militia manage to turn back the Persians.

But…" Her smooth face was suddenly wracked with fear, and it quelled his anger.

Pheidippides placed a hand to his mother's shoulder. "You are not sure there will be an Athens to return to," said Pheidippides quietly, his thin face sincere.

Symethra walked slowly back to a chair at the table. "I have listened to…your father speak on this. The Persian king has such an army it will cover the hills between Marathon and here like ants."

Pheidippides stood frozen, unable to speak in the stark reality of her words.

Symethra turned her gaze on him firmly. "I am sure, though, that your friends from the Kaboni will all find a safe place away from Athens to hide…"

He blinked at that but said nothing.

"I understand that Athens and its *Boule* Council have not always treated those of us they do not regard as citizens with fairness, or even kindness, Pheidippides." She clasped her hands together as she spoke, her thin fingers tightening with tension and worry, though her voice remained soft and filled with quiet passion. She drew a long breath. "I might even have found myself among the Kaboni's lot…for my own mother was among the haetera."

Pheidippides felt his knees buckle at this first-time admission from his mother. But he had no words to offer and knew best not to interrupt now, as he sensed she had great need of what she wanted to continue saying.

"The man who fathered me was a citizen of wealth, one of the Ecclesia who hold the right to vote at the Pnix hill near the Acropolis itself. But unlike your father, this man cared nothing for my mother, other than the service and pleasure expected of a haetera. And she was but one of several he enjoyed...only briefly." Symethra's eyes dropped, and she choked back a sob.

Pheidippides eased back over to the table and touched her hands before sitting down opposite her.

When she looked up, her eyes were moist. "I knew nothing more about him than that. He left and went back to his Ecclesian life once my mother told him she bore his child...me." Her head shook softly. "I don't even know his name or where he is now."

Pheidippides felt a heave in his throat at his mother's struggle with those last few words.

"But I swear to you, my son," she said with a tone of gentle conviction, "your father loves us both...and suffers in his own way for us too." A silence followed as they stared into one another's eyes. "He has urged that we both go somewhere safe until the Persians are gone, or..." Symethra drew another long breath, leaving the last thought as it was. "Delphi, he said, would be best. It seems even King Darius would not dare violate the land of a sacred oracle."

Pheidippides nodded, more in deference to her feelings than in agreement. Finally he mustered what he could not withhold: "Would that not make me a coward?"

Symethra's eyes widened in surprise; she had not anticipated such a response. She smiled, feeling a surge of pride, yet answered, "It would make my son alive instead of dead."

Pheidippides squeezed her hand gently, then rose and stalked over to his trundle bed, bewildered and embarrassed. His eyes fixed on something lying on one corner of the bed...the cracked tablet containing the poem he had written, seemingly so long ago, when Barthus had teased him about it at the agora pool. He picked it up and began reading from it in a voice barely more than a whisper.

"My Athens, my home...She stands here before me, sparkling in the sun..."

Softly as he spoke the verse, Symethra heard it, just the same. She wiped at her eyes but did not look over at him.

Chapter Nineteen

Decisions

The rustic old Kaboni den where Garathi and his legion of outliers gathered, plotted, and celebrated their dark escapades lurked in the usual shadows that always blanketed it, day or night, fair weather or poor. But this night its brooding outer appearance paled in comparison to the tension it harbored inside. The stone walls themselves seemed to reflect the rising tumult within.

"If you come with us into the hills, you will be hid in the safest point of the Attica region," said Barthus, one of several hovering over Pheidippides, who sat on a stool near the fire and hearth of the dusky quarters. "The entire Persian army could not follow us there without losing its way."

Azelina, stroking her wolfish canine companion round the neck, stood on the opposite side of Barthus, while the lanky Garathi stood directly in front of Pheidippides, arms folded formidably, his face both troubled and puzzled. Others lurked behind their leader, none looking sympathetic or understanding of the young foot courier recently turned Kaboni thief.

"You might at least heed your mother's words and flee with her to Delphi," Azelina said gently, trying to force an air of persuasion into her words.

"And hide there like a coward?" said Pheidippides, the words coming out faster from his heart than his tongue could contain. An icy silence gripped the large room filled with rough men of all sizes and fiery-eyed women, whose faces suddenly took on a dangerous predatory look. Unable to restrain his passion, Pheidippides recognized right away how that remark had generated instant resentment.

"You are calling us cowards?" said Barthus, fists clenched, eyes suddenly dark slits.

Pheidippides glanced around at faces that had all gone unfriendly, Azelina herself shaking her head in frustrated disappointment. Even the dog Atlas seemed to curl his upper lip coldly. "I...no," stammered Pheidippides sincerely. "No, I understand why you all feel as you do about Athens..."

"And you should feel no differently," Garathi said smoothly, his lean strong arms still folded.

"You did not seem so loyal to Athens when you watched us rob that house," Barthus sneered.

Pheidippides shifted uncomfortably. "I...I was wrong to do that," he mumbled.

A chorus of unpleasant grunts and curses broke out in the rough crowd, and Azelina reached a long-fingered hand over to Pheidippides' shoulder in a gesture of caution. Scowls covered the hard faces that only moments earlier had been warm with welcome for the teenage boy when he entered their meeting quarters. Garathi shook his head sternly, his steely eyes shutting as he all but winced.

"Oh, so now Pheidippides is too noble to live as a Kaboni ostraka!" Barthus quipped sardonically. He glared almost savagely at him, and the ring of men and women surrounding the fireside stool drew in closer, menace in their eyes. Azelina and her dog edged closer, as if trying to shield him from them. But then Garathi raised a hand, staying them all.

"This boy is not wrong to want a better life," the gaunt leader proclaimed quietly in a commanding tone all of them knew well. They halted in their advance, some even taking a step back. Garathi's strength of leadership came in the form of an authority he commanded through having guided so many of them from their shame at being deemed outcasts and into a proud defiance of those who had claimed superiority over them. There was not a man or woman of the Kaboni culture who did not feel a powerful debt of allegiance to the man. So they watched in silence as Garathi gestured them back, nodding gently to Azelina to step back as well, as he gripped hold of an oaken chair and pulled it up in front of Pheidippides, then sat facing him.

The young boy's eyes widened, seeing something here he had not witnessed even in the people at the agora when Archon Kallimachos spoke. Perhaps it was because he had never seen the Archon of Athens address anyone else so personally.

"Pheidippides, do you think any of us would live as we do if we had another choice?" the man asked, his dusky eyes locking firmly onto the boy's in a penetrating gaze. Not another body in the room moved now, and not another voice dared as much as a whisper. "Athens is free and generous," Garathi continued hoarsely, his voice low but powerful, "but only for those of the right birth." The Kaboni leader pursed his lips, as though weighing his next words in some private debate with himself. "But sometimes that may not be enough, eh, lad?"

Pheidippides gaped, startled by the man's intuition. His chestnut eyes opened wider. Garathi nodded, knowing the chord he had struck. They held each other's gaze a moment longer, Pheidippides' eyes moistening. How could this man possibly know so much?

"Do you know why they call us ostraka?" Garathi asked quietly. A soft bristle rippled through the room. Pheidippides shook his head no, spellbound. "Some time ago," the clan leader continued, leaning in closer to the boy, "when the citizens of our great city wanted to rid themselves of certain corrupt leaders, they broke a number of vases, and everyone wrote down on the broken bits the names of the leaders they wanted cast out..."

Some of the rogues turned and nodded to one another, knowing the saga well, while others appeared to be hearing it for the first time, right along with Pheidippides.

"They called the broken pieces with the names on them the ostraka," Garathi said flatly. "And those onetime leaders were cast out of Athens—even from the entire Attica region—never to return." He paused and a mounting bitterness crept into his rough voice. "In time, that term would come to include anyone that the highborn wanted shut out of Athens' finer ways. So when such a lowly stray of our city's outer quarters was seen, the eupatridae—those 'well-born'—would cry out: 'No ostraka!' "

Low muttering and grumbling rose up, though quietly, in deference to Garathi, who was not done. The tall leader rose, his strong gaze still fixed on the teenage boy sitting meekly before him.

Garathi then turned to include everyone else as he spoke in a firm declaration to them all: "No, it is not wrong to want a better life." He gave a long mournful sigh, then eyed Pheidippides sadly. "But it is wrong to think an ostraka will ever be given such a chance."

A number of the rogues appeared as though they wanted to speak, but instead exchanged looks that spoke of the camaraderie existing only between those of a similar lot. Pheidippides, too, let his eyes roam the room, briefly finding Azelina, who slipped cautiously closer to him under the watchful gaze of Garathi. Barthus, meanwhile gave Pheidippides a long, probing stare.

Pheidippides rose carefully from his stool and met Garathi's hard gray eyes again. "You took me in when others cast me out, and for that I will always be grateful...and loyal to you all." He summoned his nerve fully, drawing himself up with a pride that surprised even himself. "But there will be no Athens left at all if there are not enough of us to stop the Persians at Marathon."

The mix of reactions that filled the stony quarters of the fierce legion of rogues could not have varied more. Some leaned back in their seats, stunned by the lad's sheer courage and pride; others snickered, while some grumbled angrily, insulted by what appeared to them as a brash pretense of bravery meant to invoke a sense of guilt amongst them; yet others regarded the young boy with a renewed respect. Azelina was among those eying Pheidippides with a mix of sorrow and pride.

Barthus, however, did not harbor any kindly feelings at all toward him after hearing the words that had jolted them all. He sidled on up to his recently found new peer, dark eyes cold and unfriendly.

"You are a fool, Pheidippides. Do not expect the Kaboni to ever welcome you back."

Chapter Twenty

Mobilizing

The Acropolis, a fortress built upon the highest hilltop in Athens, served as the greatest military post for defending the heralded polis. It was accessible only via a narrow, winding strip of stone-and-dirt road that climbed a steep, walled knoll, otherwise impenetrable.

Years earlier, after Hippias had been deposed and exiled by angry, frustrated Athenians, he was later followed by another dictator who barricaded himself within the summit walls of the Acropolis fortress after the city's denizens again revolted and besieged him and his small force of rogue Spartans who had helped him seize control. It was a short-lived resurgence of tyranny that resulted in the casting out of yet another would-be despot, thus freeing the way for democratic-minded thinkers and statesmen like the legendary Kleisthenes.

Those of ranking military significance knew this history well, and only a select few bore the privilege of immediate access to the Acropolis and its armory. Captain Boros of the Elite Athenian Guard was one of them.

Standing now in the Acropolis armory—where key weapons and armament quarters were built within the high-walled fortress—the doughty captain inspected a number of the javelins and spears he knew would be utilized for the coming battle. So preoccupied was he in both his thoughts and his inspection, he did not pay heed to the trod of quiet feet as they breached the privacy of the restricted hall.

Boros held up a sturdy metal shield trimmed with bronze molding and sporting the rough image of an armored hoplite wielding a battle spear. He grinned with approval, caught up in the martial air of the moment, and failed to hear the trail of shuffling sandaled feet behind him.

"Boros…" a woman's voice murmured from behind, quiet and appealing in its tone.

Boros whirled round instinctively, the heavy ornate shield hoisted into a defensive position, his other hand going swiftly to the onyx handle of the long war dagger sheathed at his hip. He had the glistening dirk tugged halfway out from the leather sheath, but halted in drawing it the rest of the way as he saw who the unexpected interloper in the restricted armory was.

"Symethra…" he gasped, both astonishment and quiet alarm marking his rugged face. "What are you doing here? How did you ever…?"

"I merely told them Captain Boros had sent for me," she replied almost smugly.

Boros' face clouded. "Do you realize the penalties you would face if—"

"I do not care," Symethra said sharply. "I am weary of such shameful concerns when more important matters are upon us."

"What could be more important than—"

"Your son is not going to Delphi. And neither am I," she said firmly, the dusty eyes steeled.

Boros' face tightened with alarm. "What

foolishness is this?"

"A foolishness I could not sway him from," she said, drawing closer to him. "He has gone to join the citizen's militia."

Boros' jaw dropped. "But...but that is not even possible. Only citizens of Athens may—"

"Pheidippides said he has heard from...friends that the Prytany Council announced today the Assembly agreed certain non-citizens who live within our city walls may be considered to serve because of the danger posed by the might and size of the Persian force."

Boros reached over and touched her on the shoulder, as though for support. She felt his strong hand tremble slightly. "He...is just a boy, Symethra. Little more than sixteen years..."

He made his way slowly over to a flat, wide stool of hard oak and sat, head lowered. Symethra followed, stunned by the impact it had just had on him. "Surely, though, they will not take him," he mumbled more to himself. "Pheid..." Boros paused, catching himself. "Surely they will see he is not the sort who..."

"*Pheidippides,*" Symethra interrupted him with an edge to her voice. "*Your son,* Pheidippides, may already have joined Athens' militia to fight for the city of his birth!"

Boros jerked his head up at the tone of her reply, his eyes swirling with a childlike confusion that surprised her all the more. He saw the look on her face and reassumed his usual composure. "This same boy you once told me could not find it in himself to kill a fish when he went out on the boats with the men...now seeks to fight against fierce Persian warriors?"

Symethra nodded solemnly. "I told him of Delphi

and what you had said." She choked back a sob. "But he held up to me the poem he wrote about Athens."

Boros leaned in closer to her and raised her head so he could peer directly into her eyes. "Go on," he said gently, touching her cheek lightly with his thick fingers.

"He…said he had no cause to call himself an Athenian if…he did not believe in what he wrote with his own hands…what came from his own heart." Symethra gripped Boros round his sturdy shoulders and held onto him tightly. The big captain of the guard steeled his jaw and shook his head in quiet amazement.

"If you wish," he said in a soft, measured tone, "I can see to it that he is kept from the depth of the fighting." She eyed him, more hurt in her gaze than offense to his words. Boros saw it clearly. He responded with concern, and pride. "The boy's heart speaks like a true Athenian, but I fear that his…"

"And do you think I want my son to die on the plains of Marathon?" she said passionately. "I would give anything to see him change his mind, but…" Symethra faltered, struggling to continue. "But to deny him what his heart says is right…?"

Boros nodded slowly, his eyes closing tightly as they embraced one another. He struggled with the words he next spoke. "I will see that…Pheidippides…is given sword and armor as befits the finest men in my command."

Symethra opened her eyes, warmed as she gently broke their embrace. She smiled tenderly.

"And I swear, by our goddess Athena, I will do all I can to see our son returns safely to Athens," he added solemnly.

Chapter Twenty-One

For Athens!

The sun shone down from the early afternoon sky,
high over the great walled city of Athens, the golden
rays beaming down brightly on the panorama of courtly
government buildings, beautiful marble houses, and the
crunch of mud-brick dwellings making up the farther
reaches of the walled metropolis. It was known to all as
the capitol center of the vast Attica region. From far
above it must have appeared to passing birds and
winged insects—and other beings of wind and air—that
what lay below was nothing more than a colony of ant
mounds with barriers built by its multitude of
inhabitants…and by the myrmidons gathered outside
those tall polis walls.

Upon closer look, those higher beings of wind and
air would have found the huge gathering below to be
the Athenian military, comprised of trained hoplite
warriors and a civilian militia, readying for a march
north to the distant plains of Marathon, twenty-six
miles—nearly nine leagues—away. The army, under
the command of General Milteades—and overseen by
Athens' highest-ranking Archon in wartime, namely
Kallimachos—was an impressive sight assembled
outside the city walls. It wrapped round Athens itself
like a massive constrictor snake guarding its precious

brood.

The esteemed figure of the Archon stood upon the summit of a high hillock where he was flanked by several elite military officers, including Captain Boros. All below, from within the city and outside its walls, stared upward and eyed this grandly robed dignitary with an air of anticipation as he readied himself to address them.

Slim green pennants decorated with the white-leafed olive tree design—a beloved symbol of democratic freedom—flapped in the light afternoon breeze. Horns blared, and a hush draped over the mass of civilians and military flocking over the rolling grounds. No dissenters were present.

"Fellow Athenians...!" the High Archon proclaimed proudly, feeling now more than ever the full weight of his wartime solitary authority. "Behold this magnificent sight here before you! Your legions of hoplite warriors who serve Athens every day of their lives—and a militia of the bravest of our city's citizens—are now joined together in one vast army, all ready to march off and cast from our lands the vile invaders who would seek to wreak death upon us and raze our cherished city to the ground!"

Within the crowd, Symethra Deglos stood surrounded by a crunch of others who had never known even a breath of citizenship, yet they too felt the powerful tug of the Archon's poignant words. Her soft eyes roamed the ranks of the city's volunteer militia, knowing what little chance there was of even a mere glimpse of her son, whom she knew to be somewhere among them. Oh, yes, he had joined, as both his mother and father finally realized would indeed happen. The slender young haetera's gaze shifted back up to the hillock where the prime military leaders were gathered near the valiant General Milteades. Her eyes fixed once again on Captain Boros Constantis. She eyed him with a surge of conflicting emotions that all but drained her beautiful face of its healthy color.

The Archon's grand speech went on, a background chatter now to the more dominant worries and dread filling her mind and drowning out his perfectly prepared address.

"But no! We shall make the plains of Marathon—where Darius will put ashore, as our worthy courier Ginakos and his fellow hemeredrome learned—into a day of Athenian reckoning with this would-be tyrant! These bold men flooding the fields before you now shall also flood the rolling plains and hills of Marathon and repel those Persian invaders, along with the traitor Hippias!"

Jammed into a knot of civilian militiamen, a teenage soldier—garbed far more exquisitely than any of those surrounding him—heard the Archon's words most clearly...and it was of some surprise to Pheidippides that the man had left out the name of the most prominent of Athens' foot couriers, Zagorus. Indeed, since the moment the renowned courier had spoken of the Elysians, he had been ignored.

Pheidippides glanced around at the rest of the lower caste militiamen surrounding him, nearly all wearing nothing more than thin, cheap leather armor and skull caps and wielding short wooden spears. Few even bore arm shields, while he himself enjoyed the splendid bronze breastplate and helm, along with thick leather shin guards and marching sandals, a sturdy shield of layered leather, and a gleaming long-sword sheathed at his hip. Yes, Captain Boros had quietly looked after the son he had never acknowledged.

****

On a woody knoll farther off from the hillocks and rocky mounds closer to the city walls, a much smaller group was assembled. Garathi, flanked by a dozen of his Kaboni rogues—which included young Barthus, along with the sleek teenage waif Azelina and her ever-present mongrel—all stared down from the leafy cover of ash and fir trees that sprouted thickly over the hillock summit. As with some of the adult men and women flanking Garathi, Barthus bore a smirk of disdain on his swarthy face in regard to the massive throng gathered below. Azelina, meanwhile, stared wide-eyed in a mix of wonder and woe, one hand stroking Atlas round his furry neck, her young mind straining to comprehend the magnitude of an actual war in the making.

Garathi stood solemnly, his lean face taut and marked by what seemed a flood of ever-shifting emotions. He eyed the mobilizing army below, the frown that crossed his hard brow betraying mixed feelings he had yet to express. "And so our grand Archon now strives to fill even the poorest of Athens with martial valor," he said cynically as Kallimachos' hearty voice droned on, dulled by the distance and by the morning breeze, yet clear enough to be heard.

"And our Pheidippides goes with them," said Barthus, a sneer on his young face that yet seemed at odds with the air of disdain he sought to effect. "Go die for those who despise you for the fool of an ostraka you are to them!" he added, lifting his voice as though Pheidippides might actually hear him.

"But he would at least die nobly," Azelina said softly. "And for what he believes."

Barthus frowned at her quiet assertion, while Garathi and several others eyed her curiously.

"What worth is nobility if you're left with only the worms to celebrate it?" snickered Barthus.

Azelina eyed him coldly. Barthus shrugged in response to her reproachful stare. "And we're left without even the Kaboni now," the young girl snapped sharply, rubbing Atlas all the more anxiously over his thick canine shoulders and neck.

Barthus looked to Garathi for the expected retort, but the tall leader appeared preoccupied in thoughts of his own. Barthus sought to engage him in the exchange just the same. "Garathi's wisdom will lead us to survive this war—whoever the victor may be. That's what matters," the young rogue said in as conclusive a tone as he could effect. He turned to face the leader. "Ay…?"

Garathi frowned at him, as though not wanting to have been drawn into the banter between two of the youngest of his outer city sect. He gazed around and saw the sizzling debate between the two teenagers had commanded more attention from the rest now. Finally he nodded solemnly.

"Yes," he uttered quietly, though in a tone rarely, if ever, heard from the man. Garathi turned and stared back down at the proud gathering before the city gates…then motioned with one arm for his group to follow him deeper into the hills. He looked anything but the picture of pride.

Chapter Twenty-Two

To Marathon

The cheering crowd of Athenians had ventured
well outside the city walls, steadfast and loud, waving
their flood of pennants—some of the pennants adorned
with the olive tree insignias of their free state, others
bearing the owl insignia of their patron goddess,
Athena. They continued blowing loudly on trumpets
and pipes, doing so even after the army had marched
off beyond the distant knolls of the Attica plains. And
then abruptly a dull silence fell over the vast
gathering...a deathly pall that seemed to take hold of
them: loved ones were going off to die so those left
behind might live. Yes, the poleis-states of Greece had
often squabbled and clashed, some conflicts more
severe than others, but nothing to the extent of the mass
invasion now bearing down on their oft-fractured lands.

In mere moments the trumpeting and cheering had
fairly dissolved into a dirge after the armored
myrmidons had disappeared entirely. Many turned their
eyes up toward the Archon for assurance of some sort,
seeking from him even the faintest of hopes. For it was
not only the seasoned hoplites—for whom battle was of
a second nature—it was also their civilian militia, many
of them young men accustomed to the practice of daily
chores and hobbies and the cultural pursuit of a free life

in a rare polis where even those lacking in the privilege of citizenship might yet dare to dream of it.

Now everything lay under a monstrous threat, capable not only of overwhelming and destroying them, but obliterating their dreams from the face of the only world they knew. So the eyes that turned up to the Archon of Athens reflected the dread of those unspoken thoughts haunting them all—a grim reality that swept over the plains, the hills, and the city itself...an emptiness shared by everyone, with the army now gone. All that remained was a small standing force left behind to man the city walls.

Symethra, too, gazed forlornly up at Archon Kallimachos, her eyes moistening at the thought of other young boys like her son Pheidippides marching off, swords and spears in hand, all of them wondering if they would ever return to see their beloved home turf.

****

The heat of the late summer sun bore down on the parade of Greek soldiers marching through the rocky pass of rolling slopes. The passage was narrow and tight, not unlike the one that courier Ginakos had raced through en route to Athens. At best, the armored hoplites and militiamen hustling through could walk only four abreast between the rising cliffs strewn with boulders at the base, where the path was one of hard pebbles and crushed stone. At the head of the armored promenade, General Milteades eyed the towering gray walls of rock, slowing slightly in his gait, his gaze shifting from one summit to the other.

"What is it, General?" asked a burly officer striding alongside him. "Do you fear ambush here?"

Milteades kept his eyes fixed on the gloomy cliff's

jagged gray walls. "Oh…not here. No," the general mused, more to himself.

"If so, it would be disastrous for us in such tight quarters. We'd not maneuver well, and with nowhere to seek cover…" said the officer forbiddingly. "Should we hasten all the more?"

Milteades smiled wryly, something else seemingly being weighed behind the craggy brow and deep-set eyes. "Aye. Hasten more, we must," replied the general. "We need arrive at Marathon by nightfall, hopefully before Darius and his hordes beach there on the morrow." He urged the marching militia on faster. "Let the men know they'll have earned a brief rest once we are clear of this pass."

The officer looked relieved at the promise of both the more urgent pace through the menacing-looking gorge as well as any rest, however brief, given the sweltering heat and humidity that was sapping energy out of them all. But he had no idea of the real reason his general had weighed so pensively the spectre of the brooding passage.

Farther back, Captain Boros urged on the rear of the procession. He knew well the strain a forced march had on the more novice militiamen, in particular those who had yet to taste so rigorous a pace while toting swords, spears, and shields and also weighted down by armor, whether the heavier bronze or the lighter leather. The heat alone doubled the difficulty of the added weight. Many were already showing the wear of the trek, which still had several more leagues—a good ten miles—yet to go. And with the notion of a forthcoming struggle against battle-hardened Persian warriors—all eager to have at the vastly outnumbered Greeks—the fledgling militiamen pressed on, but with the dread of first-time battle looming darkly over them. The stony pass added to that mounting dread.

Boros and several fellow officers had broken off to opposite sides of the narrow gorge, scrutinizing their younger charges as they trudged by, some holding up like hardy veterans, others straining just to keep up. The wide-eyed trepidation betrayed on the faces of a fair number of them gave the more seasoned veterans cause for concern, knowing they might have to rely on some of these fledglings.

Young Pheidippides ambled on wearily under the weight of his splendid but cumbersome bronze armor; the glint of imminent fear was alight in his soft brown eyes, and Captain Boros, seeing him thus, frowned in sad disappointment. The boy did not fail to catch the look as he passed by his father. He had seen it before.

****

By the time the Athenian army of several thousand—augmented by a few hundred others from the friendly northern Greek city-state of Plataia—had arrived at Marathon, all that could be seen in the already mounting dusk were the lumpy shapes of rolling hillocks that General Milteades hoped would mask his huge force in the light of day from the Persian ships carrying a good five times their number.

Chapter Twenty-Three

Preparations

Through a late morning fog steaming up from pale warm waters that broke gently along the jagged Aegean coastline, the prow of an ornate, fearsome-looking ship sliced smoothly toward the barely visible shore. Beyond the shoals and occasional reefs that lurked treacherously beneath the otherwise alluring coastal waters, and on the other side of the rolling rocky mounds that blocked the view of anything beyond, lay the plains of Marathon. Upon mooring and disembarking, a march through the rolling hillocks would prove to be a geographic obstacle course in that there was no steady stretch of ground that allowed for easy passage.

For this reason, Great King Darius—aboard the Persian flagship cutting its way slowly and meticulously toward the choppy shoreline—had trusted to the savvy of his sea captains. Some were familiar with the erratic Hellespont coast and how it should be approached. This stealthy advance of the Persian fleet would be concealed by the thick foggy mists and the range of high hillocks blocking sight of a seafaring invader. Victory would soon be at hand over this country of disjointed city-states that had dared send aid to challenge the rule of Persia's King over his own colonies. The Athenian's Eretrian cousins had already felt the full impact of meddling in Persian affairs, mused Darius as he peered menacingly into the steamy fog. Athens would be next...and with the utter destruction of Greece's most prideful and refined culture, the rest would crumble too. This Hellespont was a widespread territory soon to be absorbed by an empire destined to establish worldwide rule.

"We will beach on the shores here, but remain on board the ships until I announce it is time for the march," said Darius to his fleet captain and the two satrap governors. "With our worthy assassins having slain those messengers, there should be no hint of our presence now to outlying villagers, lest there still be surviving couriers or wandering bards who might yet alert Athens of our advance."

"A wise decision, Great King," said Datis, the taller of the two satraps. "Our conquest of these feuding Hellespont lands shall be one of ease, once Athens and its rival Sparta both fall."

Darius smiled coyly, always satisfied with the appropriate flattery expected of his subordinates. Rare it was that any deigned to speak otherwise of an action chosen by their liege and master.

"Eh, my lord...?" the shorter, stockier governor, Artaphernes, queried meekly.

Darius eyed him curiously, then raised his head in indication for the man to go on.

The stocky satrap bowed his own head and looked away discreetly and with a clear deference. He spoke carefully. "Our General Mardonius is aft with Captain Kazek and the Athenian traitor..."

The satrap felt rather than saw the Persian king

give him a hard cautionary look that froze him in mid-sentence. Datis nudged his fellow satrap subtly, frowning in alarm. "Eh, sire, that is," fumbled Artaphernes, "I mean to say that our general and the fleet captain are with our ally—the former Athenian ruler who was unjustly exiled by traitors within Athens." The man waited, holding his breath as Darius considered the amended statement.

"Send word now to General Mardonius to bring our trusted new ally, Lord Hippias, here to speak with me," said Darius firmly. "And let it be remembered that it is *his* knowledge—not only of the grounds we shall soon cross, but from his prior, rightful rule of Athens—that will help secure us a victory so expediently." The Persian King strode imperiously over to the stocky satrap and, with one hand, gripped hold of the man's bearded chin and lifted it with a surprising gentleness so the quaking governor was now staring directly into his liege's mud-brown eyes. "It is fitting, my valued servant, that we acknowledge the friendship and aid of those whose allegiance to our Empire is unquestioned."

The satrap dared not wrest his gaze from the kingly dark eyes that bore into his own. He nodded under his lord's penetrating stare, as much as the thick hand gripping him by the chin would permit.

Darius smiled ever so subtly, then released the satrap's chin in acknowledgment of the man's acquiescence. "Now go summon our good ally Hippias yourself…then inform Fleet Captain Kazek that I would speak with him, too, of our disembarking and of our course for Athens." He spun Artaphernes round gently and ushered him firmly on his way. A quiet nod in the direction of the taller satrap, Datis, indicated that he accompany his comrade. Darius then turned back and stared outward at the misty shapes of the shoreline knolls, mere shadows still in the lingering fog.

"With Mithra's blessing—and the guidance of that hapless Athenian outcast—we shall be upon Athens and breaching its city walls while the day is still bright and fully to our advantage." He smirked quietly to himself. "And their Spartan kin shall also discover it is wiser to submit than fight."

****

Beyond the sloping hillocks the Persians had glimpsed, through the thick ocean fog, the plains of Marathon…accessible from the Aegean shoreline only through a few narrow passes that cut between the range of steep knolls. An Athenian scout lay prone atop one of those knolls now, his keen eyes alert as he peered through the morning mist and beheld the shadowy silhouettes of massive war ships lurking not far off the coastline. Had he, in fact, been less perceptive and not so attuned to detail, he might have mistaken the fleet of Persian ships for huge breakers rolling in from the ever-churning sea, or perhaps mistaken it for a pod of whales, or seen it as nothing more than misshapen shadows within the constantly shifting mist. But the seasoned scout had been sent to the hilly summit, even before the sun rose, specifically to catch sight of an enemy fleet advancing on Marathon.

And there, but several hundred yards from the jagged shoreline, did he spot the floating terror stalking his Greek homeland. The scout gasped, perspiring from far more than the intense heat and humidity as he scuttled back down the sandy knoll, wondering what kind of uncanny scheme General Milteades and his chieftains might possibly have in store for this monstrous invasion.

****

From the opposite side of the knoll where the Athenian scout had spied the massive fleet only moments earlier, Darius and his sea captains waited eagerly for the morning mist to lift. Then they would slip in closer through the troublesome shoals and reefs and disembark. But for that heavy mist, the Persian force would already have been ashore and, under the command of its ground force general, Mardonius, en route to Athens. The Greek hoplites and civilian militia would not yet have made their way out from the cover of the coastal knolls; rather, they would have been accosted on the wider, more open inland plain of Marathon…where they would likely have been destroyed by sheer force of numbers. Instead, the entire force of Athenians, and their Plataian allies, would now have time to deploy in accordance with General Milteades' crafty designs.

The spry scout now entertained a tight squadron of officers, headed by General Milteades. Strategies were being determined, debated, and solidified as the scout was grilled repeatedly by a mix of commanders regarding the size and position of the Persian fleet.

Farther back in the ranks of Greek hoplites and militiamen—little more than dark silhouettes in the tediously lifting mist—the youngest of Athenian recruits, supported by a smaller contingent of veteran soldiers—huddled between the banks of two hillocks, finishing the last bits of breakfast they wolfed down nervously while strapping on their armor and weapons.

Captain of the Elite Athenian Guard, Boros,

approached one of the squads nestled in an overhang of sand-stained rock. The wide-eyed young militiamen, most in their early twenties and some even younger, all rose sharply as a hardy veteran hoplite motioned toward the captain's approach. One in particular among the very youngest bristled uncomfortably as Boros emerged out of the mist.

"Worry not, lads," the tall captain said in a most assuring tone. His deep-set hazel eyes scanned the group of raw recruits, halting as he caught sight of the youngest, Pheidippides, garbed in the splendid bronze armor that marked him clearly apart from the rest. Boros gave no sign of recognizing the lad but gestured them all to sit back down.

"We've some time before we strike at these Persian swine. Be assured you'll not be going into the fray without guidance from battle-hardened veterans. Heh— it's our foe who need worry this day!"

The young men eased themselves back down onto the ground as their captain had indicated. He looked them over with a quiet scrutiny, trying not to let an added bit of his focus on Pheidippides be noticed. The boy could not help suppressing a tiny smile, knowing that for one of the few times in his life, this man had stared directly at him...and, for the first time, seemingly as more than a stranger.

Boros' eyes roamed again over the group. "Eh, it is of course for many of you a first time?" His gaze fell on Pheidippides once more, noting clearly how the boy struggled with his own fears. Yet the young foot courier was not the only one consumed by the tremors of pre-battle. He nodded knowingly and offered the band of young militiamen a soft smile of assurance.

"Sir?" one of them queried cautiously.

Boros saw it was none other than Pheidippides. The lad made to speak, then shook his head as though changing his mind. Boros took a step toward him and bade him rise, speaking quietly.

"Go on, lad. 'Tis all right."

Knees trembling, Pheidippides rose slowly and eyed the stalwart officer, his father. The two locked eyes, longer than at any time ever in the past, and Pheidippides wondered what in all Olympus had compelled him to assert himself thus.

"Captain...Boros, sir... Is it of any disgrace to confess to...fear in such a moment?" Pheidippides heard the undercurrent of voices within the ranks of his fellow militiamen at so candid an admission. And he caught the abrupt surprise in Boros at such open candor.

Silence reigned in the ensuing moments. Boros stared long and hard at the thin lad before him, garbed in the splendid bronze armor no other of this squad boasted. The tall captain drew a long breath, then gestured for Pheidippides to sit once more. The lad did so... Then he and every other member of the young militia group all but gaped as Captain Boros dropped to one knee and faced them all.

"A worthy question...young man," said Boros with all respect. "And one I will indeed answer." To the surprise of every one of the young militiamen, Captain Boros gestured them to all draw in closer. The senior hoplite and other officers present all eyed one another in equal surprise at this unexpected break in protocol by one of their army's most highly regarded leaders. They too drew in closer, eager to hear what the renowned captain of the Elite Guard had to say to these raw young men who commanded neither rank nor reputation in service to Athens.

"It is not so very long ago that I have forgotten those early battles where every fledgling soldier, myself included, felt the tremors of the coming fight," he said quietly. "Feel no shame in it at all."

There was a moment of stunned silence, and then one of the younger soldiers spoke up. "But you are Captain Boros, and you bear the honor of bravery in so many battles."

"Bravery is oft accompanied by fear," said Boros, turning his eyes in the direction of the recruit who had spoken, then letting his gaze slide once more back over to Pheidippides. "Many a young soldier, myself included, has felt those early fears and gone on to do much in the service of his city." The hazel eyes now held the soft brown of his son's in a near trance between the two. "Why, I can recall my very first march off to a battle with none other than our fierce Spartan cousins...and thinking I might never again see the young girl for whom I cared so deeply, feeling that all I wanted was to return and be with her again on a warm day in our blessed agora."

"And did you see her again when you returned?" Pheidippides blurted out suddenly, his mind flashing back to the last time he had seen young Azelina of the Kaboni clan, standing there in all of her lovely reckless splendor, rubbing a slender hand round her dog's furry neck. How he longed to be with her this very moment, and how he missed his little home and his mother's kindly assurances that his life was worth the living. No, he did not want to end it here this coming day.

A good many of the young recruits turned and eyed

153

Pheidippides, then Boros, the poignant exchange between the famed hoplite captain and this barely ripe teenager—who seemed so much akin to themselves—moving them all deeply.

"Aye, lad," Boros responded gently. "Though, like all of you, I scarcely believed it that day. So quell those fears and recognize that our war goddess, Athena, looks over us this very day as we move to defend the city we honor with her blessed name." His eyes roamed the ranks of the militia and of the veteran hoplites as well, generating a light of greater assurance in them. And when he gazed once again upon Pheidippides, he saw in those eyes, too, what only a father can bestow upon a son.

Every one of his young Athenian charges nodded firmly in response, eager now to appear confident. Boros rose and looked them over once more, then raised a solid fist. "Wear your armor and shields well, men, and let the fire of freedom burn in your swords!"

Before turning to stride off, Boros made eye contact with Pheidippides one more time, gave a reassuring nod of approval, then turned and marched off proudly.

Pheidippides rose and stared back gratefully, long after his father had departed.

****

A tiny fire burned discreetly behind one of the high hillocks where General Milteades, Boros, and several other officers conferred. The sun was rising in the sky, and its bright rays peeked through the drifting clouds and last bits of foggy morning mist finally starting to lift.

"We'll catch our foe as he disembarks and have

him at our mercy," Milteades said craftily, "though fiercely outnumbered here."

"A good five-to-one from what Ginakos was told, and what our scout also reports," said Boros.

"Aye," said Milteades. "But a smaller force can vanquish a larger one if we mystify and misguide them into a dread surprise. The Persians still expect to be marching, not fighting. And this hemmed-in plain won't be to their liking." He stooped over and illustrated his plan using a handful of small stones and a bent stick to etch out the maneuvers. "Now, if we send the bulk of our strength to the flanks, we can then swoop down upon them after feigning the front as our point of fury."

Boros and the other officers all nodded at the daring but tactical sense of the general's ploy.

"And by all the gods of Olympus, let our fury make them pay for their crimes at Eretria," General Milteades added.

****

Well above the Greeks and Persians on the Earth below, Queen Keres and Lord Pan gazed downward. A smile crossed the nymph queen's delicate face, the ever-present gleam of mischief twinkling in her golden eyes and indicating her thoughts before she even spoke them.

"The Persians are far too many," she quipped. "Sparta will never depart in time, and even so..."

"Ah, sweet Keres, so little you know of military cunning," Pan said arrogantly.

No sooner had he uttered those words than Keres shot him a haughty look, at which he all but cringed, as though admitting guilt of some sort. "My apologies.

Even I forget sometimes." He offered a meek smile that seemed out of place on his craggy face speckled with bits of animal fur.

Keres nodded in cordial acceptance of his apology.

"But…" Pan followed up in his usual smug tone, "did you not hear the most splendid strategy Milteades has in store for surprising these foul Persians who suspect no ambush?"

"Oh, this General Milteades talks a most splendid plan indeed," she responded, unimpressed. "But on the field where swords are crossed instead of words, his fine army of hoplites will have to rely too much on that rabble of 'citizens' and the like, ambush or not," she replied acidly.

Pan took note of the simmering bitterness in her tone and merely shrugged. He knew where this exchange might lead and did not want to let their talk fall into the murk he wished to avoid.

"Eh, perhaps we might have another wager here?" he said lightly, hoping she might be swayed from a topic he did not want to see surface.

Keres eyed him sharply. "If it were anyone other than Greeks making so futile a stand, you would most certainly admit a Persian triumph is at hand."

"Are you yet so disdainful of those you once…" Pan let his own words trail off as he caught a flash of golden fire resurfacing in her eyes. "Ah, but such eris—such strife—is no longer the concern of those who dwell far above it…eh, my sweet Keres?" His face broke into a broad smile, hoping he might lighten their discourse again. "So…have we another wager?"

Keres sighed. "Oh, but we do," she said smugly. "And for once it will not be Queen Keres who parts with any nectar or ambrosia. I say the Persian tide floods the plain of Marathon."

"And I say it ebbs," said Pan, altogether pleased with himself.

Chapter Twenty-Four

The Battle of Marathon

The Persian fleet stirred with life as gangplanks were lowered from a number of the sleek serpentine ships. Soldiers garbed in fearsome armor characterized by horned helms and demonic designs etched over the shields and face guards disembarked, battle lust in their eyes. Tales that had been told of Persian warriors being seen as monstrous demons summoned by Darius himself for the purpose of sacrificing enemy soldiers to their god Mithra had not escaped any of the raw Greek lads who comprised much of the civilian militia. And indeed, the ornate helms worn by the Persians now disembarking, the gaudy shields and breastplates decorating these legions of Great King Darius, all bore the look of monstrous beings of myth and lore, stirring long-held superstitious fears.

Those who engaged the Persians in close-quarter combat oft panicked at the mere sight of such myrmidons charging at them and shrieking like fiends. Many foes fled in terror rather than face Darius' "Hordes of Hades," who were said to feast on the flesh and souls of victims. There was no cause then for Darius, General Mardonius, or the satraps and their officers to believe anything different was to take place here in the outer regions of this northern Attica territory...or at Athens itself, where a vastly outnumbered defense of state and mere outlier townships might offer no more formidable a resistance.

From high above, spying down on the Persian troops disembarking their massive flotilla out onto the sandy shingle of beach, keen-eyed scouts of the awaiting Athenian force quietly signaled the progress of the enemy's march toward the narrow cleft at the foot of the steep rolling slopes. A large contingent of the Greek force lurked just below its scouts on the rocky mounds overlooking the plain beyond the hillocks. They waited tensely, eager for the command to attack.

The majestic figure of General Milteades listened intently as a hoplite sidled his way down from the summit of the mound and spoke earnestly to another officer of high ranking, Themistokles, who then carried the word to the awaiting Athenian general.

"The Persians make their way into the pass now, General Milteades," said Themistokles. The veteran officer's deep-set eyes flickered with admiration of his commanding general. "It appears you were right in expecting they would try using these hills as cover for concealing their landing from the eyes of outliers or scouts who might see them gathering here to march for Athens. Only now, they have unwittingly hemmed themselves in and become vulnerable in a pass that will hamper them before they can spread their numbers out onto the plain," Themistokles added, a wry smile on his aquiline face. The light of battle was already aglow in his dark eyes, and Milteades regarded the man with a look of approval, sensing already this fellow was above the cut of most officers assigned this battle today.

"What is your name, Commander?" Milteades

asked quietly.

"Themistokles, sir," the officer replied proudly.

"You are versed, I take it, in the lore of our poet Homer's grand heroes of the *Iliad*?" Milteades queried wryly, his eyebrows narrowing as he studied the man further.

"Of Achilles and Odysseus and their bold cohorts... Why, yes. I should say all Greeks who deign to prevail in spite of opposition should be of such mettle, my general."

Milteades turned to the Plataian commander, and they exchanged an approving nod. He laid a brawny hand on one shoulder of Themistokles, then drew forth his broadsword. "It is nigh time, then," he proclaimed solemnly, a grim smile on his bearded face. "Once enough of Darius' marauders have cluttered the pass below and found their maneuvering to be harshly impaired, we will signal Captain Boros to direct his hoplites and our militia to the attack. If the fortune of our past heroes—and that of our Olympians—is with us, we may then match their heroics with a cunning display of our own."

"And thus preserve the future of Athens' democratia," added Themistokles. "For if we fail here, Darius will surely go on to execute or exile all who cherish that splendid dream our own Kleisthenes fought so hard to bring us. 'Tis more than military conquest at stake this day."

General Milteades gave the man another long, thoughtful look.

"Well...we'd best effect our attack, else our fine dreams for the future may indeed be for naught," the general quipped solemnly. "Time now that we signal our ground force to pour into that pass and deal those Persian devils a blow from which they will not recover."

"And then...?" asked the Plataian commander.

"Then we shall swoop down upon them like a rain of boulders rolling over a bundle of sticks. Too late they will discover that Captain Boros' single force is *not* all they are facing," said Milteades. "And with Athena's help, the 'Great King Darius' and his vaunted commanders will watch helplessly from their ships and behold the slaughter of their men trapped in the pass— while the bulk of their forces cannot even disembark to join them."

"A bold and worthy plan, General...if our citizen militia and Plataian allies can support Captain Boros' hoplites long enough to contain the Persians hemmed in there, and keep them from breaking through before those on the ships can join them," Themistokles said, a hint of skepticism in his voice.

"My Plataians will not shirk their duty," the commander said sharply.

Themistokles raised a hand in polite acknowledgment.

"And let us also hope that your militia of citizens, with those rousted from your city's darker quarters and outlying hinterlands, will fight with the same zeal," said the Plataian just as skeptically.

Themistokles shot a look at the Plataian. "Men who yearn for freedom will all fight," he said.

"Darius' generals will suffer the shock of our sudden ambush, but will fight nonetheless...believing the lesser numbers there to be our full strength," said Milteades. "And once they finally push Boros' hoplites and militia—and our brave Plataians—out onto the plain, then shall we swoop down upon them from the advantage of these slopes and cut them off from their ships." The Greek general's face darkened with a cold glee. "With Athena's help, no Persian engaged shall live—and no others shall disembark in the limited quarters we leave them."

"And so grave a shock at seeing their own men slaughtered in such a manner may well break their resolve, General Milteades," the Plataian officer deduced, drawing a wry smile from the general.

"In all hope, yes," said Milteades. "But if not, we will await them on the shores and in the nearby swamp pools and give them cause to regret joining their ill-fated comrades in a journey to Hades."

The Plataian commander and the small group of Athenian officers all eyed Milteades at that moment, as though a god—or at least one of the old heroes of *Iliad* lore—had just spoken.

"So much now rests with brave Captain Boros and his stalwarts fighting within the pass. For if they falter, the Persians will break out freely onto the plain, while those on board the ships will then pour forth with no seeming end," Themistocles added grimly.

****

Crouched outside the passageway that marked a break in the hillocks leading to where the Persians were disembarking onto the spit of a beach, the Elite Athenian Guard of the city's finest hoplites—and the raw militia of citizen volunteers—awaited the line of cramped Persian warriors advancing directly toward them. The tramp of many feet marching in rhythm over the hard grainy sand reverberated throughout the morning air. Boros and his guardsmen all lay pressed against the rock-hard cliff base, stern-faced, eyes filling with the fervor of having known battle previously; yet tremors of fear still quaked in every one of them, not uncommon even with those who had tasted warfare in the past.

Boros' eyes locked with the Plataian captain's, both men knowing the mounting clop and crunch of booted and sandaled feet signaled numbers far greater than any they had engaged in the past.

"It is said these Persians are frightful to behold in close quarter," the Plataian uttered softly.

Boros acknowledged with a sardonic smirk. "Looks do not win battles."

The Plataian allowed for a wry smirk of his own, then gripped his thrusting spear more tightly. Boros turned his head away, and his eyes roamed the ranks of his Athenian militiamen and the Plataian force, all pressed in tightly against the sloping cliffs to conceal their presence outside the narrow passageway. He knew it was near futile to try glimpsing any sight of Pheidippides within the mass of crouching armored bodies, but he swore to himself that he would not fail to find his son at some time during the course of the coming battle, however perilous it might prove.

The tromping of enemy feet drew ever closer, and the steady clop of so many foes rang in the ears of veteran and raw recruits alike. The brewing spectre of it all was, of course, known by those who had wielded swords, spears, and shields before—and would soon come to be known by those who had never thrust or slashed with such weapons of warfare. All felt the rising tension. Captain Boros himself knew those very tremors that always preceded battle, and how they were enough to raise doubts in even the boldest of battle-hardened warriors. He wondered now, with this onslaught of so feared an empire's finest fighters, if his own raw militia would hold true to the test.

He gazed upward at the high hillock summits where he anticipated, in the next unnerving moments, the waving of the Athenian olive leaf and owl pennants that would signal the initial ground charge—he and his awaiting legion—from concealment within the tight crunch of knolls.

"May Zeus and Athena guide us, eh, Captain?" Boros heard one of his officers crouched near him utter. He nodded assuredly in response to the man.

"May all the gods of Olympus be with us against this horde," he replied hoarsely, his eyes never leaving sight of the knoll summit from which the anticipated signal would come.

And there it was!

The white and leafy green pennants snapped sharply in the early morning breeze. Boros knew not to hesitate. *"Elate—*All of you!" he cried with fierce Greek pride, and led them out from their rocky cover and directly into the teeth of the oncoming Persians.

Farther back in the ranks of young militia volunteers, and pressed tightly against the grainy slope that hid him and the rest of the Greek assault force from the unsuspecting Persians marching into the pass, Pheidippides stared wide-eyed, anticipating the moment when his mettle as a man and as a soldier of Athens would be tested. He bit down on his lower lip, the salty taste of his own blood coursing through his mouth. He felt eyes studying him suddenly and glanced around anxiously. He wondered if he had fallen under the scrutiny of some nearby officer scanning for a weak link. To his surprise it was another youth, close to his own age: a Plataian, based on the tan hue of his cheap leather armor and the crude thrusting spear and animal hide shield he bore. The dark-haired youth was deeply browned by the sun, wiry in build, and his eyes flashed with the same cold fear as his own.

"Your first battle...friend?" the youth asked almost apologetically. Pheidippides forced a thin smile and nodded. The Plataian eyed the young Athenian's elegant armor and weaponry. "Your armor is most fine," he said awkwardly.

Pheidippides made to reply but simply nodded again in acknowledgment. His father had meant this splendid bronze armament for him to survive a battle that would determine not only his life but also the lives of everyone he had ever known and loved. It meant the very streets and homes and shops he saw each day, the splendor of Athens' temples...and the marvel of the agora he so loved. Persia would destroy all of it forever if left unchecked this day.

An abrupt rage filled him suddenly. "Fear not, my friend," Pheidippides heard himself mutter, the surprise of his own words filling his ears with quiet pride. "We will not let those devils of Darius claim any more Greek states as unholy prizes." His eyes flashed with a rising confidence—the private knowledge that he himself was the son of Captain Boros of the Elite Athenian Guard. He would earn that unspoken title this day, here on the plains of Marathon.

The Plataian youth flashed a smile of reassurance. "Aye, we shall..."

"Pheidippides."

"Pheid-ipp-ides," the boy repeated, pronouncing it carefully. "And I am Kretus," he proclaimed. There was no time for more. They found themselves swept forward roughly as their entire regiment surged abruptly toward the tromping of footfalls advancing from within the hillock passageway.

Captain Boros had seen the battle pennants hoisted high on the thin hickory staff by the Athenian scout, signaling the charge round the bend and into the narrow pass between the hillocks. No sooner had he gestured with a brawny sword-wielding arm and called out "Elate" than the entire force he commanded thrust itself forward like a surging tide, sweeping men, sand, and stone along with it. The battle cry of "Athena" roared through the gully, lending more courage and fury to the charging Greeks...an utter shock to the astonished Persians marching in what they all had believed to be a routine trek.

On board the flagship, none other than Great King Darius stared in complete awe at the spectre of his infamous troops so unexpectedly ambushed...and so drastically unprepared for it. Before the full impact of the ambush had gripped him or the stunned commanders and satraps on board, the follow-up avalanche of enemy myrmidons pouring down from the hillock summits on either side of the gully slopes turned the Great King's astonishment to horror. Darius gawked like a child who had just had his prized possession seized from his grasp. The gold spiked crown that always rested comfortably and snugly on his head tottered to one side, while the bearded face beneath it wriggled violently in disbelief. His thick shoulders, wrapped in a purple silken shirt, jerked backward, causing the flowing cape made of exquisite leopard's skin to flap sharply, as though a sentient force had suddenly possessed it. His eyes raged with fury. "By Mithra, what madness is this!" he gasped.

The gray morning mist still hung over the water, reluctant to lift as though reveling in some mystical ability to hold back a clear view of the shore. It lingered in a fog of obscurity. And though the shadowy shoreline revealed little more than a jumble of silhouettes colliding in a clash of hostile clamor, it was clear enough to those on board that the ones pushing from farther back in the passage and those pouring down from the hilly summits had seized an instant advantage, shaking the stunned figures who had disembarked the ships and marched directly into the teeth of a deadly ambush.

Those on board the flagship had also caught the uncharacteristic tremor of doubt that eked out from their liege and master. Darius felt their looks. He mustered back his nerve, then turned a hard gaze on his two satraps, who stared squeamishly down at the deck. Then he fixed a cold eye on General Mardonius and on the flamboyantly armored captain, all swagger gone from both.

"They knew our course," the Persian king hissed like a coiled cobra. "*A courier got through.*"

Chapter Twenty-Five

The Seeds of Courage

Striding solemnly toward the foredeck where
Darius was still scowling reproachfully at his
subordinates and lashing out in an ongoing tirade, the
huge, bearded assassin Rojese, of Macedonia's tribal
clans, exchanged a look of curiosity with his equally
large Nubian comrade, Jamjon, whose ebon features
bore a curious frown. Rojese raised a gnarly hand
slightly, indicating they slow their pace and capture
more of the tongue-lashing Darius was dealing his
military and fleet commanders. Jamjon raised an
eyebrow and nodded as they continued more slowly. As
with his fellow assassin, the Nubian was quietly
amazed by the Persian emperor's unfettered angst.

"How is it possible that our spy ship and our scouts
failed to see there was one more courier!" Darius
roared, his tone approaching that of a tantrum. "Have I
not made clear my thoughts on the danger of outliers
and couriers—and those sly roving bards who spread
nothing more than lies?"

Not an officer or satrap standing anywhere in the
scope of the red-faced emperor's eyes dared react. Most
simply bowed their heads in acquiescent shame, though
it was unlikely any of those present were truly
accountable in any reasonable way for a Greek foot

courier having slipped away unnoticed along the misty coastline. The many wispy shapes and shadows there usually proved to be nothing more than prowling beasts or grainy sands shifting and whirling in the wind. But such explanations would prove futile here when Lord Darius was festooned in such wrath. It might even prove perilous for anyone foolish enough to interrupt or disagree with him under such circumstances. Gods were to be obeyed, not contested. So they remained silent, even the debonair fleet commander, upon whose shoulders the consequences of this campaign would fall.

"It seems only my loyal Hippias here considers my wishes and demands accordingly," Darius pressed on with a sweep of one robed arm toward the aging, deposed Athenian tyrant. The elder Greek regarded Darius with as suppliant an air as he could project. Ever since seeking asylum from his former subjects of Athens—due to his ill treatment of its people while ruling there—Hippias had measured well the means of flattery and obedience desired by the Persian King…and how best to benefit from it.

"Was he not victim himself of the falsehoods spoken by rivals," Darius continued, "who then sent forth bards and heralds spreading lies about his efforts to bring order and prosperity to Athens? Good Hippias did strive to direct his fair city into a center of commerce and prosperity and peaceable rule. But his enemies ever spoke ill of him through their couriers and the like, and through the writings on tablets by men who sought to belittle and defile him. And these same traitors did ruin the reputation of so good a man as Hippias here by denouncing him before crowds of gullible Athenians, telling them terrible rumors that were not true. Thus did it have the desired effect in that a true leader who might have commanded peace and friendship with Persia—as when he presented our own emissaries with the submissive Tribute of Water and Earth—was instead wrongly deemed traitor by his own people!"

Darius turned grandly to be certain his gaze made a sweeping arc of everyone standing at the prow of the fleet flagship, as would a sly prosecutor to a jury already conditioned to his will. Every man on the foredeck knew the response and every one of them nodded in respectful acknowledgment.

"Now we learn that a courier escaped our vigil and brought word to Athens of our most carefully wrought campaign here." He gestured darkly and ostentatiously with a long, robed arm toward the shoreline of Marathon. "Our advantage of surprise was thus lost..." Darius' voice trailed off.

Rojese and Jamjon strode up in full view of the men gathered on the foredeck. The pair halted, standing stock still like a pair of stoic sentinels, impervious to anything but whatever orders awaited them. Both had overheard much of the Persian king's rant, but neither gave hint of it. *They* would not be blamed, for their responsibility had been to slay whatever couriers and the like had been spotted from the scout ship—which they had done, then rendezvoused with the ship afterward, as instructed.

Darius acknowledged their presence with barely a nod, though a tiny frown flickered on his brow, perhaps because neither of the two mercenary killers seemed cowed in the least (perhaps not even humbled) by his grand presence. Dismissing this observation as more a byproduct of his current angst, the Great King continued with his tirade, now a quiet rumble, yet containing menace. "Unless you are all wont to see this dread 'Rule of the People' take further root and spread beyond this day's campaign, then here it must end, never to fester in this or any other land again."

Again the two assassins neither moved nor reacted. Darius glared sharply at General Mardonius, who then turned to the silent duo. "Rojese, Jamjon," said the general, "we have need of your services again to make certain none of the Athenian rabble along this shore slips off to forewarn Athens of our...change in tactics here." Both assassins nodded, turned, and departed in silence.

Darius watched them go, rankled still by an apparent absence of awe, in the Macedonian or the Nubian, of his regal presence. Though both their homelands were under Persian domain, neither had appeared suppliant enough to him. Yet he said nothing as they left, for at this point the services of both were needed. Besides, had either displayed a mere hint of disrespect, they'd not have drawn an ensuing breath of life, he rationalized.

So the stolid demeanor of his hirelings could be overlooked...for now. They had pleased him earlier with select body parts of the couriers they had slain, serving both as proof of their success and as due tributes to their King. And they had succeeded previously where others had failed. The two were now charged with seeking out and hunting down any more foul couriers en route to Athens. The city could not be informed in the least of whatever took place here.

Surprise and morale were key factors in battle, along with superior numbers. He needed his assassins.

"Eh…sire?" He heard the voice of General Mardonius imploring him.

Darius turned and gestured regally with one hand for the man to speak. The general bowed his head accordingly and turned his gaze in his King's direction, mindful of not looking him directly in the eye. "Great King…as commanding general of your armies and seafaring forces, I believe I speak for all in saying we are abject in our sorrow to have disappointed you in this first…skirmish with our foes. These impudent Greeks, who dared defile Persian lands and so brought on these conflicts, must feel the weight of justice. And we *shall* mete it out to them. Errors made earlier shall not be repeated."

Having heard precisely what he expected of subordinates, Darius gestured with a lift of his chin to the collective of commanders and guardsmen, then strutted off the foredeck, Hippias in tow—leaving General Mardonius, his satraps, and Fleet Captain Kazek eying one another in silent angst.

****

The abrupt charge of the Greek hoplites had thrown the Persian force into near chaos, most of the outlandishly garbed warriors not assembled in a proper battle formation but for a long march instead. It would have been far more devastating for Darius and his satraps and commanders to have been there on the beach and witnessed, in close quarter, the utter disarray of their vaunted troops—all caparisoned in their signature attire of helms shaped like the heads of ferocious beasts and unworldly demons, and with vile etchings and painted designs and evil runes decorating their purple-gray armor—now discombobulated and colliding with one another almost comically. It would have sent the Persian king into a rage worse than he had displayed before everyone on the deck of his flagship.

The cunning ambush calculated masterfully by General Milteades had effected confusion and panic in soldiers who normally had done the same to all others with whom they had previously been matched. And other than the twisted tangle of shadows and the haze of shapes visible from the ship's decks, it was not possible for those on board the cluster of war galleys squeezed into the rocky strait to determine the extent of the fierce Athenian attack. So the denizens of the Great King, tramping down the gangplanks and onto a shingle of beach—then into the confines of an even narrower passage that cut through steep sandstone cliffs—did not realize their actual peril. Neither did Darius.

****

The avalanche of Greek hoplites pouring down the hillock slopes hemmed in the Persians, cramming them into a veritable crunch of heavily armed bodies that made maneuverability fairly impossible...barely able to withdraw their sheathed swords or even hoist their long-shafted spears or thick-hided shields into play. But the charging rush of howling Greeks, shields raised high, swords and spears thrusting and swinging, entertained no such dilemma as they closed on their stricken victims—the added advantage of complete mobility aiding their charge. It forced a number of the startled Persians back onto the narrow spit of beach, thus clogging the base of the ship's gangplanks and preventing any number of warriors from disembarking.

Astonishing enough, the Persian soldiers on the beach and in the pass were, at the moment, outnumbered by an enemy whose total force was but one to their five. With most of Darius' warriors unable even to disembark—and the officers on the strip of a beach and those trapped inside the passageway unable to coordinate or rally their men effectively—the charging Greeks, spurred on by the impact of their powerful ambush, slashed, hacked, and thrust their stunned enemy into an immediate retreat.

Milteades yet held back a fair number of his hoplites, who lay flattened against the rear slopes of the hillocks, just shy of the summits and readied for a follow-up surge down the sandy knolls once the Persians did manage to dispatch enough warriors from the ships. The number of them rushing down the gangplanks would still be limited, though in droves enough that would indeed outnumber the Greeks. It would be only a matter of time before the advantage of surprise had passed. So the cagey Athenian general held back a portion of his seasoned fighters, still concealed on the far side of the rolling sandy mounds…and by the clammy fog that refused to lift and melt away with the steaming heat of the morning sun. So long as the heavy mist persisted, the Persian fleet commander could not coordinate efficient moorings to release all of their legions.

Milteades knew it depended entirely on the disunity and disarray his own charging hoplites could unleash in these precious opening moments of skirmish, where the entire tone of the battle would be cast. So he crouched down atop the slopes, along with the other men he had assigned to command, and waited there to signal the next charge he hoped would prove to be the coup de grâce. The hemmed-in Persians would likely have to retreat back into the shallow Aegean waters, thus clogging the few gangplanks lowered and keeping the rest of the enemy fleet in deeper waters—while on the other end, those who had entered the pass leading out onto the plain of Marathon would be facing a charging horde of civilian militia rallied by Captain Boros and his elite veterans.

****

No sooner than he had uttered the Athenian battle cry of "Elate!" urging his guardsmen and militia through the cleft between the towering hillocks, Captain Boros rushed ahead, bronze shield raised high, slashing powerfully with his broadsword at the Persian officers who unknowingly directed their unsuspecting infantrymen into a fateful ambush. The fury of the Greek charge halted the Persian march so abruptly that many of them, more than two or three striding abreast, collided with one another, some even tumbling over.

The raw Athenian and Plataian militiamen—some barely more than teens or early twenties, others older but still tasting the rigors of combat for the first time— followed the gallant captain and his elite guardsmen, who had hurled themselves at the enemy forerunners, cutting them down. The seasoned hoplites, who had seen battle in heated skirmishes with rival city-states— including fabled accounts against their all-powerful Spartan kindred—introduced themselves to their Persian foes with a ferocity the denizens of Lord Darius may never have known in an enemy prior to this conflict. Between Boros' battle-hardened veterans and those pouring down the hillside and into the narrow passageway, it was certainly not the manner of battle the Great Persian King had envisioned.

Farther back in the militia ranks, Pheidippides and his young Plataian comrade, Kretus, had found themselves caught in the crunch of their own ranks pushing forward but unable to squeeze into the passage itself, which was jammed tight with soldiers of both sides, gnarled in close-quarter melees. He did not feel any strains of disappointment as the clash and clatter of swords and shields and the morose howls and cries of men slaughtering one another filled his ears, as though a legion of banshees battled not far from where he was jammed against other sweating bodies. The odor of blood and sweat was already staining the hot August air. Pheidippides wondered if he would soon be among those caught up in the fighting ahead…when, as abruptly as the charge had begun, the morning mist lifted.

****

Along the bay shoreline, the massive fleet Darius had led all the way from the Ionian coast of Persia's heartland and into the soul of the Hellespont territories was now revealed, as if a dark curtain had been yanked away. Off the grainy shore lurked a veritable flock of war galleys, like sea dragons that had been waiting impatiently for a clear sight of their prey. Three of the huge ships were already moored, with gangplanks lowered in water too shallow for maneuvering in closer, while no other men were able to disembark due to the flood of enemy soldiers blocking their way. Now that situation had changed.

More galleys sliced in toward the shore, oars from scores of rowers cutting through the murky green of coastal waters now filled with bulky crafts finally able to maneuver without ramming one another. The flap and splash of oars was soon joined by the clink of armor and shields and the clang of more gangplanks being lowered...while from a distance, the clamor of battle rang loudly and vividly. Magnificently armored men wearing helms of bestial designs and wielding swords, pikes, and axes hustled down the wooden ramps, eager to ford the shoreline shallows and rush into the fray within the cliff passage, where their own brethren fought against the ambush of a foe cagier than expected.

****

Pushed finally into the narrow pass where the fighting had ripened to a mass of close-quarter brawls, Pheidippides had not yet engaged a single foe, as only his own allies loomed before him. But the smash of swords on shields and the crunch of bodies laden in leather or metal armor were close enough so the force and weight of men pushing and thrusting at each other rocked him to and fro. If the ranks of Greek militiamen gave way to the enemy onslaught, he might soon be staring into the cold eyes of a foreign foe. Would that foe be a raw recruit as he was—one who had never swung a sword or even held one till these past two days? Or would he soon see before him a bloodied, battle-tested warrior to whom fighting for one's life was commonplace? Pheidippides had had only few boyhood skirmishes...one being but a week past when he had failed to keep even a fellow street teenager like Barthus from bullying him. What, in the name of all gods, could be expected of him if...

And then the thick wall of sweating human flesh

rammed against him like a vicious tidal surge, hurling him back and into the crunch of those crammed behind him.

****

Once the Persian galleys had maneuvered closer to the beach area and into the shallows—lowering more gangplanks—the Greeks on the shore found themselves too few to intercept all of the outlandishly garbed sea invaders, and so fell back under the weight of the onslaught. They retreated and held their ground at the passageway—the most accessible path leading onto the plain of Marathon. But valiant as the bold hoplite defense was—causing frustration and angst among the more heavily armed intruders—it was only a matter of time before the pass was breached.

****

Pheidippides and the young Plataian, Kretus, still directly in back of him, were flung out onto the plain, as though a massive battering ram had been propelled through the other end of the hilly tunnel. Only the weight of the other militiamen, crammed so tightly against one another, had kept him afoot. And no sooner had they been jettisoned out into the open flats, like corks being sprung free from champagne bottles, than Pheidippides and a number of others stumbled back, spread instantly apart from one another and landing unglamorously on their rumps as the loss of balance and bodily control took hold. The sweltering sun pelted them like a hot sponge as they plunged out onto a weedy turf, baked brown from the persistent August rays.

Encumbered by the weight and bulk of his thick bronze armor and shield, and the sword sheathed at his

178

side, Pheidippides landed hard, his right hand dropping the metal thrusting spear he had tugged free upon hearing Boros' "Elate!" command. But he had little time to contemplate how he might make use of the splendid weapons and armor his father had covertly provided for him. Emerging from the cave-like opening of the pass came a harrowing sight—the likes of which he had only heard tales.

A huge Persian warrior, his height and girth giving him more the look of a hulking beast than a man—made all the more menacing by his scaly armor and helm that sported the facial design of a wild boar—had burst through the wall of young Greek militiamen and scattered them like so many splinters from a flimsy wooden fence. Behind the massive brute, others of his ilk had also smashed through the narrow opening, knocking the Athenian and Plataian defenders asunder, while forcing the assault out into the open where the Persian numbers increased at a frightening rate, the fighting now transcending the spatial limitations of the slim shoreline and tight gullies of the sloped passageways.

The initial advantage of the morning mist and surprise ambush had finally been compromised.

Still sprawled on his backside, not far from his Plataian comrade, who had been slammed to the ground mere feet away, Pheidippides beheld, to his own horror, the boar-faced Persian charging in their direction. Kretus, straining to rise back to his feet, had drawn the sword-wielding brute toward them. The cries of men earnestly in combat—steel meeting steel, their yowls and grunts filling the steaming air of the wide plain—drove a barb of fear into Pheidippides' heart. A wave of shameful relief swept through him as the Persian giant charged right past him...and an urge to remain on the ground and feign death tempted the Athenian lad. But now, there was his comrade-in-arms, Kretus, on his feet finally, raising a thrusting spear in one hand, his cheap leather shield held high in the other, and his eyes muddied with fear at the sight of the rampaging brute bearing down on him. Pheidippides knew his newly found friend had no more a chance against so seasoned a soldier than he would himself. He could not ignore that a decent young man was to die savagely here before his own eyes.

****

Inside the tunnel between the two tall cliffs, and entirely unaware of his son's plight, Captain Boros sliced, slashed, and thrust from within the snarl of armored men, mindful that he aimed his lethal blows at those garbed only in the gaudy gray-maroon of the enemy. He proved, as always, an armored demon whose ferocity and strength was unmatched by few of his foes, many drawing back at the sight of the tall captain in the elegant green-plumed helm. Boros knew of Milteades' next battle tactic, but knew also that more of the enemy needed to be drawn into the narrow passage before it was time to pull back. *Soon*, he thought, as he ran his heavy broadsword just under the pearl stone gorget encircling the neck of a Persian footman and penetrating his throat.

Several other warriors garbed in the maroon-and-gray of Darius' dread legions grouped closer together in an attempt to forge themselves into a closely knit fighting unit in order to better face the powerful Athenian commander. Boros raised his huge broadsword, then braced himself into position for whichever of his armored foes drew closest to him first. The tight enclosure lent him an edge he might even exploit by maneuvering so they had to scramble over the men he had already slain. The men in the Persian unit paused—then all three lurched forward involuntarily, tossed off balance. The added cries and clamor from behind them told Boros that what he had been awaiting had just struck.

****

From atop the hillock nearest the beach, Milteades watched as Darius' legions disembarked now without facing impediment by the Greeks, who had been forced farther back on the beach. An overwhelming increase in Persian fighters pouring down the mounting number of wooden ramps from the many ships that fairly clogged the shoreline was far too vast to face in open quarters, phalanx fighting formation or not. Numbers would soon overwhelm their triangular wall of armored men. So the Athenian hoplites gave ground to the onslaught of enemy soldiers who drove them back toward the passage where the first wave of Persians had previously found themselves hemmed in. Now this abrupt reversal of circumstances gave new life to Darius' soldiers trapped within the pass. The swarm of armored warriors charging down from the ships and onto the beach slammed into the retreating hoplites with such momentum it was felt all the way back inside the tight pass and hurled the Greek militiamen closest to the other end sprawling back out onto the open weedy plain.

Captain Boros and his corps of elite guardsmen, who had entered the passage and taken the fight so valiantly to the Persians inside the narrow enclosure, now found themselves in a forced retreat—while the hoplites of General Milteades were suddenly bottled up, Darius' denizens on either side of them—all due to the abrupt lifting of the morning mist. And still the swarm of Persian infantry poured down the ramps—Darius, his satraps, and the Persian commanders eager now to release the cavalry units, also waiting in reserve on board the ships, once the passageway was cleared.

****

Out on the plain, where the Athenian and Plataian militia had been thrust back, Pheidippides gaped in horror as he stared up at the sight of the massive Persian warrior thundering down on his young comrade, Kretus. The young Plataian trembled as he hoisted his thin leather shield up to try warding off a war axe swipe by a man outweighing him by nearly a hundred pounds. The Persian behemoth chopped down viciously at the Plataian, whose shield arm shook, then gave way, as did the shield itself under the force of the man's massive war axe. Down young Kretus went, flat onto his back, his head slammed hard into the grassy turf, his leather cap squirting off his head like a cork. The Persian chortled in triumph as he hoisted his axe over his head for the death blow.

****

No sooner had the Persians swarming up the beach poured into the passage, separating themselves from those still racing off the ships, than General Milteades finally roared out the command for the remaining hoplites stationed atop the hillocks along both sides of the sandy strip to charge down the slopes and onto the beach—splitting themselves between the Persians still on the ship ramps and those now pressing the passage. It was yet another sly maneuver on the cunning Greek general's part, one the enemy failed even to fathom, let alone anticipate.

Down they charged from the hills, half of them veering toward the shingle of beach or into the Aegean shallows, once again bottling up the startled, beast-masked warriors and restricting them to the gangplanks—while the ones who had hurled themselves toward the passageway were yet unaware of the raving Greek hoplites storming them from the rear. And even as those same Persians pressed their way into the pass, forcing Boros' unit back out onto the plain, some were already being cut down from behind by the second wave of Athenians that had charged down both hillsides. Just how long a fighting force outnumbered a good five-to-one might contain so huge a number of invaders would determine who would ultimately prevail. Milteades himself knew his limitations here in trying to repress the horde of Persians still disembarking the massed fleet of war galleys.

****

Young Kretus turned his head to one side, not wanting to see the deadly axe chop by the boar-masked Persian giant that would end his life. But a bloodcurdling yell suddenly distracted his assailant, and the man shifted like a great beast of prey to face whatever new threat was upon him. Too late, a shining sword of tempered steel sliced into the big warrior's hip. He bellowed, more in surprise and rage at this unexpected assault from his blindside. So caught up had he been in dispatching his seemingly helpless foe, the man had forsaken the standard caution all infantrymen were wont to take, especially in the heat of a melee where unexpected blows might come from anywhere and at any time.

The Persian brute roared again like an infuriated beast. And there before him stood...Pheidippides, stunned by his own action, his long sword dripping with fresh blood. The rage that had possessed the young Athenian boy only moments earlier had washed through him here in the immediate wake of his own actions...and he now stood agape at what he had just done. The Persian stared down in disbelief at the young battle pup that had just wounded him—a puny whelp who had dared attempt such a sneak attack.

His full attention now directed entirely at Pheidippides, the brutish warrior lifted his bronze war axe high over his head and brought it thundering down on the terrified young foot courier who barely had time to raise his thick metal-and-hide shield over his own head in defense. The axe smashed down onto his shield with the might of the man's full weight behind it, sending shock waves through Pheidippides' thin arm and rippling through his entire body. He lurched back several steps, then went sprawling onto his backside, his sword and shield both wrenched from his grasp and sailing off as the impact of his landing knocked the wind completely out of him. His head rammed hard into the turf with the same amount of force, whiplashing him nearly unconscious. Peering up from where he lay, unable to budge, Pheidippides squinted into the blistering sun rays and beheld the glossy image of the massive, armored brute hoisting his war axe once more for a finishing death blow. But it never fell.

Pheidippides blinked as the Persian lurched back,

one leg buckling suddenly as he let loose with a roar that split the air. The man toppled over backward, a crude wooden spear jammed into the back of one knee—unprotected by his leather vambraces—the point poking out obscenely from the kneecap itself. And kneeling right beside the mammoth warrior was none other than the Plataian youth, Kretus. Pheidippides gaped at the incredible sight of their frightening adversary—now sprawled there and bellowing curses as he wrenched savagely at the spear impaled in one leg and leaving him trapped on the ground in so debilitated a state.

Kretus helped Pheidippides back to his feet as they continued staring down at their stalwart enemy who might just as easily have slaughtered both of them at the same time yet now lay there helpless, a victim of blindsiding strokes by a pair of frightened boys. Neither of the two raw young Greeks spoke as their baptism into the ranks of war's realities washed over them. Neither knew whether to feel proud or ashamed at the sight of the wounded man writhing in impotent rage at his complete inability to rise and retaliate.

Pheidippides glanced about, realizing all at once that he was empty handed—as was Kretus, whose spear was still firmly affixed in their victim's leg. Kretus eyed the Persian's war axe lying just out of their fallen foe's reach. He nudged Pheidippides, who was still groggy and scant of breath from the blow he had suffered only moments earlier. The young Plataian was still wobbly, but steadied himself, then nudged Pheidippides again and pointed to where the young Athenian's sword and shield had been flung. Amidst the roar and thunder and wails of a battle being pushed farther and farther out onto the open plains of Marathon, neither boy was yet able to take the next step into retrieving an available weapon to finish off their stricken foe. But to stand there weaponless and foolishly await the next Persian marauder to come and make light work of them made no sense at all.

So, steadying one another, they limped their way over to where Pheidippides' sword and shield had landed, Kretus reaching down to the ground and retrieving a short spear that had been lost to some soldier on one side of the conflict. Pheidippides wondered if Kretus was going to use it on the big Persian who still lay on the ground struggling to rise. The young courier drew a long breath and reached down to grip hold of his own sword and shield again, then turned back to once again regard their Persian adversary, who moaned furiously at his damaged leg's inability to support him at all, his hip now bleeding badly too. The big warrior reached up and wrenched his boar-masked helm away, revealing a coarse hard face that had seen many battles. The dark eyes burned like coals as they glared accusingly at both boy soldiers. Had these mere striplings done this to him?

Neither of the two lads moved—but in the next instant, someone else did.

A tall, seasoned Athenian hoplite had emerged from the surrounding melee that, by now, had squeezed out entirely from the passage between the steep cliffs. He spotted the two young militiamen struggling with what action they should take. The hoplite eyed the pair, appraising the situation instantly and knowing well the duty expected of them. Both had spied the thickly armored hoplite bursting out from the throng of fighting men; both gasped as he sprang forward and plunged his already bloodied sword mortally into the lamed Persian warrior.

The wounded giant had been struggling to rise into a kneeling position, only to tumble back over each time as his sliced tendons had made it impossible to gain his footing again. His head jerked round with the force of the hoplite's blow so he made one last eye contact with both youths. Pheidippides saw more in the gleam of that man's eyes than anything he had ever beheld in the stare of another human being. Angst, betrayal, accusation—*contempt*—all poured forth before the big Persian pitched forward and died face-first on the weedy, bloodstained turf. The hoplite who had run the man through nodded in acknowledgment of his own lethal deed, then turned and eyed his two shaken young allies, calling out "Elate!" for them to come charge back into the fray with him.

Pheidippides and Kretus stared solemnly at one another; then the Plataian youth held aloft the spear he had scooped up from the ground. "We need join the battle again, my friend," he said softly.

Pheidippides nodded gravely, reluctantly, in response. "He was brave, this fellow," he reflected, seemingly more to himself as he gestured toward their slain foe.

"Aye," agreed Kretus, looking more disturbed the longer the two of them remained there standing over the man's body. "But now we must fight or we will soon be lying there ourselves," he added. And with a soft touch of one hand upon Pheidippides' shoulder, he turned and ran off into the battle that raged furiously over the heated Marathon plain.

Pheidippides gripped his sword more tightly and made to follow Kretus, then paused, gazing down once more at the Persian warrior whose untimely death he had helped bring on. The man still lay on the steaming turf, face flat, his great war axe lying several feet away. Finally, he nodded to himself as though making a silent vow. "Too brave a warrior to be left here like this," Pheidippides heard himself say. He glanced round once more at the fighting that had spread everywhere, Greeks and Persians all seeming more like so many silhouettes in the hot sun's stabbing glare. He felt quite alone for the moment with his dead foe and, on impulse, Pheidippides knelt, laying his sword and shield down on the ground. With a grimace and a loud grunt, he leaned over and gripped the spear that was still poking out from the dead man's hamstring, then yanked it free. Pheidippides rose and held it aloft a moment, then cast the cracked weapon away. He turned back to the sprawled body and gripped the man by his huge shoulders and, with a massive effort, flipped him over laboriously onto his back.

Pheidippides glanced round furtively, perceiving no further threat for the moment, then rose and stumbled over to where the Persian's war axe lay. He hefted it into his own hands and brought it back, resting it over the big man's chest. Solemnly he took hold of the warrior's thick calloused hands and wrapped them round the weapon as though readied for battle once more. The youth stared again into the lifeless eyes...then closed the lids over them gently. "I am sorry," Pheidippides whispered. The fearsome boar-faced helm lay right next to the corpse. Pheidippides reached over for the metal mask, gripped it, and placed it back over the Persian's head. "You were a very brave warrior," he said quietly as he gathered up his own sword and shield and limped off toward a nearby hill.

The young man had had enough of battle and courageous company for the moment.

Chapter Twenty-Six

Resolve

General Milteades could not believe the good
fortune of his proud fighting legion. He had hoped, at
best, simply to have cut off the flood of Darius'
warriors charging down the ships' gangplanks, and to
separate them from the ones who had disembarked
previously and marched up the beach toward the
passage. He had also known that Captain Boros and his
Elite Guard and raw civilian militia needed to hold the
tide of seasoned Persian infantry long enough before
being pushed back out onto the open plains of
Marathon…where conditions greatly favored the
enemy. But Milteades was more than pleased with the
manner in which his regiment of hoplites had powered
their way into position on the narrow spit of beach, and
in the shallows of the Aegean—impeding the advance
of Darius' troops. So long as the barrier of Greek foot
soldiers held strong in their human blockade against the
tide of Persians clambering down the ramps, the
enemy's advantage of superior numbers would be
quelled. For how much longer he dared not surmise, but
every moment they kept them at bay lent hope to a
situation that cried out for every conceivable advantage.

****

Darius stared out from the deck of the fleet's

flagship, his mud-brown eyes gaping in disbelief as once more he beheld the impossible. How could so few hold off—and even outmaneuver—so many? The two satraps, Datis and Artaphernes, also stared out at the cluttered shoreline, aghast at the stunning manner in which the crafty Greeks had so adroitly intercepted and disrupted the Persian landing and had also split the invading force in two. What gods—or devils—aided them so?

"It cannot be," muttered Kazek, the fleet commander. "What makes them fight as they do?"

General Mardonius all but gasped at the ferocity with which Milteades' hoplites attacked the beast-masked, heavily armored Persian marauders. He could not help seeing it akin to wild wolves ravaging a herd of much larger oxen.

"It is in their blood…and in their many years of such warfare," said the wizened old Hippias, peering out through the slits of his ash-tinted eyes, hate spewing forth from them.

Darius grunted in perturbation, and the wiry wisp of a man gripped his own ram-skin robes tightly as he turned sheepishly to face his Persian lord. "The lands of the Hellespont have never been as one, sire…only a vast cluster of poleis, some of them allies, others longtime enemies." Hippias turned his gaze back toward the shore, where it was now clear the Athenian hoplites had effectively assembled themselves into a veritable armored phalanx, three-deep in its ranks, that could not be penetrated by the Persians. Darius' legions suffered a position of grave disadvantage…while the Greek general's other squadrons hounded those still outside the passage between the high cliffs. "We have long known such struggles, ever since men first settled these mounts, plains, and valleys. They are prepared to fight on here eternally if need be," he seethed, hating his own kindred, but quietly, bitterly, admiring them too.

Darius' eyes smoldered at the words of his turncoat lackey. "And a pity that an old leader of its grandest state did not have the foresight to anticipate such military cunning," the Persian lord said with a dripping sarcasm. Hippias quailed at the comment, mortified at how abruptly he apparently had plummeted in the eyes of his current liege.

"Fear not," said Darius. "We yet have suitable use for you, dear Hippias. This engagement shall not in the least send us scurrying home in disgrace." The Persian lord turned to his fleet commander. "Captain Kazek, have we a fair wind?"

Kazek frowned and turned his head to Darius, ever avoiding the darkly gleaming imperial gaze.

"Aye, sir," the fleet commander answered quietly.

"Then recall the men who have yet to engage," snapped Darius.

"Sire?"

"Is my order not clear?"

"Aye, Lord. But…" Captain Kazek cleared his throat discreetly, hesitant to press the point.

"But what of our men still engaged in the fighting, Lord Darius?" asked General Mardonius, stunned by his king's command.

Darius smiled thinly. "They will keep this Greek rabble here dutifully occupied while we sail south with the fair wind."

"*South*, Lord?" Mardonius said perplexed.

"Aye," Darius replied flatly. "For *Athens*."

Chapter Twenty-Seven

Open Warfare

Forced back, out onto the open plain, Captain Boros rallied his hoplites and his civilian militia into a frenzy that fairly bedazzled the Persian infantrymen. They generated a ferocity Darius' seasoned warriors had never encountered in the past. For here was an enemy seemingly unafraid and not the least bit daunted by the world-renowned Persian fighters, all garbed in their maroon armor and bestial helms. With Boros' regiments the first to engage the charging enemy soldiers who wielded their curved scimitars, war axes, and spears, the raw militia flanking the Athenian guards felt heartened by the time their foes broke out onto the plain to engage them. With the hoplites pressing forward and leading such a ferocious charge, it became instantly clear these self-proclaimed invincible Persians could indeed be cut down like mere mortals. They were not underworld beasts or demons or warriors of some supernatural design.

These were men…just as they themselves were.

Gone was the myth that had mottled the nerves of so many others. The Athenian and Plataian militiamen rallied their previously frayed nerves—and charged.

Boros swung his long steel broadsword in a devastating arc, disemboweling yet another of Darius' invading denizens—the mere premise of these Persian butchers who had only days earlier slaughtered Greek Eretrian kinfolk of the northern isle of Euboia enraging him all the more. Now, here on this very soil of the Attica regions, they sought to do the same. Not while there was breath in his body and fire in the swords and spears of himself and his men. He glanced about at the swarm of enemy soldiers wavering now under the wrath of Greeks who would not be so cowed and annihilated as the ones this same Persian horde had devastated days earlier. But no sooner did that prideful thought fill his heart and mind than another one crept over Boros and gave him cause for worry.

Pheidippides. How had his gentle-hearted son fared on this field of fury and death? His eyes scanned the plain like a great-beaked hawk seeking its nest among a tangle of impenetrable trees.

****

Pheidippides scrambled up the sandy banks of the nearby knoll, sucking in hot breaths of the steamy air that now approached one hundred degrees. He had yet to regain a regular breathing pattern in the wake of the blow he had suffered at the hands of the big Persian earlier. The weight of the cumbersome armor that had helped save him from being battered into oblivion now felt a good deal heavier. He dropped to his knees and crawled toward the summit of the knoll. How in the name of all gods had he even managed to find himself in so dread a situation?

"How indeed?" he heard a sardonic voice suddenly chime in like a taunting echo. Pheidippides glanced round anxiously but saw no one else on the grainy slope. Thinking the sun and its writhing heat and humidity were both at work on his already muddled mind, he shook it off and continued his ascent. The voice made him think suddenly of Azelina, the spry and sensuous street scamp who had first brought him to Garathi's band of rogues in the dark Kaboni quarters of Athens. Oh, how he would have welcomed the sight of Azelina, and her canine companion, Atlas—and even that entire gaggle of street thieves who had departed their great city upon learning of the Persian peril. How wise Garathi especially seemed now…and how foolish Pheidippides himself now felt in his patriotic instinct to fight for a state that had deemed him and his mother ostraka.

"Indeed it did…yet they called upon you and yours to defend them, just the same," the musical voice chimed in again.

Pheidippides' head snapped side to side once more, seeking the source of the voice, but catching only the sun's glare and the bright steamy shadows that came with it. He shut his eyes and, in his mind, again saw the lithe, tanned form of young Azelina. He imagined her now in his arms as he realized fully how utterly fond of her he truly was. He hoped upon hope he would live through this horror and return home to tell her so.

Finally, he crested the sandy summit and collapsed there, his mind drifting back to the rustic but comfortable little hovel he shared with his dear mother, and he wondered how Symethra herself fared.

A distant chorus of heavy cheers disrupted his thoughts, and Pheidippides forced himself to his feet to see what had provoked it. He squinted, straining to see through the muggy haze of the dust-clogged plain. And there it was: the Persians were in a full retreat, scores of them lying dead everywhere, their maroon-gray armor all but changing the hue of the ground itself. Those that remained fought fiercely in their retreat. No cowards these invaders, however barbaric their reputation. No cowards, Pheidippides thought to himself. He half-expected that haunting feminine voice to mock him once more.

Pheidippides wondered where he had found the courage earlier to stab the huge Persian in the hip when the man had been ready to slay his comrade-in-arms, young Kretus. And where now was Kretus in all this cluster of soldiering on the steaming tundra? Where was his father, the gallant Captain Boros? His exploits this day he was certain had been hardy and brave. The young courier turned his head away from the battlefield and toward the Aegean waters. And he gasped. It was not possible! But yes, his mind and eyesight could not be so muddled.

The Persian fleet was putting out to sea!

For there were the dark, square-shaped sails that had been described to him so many times by those who knew them…all sailing south. His heart leaped with joy and relief. *They had beaten Darius' dread legions!* The Persians were heading…south.

It took but seconds for the truth to creep over him. In spite of the blistering heat, a sudden chill bit into the young Athenian boy. The Persian fleet was not sailing for home, north.

It was sailing for Athens.

Chapter Twenty-Eight

Dread Choices

Still in his fine bronze armor, his shield strapped to
his left arm and the keenly wrought steel sword gripped
firmly in his right, Pheidippides descended the knoll,
his sandaled feet striding faster than he'd intended. He
peered ahead and saw that a good portion of the
fighting had rescinded with the Persians' retreat back
into the passage. Pheidippides mused in grim irony that
the retreating Persians here had no idea they had been
abandoned by their commanders, who now sailed for
Athens.

He doubted that any ships had remained behind to
board them. Would his own generals and their officers
have done the same had the Persians prevailed? Not a
man such as his father, Captain Boros. Never. Then a
dark thought tormented him as he hustled along through
the corpse-riddled field, some of the bodies—both allies
and enemy—still moving, either in death throes or
badly wounded and in desperate need of aid.
Pheidippides tried suppressing a nagging thought that
would not let him be. If his father had not
acknowledged him as his own son all these years—
recalling the humiliation of that cruel day at the agora's
stoa center—why would the man risk command or
reputation if one such as General Milteades ordered the

abandonment of Greek militia trapped by the enemy?

He gritted his teeth bitterly as yet another cruel thought swept into his mind. Would not the loss of an illegitimate son save him other embarrassing issues too? Pheidippides shook his head savagely, refusing to believe his own father—the man he had finally spoken with in person but a day ago—was of such ilk. So he forged on, drawing closer to the scattered fighting that remained just ahead, and nearly tripped over a body that appeared all too familiar to him.

He recognized the tanned, lanky body, the innocent teenage face, the plain leather armor…now bloodstained due to a gaping wound in the chest. Pheidippides dropped to his knees, tears welling instantly in his eyes. "Kretus…No!"

The dying young man's soft brown eyes opened with a painful effort. "Why, Pheidippides. How is it you are here?" he barely eked out.

"I…I was recovering, Kretus," he replied, pressing his friend's hand gently. "Now I wish I had just stayed with you. Perhaps then…"

"No, Pheidippides. You saved me once already."

"As you saved me. And if only I had—"

Kretus gripped him weakly by his breastplate. "You gave me more than that. You gave me a friend in my hour of fear. Even now."

Pheidippides fought back the tears, striving to remain strong for his dying friend.

Kretus struggled in gasping out his next few words. "And how did we fare this day?"

Pheidippides lowered his friend's head gently to the turf. "Rejoice, we conquer," he answered firmly. "The Persians flee."

Kretus reached with one hand and squeezed Pheidippides' palm as tightly as he could, smiled, then closed his eyes and died. As with the Persian warrior he had honored earlier, Pheidippides searched and quickly found Kretus' spear, split and lying close by him. He crossed his dead friend's arms over his chest and wedged the broken spear under them. Then the young Athenian raised his eyes and stared straight ahead where fighting near the entrance to the passageway was still ongoing.

He rose and charged.

Not fifty strides from where he had laid Kretus to rest, Pheidippides saw a stout, armored Persian emerging from a scrum of men, all fighting earnestly. It mattered not whether this particular warrior had had anything to do with his friend's death. He was Persian and would serve as focus for his rage. It mattered even less at that moment to this Greek youth that the Persian Empire had invaded his own Greek homeland or that the fate of Athens itself—and all the other city-states of the Hellespont—was at stake this day. What burned more fiercely in his breast was that his comrade who had crouched, stood, and fought right next to him when fear and indecision had been upon them both, had been slain. And the culprits were right here before him.

With a shrill cry he could hardly believe came from his own throat, the slender teenager launched himself fiercely into the fray, sword swinging at an enemy soldier a good ten years his senior. He caught the stocky, maroon-armored Persian clean on the shoulder with a solid swipe of his sword, cutting between the metal sleeve and the breastplate, drawing a spurt of blood and a shriek of pain from his startled foe. The man turned. His bronze helm sported the insignia of a snarling demon, and its fearsome design had the desired effect on the young Greek courier. Pheidippides paused briefly in his assault, startled by the fiercely featured helm that had shaken many a past Persian foe, the intent of its design. The raw young Athenian was no exception. And that pause was all that the seasoned warrior needed. He lowered his good shoulder and rammed into his much lighter enemy, knocking Pheidippides to the ground. The Persian raised his sword in his healthy arm for the finishing blow.

Through the haze and glare, young Pheidippides made out the sweeping arc of the curved scimitar descending on him—then heard, abruptly, the sound of slicing flesh, then bone. The hideously designed helmet worn by the Persian warrior flew off the man's neck— the head along with it. Pheidippides gaped in shock as a now headless armored body jiggled obscenely for several moments before collapsing onto the grainy turf. The helmed head landed separately, blood spurting at the point where it had been lopped off.

A tall hoplite loomed over Pheidippides and over his now headless foe. The hoplite shifted left, then right, like a wary jungle cat readying for attack. But none came. Satisfied, the hardy Greek warrior reached a strong hand down to the stricken boy and tugged him lustily to his feet.

"You were brave to engage that brute, lad … but be more mindful of tactics with such foes!" boomed a voice that rang of familiarity. The hoplite removed his own thick bronze helm, and Pheidippides stared in awe as the green-plumed top-piece revealed a hardy face he knew.

"I owe my life to you…Captain Boros."

Chapter Twenty-Nine

You Can Run

The two stared awkwardly at one another, standing against the raging backdrop of spear-to-spear, sword-to-sword warfare, where the clang and thud of weapons upon arms and shields resounded gruesomely—men crying out in triumph and despair like a bleak chorus of discordant heralds. With no immediate threat to either of them at the moment, father and son stood in solemn silence, neither ready to break the long, unspoken pact between them. Another victorious roar from the Greek hoplites turned Boros' head suddenly in the direction of the now waning battle.

The Persians were in full retreat, bordering on a rout as it seemed they could not cram their way fast enough into the cleft between the steep cliffs in hopes of escape.

"Hah…The great Persian army!" exclaimed Boros, as much to himself as to the boy standing there eying him in confused awe. "If our General Milteades has had his way on the other side of that passage, as we have here, then Darius will behold the doom of his finest legions." He turned back to face Pheidippides, a smile forming on his grizzled face. He was taken aback, though by the look of seeming terror growing over the boy's young face. "What, lad? What is it?" Boros asked eagerly.

Pheidippides paled, his mind now flashing back to what he had seen from atop the knoll. It had been eclipsed by the untimely discovery of his dying Plataian friend and the ensuing rage that had gripped him and sent him hurtling impulsively back into the fray. Now that it had worn off in the wake of his father rescuing him, and the reminder that the entire Persian land force had been beaten back, a harrowing image of what he had witnessed earlier came back to him in a roiling rush.

"Sir…the Persians…they move for Athens!"

Boros frowned, shaking his head with an assuring smile. "Why, no, lad. Do you not see they are in full retreat now? And though we cannot catch sight of it from here, you must remember how our good General Milteades crafted his ambush cleverly for a rear assault that would cut them off from their ships and—"

"No, Captain Boros!" Pheidippides cut in, surprising both him and his father with a sudden assertiveness. "They have set sail," he added in a tone of deference. "I saw it from atop that knoll," Pheidippides said, pointing back to where he had retreated earlier.

Boros frowned again, ignoring that the boy had openly admitted to an unexplained absence from the fighting. At that moment, the Captain of the Elite Guard did not want to know why.

"Why, yes," he acknowledged with an impatient nod. "It would not surprise me that one such as Darius would sacrifice a rabble of his own men if they had lost and he cared not to risk more of them."

"They sailed *south*, Captain Boros!" Pheidippides

exclaimed.

Boros grimaced as the reality of what he had just heard slammed into him with the impact of a sword blow. There was a prolonged silence in which the background battle clamor was now but white noise. "South…" he uttered. "*For Athens.*"

Pheidippides nodded.

Boros eyed the boy curiously. "And how was it you were in position to know this?" the big man asked quietly, his hardened eyes locking onto his son's.

Pheidippides swallowed and tugged off his metal helm, as though signifying he was unworthy of it. "I…fled there," he answered hoarsely.

The words struck Boros nearly every bit as hard as learning of the Persians' sudden new ploy.

"I…I am sorry," Pheidippides choked out. "It was after…" And he blurted out in a rush the account of himself and Kretus and the big Persian warrior whose death on the battlefield they had both brought on—and of their splitting apart.

Boros listened patiently to all of it, with its ending of the boy's flight to the knoll summit and what he had witnessed there. "And you are certain of what you saw?" he pressed eagerly. "You are certain the Persians were sailing south?"

Pheidippides nodded firmly.

"Then I must find General Milteades," Boros said urgently, casting an eager glance back toward the fighting.

Pheidippides cleared his throat and forced himself to meet the eyes of his father. "I…am sorry I failed to show…"

"Nonsense, lad," Boros interrupted. "You are far

too much in judgment of yourself here. Many a young man suffers those early fears in battle. But you overcame them by helping your friend, your comrade-in-arms. And you honored a fallen foe. There is never shame in that...*Pheidippides*."

The name had passed through Boros' lips so softly that it seemed more a whisper of the wind. But Pheidippides had heard it clearly, and a sliver of a smile cracked his thin lips.

"And you fought on bravely for your friend too," said Boros, following up quickly as though covering for his own utterance of his son's name. "But now I must find our general and urge him to finish here so we might force-march to Athens, lest those treacherous Persians find a fair wind and—"

He caught himself. A myriad of thoughts and emotions seemed to cloud the big man's face; he bit his lip, frowned, and shook his head several times.

"What is it, sir?" asked Pheidippides, vexed by the man's abrupt change.

"It is all too plain to see now," Boros said finally. "Darius sacrifices these brave souls who fight on here because he and his accursed generals know we dare not leave them behind where they can still wreak destruction on our outer villages—and even hound us as we try marching back to protect Athens."

Pheidippides shivered at the grim truth of what his father feared.

"And by our staying to finish off our enemy here, Darius and his fleet gain the time they need—especially with a fair wind at their sails," said Boros, his ruddy face darkening all the more.

"Then all is lost?" asked Pheidippides darkly.

Boros drew a long breath before responding. "You are a courier," he said finally.

Pheidippides blinked, a sense of disquiet creeping over him as the man's hazel eyes scrutinized him. "Yes...I run short treks from village to village on well-known paths making deliveries," he explained rationally, knowing his father was fully aware of it.

Boros measured him, his eyes boring into those of his son. "I...have seen you run, and your stride is a strong one."

"You have then seen me finishing nothing more than two leagues, a six-mile run, Captain Boros."

They stared for a long time at one another; then Boros reached over and laid a hand on Pheidippides' lean shoulder. A father's touch. "And such a run that lies before you now, oh, Courier."

The boy shook his head in disbelief and abject protest as the reality of what the man clearly expected of him could no longer be denied. "Athens is nearly nine leagues from here...a good twenty-six miles. It is far beyond anything I have ever dared try on my own," he added, dreading the mere thought of the distance he had just expressed. "Surely there must be others among our army here who might—"

"There is no time to seek them out," answered Boros, glancing back anxiously toward the passage. "This task is for you, Pheidippides." And with that, the husky captain of the Elite Athenian Guard reached down to unstrap the boy's bronze breastplate. "A courier need bear no armor on a task that demands mettle of a different nature."

Pheidippides said nothing, unable to fathom all that had taken place here in mere moments—the most time he had ever spent with this man in his entire life.

"Run as bravely as I saw for myself when you ran back into battle here for your lost friend, and you shall prove yourself more than courier, lad," said Boros, squeezing his son's shoulder in assurance. He cleared his throat and held the boy's eyes with his own iron gaze. "Warriors are cut from many different kinds of cloth," he added stolidly.

Pheidippides wanted dearly to say something but could not form the words. He felt a soft lump in his throat as he wondered if he had perhaps died and this was, instead, some spiritual image of the man who was his father, now reassuring him of a value he had never truly believed he harbored within himself. Other than his dear mother and the little creatures of the agora pond, only Garathi and his ostraka band had ever lent him such a feeling as now filled him.

Boros continued removing his son's armor so all that finally remained was the light, cut-down muslin britches, his sandals, and a sleeveless cotton chiton. At his waist were a sheathed dagger and a waterskin. He gathered his resolve. "Sir, I am no Zagorus…no Ginakos, but I shall run for my city's salvation as if I were," Pheidippides said solemnly.

"I know you will," said Boros. "Both those men proved themselves as brave as any hoplite or militiaman bearing sword or spear…as will you."

Pheidippides nodded, hoping at least his willingness to accept so daunting a task might lend him the strength to endure it. Boros tugged free the waterskin from his own waist satchel and handed it to Pheidippides. "You will have greater need of this than I," he said.

Pheidippides accepted it without a word and waited. Boros drew one more breath, then spoke. "My part is all but done here...my boy. Now you must run." And with his great hands he turned and gestured Pheidippides in the direction leading home.

Pheidippides paused, gave his father a brief wave, and ran off.

"May our goddess Athena guide you, my son," Boros said quietly to himself. He swallowed, watching the boy striding away. "And I hope I've not sent you to your death," he uttered more softly.

Chapter Thirty

Elysian Wagers

Peering downward through the misty haze of puffy white clouds, the two Elysian gods, Pan and Keres, both watched the earthly drama below with a mix of growing curiosity and intrigue. Lord Pan's rough-cut facial features were pensive, yet marked with an air of satisfaction. His dear Keres wore more a smirk over her tan features. The golden eyes that normally twinkled with a perpetual mischief now flickered with a lessening luster. She quivered with a degree of agitation.

"Oh, but this tender saga must feel so fitting to your taste, my dear Lord." She shook her head side to side, the long shoulder-length locks as golden as her eyes seeming to shimmer in annoyance. Pan regarded his beloved nymph queen, a sliver of a smile crossing his hard lips in a hint of amusement, though mixed with concern. He knew well both her sweet and bitter tastes, her mix of passions and moods too—and he knew of the disturbing dark shades that still drifted through her. The moment of father and son they had witnessed only an instant ago had affected her more deeply than she had indicated, and he moved to distract her from it.

"Eh, Keres dear… It does appear you owe me more food of immortality," he quipped, a smirk of satisfaction on his lips.

Keres blinked, as though rustled from a dream. "What is that?"

"Why…sweet ambrosia to dine on, along with the past batch I already won. Perhaps even a goblet of divine nectar I might sip as well…"

"Oh, how you love to gloat, my gracious Lord of Elysia." Her eyes launched tiny golden barbs his way.

"I merely remind you that the 'Persian Tide' has indeed been pushed back at Marathon."

"Perhaps, then, a more fitting wager is in order?" she sizzled back at him.

Pan turned his head slightly, concealing a knowing, reed-thin smile that he had succeeded in diverting her attention from gloomier thoughts that had crept over her. He turned back to her, smiling.

"And what new foolish wager might my sweet Keres dare put forth? For I'll remind you that a goblet of nectar, or a bite of ambrosia, is ever a drain on the stores of energy enjoyed by us immortals…both of Elysia and Olympus. So perhaps you might want to reconsider?"

"Oh, stop with your jester's babble, coy old Pan! Will you or will you not dare risk a wager to settle our tally?"

Pan raised a thick, furry eyebrow. "Why, whatever wager my eager young queen cares to put forth. But do consider the store of effort it costs to produce the ambrosia already owed me." He stared at her through his stone-gray eyes, folding his furry arms as though already having won the bet. "So what is this latest, most futile of hopes you hold for regaining lost food and drink of immortality?"

Keres lifted her chin in pert acknowledgment, then raised an arm and gestured with opened palm toward the secular world below. Pan followed her hand. Through the filmy portal, he beheld the earthly realm where the slim figure of Pheidippides trotted slowly back up the knoll where he had earlier spied the Persian fleet setting its sails for the south. The Elysian lord gulped—as only a goatish man might gulp.

"Eh, the lad's journey to Athens?" he asked meekly, all swagger gone suddenly from his bearing.

Keres nodded smugly. Pan closed his eyes, shaking his head side to side. "Done," he said ruefully.

"And none of your tricks!" she said with an air of haughty assertion. "I wager this Athenian messenger boy surrenders to the heat and trials of his journey and does not see Athens this day."

Pan stared down at the seemingly more-frail-than-ever figure of Pheidippides ascending the hill. "And I say he…prevails," he answered with absolutely no conviction and wondering exactly why he had let himself walk into her trap.

****

Boros had swept through the crunch of fighting men still locked in combat on his way to the narrow cliff tunnel leading back to the beach. His great broadsword had cut a swath through the Persians lingering in his path; they fell back before his wrathful urgency. Their fearful helms shaped into horrid images of demonic design now appeared almost comical in the chaotic retreat brought on by the Athenian captain's storming attack. His battle cries of "Finish them and hasten through the passage…" had worked his own militia into an even greater frenzy as they followed his lead in routing the now fleeing Persians. Shaken already by the unanticipated Greek ambush, the invaders broke, all sense of military discipline gone.

Captain Boros knew the Battle of Marathon had already been decided, but only he, of all the Greek military officers, apparently knew of the enemy's pending assault-by-sea that now threatened Athens. He felt certain that only his son Pheidippides had been in a vantage point on that high inland knoll to see beyond the lingering bits of coastal mist that had all but masked the southerly direction of the departing fleet. He had to find Milteades soon!

****

Pheidippides stood upon the knoll summit in the very spot where he had first sighted the Persian galleys pulling away from the shores of Marathon. Now, garbed only in a sleeveless white tunic of light muslin and green britches that came down just below his knees, the leather marching sandals on his feet, he stared out at the foggy waters. Through the glistening early afternoon haze, he made out the silhouetted shapes of enemy galleys reforming for a southward course.

He shivered despite the rising afternoon humidity and heat as he envisioned the absolute horror of those very warships beaching at the port of Phaleron, only a short march from Athens. He thought of the many inhabitants of that grand city as the massive Persian army descended on them. And he knew, in his heart, it was unlikely the Athenian army would have time to mobilize here in the wake of so violent a struggle and hasten homeward in time. The young foot courier trembled in the knowledge that he alone was the one hope for Athens to muster a standing force that might yet hold Darius' savage hordes at bay till Milteades and his militia arrived to mete out Greek justice once more.

Perhaps.

In all truth, the numbers were still far too heavy on the side of the Persians aboard the sailing ships. And enemy stragglers left behind might even harass and impede the army's march home. But morale was on the side of the Greeks now, having already bested their supposedly invincible enemy. Could the strength and resolve of those defending their own home deter so massive a foe again, in spite of such numbers? Or did these Persians believe strongly enough in the designs of Darius that it would drive them sufficiently into overwhelming a people fighting for their own existence?

And did he, Pheidippides, have the resolve to match those who had already fought so hard this day defending all they held dear? It seemed his father thought so...or so he had said. Pheidippides bit down on his lip, knowing his father would not fail in his own dash back to the beach to alert General Milteades to finish here at Marathon and start the march back. His chestnut eyes shifted to the grainy slope leading down to an open stretch of steaming sandy tundra. Could he hold true to his own task? Run as the swiftest of Olympus—Lord Hermes himself—fabled god of the hemeredrome? And in thinking so, he sank impulsively to one knee and prayed. He could not help speaking the words aloud as he envisioned himself undertaking a grueling journey unlike any in the past...other than those that had taken place only in his own mind.

"Lord Hermes, swiftest of the gods...guide me as you did the great Zagorus on his gallant quest to Sparta and back. Lend me the speed of thy winged feet that I may be safe from the perils of this deathly heat...the bandits and the dangerous beasts along the way...the harsh hills of Pallini..." He stopped, pausing to consider his prayer, then rose up tall, shaking his head scornfully. "Wretched little gnat Pheidippides!" he spat. His lean features hardened in self-loathing. "To dare beg aid of Hermes himself—and never having done deed nor quest to merit such aid as his?"

Pheidippides smirked, the twisting of his lips unfamiliar to his face, for his soulful nature resisted the cynical, whether he chose so or not. His mind reviewed the day's events and, in spite of how his father had tried filling him with reassurance, even that could not dismiss the doubts that plagued him. What deed had he ever done that might truly command the respect and trust of one so bold and accomplished as his father—or any other Athenian of merit—let alone gain him the favors of the gods?

"No!" Pheidippides proclaimed suddenly, as though all of those who had ever mattered now stood before him: his parents, the militia in which he had served, General Milteades and his brave hoplites, the stoics of the agora, the Archon of Athens, even the band of wayward ostraka with whom he had bonded so closely of late...and especially the spirit of his Plataian comrade-at-arms, brave Kretus, who had fought side by side with him against the enemy. Even the gods themselves...

"Lend me no aid, good Hermes, God of the Hemeredrome, *till I prove myself worthy!*" He raised a clenched fist high in the air. "'Tis for Athens I go forth this day...not Pheidippides! I shall trouble no Lords of the Higher Worlds with my wailing cries for help. Let my very run serve as prayer on this day. Then lend what aid you will, if you see fit!" And with that, the young courier shot a spiteful glance in the direction of the Persian fleet, and trotted down the hill, a surge of confidence filling him.

He was unaware of hostile eyes following him.

Chapter Thirty-One

To Athens

While the Athenian hoplites hewed down the
remnants of Darius' detachment of warriors that had
been intended for a land invasion of Athens, twenty-six
miles away, Boros had fought his way through the
ranks of enemy and ally alike, hacking and thrusting
with a ferocity that would have impressed even the
fierce Spartans. Now he stood atop the knoll from
where General Milteades commanded his Greek
legions. Boros was pointing with his sword toward the
long shadowy shapes of Persian galleys creaking slowly
through the shoreline's lingering mist. Both tall men
peered out into the choppy coastal current, seeing the
whitecaps pushing the lead galleys of the enemy fleet
along with an increasing southerly wind. The general's
sunbaked features stiffened as the dark ships glided
downwind with the precision and cold grace of giant
swans seeking prey.

"A fair wind," muttered the general, his dark eyes
smoldering into hot coals. He turned to Boros. "See to it
that no Persian that Darius abandoned here lives to
follow after us, or slips aboard the few crafts still
hauling in their anchors. I want that devil to think us
unaware of this foul new ploy of his."

Boros saluted and turned to rejoin the men still

engaged in battling the Persians.

"Who was it that first took note of the Persian fleet slipping off thus?" Milteades asked abruptly.

Boros' hazel eyes clouded like churning eddies. "A raw young militiaman, General," he answered softly. "Pheidippides is his name. He is also the courier I ordered to bring word of our victory and this new peril back to Athens."

Milteades nodded with an air of respect. "Athens dearly thanks you both," he said, clasping Boros by the forearm before he hustled on down the hill to mobilize his troops.

Boros' gaze followed the general as he left, then he uttered softly, "He is *my son*, General."

****

The Persian fleet commander, Kazek, nodded to his first mate to veer the lead vessel away from the sandy coast of Marathon and its fennel fields where he had just beheld the impossible. Great King Darius not only having failed—though he would never accept blame for it himself—but also fleeing the fight and leaving his own denizens to die violently at the hands of the enemy. Kazek's mind whispered to him the silent words he knew best not to speak aloud to anyone. Men did not do this to their own, let alone was it the action of a king. And most certainly it was not the behavior Persia's own sacred deity, Mithra, would expect of a ruler who had deemed himself a "God on Earth." Yet here they were, with Lord Darius doing—

Kazek's thoughts were interrupted suddenly by a movement along the high coastal hillocks. He blinked, his hawkish features casting a deep frown, and stared more fixedly into the early afternoon haze. Unless his own eyes played tricks with his mind, he thought he had glimpsed a slender figure trotting down the slope of one of the shoreline hillocks. His strong hands gripped the starboard wooden rail of the war galley, and he leaned his shoulders and head over it, squinting for a better look. Yes…he was sure of it now. Someone stripped of armor and weapons was running down the knoll's sandy slopes. Captain Kazek shut his eyes tightly and drew a long breath, contemplating.

"What is it, Captain?" a thick voice spoke from behind him. Kazek shook his head as though woken abruptly from a brief slumber, shifting his sinewy frame to one side so he might identify who had broken into his thoughts. He saw the burly figure of General Mardonius regarding him curiously. The man's bushy brows that topped his fairly square, bearded face were furrowed in a deep frown.

"Eh…something on the shore, perhaps an animal of some sort," the fleet commander mumbled almost dismissively.

Mardonius squinted in the direction of Captain Kazek's gaze, scanning the shoreline. And then his eyes widened sharply. "Why…that's no animal!" Mardonius exclaimed gruffly. He pointed a gnarled finger toward the base of the hillock. "It's a man!" The grizzled face darkened like a storm cloud as full recognition of the situation dawned on him. He placed a hand to Kazek's shoulder, the fleet commander's sudden disquiet evident from the bristle Mardonius felt in his touch. "*A courier has been sent on from the battle!*" He gripped the captain's shoulder more tightly.

Kazek eyed him back, nodding grimly as though realizing it all for the first time.

"We must alert Lord Darius!" the general barked in mounting alarm. He hustled off, leaving Captain Kazek in silent contemplation. The fleet commander's eyes followed the shape of the striding figure along the shore. "Yes indeed," he whispered prophetically, "one more desperate courier."

Chapter Thirty-Two

A King's Anger; a Courier's Ordeal

Darius glowered savagely out into the steaming
afternoon that was heightened by the sun's stabbing
rays reflecting off the glistening tidal waters. He was
not sure which infuriated him more: the Greek foot
courier his fleet commander had glimpsed slipping
away from the battle and surely on his way to Athens to
foil the surprise of their planned sea assault, or the
added time it took, delaying their hastened course round
the coast, to dispatch their two mounted assassins down
the gangplank and onto the mainland to pursue and kill
yet another courier that had been missed.

The delay was costly, especially in the wake of a
humiliating defeat. The devastation they had wrought in
annihilating the Eretrians on the isle of Euboia would
diminish after being beaten back here by these upstart
Athenians. This Hellespont was a land of squabbling
city-states that could find unity in nothing. Or so he had
been told by his lackey Hippias. Yet the Greek traitor
had clearly lacked the foresight to warn General
Mardonius of the sort of ambush their sly foes sprang
on them this day. The thundering defeat suffered here
might even be seen more as one against Great King
Darius than as one over Persian military commanders—
as truly it had been. How could anyone not realize it

was the fault of bumbling generals and fleet commanders and satraps? He would be certain everyone understood that; even if it meant denigrating his military underlings, along with his two satraps, Datis and Artaphernes…and that fawning jackal, Hippias.

All had failed their Great King—and the entire Persian Empire as well. But he, Darius, would see to it that those mishaps were corrected with a cunning ploy of his own. For, in sailing round the Hellespont coast and surprising troublesome Athens with a successful assault by sea, this defeat at Marathon might then appear more as a clever tactic to separate the walled city-state from its own army. And the ones left behind on the fennel plains, those who survived, might even follow and harass the Greeks in their force-march home, thus slowing the enemy down all the more. Those he had stranded might then redeem themselves for so humiliating a defeat at the hands of a foe they had greatly outnumbered. As for the ones slain, so be it. King Darius preferred warriors who were not captured or killed.

The Persian lord smiled to himself, knowing that once this day's work was done, they might finally celebrate a fitting end to this fledgling but dangerous new 'Rule of the People'—this democratia the intrepid Athenians had dared introduce into his world. Today it would die in a most furious fashion, never to surface again. He would see to it. And he would, of course, heap ample praise then on all his generals and satraps, and even Hippias, for redeeming themselves, thus reinforcing their loyalty to him. Hippias would be reinstated as overseer of *all* these disjointed Hellespont states, which would fall one by one in the wake of the destruction Persia's hordes would wreak on Athens. Powerful Sparta would follow. The people of these hill-infested lands knew nothing of unity.

Darius sighed deeply, pursing his lips as his attention shifted to the shoreline. His gaze settled there on the huge mercenary, Rojese of the northern Macedonian tribes. They were not true natives of the Empire itself, their lands having been seized only recently, but their clans functioned as trustworthy mercenaries when called upon, this one especially reliable. As was the husky Nubian, Jamjon of the black-skinned tribes to the south of the Aegean—a people who had never quite acted as a conquered folk, but were yet compliant and also reliable.

Both assassins now galloped along a grainy shingle of beach in the direction taken by the Greek foot courier sighted earlier. Their reputations were predicated upon a cold efficiency exemplified when assigned to the task of capturing or killing at the behest of the Great King, who also heaped generous rewards, along with praise, for those who succeeded in his service. The mercenary duo of the Macedonian and the Nubian had gained notoriety throughout the Persian Empire as the very best.

****

Pheidippides trotted briskly over the sandy strip of path that banked the warm Aegean waters breaking lightly on the grainy shore. The weedy plain to his right stretched beyond his scope of vision. With no knowledge of the routes to Athens trekked by the hemeredrome, he would have to negotiate his way back along the trails taken previously by the army…if he could gauge all of it. He was testing a pace he might sustain, though entirely unaware what that right tempo might be, as he already was on a ground, both figuratively and literally, which he had never before attempted. A trek of five or six miles—perhaps even seven or eight—he might have plotted out successfully. But this? Pheidippides once again heard his own words of protest, then reluctant acquiescence to his father's insistence that he undertake so lengthy and solitary a venture. But with so feeble an outlook on how he might fare, here in the most meaningful hour of his young life, doubt descended on him.

The young courier shut his eyes, as though it might shut out the grave circumstance in which he now found himself. He listened to the soft tromp of his own feet on the hard, baked sand, hearing also the choppy rhythm of his own breath. And, as he ran on, unaware hostile eyes had already spied him and mounted predators pursued him, he could not shut out glib voices of his past surfacing to haunt him. Pheidippides heard them, along with the hazy shapes of faces forming in his mind's eye as they spoke inside his head.

"*Are you ready for a try at the discus now?*" a hardy teenage voice chimed eagerly.

Pheidippides flinched, his soft brown eyes darting side to side as though someone lurking unseen along the pebbly trail had suddenly made himself known.

"*Aye,*" answered a second voice of the same nature. "*I shall hurl it so far at the Games next week, those Spartan lads will groan when it sails past their longest marks!*"

Pheidippides drew a breath and sighed deeply. He nodded grimly to himself, knowing the voices well, recalling those times past when he had heard them, and knowing, too, what meaning they bore. He shook his head and picked up his pace, trying in vain to dismiss them but knowing he could not. He shut his eyes tight, the images of two well-muscled Athenian boys, their tanned beautiful skin reflecting the olive ointments—the *strigil*—rubbed over them previously, making him realize the envy with which he had long held the luxuries granted children of known citizens.

When he opened his eyes again, Pheidippides all but swore they ran alongside him now…

"I would like a try at throwing the discus!" Pheidippides blurted out suddenly, not unlike that very day long ago. The voices seemed as real to him as before. And then came the laughter…cruel laughter he had heard from them. Laughter that had stung and did so every bit as much now.

"*You, Pheidippides?*" snickered the taller of the two, both phantasms sidling in closer to him.

"*With those arms and legs as thin as sandal strings?*" cackled the other, shorter and huskier than his companion. The huskier phantasm closed in on the young foot courier so their ghostly shapes boxed him in completely. An ethereal hand reached over and gripped Pheidippides gingerly on the left bicep and squeezed. Pheidippides winced exactly as he had back then, more from the sour memory of the moment than from any seemingly tangible pain meted out by the phantom boy trotting alongside him.

"*You are best keeping to your running,*" the huskier lad said derisively, removing the hand.

Pheidippides gasped out in frustration, the phantom runners keeping pace with him and more real than before. "But they would not let me run in the Games!" he protested. "I am—"

He stopped abruptly and doubled over, realizing his pace had increased to a sprint and was costing him precious breaths in the rising heat. "They will not let me run because I am…ostraka!"

Pheidippides peered up, hating to hear himself utter the very term that always reminded him of the outcast status that had stigmatized him from birth. He recalled it all too vividly as he lifted his head and beheld the two phantasms who stared down at him disdainfully—just as those they represented had in the past.

"*Ah…but you may run…for us, Pheidippides.*"

"I…run for you?" he said in the flat tone of one already aware of the answer coming, recalling that day, and others like it. He grimaced as the taller phantom boy snickered.

"*Why, of course, oh, swift courier,*" the phantasm from his past quipped. "*Each time we hurl the discus, you may run and fetch it. That will give us more turns at tossing it and getting ourselves ripe for competing against the Spartans next week!*"

Hollow, ghostly laughter followed. Pheidippides blocked his ears and rose to his feet, dismissing the phantasms and the cold memories finally. He forced himself into an earnest walk, seeking to clear his mind of further haunts. He felt sure it was the oppressive heat of this Hekatombion—the late summer season—that had brought it on. It was not the first trek where his mind had wandered thus, though on his village jaunts of no more than two leagues they had been mere fantasies he'd envisioned willfully, seeing himself back then as the bold distance courier he was now truly expected to be.

Pheidippides measured his steps, his leather-sandaled feet scraping lightly over the turf that grew stonier as he trod farther from the sandy coastal area and veered inland. And another past haunt played out in his head, every bit as vivid as the one he had just endured. He tried blotting it out, but it reared up before him: the day he had crouched outside the window of the modest little house where he and his mother resided. And on this day of all days, Captain Boros had chosen to have a discreet visit with his haetera…both he and Symethra sure their son was not soon to return. But return early he did. And he had heard…

"He…chased the discus, you say?" Pheidippides had heard his father's inquiry, the sardonic tone in the man's voice unmistakable. The boy had crouched there by the unlatched, wide-open window, fists bunched in angst at the discussion he was hearing.

"They would not let him throw it with them," she had declared in his defense.

"Perhaps you should see then that he does more than read by the pond and play with turtles," the caustic reply had come.

"It does not make him weak because he wishes to be more like the stoics who think more deeply than others," Pheidippides had heard his mother retort. Crouching beneath the windowsill outside, he had smiled in spite of it all—for she had always stood by him. He had shut his eyes tightly then, as he did now, here on the grueling path back to Athens, knowing that, in the heart of his mother, neither of them were ostraka. But he also recalled, glumly, his father's response when she had tried vainly to draw forth a sliver of pride from a man who could not bring himself to acknowledge, by name, the son she had brought forth to him.

"And he can run, Boros!" Symethra had insisted to no avail.

Having heard the choking plea in his mother's voice, the boy's teenage mind had pondered what sort of man could be so cold—so callous—in such a moment. His reply had devastated the youngster.

"Aye, he can run…as he did today when he chased the discus…much as a dog might do."

Pheidippides had not seen the sharp glare in his mother's suddenly darkened gray eyes and how it had affected Boros enough to show he had not truly meant so unkind a barb as he had delivered. And Symethra had recognized the instant regret of his words…but Pheidippides, crouched outside, had not seen his father's face, or the regret it had conveyed. The boy had only heard, and so all but crawled away, much like a dog whose master had refused him any sense of approval or affection.

****

Pheidippides opened his eyes wide again, the hazy world of past times fading away—but the hard voices he had allowed to be dredged up from those days had renewed the damage done to him. He shook his head, as if trying to shake away the painful memories, and pressed on. The coastal surf was soon lost entirely as he veered more inland. His eyes scanned the bleak terrain of rolling hillocks and dust gray turf that now dominated his scope of vision. He felt more assured by it. Pheidippides threw back his head, the long brown locks tickling his lean shoulders.

"And what say you now, Father!" he proclaimed

defiantly, as though the phantom Captain Boros from that sad day might somehow hear him. "I do not play with pond turtles now, nor do I chase the discus for others, do I! No, I run against the Persians! *I run to save Athens...* commanded by none other than Captain Boros of the Elite Athenian Guard! And I—"

He stumbled suddenly and shrieked, tumbling to the ground as a streak of searing fire ripped into his lower leg and exploded in a bolt of furious pain. He'd known leg cramps, pulled muscles, even a tendon tear on past runs...but nothing so painful and disabling as this. Pheidippides rolled over on the gritty turf, the spasms in his leg dominating his every thought. He howled morosely and kneaded fiercely at the throbbing that felt like hot stones roiling through his muscles. He grew faint.

After a matter of moments that felt longer than perhaps the minute in which he had twisted and writhed, the spasms in his lower leg eased and passed, as though knowingly having paid him a temporary visit to remind him of the futility of his quest. Finally, he rose back to one knee, hesitant to ascend completely to a full stance lest the cramp revisit him for his effort. Once more, young Pheidippides eyed the heavens and cried out as though the gods themselves might hear him.

"By all the gods of Olympus, couldn't one more worthy have been chosen for this task?" He raised both hands skyward. "Oh, Great Athena, Goddess of Athens herself, and swift-footed Hermes, and Zeus, mightiest of all gods! Could you not have made our Spartan cousins listen and pay heed to valiant Zagorus and come to our aid? Or even Pan, Lord of the Elysian

Fields, whom so few honor as we honor Olympus! Would you, oh, Pan, have come to Athens' aid had the Archon ordered a temple built in your likeness—as Zagorus did urge? And why let the fate of so many now lie with feeble Pheidippides?" He kneeled again and pounded the ground with one fist.

The slender youngster held that position for several moments—a bizarre tableau of anguish—then slowly raised his head skyward again, his brown eyes smoldering like ashes kindling into flickering flames that had caught a sudden spark. He rose completely to his feet, a single fist clenched in front of him. "No," he uttered hoarsely, something else stirring within him…something that came from a place unexplored inside his soul. "I will not be defeated by you silent Lords of the Heavens, wherever you might be." The voice he heard coming from his own lips was one he barely recognized.

Pheidippides broke into a slow but steady jog. He stared up again at the sky, at the surrounding hillocks and the shadows that seemed to dance in the sun's stabbing glare. "Nor will you cruel voices of the past deter me," he muttered with defiance, as though daring another phantasm to revisit him. His pace increased, knees flexed and falling into a steady rhythm, arms bent and pumping on either side of his ribs. "If I but keep one foot moving before the other"—he drew a strong breath and proclaimed—"no power of man or god shall ever stop me!"

Pheidippides heard his own voice ring out those words of youthful defiance and, emboldened by the very sound of them, added in for good measure: "Send me your trials and taunts—I run for Athens!"

Chapter Thirty-Three

Adversaries...Allies

From high above the rolling sandy plain where Pheidippides had once more rallied and spurred himself on in defiance of fatigue, self-doubt, and futility, Lord Pan of Elysia shook his horned head in amazement and awe. He turned to regard the winged young beauty fluttering alongside him—Keres, Queen of his Dryads.

"Eh, the lad does show resilience, my dear," he remarked playfully, yet with an air of conviction.

Keres gave a mild shrug of her wings. "He is but early into his trek, dear Pan, and he has already faltered more than once," she quipped, unimpressed. "And the way ahead shall prove far more formidable," she added.

Pan floated down outside a long gray cave, unseen by any living in the earthly realm of mortals. He settled his strong, knotty back snugly in the nook of a wide oak, shaped seemingly to accommodate him. Keres alighted next to him on a large boulder that loomed over a pale blue grotto, all of it the enchanting landscape of their Elysian realm. As always when the fairy-like wisp betrayed the deeper feelings she harbored, she stooped down onto the smooth ledge of her rock and wrapped her shapely bronze-tinted arms round her beautiful long legs, fairly hugging herself.

"I will taste of the sweet ambrosia this time, oh,

cunning lord of this realm, and will sip of the golden nectar too…for that frail Athenian boy is ill-equipped to meet even the most natural of perils, let alone those of a more fearful sort he has never seen in his sluggard of a life."

Pan's thick brows furrowed with a shimmer of disturbance. "Now, you understand our pact that to interfere or hinder—"

"Oh, do not fret over such trifles, my lord," she snipped at him like a flustered kitten. "You know well of what I speak, and what awaits him. And that it has nothing to do with either the mischief of Keres or Pan. Even their gallant Zagorus lacked the fiber to face such foes alone. What mortal could? Certainly not this pitiful one here," she said, untangling herself and rising. "And even so, what matter if he could? Did any in Athens bestow belief in Zagorus once he returned? No…Greece is doomed by her foolishness alone. And no pompous or fickle Olympians can change a people made of such arrogant gods' own flawed ways."

Pan placed a cloven hand to one of Keres' shoulders. "Did we not make our wager in a spirit more light than this, my sweet Keres? We need not fret so over a world in which we ourselves have no true part, eh? Why not let our mere wagers be the only concern we hold for these simple—"

"Not all is as simple as it may appear," she said with so quiet and assuring a conviction that it silenced him. Her golden gaze met the pensive gray of his own. "And not all can reflect on the lives of mortals—having never lived such a life," she said in barely a whisper. "There are ways in which gods themselves are powerless to understand others."

Pan merely nodded, understanding well the depth of her feelings. He rose from the comfort of his rocky nook. "Well, then, dearest Keres, it appears that mortal doom does indeed stalk these lower worlds…even as it stalks this boy." And with that, he gestured toward the menacing shapes looming up on horseback from where Pheidippides had passed already.

****

The two armored horsemen had heard the wailing cries ahead of them, somewhere on the path guiding them across the plain and away from Marathon. At first it had sounded like an animal of some sort that had perhaps been wounded. Rojese was fairly certain of it, remarking that the advancing hillocks and woodlands were home to wolves and foxes and goats and boars and even large wildcats that preyed on most anything. "A goat or unfortunate deer sounds to have met its end," mused the husky Macedonian.

Jamjon reined in his powerful ink-black stallion, his own ebony skin glistening in the steaming sun as brilliantly as his mount's. The tall Nubian shook his head, the gold-colored plume on his bronze helm waving in the same way. "'Twas no beast, my friend," he said solemnly.

Rojese frowned, staring across from the back of his huge roan. "Then what…?" He enjoyed the company of the big Nubian and was pleased how the two of them were often paired together by chieftains who paid handsomely for services like theirs. They had worked well together, always snaring their quarry, always too crafty and fierce to be thwarted. Persian lords paid willingly and handsomely for such results.

Jamjon reined in his powerful steed, then slid

silently down from the leather saddle and stepped onto the grainy turf that yet sprouted twisted mesquite weeds scattered over its surface. He knelt and ran a hand over the battered path that was still visible due to the scores of booted and sandaled feet that had marched over it only the day before. "Not close…but not terribly far either," the Nubian mused, more to himself.

"I've seen you track man and beast where no sign of either was to be seen at all, my friend," said Rojese wryly. "But here, with a whole army having tramped this way over sand and stone and grass…"

"These prints were made most recent, my brother," said Jamjon. "And the ground ahead may bring him the peril of wild beasts that may earlier have been shy of many fierce men carrying weapons. But such beasts rarely shy from the few…nor especially from a single one who poses little or no menace."

Rojese grunted in acknowledgment. "Best we hasten, then."

"Best we do," agreed Jamjon, "lest our courier finds his way into the hills and forest that lie ahead and cheats us of our catch." He rose and put a thick hand to the pommel of his horse and mounted.

Rojese surveyed the mountainous horizon thoughtfully. "Hmmh! Once our Great King Darius seizes these lands for his own, there will be less of those forests and even less wild creatures prowling there. He will most surely clear trees and beasts between here and Athens to build monuments and temples and the like that might boast of his bold conquests…as we have seen him do in other lands."

Jamjon threw back his broad shoulders and considered the words of his comrade. He nodded almost sullenly. "Aye," he said softly.

Chapter Thirty-Four

The Home Front

Symethra sat by the small fish pond not far from the Bouleuterion—the tall columns of that nearby Athenian Council House lording over the most prominent sector of the agora like sentries. The grand public gathering square was virtually deserted, the usual flood of citizens and non-citizens alike reduced now to a few scattered souls who slipped along the usually well-trafficked road that was all but barren. The roofed stoas and vendor stalls were empty. Here and there were the shapes of those who passed by quickly, either the rare few out on errands of great necessity, or fleeting figures scurrying through the shadows, eager to soon be behind walls and doors. No word had come from the plains of Marathon—nearly nine leagues away—where the fate of a now troubled land was at stake.

No courier had yet brought back word of the great battle everyone living in the Attica region of the Hellespont knew was taking place; and little, if any hope was there that the brave souls fighting had any chance of being little more than a living rampart against the Persian hordes. For the vast army commanded by Great King Darius would most surely smash through them as lions would power their way through brave but smaller dogs.

So most of Athens' population stayed hid now, awaiting the inevitable—some even heeding the whispers (that gradually grew louder) of underground dissidents within the city: lingering loyalists to the exiled Hippias, who had sent word—via his own spies posing as metic outliers—that surrendering and swearing fealty to the Persian King was the only hope Athenians had of avoiding the gruesome fate that had befallen the hapless Eretrians of Euboia. They, too, had dared defy Darius, and now their northern island home lay in smoldering ruins...the very fate that awaited Athens, as the dissidents and spies of Hippias had quietly assured all who would listen.

The ploy had proven most effective, as few ventured out and most remained hid inside their homes. Symethra therefore, all but had the agora to herself now. She sat alone on the low stone wall that surrounded the pond...resting in the very spot her son always enjoyed. The lean, longhaired beauty stared down into the flat sunlit water that was home to the fish, turtles, frogs, and eels that had been stocked in it over time. She smiled as an occasional rustle or splash revealed one pond inhabitant or another. In her hands she held almost reverently the cracked wax-covered tablet on which Pheidippides had etched his tender poem about Athens. Now it all seemed so long ago, practically from another lifetime, she thought solemnly to herself.

"My Athens, my home...She stands here before me, sparkling in the sun..." Symethra read aloud in barely more than a whisper. She continued reading silently, a tiny smile on her face at the soft, heartfelt verse created by her son. Now and then a turtle or frog paddled or kicked closer to her, curious of the woman sitting by their specially created habitat, as though she were one of them herself.

A chorus of voices and the tromp of feet amidst a clatter of armor drew her attention abruptly from her reverie. She had been waiting for this moment and rose from the stone wall, hustling her way toward the Bouleuterion. Men were emerging from the great Council Hall. She spotted them heading down the marble steps—tall, brawny men garbed in thick armor, their hands on the pommels of sheathed swords ready to be drawn at the slightest provocation. Symethra put a hand to her chest, taken aback by their grim demeanor, then noticed a regally clad figure flanked by the guardsmen: Archon Kallimachos. He strode elegantly down the marble stairs, surrounded by the hoplite guards, who all bore the swagger and pomp of superbly trained dogs.

Kallimachos and his carefully chosen entourage were all keenly aware of the rumblings and mutterings within the city's walls by dissidents such as the troublesome Hahnitos. For, even in exile, the smooth talking Hippias still held sway over many blindly devoted loyalists who yet yearned for his return. They too despised the rise of the germinating new government of democracy, for they all believed precisely as Hippias had instructed them. Little did it matter to any of his dedicated followers that their onetime trusted lord and master had now become supplicant to a harsh despot. They would obey him regardless. And men such as Hahnitos knew *they* would benefit most from his return.

The danger of such minds being at large in Athens therefore made everyone in the city suspect. Kallimachos could ill afford to take chances. So when a cloaked woman of obvious peasant stock appeared and began walking in the direction of the High Archon himself, it was of no surprise that the magistrates and soldiers accompanying him formed an even tighter wall around him and drew their weapons. Suspicion of this raggedly clad woman climbing the steps of the Bouleuterion so earnestly and possibly bearing the concealed "gift" of a sharp dagger for her Archon was not farfetched.

"Archon Kallimachos…may I have a moment, please?" Symethra called out softly, urgently.

The lead hoplite guard stepped out in advance of the tiny phalanx surrounding the Archon, the man's sword drawn fully from its scabbard. "The Archon is busy, woman!" barked the guard, stepping into her path and nudging her aside less than gently with his free hand.

Symethra nonetheless eyed the man defiantly. "And my son is busy fighting at Marathon!" she snapped back in a tone not unfamiliar to her of late.

The magistrates and guards all regarded her more closely. "So are the sons of many others," the lead guard said dismissively again, moving to brush her aside…and again meeting with resistance. Symethra stepped back assertively in front of the procession and this time held up the clay tablet with Pheidippides' poem etched on it.

"And did they put into such words why their city is one they would fight for?" she demanded passionately.

The hoplite guard stared in surprise, having

anticipated some sort of weapon to have been brandished instead. He shook his head with an air of embarrassment and sheathed his sword. "Eh, perhaps later," he uttered somewhat flustered and unable to manage a more suitable response. He made to nudge her aside again, only his demeanor more gentle than previously.

"Stay…" said a calm, dignified voice. It was the Archon. He stepped assuredly through the ranks of his entourage and continued toward Symethra, his magistrates and guards shadowing him protectively just the same. Though the slender woman apparently posed no perceivable threat, others lurking nearby might harbor menace toward the city's highest of council members. "What is this written work you wish me to see, young woman?" the Archon asked gently, his eyes soft and sincere as they probed hers.

Symethra choked back a sob and a tiny smile crossed her lips. She could not resist shooting the lead guard a smug look of triumph as she stepped in closer to the Archon and handed him the tablet. Her thin fingers trembled as the clay piece left her hands and was accepted into the graciously clean grasp of the man entrusted with the well-being of the entire Attica region. She stared anxiously as his wise features perused the contents of the tablet. A moment more and his deep-set eyes peered into hers.

"Your son wrote this?"

Symethra nodded in quiet acknowledgment.

The Archon eyed her thoughtfully, then nodded back, a smile forming on his handsome face.

Chapter Thirty-Five

Predators of the Hills

Pheidippides strained as he forced his way up yet another steep hill laden with misshapen boulders strewn over the stony path of pebbles and dust. Heavy winds often swept through these coastal mountain passes and always left heaps of lumpy debris scattered everywhere —ankle traps for anyone trekking through. The going was rough and the toll on his breathing costly due to the erratic footing. He veered farther inland, retracing the path taken by the army only the day before. All view of the sea itself had fallen from his sight, and only the sloping range of hills and the sun's persistent glare now filled his scope of vision.

His knees ached and his sandaled feet felt the coarse surface more now than on the way to Marathon with the army, as the scuffling throughout the battle had worn the leather soles down a bit. Ascending the cracked, hilly path and garbed only in the sleeveless muslin chiton and britches, with a dagger and two waterskins attached to the sash round his waist, sixteen-year-old Pheidippides did not resemble in the least a soldier who had just fought in a brutal battle.

A chill, mournful howl broke the hot afternoon air suddenly.

Pheidippides froze. He'd heard the distant howling

of wild wolves in the past, but only from within the confines of city walls—or from far off while finishing one of his many short delivery treks over the quiet, well-used paths traveled regularly by those dwelling in the Attica region. Athenian citizens and merchants, commoners—even slaves and outliers—who trod those routes never worried about the presence of dangerous predators. The only wild beasts seen there were occasional foxes, birds, rabbits, and rodents, or perhaps a mountain goat wandering down from the hills, but nothing of a frightening, predatory look—not even Kaboni rogues, who kept more to their own interior city haunts. This cry that had come wailing out from the steamy mountain breeze was one that spoke of the hunt. It raised images in the young courier's mind of the chilling lore told by hard men who had traveled such eerie wild lands. But nothing those men had told him compared to the sound he'd just heard, which instantly raised hackles over his entire body.

Wolves.

Among the fiercest and most fear-evoking predators known, the dark wooly canines prowled not only the forests and hills that bordered the rim of civilization, but also the very borders of one's sleep. Their long, loping strides and lolling red tongues, their glistening yellow eyes and dagger-sharp teeth had earned them the fear and enmity of those who knew very little of wolves as natural predators.

Pheidippides was among the many who believed and feared the dread legends created entirely by men. And that fear enveloped him now as he stood virtually naked and vulnerable, hearing the howls echoing throughout the hilly range. His eyes darted in every direction. "Wolf?" he whispered hoarsely, at any instant expecting to see great wooly shapes bounding out from behind the lumpy boulders.

From somewhere came the scamper and scrape of feet treading over the pebbly surface of the hillside…and then a low growl filled with menace. He tried determining from which direction it was coming, when another howl broke the mountain air, then another, and another. Pheidippides had no idea where the creatures lurked, for he could make out nothing more than hazy shapes in the glare of the glistening afternoon sun. The scrape and shuffle of scurrying feet caught his ears again—padded feet, it seemed, followed by the clatter of hooves galloping over the hard ground. He glanced left, then right, his eyes straining for a rock, a log, even a shrub he might hide behind. The nearest possible cover was only a boulder pathetically too small to conceal his body. With no other option in sight, Pheidippides clambered over to the rock and squeezed himself behind it, the effort almost comical.

The howling increased. And then he saw clearly the first of several canine shapes loping like long gray shadows into his scope of vision among the scant bushes and rocks—finally he beheld his first wolf in the wild. It bounded out into the narrow clearing, husky and ash gray, the thick fur covering a muscular frame that flaunted the natural beauty of its wild existence. The bright yellow eyes harbored a primal intelligence all too willing to challenge either man or animal for mastery.

Pheidippides stifled a gasp at the sheer grace of this huge canine that fairly lorded over the stony mount. He held back his straining breath as several more of its wooly kindred joined the first, emerging from the surrounding shadows as though materializing from the very mountain air. Four in all stood there majestically, facing one another as though in council.

Crouching lower behind the rock that was far too small to conceal him entirely, Pheidippides felt every muscle in his lean body cramping the more he tried compressing himself into a smaller mass. The rumble of quiet growls that drifted in his direction caused his stomach to tie into a knot. It was as if the lupine voices were speaking to him—their soon-to-be victim—a prey too easy and insignificant to even bother snaring. "*What timid, small creature do we have here?*" the eerie mix of mountain breeze, howls, and snarls seemed to coo at him. The added blend of padded feet and the clack of harder soles treading the stony mountainous path intensified the mocking taunts that rang inside his head like discordant voices: "*There is nowhere to run…you cannot hide from us!*"

The clack of hoofed feet hustling away from the site, and the loping gait of padded paws in pursuit, filled his head now, and the trembling teenage boy could no longer take it. More primal…more terrified did he feel in this element than when engaged in the crude clamor of the battlefield earlier—where at least he could see his foes—that it caused him to burst up from his spotty cover.

Pheidippides hollered like a beast of prey, rose, and staggered over to one side of the pass, the growls of the small pack of wolves mixing suddenly with loud bleats of terror from somewhere else. He ran, catching a glimpse of a cream-colored body, horned and fleeing in the opposite direction—a pair of husky gray shapes in pursuit. Then he found himself staring straight into the golden orbs of a lupine face, fearful to behold, yet majestic in its own right.

For one bizarre instant, Pheidippides was reminded of the evening in the Kaboni alleyway—which seemed like a distant lifetime ago—when he had stalked through the outlaw neighborhood of Athens and come face to face with the wolfish canine companion of Azelina. The dog Atlas had regarded the lad guardedly, but without menace, its eyes having gleamed with the same feral intelligence he now beheld in the gaze of this full-blooded wolf before him. Pheidippides' throat clogged, and he could not breathe for several seconds. The wolf raised its thick muzzle, displaying the glistening white fangs that curled out from its upper jaw and down the sides of its mouth.

The boy's heart stalled between beats…and then to his utter surprise the wolf rolled its furry head to one side and sprang, veering off and dashing gracefully away. Pheidippides did not budge. He was suddenly aware of a shrill bleating, followed by a fierce predatory howl that appeared to command the other wolves of the tiny pack. The bleat of terror he had heard earlier sounded again…but was snuffed out abruptly. The crunch of jaws snapping and the rending of flesh ripped through the air. Nature had spoken.

Pheidippides did not need to turn his head to know what he would see. Nor was there any doubt in his mind that the wolves had simply executed as survival in the wild dictated. Their prey all along had been the mountain goat, not a boy frightened by his own fears and the outrageous tales of his human kindred…who knew less of such creatures than they would ever realize. Drawing a long breath, and without looking back, Pheidippides steadied himself into a silent measured hike up the rest of the slope, while the wolves behind him continued to feed, paying no heed at all to the young human stalking his way up the hill.

Chapter Thirty-Six

As Gods (And Others) Watch Again…

Queen Keres of the Elysian Fields gave a shake of her golden-haired head, while her equally gold-hued eyes flashed in dark merriment. She stared sardonically at her dear Lord Pan. Both peered, unseen, through a filmy wall of mist at young Pheidippides hiking steadily up the hilly slopes.

"Most impressive your lad appears now, my lord…mmm?"

Pan frowned, his furry eyebrows knitting together like an agitated caterpillar. He made to speak, then merely pursed his lips into a sliver of a smile, knowing she was trying to bait a retort from him. He instead shook his horned head subtly. Both continued watching the struggling boy as they peered through what amounted to a glossy one-way window.

Pheidippides trudged on, oblivious to the ethereal presence of the two Elysians taking in every step of his tedious trek up the steep slope. He spoke aloud to himself with disdain. "It seems there are more worthy morsels in these hills for hungry wolves to feed on than boys frightened by myths." He glanced round, embarrassed more by his having swallowed such silly fables than from his natural fear of a wild predator. "How sad that we see such creatures of might and grace so dastardly…when we ourselves prove far uglier," he quipped to himself. "Perhaps men of Garathi's sort have cause for their bitter ways toward 'civilized' folk."

Pan and Keres eyed one another, she more surprised than the Elysian lord, who merely smiled and nodded in silent agreement.

"Our unfortunate lad is soon to learn the truth of what he has just stumbled upon," Keres said with a shake of her head. "There are indeed predators that seek him now—and of a more dangerous sort."

Pan nodded gravely.

Pheidippides strained as he forced himself up the pebbly slope, his legs aching with every painful stride. Where his encounter with the wolves earlier had left him drained emotionally, now the sharp grade of the hill threatened to drain his muscles, unused to such an unrelenting incline. As he had proclaimed to Boros, he was accustomed to well-worn flat paths on treks totaling no more than six miles. How he was to drive his failing muscles, his bones and lungs, into enduring an ordeal of constant motion over four times that distance was beyond his comprehension. So the young foot courier pressed on, the depth of his journey weighing on him, as well as the dread of what more— other than the grueling heat and spectre of wild beasts of prey—might plague him.

****

Rojese and Jamjon guided their war steeds slowly over the choppy turf that was littered in places with misshapen rocks and snapped branches. A fractured overhang of gnarly old cypress trees was all that comprised the sparse concave of leafy boughs which yet masked the view the two assassins might have had of the more open terrain ahead. And as they broke out from the cluster of trees, Jamjon peered outward and pointed a long, thick finger ahead. Rojese followed the Nubian's gesture and spied the distant tiny figure of the struggling courier, hunched over and working his way laboriously up a steep hillside. They exchanged a smug look and a nod of satisfaction.

"Hah! Our courier is poor on stealth!" quipped Rojese. "By Mithra, we'd have had him already if not for all the rocks in these devil hills."

"Mmm!" agreed Jamjon. "We'll have to dismount and lead our good steeds on foot soon. They'll not be able to pick their path safely with us atop them."

"He does not yet know we follow. So we'll show some stealth ourselves while we press through these boulders and he strains in his climb," said the bearded Rojese. "By the time he knows of our pursuit, it will be because he hears us riding down on him."

****

Unaware of his peril in the form of the deadly assassins behind him, Pheidippides forced himself onward against the grinding protest of every part of his body, surging ahead like a man wading through the grog of a dream. He raised his hand in woeful weariness, hoping to behold the summit of the grueling Pallini Hills nearing the scope of his foggy vision. What he saw dejected him all the more. The boy shook his head in disbelief. He had indeed drawn close enough to glimpse the crest of the ever-rising slope, no more than fifty more steps from its seeming summit…and near enough also to catch the looming shadow of…the *next* summit.

"What cruelty is this!" he wailed in agony. For he

had forgotten that during the march from Athens to Marathon how the hills of the Pallini range had dipped and risen frequently, but ever on a downgrade as the army had approached its destination. Little thought had he given to the torturous climb that would mark the way back. Pheidippides could not recall how many trick summits these rolling hills actually contained. He dropped his head back down, not wanting to glimpse again the steady climb that awaited him once he managed to scramble his way atop this first summit. He dropped to his knees, gasping as he stared down at the rock-encrusted turf that barely resembled a path. His thin fingers groped for the leather waterskin that was already more than half drained. He choked on the boiling, humid air.

****

"He is frail, my lord," Keres all but snickered, the coarseness in her voice belying the vixen-like beauty of her tan features.

Pan shook his head in an air of seeming disappointment, the curled horns above his bestial brow creaking as though in solemn agreement. "Why so scornful of the boy?" he asked quietly, a sad frown showing. His cloud gray eyes seemed on the verge of moistening.

"He is pitiful...this Athenian foot messenger is unworthy of the honor he desires."

Pan stared at her hard. "Unworthy? That has been said of others who yet deserved honor, but were denied." Keres eyed him back sharply but said nothing more on the matter.

Pan meanwhile peered down once more through the rift that separated the realm of the Elysian gods from Earth. "The worst of the trek will be behind him once he attains the final summit."

"*If* he sees it," she retorted, eying the all but broken form of the lad lying on the rocky trail.

****

Pheidippides lay sprawled on all fours, his hands, elbows, knees, and stomach scraping the steamy turf of the rocky knoll as he peered downward into a wide crevice between a pair of box-sized boulders on the narrow path. A sticky tangle filled the space there between the two rocks. And as his vision cleared, a soft buzzing caught his ear. Pheidippides blinked several times and saw a gnat stuck inside a web strung between the two rocks. The gnat's tiny wings fluttered and flapped rapidly while the insect's crooked little legs strained in a futile attempt to break free of the gooey netting. The reason for the gnat's panicky effort loomed above it menacingly…a hulking brown spider many times the size of the winged insect. The huge arachnid's hairy legs drove it slowly, steadily in the direction of the hapless little creature.

Again the gnat beat its wings and strained with its thin legs against the gray webbing that suppressed all hope of escape. The adhesive holding the gnat prisoner seemed all-powerful. Closer the spider's furry blob of a body crept, the eight-legged predator sadistic in its stalking approach. The gnat squirmed furiously and beat its little wings again in a panicky flurry. The huge arachnid closing on it paused, as though savoring its tiny prey's predicament.

In spite of the trauma of his own situation, Pheidippides felt riveted to this vivid micro-drama taking place just below his own eyes—as though he

251

were some god of the heavens eavesdropping on lesser beings. He shivered in spite of the oppressive humidity and heat, utterly taken with the gnat's futile denial of its own impending fate. This plucky insect deserved to be more than a mere hapless victim of so gruesome a predator that seemed intent on savoring its conquest before even finishing off its quarry. Pheidippides raised a hand, ready to end the gnat's plight by freeing it with one godly strike…then paused abruptly.

The gnat had instead taken command of its own destiny.

Whether such a minute and seemingly insignificant form of life was even capable of such an assessment or not, the diminutive insect kicked savagely again with all six legs and wriggled its chitin-layered shell of a body so desperately that a small tangle of the sticky web was snapped apart miraculously. *One more great thrust and it might break free.* The great blob of a brown spider saw what had just happened and rasped in predatory rage. It scuttled with frightening speed across the gooey network of its self-spun webbing. The gnat kicked out again at the webbing and flapped harder, loosening one wing and several of its crooked little legs.

The spider lunged down, its hairy legs stabbing savagely for the gnat's head—but the force and impact of its very attack split the webbing all the more, jarring the gnat to one side and tearing the web asunder. Now but a single strand held fast to the dangling gnat. The spider's beak grazed its prey's tiny body as the winged insect gave one more desperate kick, freeing itself from the fractured web. The gnat plummeted downward, then flapped its wings frantically one more time…catching enough semblance of a flight to pull itself safely out of range of the eight-legged horror that sought to devour it. And by the time the spider had whirled back around, the plucky insect had managed to soar off into the freedom and safety of the hot August air.

Cheated of its prey, the huge brown recluse spider rasped out in fury and frustration...then finally recomposed itself and started reconstructing its ruined web, its primal instincts assuring it that another creature of prey would be along in time.

Pheidippides started incredulously at the bold and fascinating drama he had just witnessed. He eyed his right hand, which he had raised but moments earlier in the presumed intent of helping the trapped gnat, a smile forming on his lips in the knowledge that the tiny insect had needed no help at all. Acknowledging the spider as it rebuilt its web for a chance at another victim, the young foot courier rose to his feet again and pressed on.

Chapter Thirty-Seven

Relentless Trial and Pursuit

Farther down on the lower slopes of the same Pallini Hills, the two enlisted assassins, Jamjon and Rojese, led their horses over the treacherous terrain, ever mindful of the rocky turf that could prove devastating to the narrow-hoofed equine legs. A single step in the wrong place might result in a twist or snap, and a broken bone that would spell disaster. So the going was tedious and slow and especially frustrating to them. Both men could see the stumbling, crawling form of the lean foot courier they had been chasing, knowing they could do nothing more at the moment to hasten their pursuit. And yet the straining Greek messenger also knew nothing of the assassins trailing him, assuring them both he would soon be in their grasp.

****

Pheidippides had drawn himself up valiantly, willing his tired legs to force their way up the final rise of these harsh Pallini Hills. He was a good eighteen miles into his twenty-six-mile trek. On impulse, he threw his head back and hollered defiantly up to the heavens: "Wretched Pallini Mountains—I have beaten you!" He balled his right hand into a fist and waved it fiercely. Triumph filled his heart in knowing that these rolling summits which had deceived and teased him earlier had failed to stop him.

Much farther back on the slopes, his pursuers exchanged looks of begrudging respect for the dogged courier they chased.

****

Pan smiled as he stared down through the glossy portal and into the corporeal world of earthly struggles where young Pheidippides had crested yet another of the mountains' multiple summits…overcoming the visual illusions that had fooled many a traveler into believing they had completed the arduous climb. Now the exhausted youth recognized clearly the peak he had just crossed was the final summit. Pan and Keres both watched in amazement as the lean courier raised his arms in joyous triumph atop the very mount that had nearly snuffed out all his hopes.

"Well…?" crooned Pan.

Keres frowned in response to her lord's revived confidence in the boy's quest. "Do not taste of that ambrosia we wagered on just yet, my dear lord, else you choke on it and spill precious nectar down onto your hapless lad!" she chided.

Pan shook his head and sighed.

"Remember," she added, "he has yet to meet his worthy pursuers."

She made a sweep of one shapely arm and a band of fairy-like wood nymphs, dryads, appeared magically behind her and laughed musically, great mischief covering their delicate faces. "And he has yet to face Keres…and all of Elysia!" Fluttering in midair, she readied her beautiful minions to follow her.

Pan scowled. "And *you* remember, it is our agreement that you may *tempt* him…but not hinder."

"Why, of course," she chirped playfully. With a sorceress' wave of both hands, Keres and a gaggle of dryads fluttered off in a rush of laughter and wind.

Lingering there alone, Pan again questioned the wisdom of his own wager.

****

The triumphant figure of the young Greek courier jumping gleefully atop the summit of the last of the Pallini Hills, arms stretched upward, was not as solitary a moment as he thought. He was being watched...not only by the eyes of coy Elysian gods but by the ever-persistent assassins serving at the behest of the Persian king. They followed more swiftly now as the choppy mountainous terrain grew less treacherous for the hoofed feet of their steeds. Allowed to mount again, they hastened the pace of their pursuit. The going was yet laborious and plodding, but a fair increase over the previous pace where frequent boulders, crevices, and debris from brambles and fallen trees had hampered them.

The two watched from below as the boy celebrating up on the summit took a hearty swig from his waterskin, then disappeared from view as he started down the other side of the mount. His pursuers were less than a *stade*—a quarter-mile—away. They exchanged a glance and a nod of satisfaction.

Chapter Thirty-Eight

Outliers in Waiting

Little more than a single league—some three miles from Athens, up in the hilly open woodlands, Garathi sat on a flat-topped boulder, his back against a thick oak as he surveyed his band of over thirty rogues who had vacated Athens only days earlier. They had wanted to put the matter of hostile Persian invaders plaguing their Greek homeland behind them. Having departed under the cover of night, unnoticed by any of the city's hierarchy or its prominent citizens, they had all declared with great resolve and conviction that whatever outcome came of the pending clash, it would be of no significance to them. Ostraka…outcasts they would still be, whether the Archon or Darius ruled in Athens. No, they owed no allegiance to a state that had long deemed them unfit to be citizens.

Garathi frowned as he surveyed his clan of outliers that ranged in age from teenagers to seasoned adults. In particular, he eyed young Azelina, who had befriended Pheidippides, whose departure with the civilian militia had disappointed the bandit leader immensely. Azelina was among the few who had accepted the young courier's choice, though she certainly had not liked it.

The girl now lay stretched out, one shapely knee raised, her supple back and shoulders supported by the furry bulk of her wolfish dog, Atlas. Not far from Azelina, young Barthus stood leaning against a tree, his tanned face smug and defiant as always. As with the adults who had dwelled in the seedy Kaboni quarters within the walls of Athens, the teens felt no loyalty to a city where leaders had never embraced their lot…including past tyrants and dictators who had regarded them just as poorly.

"How do you think our bold defenders have fared, Garathi?" asked a crusty elder sitting several feet from his clan leader.

Garathi allowed a sliver of a smirk to cross his face, a mix of knowing and irony etched on his thin lips. "Regardless, it is but one overlord or another… though with our good Archon Kallimachos and his ilk lording over Athens, we were at least certain what tolerance was afforded our lot."

"And if this Great King Darius does indeed prevail…?" asked another voice from the group gathered beneath the umbrella of willows and firs that formed a near-cavernous roof over the hilly glade. "Might he perhaps see us in a fairer light than those who now rule?"

"Not if he is of a mind that is like his puppet Hippias…who we're told now serves the Persian King," the lanky bandit chieftain answered. "Remember the tales of when Hippias first seized control of the city after his father Pisastratus' death, and how he spoke of fairness and just treatment for all?"

"Which we have been told by many elders was a lie," Azelina said boldly, her dark eyes alight with an air of defiance. All turned abruptly to the saucy teenage girl. Her thin fingers ran more firmly round Atlas' muscled canine neck, as though the action might imbue her with greater confidence and conviction. "Many a tale is still told of his cruelty and scorn toward any who failed to earn his favor," she added. "And poor as life has been for us in Athens under the city's archons and their council, we still live without fear of torture or death just for being who we are."

Garathi raised a lean eyebrow at the girl's bold statement made before so many adults.

"But why should we not at least welcome what the Persian King might offer those of us who did not take part in opposing him at Marathon?" insisted a stocky man among the crowd.

"*Because we are still Greeks*," Azelina retorted firmly.

A palpable hush fell over the woody glade as every eye locked on the teenage girl, now fully aware of the undivided attention she commanded from all her companions. She trembled inwardly under the weighty stares leveled her way. She pursed her lips and eyed them all back with an effort to convey a confidence she did not truly feel at the moment.

The stout rogue to whom she had directed her remark glowered at her. His face seemed to ask, "How dare this whelp of a girl chide him? And what say the rest of those gathered here?"

Azelina clutched Atlas' mane more tightly, and the big dog rose from his haunches, a low growl rumbling in his throat while his pale eyes roamed the crowd.

Garathi stood up from his seat on the large rock and lifted a gnarled hand to end any further discussion. He eyed Azelina curiously, not having expected such a display of *philhellenism*, such Hellenic pride among his own. And certainly not from one he had long ago found abandoned on the side of a dark road when little more than a child. He made as if to speak, then just nodded solemnly.

Chapter Thirty-Nine

Struggles on the Trail

Pheidippides' legs ached horribly as he pushed on against the grinding protest of every part of his body. The rolling Pallini Hills had thrown the muscles in his thin legs into complete disarray with the constant shift of climbing and descent. With nearly twenty miles of his trek gone by, the erratic rise and dip of the terrain filled him with a mix of muscular confusion and ache. But he could not give way to the overwhelming demands of his body to pause and rest…not with the knowledge that Persian ships churning toward Athens would not be seeking respite. So in spite of aching feet that felt afire, legs that could barely hold him upright, and hips that tightened like burning rings, Pheidippides urged himself on. The gleaming rays of the blazing sun overhead burned his face and forced his eyes into little more than slits, while his throat was parched, as though his lungs were nothing more than dried rags. But he surged ahead, finally reaching more level ground.

He strained his way through a weedy stretch, like a man wading through the fog of a dream, unable to discern between reality and fantasy. And then his tired eyes caught sight of what his equally worn mind felt sure must be a cruel hallucination. He blinked several times and fought off an unyielding urge to tug free the waterskin from the sash round his waist and gulp down the two or three mouthfuls left. Pheidippides stared hard again…and now his eyes beheld, in the near distance, what seemed a lush woodland that curled over a narrow trail. He shook his head in startled disbelief…for there it apparently awaited him, just ahead!

A soft piping sounded faintly, and delicate feminine voices beckoned him from within the grove of trees. Slim paths appeared as he staggered ever closer, though he doubted his own senses, convinced he was seeing and hearing perhaps only what his desperate mind yearned to perceive.

"Rest, oh weary traveler…Lie down and suffer no more…Rest, drink of your water…Quench your mighty thirst…" The voices continued, promising if he but lie down and rest, his suffering would end, and he might then bask in the comfort of shade and gentle grass and never again feel the pangs of hunger and thirst…

His legs buckled suddenly, and Pheidippides nearly toppled over onto the weedy turf. He righted himself with a tremendous effort, his eyes darting about and straining to catch some glimpse of where those who coaxed him so lyrically (but perilously) might be lurking. Surely no such creatures dwelled out in this hazy waste. So hot and humid had the air grown he could no longer see far ahead enough to determine if the woodland he had seemingly sighted earlier was still in the scope of his vision.

Again the sweet voices beckoned him, now in a ghostly chant: "Drink…Rest…Sleep…Lie down and suffer no more. Drink…Rest…Drink…"

Pheidippides dropped to one knee, then tugged free

his waterskin once more. He raised it to his lips—and then he heard another voice: older, deeper, more masculine… "*Do you know why they call us ostraka?*" Pheidippides paused, recognizing the gruff, wistful voice in his head as that of Garathi, when the rogue leader had explained so lucidly the term Athenian citizens used for those deemed outcasts.

He considered those words spoken that day in the rogues' den…and then another voice, younger and more pointed chimed in: "*Read of your precious Athens before the Archon himself,*" snickered a cruel distortion of young Barthus' voice the day he had mocked the cherished poem Pheidippides had written by the agora poolside. "*He might even let you pretend you're a real citizen for a day!*"

Pheidippides lowered the waterskin as anger flushed over his face. "I *am* a real citizen of Athens!" he cried aloud in defiance as he had that day, which now seemed so terribly long ago.

"*You are a poor little messenger, Pheidippides… with stupid dreams!*" the voice quipped.

"No," Pheidippides insisted, barely able to eke out the word.

"*And your Athens cares only for those who are well-born—not fatherless rogues like us.*"

The exhausted young courier dropped to all fours, choking on the hot air as he tried breathing in so he might retort again, but failed to eke out a single word.

"*It's that ostraka again, Stoic Rolios,*" snapped an even younger voice from his past. And the dejected teenager recalled that painful day at the agora when the refined Athenian youths who were gathered round the stoic had belittled him so…which Boros had witnessed.

"*Do you know why they call us ostraka?*" he heard Garathi say again.

Pheidippides rose to his knees and held the waterskin up to his lips once more. The feminine voices chimed in: "Drink...Drink...Drink!"

He popped open the tiny nozzle and pressed it to his lips, but then opened his eyes more and saw, through a now-clearing haze, a solid, tangible woodland not even a stade away...less, perhaps. He blinked, then stared again, his tired eyes widening as he beheld what appeared to be a mix of oaks, firs, cyprus, and ash trees—with paths seeming to lead inside the welcoming shade of branches and leaves. Pheidippides corked the waterskin and stuffed it back into the sash at his waist.

"Oh, Great Zeus...the blessed woods!" the young courier cried. He righted himself and staggered on in the direction of the woodland, certain that he may also have heard the sigh of a male voice...as well as the scorn of a feminine one.

****

Suspended in midair, Lord Pan scowled, his furry arms folded across his wooly chest, his very horns seeming to wriggle in annoyance. He stared through the filmy portal from his own enchanted realm of the Elysian Fields to the earthly world where Pheidippides was celebrating his discovery of the lush little forest that beckoned him into its comforting shade, where vegetation appeared thick, and gentle life forms romped about.

" 'Great Zeus,' eh?" Pan quipped to himself. "Hmmph! Best learn whose wood this is, lad, and who it is that can serve you here. You'll not get much help from that bolt-throwing bag of pomp, Zeus...or any other of those Olympus louts." He watched as Pheidippides struggled onward, straining just to remain upright as he staggered closer to the woods. Pan's gaze drifted farther back along the steaming path and up the last of the rolling slopes, where the boy had been only a short while ago.

Two armored men mounted on huge war horses caparisoned for combat galloped down the hillside in earnest pursuit of the stumbling runner—who was yet unaware of their presence, no more than two hundred yards behind him. "Well, my lad, it does not appear those dear gods of Olympus you've given such praise are paying much heed to your plight," Pan mused sardonically.

****

Nearing the base of the slope, Rojese and his fellow assassin, Jamjon, eyed their unsuspecting prey eagerly. "We must seize him before he enters those trees, Jamjon," said Rojese firmly, "or he might hide in the thick of that wood as long as he pleases."

"Then he'll not warn Athens in time," Jamjon said glibly.

Rojese frowned. "I would rather we made sure of that, my friend." And they urged their horses on faster, closing the distance between themselves and the weary runner on the narrow path ahead.

Still unaware that Darius' assassins had trailed and stalked him since the outskirts of Marathon, young Pheidippides forced himself onward, every limb of his thin body pathetically out of control now. His knees buckled and his arms flailed like broken bird wings as the abrupt clopping of hooves caused him to turn sharply and step into a rut on the pebbly path, spinning him nearly all the way around and into a momentary backward trot. The glaring gold rays of the sun stabbed at his eyes, and Pheidippides raised a hand to shield them—allowing him to glimpse the silhouettes of a pair of horsemen charging toward him in the near distance. He gasped and lurched back several steps, falling back hard onto his rump. A burst of uproarious laughter rose above the din of the horse hooves, drawing a strain of embarrassment and impotent rage from the boy.

Riding stride for stride with Jamjon, Rojese turned his helmed, bearded face toward his comrade and snickered loudly, saying, "We'll give the Lord Darius cause to grin wide when we meet him with this dainty strapped to my saddle!" Jamjon nodded in acknowledgment as he too urged his steed on.

Pheidippides' eyes widened in horror as he heard their booming voices, beheld the bright gray-maroon colors of the Persian Empire, and trembled at the violent approach of the charging war horses. He scrambled to his feet, finding great strength in his fear, and stumbled blindly toward the cavernous woods with its faint hope of refuge. Behind him, both assassins smirked in triumph—smirks that disappeared almost instantly.

Not fifty feet away, a mad flurry of talons and feathers was swooping down toward them with predatory deliberation. There was no mistaking that a large golden eagle was on the attack and they were the object of its aggression. Where it had come from, neither assassin could fathom. Perhaps from the nearby woods, for this huge predatory bird had seemingly materialized out of thin air.

"What beast of the hell-worlds is this winged

monster?" growled Rojese, raising one thick forearm to shield his face, the other gripping the leather reins in an attempt to manage his spooked horse. The great bird swooped down at him and Jamjon—its massive golden-hued wings making it a match in size to either of the men's steeds. The bird did not hesitate. Its loudly flapping wings caused Jamjon's stallion to rear onto its hind legs in panic, while the beak snapped viciously at Rojese's bearded face. Neither man paid further heed to their fleeing quarry.

Farther up on the path, Pheidippides was completely oblivious to the abrupt attack on his pursuers by the great flying creature. Knowing they were bearing down on him, the young foot courier felt no need to glance back at the fearsome duo. He was sure of their intent. Terror gripped him like a pair of cold fingers. Even if the mounted brutes did not slay him, he knew that whatever fate their dread King Darius had planned for him might well prove worse than death itself. So he raced with every ounce of energy he could coax from his weary, aching body. And then he gaped.

Straight ahead he caught the hazy shape of some sort of ethereal being beckoning him from within a tangle of cypress trees…but where he could discern no path of entry. He blinked, unsure of his own eyes as he beheld what appeared to be an impossible mix of a lithe woman and a woodland cat. The bizarre creature beckoned him toward her, then turned and slipped smoothly off onto a narrow deer trail that materialized as magically as had the strange she-creature itself.

Pheidippides shook his head, squinted, and saw that the path upon which the womanly cat-creature had vanished was still there! "By all the gods, it must be Zeus Himself aiding me!" he gasped out in thankful relief. And with that he urged himself onward toward the tiny break within the thick cluster of cypress trees…not hearing the soft *thump* as they closed off the all but imperceptible slit of a path no sooner than he'd passed through it.

Chapter Forty

Mysterious Borders

Rojese and Jamjon waved their huge broadswords in bellicose fashion at the enormous golden eagle that had flown out abruptly from the strange woodland in the near distance and soared down savagely upon them. The great bird's frosty eyes peered at them with so reproachful a light it gave the husky Nubian warrior cause to shiver with superstitious dread.

"Sorcery?" Jamjon uttered hoarsely. He all but expected his comrade to snicker at so outrageous a claim—but a glimpse from the corner of one eye assured him that Rojese reacted in no such way. The big Macedonian swung his broadsword deftly at their winged assailant once more, fearful, though, that it might not have even mattered had he made contact. Jamjon shifted his gaze back slightly in the direction of their fleeing human quarry.

Pheidippides was gone.

The Nubian glanced back up and saw that the huge eagle attacking them had paused momentarily in its fury and, incredibly enough, also appeared to be taking note of their fleeing prey's disappearance into the nearby woodland, which also had materialized in as queer a fashion as the winged assailant.

"Sorcery, perhaps," Rojese acknowledged with an

air of somber reluctance. "But that shall not give us cause to abandon our task," he added grimly. The bird now gone too, he urged his huge roan on toward the woods. Jamjon, a shade less eagerly, followed on his great black stallion.

****

Within the cavernous trail of the thick woodland of cypress, oaks, and pines, Pheidippides staggered on, gasping as he lurched forward, grateful to have eluded his pursuers. How they had come upon him so abruptly, and he so completely unaware of their presence, he could not fathom...but here he was, seemingly safe for the moment. He dropped to one knee, catching his breath while taking in the welcoming beauty of the flowery woodland. Truly the gods must be watching over him, he thought. He raised his eyes upward. "Oh, Great Zeus...I thank you for your kindly aid...and I swear to you I shall finish this quest!"

Farther up the trail, within the curling branches of a tall oak tree, Pan frowned in frustration, his head still sporting the great curved beak of a golden eagle, his limbs still a bizarre mix of hairy human arms and bird wings as the transformation of one shape back into the other was still in mid-form.

"Hmph!" the Elysian god snorted. " 'Great Zeus' again, eh, lad?" His bestial face wore a pronounced scowl.

"Oh...and *who* should he praise instead?" a sassy feminine voice chided from even higher in the tree's leafy branches. It bore the tone of one scolding a naughty child.

Pan winced, knowing well the voice, yet startled to hear it. He cursed unintelligibly, as none other than his

270

nymph-queen Keres swooped down upon him from her cover within the oak's thick branches and leaves and plucked out sharply one of the long golden feathers on his still lingering eagle guise. Pan yelped at the acute ache he felt in his rump from her less than gentle act.

"And you dare even cause one of my own dryads to show that Athenian brat a secret path in here he could never have found on his own!" she shrieked, the gold-hued eyes afire with feminine fury. Pan cowered before her wrath, hastening with greater urgency now his transition from the golden eagle form back into his own shape. He did not welcome another painful snatching of feathers from his tender and still vulnerable hindquarters.

"But sweet Keres…" he implored.

She silenced him with a cross look that promised worse than another feather-plucking. "No! I'll not listen to your sly tongue, wretched Pan. *There were to be no tricks!*"

Fully back into his own form again, the goat-god eased himself smoothly onto one of the oak's limbs, his backside securely against its solid trunk. Keres remained suspended in midair, hands upon her hips. Her lips were pursed, and she narrowed her eyes expectantly, one hand extended and waiting.

"Very well," Pan acquiesced. And with a tiny wave of one cloven hand, he caused five goblets of bubbling golden nectar to appear, suspended by an outreach of branches and by the very air itself. "But if I may point out," he offered diplomatically, "this is hardly fair terms here. Those Persian riders were not a part of the wager we made."

Keres settled down within some of the oak's curly

branches and nodded for him to make his case. Pan gave a wry smile. "Our wager, if you recall, my dearest Nymph Queen, was on *the lad's will to continue*...his devotion to his task," he explained rationally. "Had those assassins caught the boy, neither of us would know how this all truly would have gone. I merely offer you the opportunity to tempt him yourself now."

She frowned skeptically, not buying into it. Pan took due notice of her look. "Eh, lest it is too great a challenge...?" The tiny but clearly perceptible smirk on his goatish face was too much for her. With a wave of her hand, Keres dispelled the proffered goblets of nectar.

"If I knew less of you, oh, Pan, I'd think you more a scoundrel than you already are."

"Why, Keres...thank you, I think."

"And it is to be agreed, here on, there shall be no interference at all!" she added firmly, as though scolding a misbehaving child. Pan nodded with an assumed air of innocent compliance. "Nor shall any of my dryads be made to do your bidding again."

"Of course, my dearest. Who is Lord Pan of Elysia to dare command the very fair nymphs over which he once made you queen?"

She responded with a snippy stare...to which Pan once more raised both cloven hands in playful submission.

****

Rojese and Jamjon had both dismounted and were beating the heavy brambles and brush just outside the woodland. Thick as it was with cypress trees and oaks, no tangible trail leading inside it could be discerned. Both men hewed at the twisted tangle of low-hanging branches and gnarly bushes, Rojese with his great war axe, Jamjon with his broadsword, but with scarcely any effect.

"With my own eyes did I see a path seem to part open for him—slim but wide enough for one as thin as he—but I failed to see him pass through because of that accursed winged beast that came upon us," said Rojese, his thick black hair and beard bristling with each word.

"And if we find entry?" Jamjon asked with uncharacteristic caution.

"Why, then, in we go," said Rojese, eying his comrade curiously. He caught a faint hint of concern growing over the man's ebon features. "Come now, Jamjon friend, let's not allow those Nubian superstitions of yours to have at you. Those of us now in service to Persia did not aid in building such an empire by being fearful of shadows."

Jamjon bristled slightly, knowing no man other than his longtime companion Rojese might speak to him thus and not truly offend him. "It is no mere shadow that frightens a Nubian."

Rojese grinned and nodded, a laugh born both of respect and mirth passing through his coarse lips. He clapped his comrade heartily on the shoulder, then turned back to face the thick tangle of trees. "Now, as our frail lad was nearly within our grasp only moments ago, let's find our way in too and end his trek homeward," the Macedonian quipped. They continued hewing at the pathless cluster of trees.

****

From the instant he had glimpsed the Elysian dryad beckoning him from the slice of path that had parted the snarl of cypress trees, and then slipped inside them

273

himself, Pheidippides marveled at the suddenly colorful sense of harmony that now surrounded him. There was no further sign of the wispy she-creature—a seeming mix of feline and human that had sprouted wings from its shoulders. So, after kneeling on the flowered path and proclaiming his thanks to Zeus, Pheidippides rose and urged his body onward along the now visible trail. His body ached less, and he attributed that to the brief respite he'd gained from kneeling, and from the utter charm of his surroundings. He did not recall any of this terrain from the army's march the day before. The woods then had appeared dark, grim, unwelcoming. But this, this was...

A rustle from within the trees caught his ear, and he stopped, harkening, then catching a faint patter seemingly on the trail behind him. Pheidippides whirled round. No one there. Another *crackle* and *pop* from within the trailside trees and brush.

He was not alone.

He fixed his gaze on a spot within a clump of drooping firs...or were they cypress trees? Perhaps oaks, as they seemed wider at the base. Pheidippides shook his head, the soulful brown eyes straining to focus. Shadows danced and flitted through the lower hanging branches, causing the thick leaves there to flutter and flap. He squinted, catching a glimpse of *something*—on foot? or in flight?—that hinted, perhaps, of a forest creature, yet also bearing a shape that suggested a human.

A soft stomping of feet sneaking up behind him caused him to whirl round once more. Again...nothing there. Pheidippides perspired, though the broiling temperatures that had tormented him only a short while earlier seemed actually to have relented within this strange spinney of trees and brush. For the first time he realized that the persistent ache and strain throughout the muscles of his entire body had lessened, just as the searing heat had rescinded. He squinted through the tangle of branches and leaves again, first on one side of the path, then on the other. So different these woods seemed from when he had passed through with the army, he thought once more.

So different.

Pheidippides shook his head, recalling vaguely something he had once heard in the talk of the hemeredrome—the fabled long-distance foot couriers who brought news of import from all over the Hellespont to its widely spread poleis—and how on those lengthy treks they were, at times, subject to tricks of the mind, even bizarre hallucinations that were known to plague them. Had not the bold Zagorus been said to have suffered such a strange tickling of the mind...with his claims of having had audience with the most bizarre of gods himself: Lord Pan of the Elysian Fields? And now, here, some twenty miles into his own lengthy courier's trek, was he enduring a brand of those same sorts of illusions? After all, his arms and legs felt less weary now, less strained than mere moments ago. His mighty thirst did not seem as great as before. Perhaps he—

A soft piping rose gently from somewhere in the eerie woodland, cutting off his speculations and causing him to halt and harken. He turned his head this way and that, seeing nothing other than the same fleeting shadows and misshapen wisps that scampered and floated through the branches and leaves of the trailside cypress, oaks, and firs but never seemed to take tangible form.

"Who is here with me?" he demanded in a near desperate tone. No reply...only the soft piping.

****

Jamjon paused in his hewing of the outer brush that yet prevented the two assassins from gaining entry into the impenetrable woods where they felt sure the elusive Athenian courier had fled. His handsome Nubian features flickered with a sharp awareness, and he listened attentively to every crunch and crackle in the surrounding underbrush. His fellow assassin had just sliced through a tangle of thick brambles, which yet gave no sign of parting wide enough for even a small man to slip through, let alone men of their size. Rojese raised his heavy war axe overhead, gripping it more firmly in his powerful hands—as though determined to shear through the thorny snarl in one violent chop— then noticed his comrade frozen still and listening, as would a wolf or a bear.

"What...? What is it?" said Rojese, glancing about to see if perhaps the accursed golden eagle had returned...or some new foe had come upon them.

Jamjon's head turned side to side, his attention more riveted to whatever sound apparently touched his keen ears. He very nearly ignored his friend, though answered as a courtesy, speaking more to himself than in response to the Macedonian. "That...music," he said softly.

Rojese frowned. He, too, listened, but no sound other than the light steamy breeze, along with his own breathing and the creak of their metal armor, reached his ears. "I hear nothing more than what is likely the chirp of birds or other forest creatures that—"

"Hsst!" Jamjon cautioned, raising a hand. "Someone nearby plays a reed...pipes. Listen..."

Rojese harkened, but could detect no sense of anyone playing any sort of music. He well respected the heightened senses of his Nubian friend...a man raised since childhood in the wild forests of southern Egypt. Jamjon was not one to give way to illusions. But in listening himself, the Macedonian heard nothing at all and now grew frustrated. He thought back to the massive eagle that had attacked just as they were about to charge down and seize the fleeing young courier. The bird had appeared so magically, delaying them in their pursuit, and had vanished just as magically, as though *sent* to aid the fleeing boy. Both men had been spooked by the incident, though neither wanted to admit it.

"Come, we've no more time for this," Rojese urged. "We've a two-legged prey to catch." He raised his axe again, readied to resume chopping at the thorny tangle. And then the cluster of branches and trees rustled loudly. A path appeared before them, the queer woodland seeming to part all on its own. Their eyes widened in astonishment as the overhang of branches spread open—as though daring the pair to enter. They eyed one another incredulously.

****

Pheidippides waited, then called out defiantly again at the eerie presence that swirled around him, while the pipe reeds cooed softly. "Show yourself!" he cried with less bravado than he really felt.

A feminine voice rose melodiously above the sound of the piping, humming and trilling, taking on a bell-like tone...then words sifting inside his head that spoke *just to him*: "Rest here, weary traveler, lie down and suffer no more…"

Pheidippides' eyes darted back and forth, searching the trailside trees for the source of the voice.

"Why do you suffer?" the beautiful voice cooed seductively. "What does it matter? Sit down and drink of your water…" More voices joined in as shapely arms and gentle hands of ethereal tenderness reached out from the flora surrounding him…seeking to embrace him.

"It is merely the sun," he said, trying to explain away to himself the persistent call of the chanting voices that now seemed everywhere.

"Pheidippides…Pheidippides…" they beckoned all the more melodiously.

"Who's there!" he demanded more assertively. "How do you know my name?"

Now wispy humanoid shapes emerged more clearly from within the brush and from behind tree trunks, only to disappear again no sooner than they had materialized—their ephemeral state of being causing him to be more ill at ease.

"Has hunger, heat, and thirst finally got the better of me?" he asked aloud, as though an answer might come from the very woodland itself. And indeed it seemed so, for even as he spoke those words, the wispy shapes flitting through the overgrowth took on the more defined shapes of Pan's winged nymphs—the beautiful dryads of which Keres was queen. From the lower hanging boughs of trees they spread their delicate wings and lifted off into the air above him, eying him with angular faces that were both coy and mischievous. Others, clad in colorful silken garb, skittered out from the trail behind him.

The bemused fairylike creatures stared curiously at the weary young man, their delicate faces showing a mild amazement at this human here in the heart of so bountiful a forestland, yet also so weary and strained. Two younger dryads giggled, and Pheidippides whirled round, catching both mischievous culprits in the act. His tender brown eyes widened in disbelieving awe.

"*Dryads…of Elysia?*" he gasped, then blinked several times. For there they stood…while two more wood nymphs flitted out from within the branches and leaves of the firs on either side of the trail. Both hovered in midair, staring back at him in equal wonder. "No, this cannot be," he uttered hoarsely. "'Tis but my own tired mind and nothing more." He thrust his shoulders back in resolve. "These false images and their haunting ways shall not deter me. I must hasten home to Athens, else…"

He ceased speaking as it was causing him precious breaths. The dread fatigue from a short while ago seized hold of him once again, the throbbing ache and strain he suffered gripping his muscles in an iron grasp. Pheidippides shook his head in solemn defiance. He struggled to dismiss the soft voices that beckoned, almost lyrically, for him to "*Lie down…surrender this fruitless quest that can only end in defeat. Perhaps if you but sip of your water and quench your mighty thirst?*"

"No!" he shouted. "Be still, you voices of false promise and you ghostly shapes of my own tired mind!" His eyes dropped to the soft dirt trail beneath his aching sandaled feet. He would no longer allow himself to behold these phantoms his weary mind most surely made of mere woodland shadows, nor let his own distorted hearing twist the chirp and chatter of insects and birds into creatures other than what they truly were. He urged his journey-beaten legs on…and then heard behind him a noise he recognized as all too real: the clop of horse hooves farther back on the trail.

****

The two assassins gawked at the narrow fissure that had opened seemingly of its own volition. Jamjon's cedar-brown eyes narrowed, and a deep frown crossed his brow. The Nubian was terribly vexed by everything that had happened from the time they had sighted their quarry and hastened their pursuit: the eagle materializing at nearly the same time the queer woodland had come into view…and now this. He shook his head, unsure as he eyed the opening suspiciously. He blinked, as it seemed wider than a moment ago. Jamjon turned to Rojese and gestured at the wider breach in the trees. The Macedonian had seen it too, but regarded it with a renewed skepticism.

"I think this is more the work of our hefty blades hewing this crunch of wood and root, and we only now noticed its wider girth," said Rojese.

Jamjon did not look so certain of that.

"Come, my old friend." The Macedonian chuckled. "Surely there are reasons for these—" His attempt at explaining this latest phenomenon was pinched off by a haunting cry that came from somewhere within the woods. Rojese stroked his beard thoughtfully, regarding the mysterious concave of trees now as suspiciously as his fellow assassin had been doing.

"You heard," Jamjon declared knowingly.

Rojese frowned. "An animal, perhaps."

"More than animal," said Jamjon.

"Then what? Some 'dread woodland demon' of your Nubian lore come here to plague us?" He chuckled lightheartedly, not wanting to offend his good friend, but still wanting to dispel all this talk of unnatural causes. These strange sightings were due more to the nature of their awkward trek and the stifling heat…that and nothing else.

Jamjon responded with a bland look that suggested a tinge of frustration with his comrade's scoffing, however lightheartedly, at what he himself felt most certainly.

Rojese offered a hearty smile and clapped his fellow assassin on the shoulder. "You Nubians are always hearing such things the rest of us don't recognize, friend Jamjon. But that's not to say *something* of a different sort is not lurking about," he added in a more generous tone. "So let's to this slim path…as it seems our only way into this queer wood. We need get on with our pursuit of that sly courier and do the task our Lord Darius expects of us. Ay?"

Jamjon studied his longtime fellow mercenary and even allowed a slight smile to form on his lips, acknowledging to himself how they had always managed some form of agreement between them. For had they not succeeded, time after time, because they knew each other as well as they knew their trade? It had made them the preferred choice, always, of their Persian commanders. They *were* the best.

"We should go in on foot, leading our steeds, then mount again once we see the makeup of the ground there," said Jamjon.

"Agreed," said Rojese, gripping his horse by the

reins. The two passed through the breach between the trees, barely wide enough for both men and their horses, one by one. And no sooner had they entered than the breach sealed back up behind them with a silent *snick*. Neither heard even a rustle as the bushes and trees closed up behind them. Both were too caught up in marveling at the quality of the thick forestland hemming them in on either side. Oaks, cypress, firs, and pines leaned over the winding path that loomed ahead, their branches and boughs so filled with leaves and long needles it was impossible to see what they may or may not have concealed. Only the chirp of birds and the soft crackle and snap of perhaps small animals or lizards scampering through the underground was heard.

There was no sign at all of their human prey. The path, though, seemed to have widened a bit. Rojese motioned that they mount again, and Jamjon nodded in agreement. "So fair a forest I've not seen before," the Nubian uttered in admiration of their surroundings.

"Aye," said Rojese, hauling himself back up onto the saddled back of the tall roan. "Pity if the Great King Darius ever comes upon this realm here. No doubt he'd have much of it hewn to the ground and laid waste in favor of grand temples celebrating his conquering this prosperous land."

Jamjon, riding ahead of his comrade, nodded grimly, bristling at the thought.

Seeing his friend's husky frame stiffen so, Rojese added: "And that would of course be after His Lordship allowed his brute of a son, Xerxes, to hunt and kill for his own pleasure whatever wild beasts might prowl this wood."

At that, Jamjon glanced back to his companion. "Pity if either was to happen." He turned forward again, and both men urged on their horses to pick up the pace.

A loud cry, clearly that of a human, suddenly pierced the warm air of the queer woodland. "No... Be still!"

Both men heard it but were unable to detect anything more. It was enough, though, to satisfy them it was the voice of a tired, frightened youth. "Our courier," said Rojese.

Ahead of him, Jamjon nodded, knowing there was no disputing this time what was heard. He slapped his stallion on the rump, and Rojese did the same with his own mount. Both broke into an instant gallop down the winding trail and, rounding a bend, they beheld...a pronounced fork in the misshapen path. Jamjon tugged on the leather reins, his great black stallion rearing momentarily onto its hind legs, Rojese's roan doing the same. The two assassins exchanged a brief look of understanding, then urged their horses down the separate paths.

Chapter Forty-One

Pursuit to *Elsewhere*

Pheidippides felt his heart turn into a knot and tighten. The clopping behind him was not the soft, gentle patter and chime that had been fairly teasing him from the moment he'd slipped inside the colorful woodland; those sounds had been peaceful, if not mischievous. But it had all felt benign...nothing of a foreboding nature. These galloping hooves bore menace. He swallowed hard and instinctively hastened his pace, fearful now.

The clatter increased and left little doubt in his mind that the horsemen he had glimpsed outside his woody refuge had followed him in and would ride him down in moments, once they sighted him. Perhaps their cold eyes were already homed in on his futile flight and all that remained was to close in on their prize. Surely someone had seen him from afar when he had first started off on his trek and sent these assassins to seize him...even murder him to prevent word of their fleet sailing for Athens.

Pheidippides' eyes scanned the trailside frantically, but the interlocking thickness of trees, knotted with so much bramble and brush, revealed no hint of tiny deer trails—or any other means of breaking through the thorny tangle for a temporary hideaway. There would be no time anyway; the pounding of beating hooves on the soft soil made it clear he would be sighted even if a break did appear somewhere. So he summoned all the strength he could from failing muscles and aching limbs, and put his trust in flight. The roar of horse hooves now filled the entire woods as his squinting eyes strained to see farther ahead. And what he beheld nearly made him stop in his tracks. He gasped!

Perhaps fifty or sixty strides ahead on the narrowing trail, a yellow haze seemed to germinate out of thin air and take on the form of a glittering sphere. Pheidippides blinked, one hand going instinctively to his side and gripping the flesh of his own waist—hard fingernails digging deep into the skin, the sharp pain it evoked assuring him he did not dream or hallucinate. And now, from either side of the path, he caught the tinkle and chime of feminine voices, pleasant sounding, but also filled with alarm: "Hurry noble courier...run!" He heard the cries not with his ears but as within his head.

The thunder of horse hooves increased, closing on him, the dirt and light grass of the trail spewing up and the earthy scent of it touching his nostrils. Fear overwhelmed him. Pheidippides found renewed strength in his limbs and forced his already spent legs on harder. Still the pounding grew louder—closer! But now, wispy, elfin-looking figures appeared on either side of him: winged ethereal creatures. *Nymphs?* That could mean only one thing. He dismissed the absurd thought, knowing for certain now that his mind was indeed overwrought with strain and fatigue. He shut his eyes and blocked his ears as he ran on, trying vainly to blot out the voices teasing him...and the hooves clopping behind.

Pheidippides refused to allow his eyes to stray to either side, nor would he glance back and glimpse his own doom descending upon him. He pumped his arms vigorously, urging on his legs. A hoarse *gasp* that came not from the lean young courier but from behind him burst through the moist woodland air. Still he did not dare glance back but instead fixed his gaze directly ahead.

And there, hovering in midair, encircled by the golden haze he had seen materializing earlier, he beheld the most beautiful creature of feminine grace he had ever seen. She was garbed scantily in the colorful leafy green-and-brown of the bountiful woodland itself; her tanned face was encircled by long golden locks that draped all the way down a body that was both muscular and lithe. Shapely golden wings sprouted from her shoulder blades, and Pheidippides knew instinctively— in spite of what his mind told him—*this was no illusion*. No more than the pursuit on horseback behind him was a trick of his own tired mind.

From either side of the trail, the delicate-looking nymphs that emerged from the bushes and trees twisted and throbbed, their shapes shifting abruptly and taking on the form of wild forest creatures—rabbits, deer, foxes, squirrels, birds. They scurried alongside him as though trying to hasten his pace. And, ahead, the beautiful dryad with the golden locks waved him toward her, urgently calling out in a language he could not make out. But her intent to help was clear.

Again he heard a loud gasp from behind, whoever or *whatever* chased him apparently having beheld the same vision, now mere strides away! The gleaming yellow haze surrounding the beautiful dryad—none other than Queen Keres herself—widened into what amounted to a portal leading from the surreal cluster of trees and brush into an even more airy woodland that sparkled with vibrant colors. The queenly beauty stretched a slender arm out toward the desperate boy, urging him on as if it were the extent of all she might offer in the situation. A frown crossed her tanned face, knowing her limited actions spelled the difference between the hapless lad falling victim to his pursuer— or escaping.

"Come to us, oh, courier... You'll be safe!" she cried out.

"*By Mithra!*" Jamjon uttered hoarsely to himself, his voice carrying through the moist air of the woodland trail. "He strides the border of—" The Nubian did not permit himself to finish his thought.

Pheidippides heard him, though...while also seeing and hearing the fairylike dryads coaxing him on as they hustled him along, mindful of not touching him. The outburst he'd heard on the part of his mounted pursuer was just the added bit of push he needed. With one last surge of energy and strength, he followed the dryads through the portal...and into *somewhere else.*

Jamjon gaped in superstitious awe as he reined in his great stallion, the hoofed beast rearing onto its hindquarters. Not only had rider and horse both beheld the strange feminine creature that had materialized here in the midst of this mysterious wooded path, but she and her hustling minions—fairies of some sort, it seemed—had beckoned on the fleeing lad and whisked him away, off into some nether world perhaps, for the spiritlike creatures were no longer visible.

Nor was the boy.

The stout black warrior shuddered involuntarily as he peered ahead, behind him, and to either side of the path that now appeared to have grown much narrower. Sweat rolled down his brow and cheeks. Jamjon had heard many a queer tale of such mystical places, but dared not allow any further thought of them to seize hold of his mind. "Rojese! Here! Come now!" he shouted.

****

Pheidippides lurched through the haze of the foggy portal, feeling a soft tingle, warm and moist, as he emerged suddenly into a world of pastoral beauty and serenity unlike anything he had ever known in his life. His eyes blinked in sparkling awe at the magnificent sight that jolted his tired, wrought mind. For not only did a forestland of dazzling color and grace flood his vision, but now every muscle and bone throughout his entire body felt invigorated and devoid of all pain.

And poised majestically within an archway of beautiful maple and olive trees, seated regally upon a high-backed throne of emerald-hued bushes and multi-colored flowers, was the most beautiful and alluring creature of golden-haired, feminine grace he might ever have imagined...the very one who had beckoned him through the portal. Flanking her were the adorable dryads that had helped guide him into her net of comfort and refuge. Also sitting on the flower-and-leaf-filled ground were several small, bestial half-men that sprouted tiny horns akin to Pan's.

"*Wood nymphs*? And, and...*satyrs*?" gasped the bewildered young courier. It cannot be!"

"Oh, but it is, dear Pheidippides," said Keres

sweetly from her leafy throne. Her amber eyes twinkled with their usual mischief as she sat back regally, her shapely tanned legs crossed. One lithely muscled arm stretched out an open hand toward him. "Welcome, Pheidippides...to Elysia!" she said almost lyrically.

"And your journey's end," chirped one of the dryads.

"If you so wish it," added a satyr, grinning.

Pheidippides gasped again, convinced he must be lying somewhere out on the narrow path, passed out...or perhaps passing into the Netherworld of Charon...Lord of the Soulless Dead.

****

Rojese found Jamjon, dismounted from his black stallion and semi-crouched in the middle of the trail, his great hands reaching forward and grasping at thin air. The big Macedonian warrior stared curiously, then called out to him, vexed.

"What of those cries, Jamjon?"

The Nubian continued making passes with one hand at the spot where he had witnessed Pheidippides disappearing through a portal that had moments earlier loomed there as a globular rift between worlds. "'Tis ancient sorcery in this place, my friend," he replied without looking back at Rojese. A long moment passed with nothing said between them. Jamjon rose and turned round to face his friend, who was still mounted on his tall roan. "We are best to leave here."

Rojese frowned. "Oh...? And let this slippery Greek boy just elude us and be on his way?"

"He is no longer on his way," Jamjon said flatly, then sheathed his sword and mounted his horse.

"I am mistaken? You have killed him?" Rojese

said eagerly. "Where then is…?"

"He is *gone*, not killed," said Jamjon.

"Gone where?"

"Beyond where you or I can follow."

Rojese shook his head and scowled impatiently. "I'll not be the one to tell the Lord Darius we failed to stop a whelp of a courier because…" He groped for words to express his frustration. "Eh, because of some old Nubian myth!"

Jamjon half-smirked, his eyes harboring far more than superstition. "He has gone to a half-world. I saw so with my own eyes."

Rojese tried not to snicker, knowing and respecting the essence of his comrade's beliefs. " 'Half-world,' eh, my friend? Erebus is the only half-world that poor courier will see once we catch him. Come…there are other paths to follow." The big Macedonian gestured to his comrade, then veered his horse round and headed back down the trail.

Jamjon did not join him immediately. He shivered, in spite of the searing heat, then finally urged his own steed in the same direction…reluctantly and without conviction.

Chapter Forty-Two

The Elysian Fields

Pheidippides blinked his eyes over and over as he gripped his own arm again, digging his fingernails into his flesh as he had done before, convinced this was truly a hallucination…or the prelude to his own death. He winced at the sudden pain of his nails piercing the tender skin of his lower arm and withheld the urge to squeal in reaction to it. So perhaps he still lived. Then these strange surroundings and phantoms were indeed tricks of his mind, brought on by the strain of heat and—

"Oh, why is it that you mortals must always wonder that you are either dead, or that you dream, whenever you cannot explain where you are?" chirped a melodious feminine voice in his head.

Pheidippides blinked again and stared inquisitively at the golden-haired beauty seated on the flowery dais of branches and foliage. Her lips had not moved, yet he had heard every word clearly in his head as if she had spoken them aloud. Her golden eyes danced with a condescending air of merriment. He made to speak but was distracted suddenly by the clop of horse hooves— the very ones that had hounded him just a short while earlier. He glanced around nervously, invoking a tinkling chorus of laughter from the dryads and satyrs, and drawing also a delicate yawn from Queen Keres.

"Fear not, sad messenger of Athens. Your pursuers cannot follow you here," she quipped. "They cannot even see you so long as you remain in Elysia."

Pheidippides swallowed. "Then truly this is the Realm of Lord Pan?"

"And Queen Keres," she added pointedly.

"I…uh, yes," he stammered. "I just did not know…" His voice fell into a murmuring jumble as he was unsure of what to say or how to express clearly what he now thought. This queenly nymph was beautiful and regal, yes, but…

"Of course you doubt your own senses, foolish courier." She laughed, reading his very thoughts. "But ask yourself why you now suffer no fatigue or ache, or why you no longer thirst…as your nearly broken shell of a body still does."

"My…*shell*?"

"Why yes," she said pertly. "Behold!" And with a twirl of one supple arm, Keres stirred up, from the fertile-looking soil between herself and where he stood, a cloudy image of him struggling vainly in a bedraggled run, and on the verge of collapse. He saw it clearly, as though it were a dusty reflection of himself running earlier along the woodland path…as drained and scorched as he had felt then. This sad image of himself plowing pathetically through the sooty August air caused him to cry out in alarm.

"Yes, dear Pheidippides of Noble Athens…that is indeed your weary *shell* of a body as it struggles even now between worlds."

Pheidippides ran a hand over himself again to be certain that here he now stood in legendary Elysia itself,

while he watched a broken image of himself in…
"Where—"

"Your straining body that you see now treads the border between the paths of the Hellespont…and the Realm of Erebus, where Charon, Lord of the Dead, lurks in wait for you," Keres said darkly. "Or…you might consider instead these blessed Elysian Fields where eternal comfort could be yours."

Pheidippides felt his knees buckle and might well have dropped to the ground had two lovely dryads and a pair of the horned satyrs not hustled to his side and kept him afoot. No sooner than they did, the harsh image of his struggling earthly form vanished. Keres rose haughtily from her floral seat.

"*That* is what you will know if you depart fair Elysia and refuse what we offer instead," she added. "Those who still pursue you can no longer see that pitiful shell of yourself you just beheld, but should you return to continue your foolish quest, they will indeed be upon you again." She smirked sweetly. "Or perhaps Charon himself will seize you for the Lake of the Dead…as he sought to do with brave Zagorus, and—"

"And would have, had we not saved the lad so he might complete his own quest!" a coarse but friendly voice rippled through the air.

A frown flickered over Keres' smooth brow, while Pheidippides fairly jumped at the sound of it.

"'Tis still my time!" the nymph queen snapped at the unseen intruder.

"A bit more, yes, but that is all," the coarse male voice responded quietly.

Keres pursed her lips impatiently in response, though quite pleased with herself. She turned, regarding

Pheidippides again. The lad was still in the gentle grip of the satyrs and nymphs who had kept him from falling over earlier. His mind was spinning in confusion, his senses altogether disrupted. Keres smiled thinly. "Here in Elysia, dear Pheidippides, is the absence of all hunger and thirst…of pain itself, of sorrow…the end of all your struggles in vain," she cooed.

Pheidippides' chestnut-brown eyes widened in wonder; he shifted his gaze from the nymph queen to her minions…who still held him aloft. He nodded to them assuredly that he could now stand on his own again. The dryads and satyrs nodded back in response and glided gracefully away from him, bowing respectfully and smiling affectionately at him.

"Remain here," Keres said quietly, "and no Persian assassin…no beast of prey…no scorching heat can harm you. Nor can any spirit of Dark Erebus. Not here in this Woodland Eternal."

"And Athens?" Pheidippides heard himself ask, the words coming abruptly from his mouth.

Keres frowned deeply. "That would no longer be your worry."

"No…not your concern at all," quipped the coarse mannish voice they had heard earlier.

Pheidippides' eyes darted wildly about in search of the source of the odd but authoritative voice he had heard several times now. Keres, meanwhile, sighed as if in resignation, and watched as the form of Pan emerged ostentatiously from the thick of the overhead trees and floated downward to join them.

"Pan—Lord of Elysia," Keres proclaimed flatly.

"Pan…?" exclaimed Pheidippides, eyes widening in reverent awe. One look at the tall, muscled figure, its goatish, horned head furry yet mannish, a whiplike tail swishing behind its thick legs that were covered partially in black woolen britches cut off just above bulging calves that tapered down into heavy feet that sprouted long toenails…this told the astonished Greek lad that here indeed was the legendary Elysian Lord of the Revel and the Din himself. And here, also, were Pan's fabled woodland courtiers of whom fantastical tales had been told by stoics and bards…the very ones Pheidippides had long imagined and even tried illustrating with his own etchings on waxened tablets. Yes, the very Elysians mocked by Athenian citizens and deemed false deities…as "more suited to the likes of servants and slaves and ostraka, and *never* to be confused with true gods: the Olympians."

Yes, here was the very Elysian lord the valiant Zagorus proclaimed he had met on his own trek back from Sparta. Pheidippides felt his stomach churn sourly as he also recalled how Zagorus—for all his heroics—had been so rudely treated by nearly everyone for his plea on Pan's behalf; how it had resulted in the renowned courier being unfairly ridiculed. Shame for all of Athens filled his heart here in this magnificent little glade of mystical beauty…for he now beheld what Zagorus had experienced. And as though it might make some small difference here and now, young Pheidippides of cherished Athens fell to his knees so he might pay homage to the Lord of Elysia in place of what his own city had failed to do—not only in the great polis' refusal to honor Pan with a temple as grand as those afforded the mighty Olympians, but failing to see those of the Elysian Fields as more than false gods.

The boy's actions surprised Pan, whose coarse

features lit up in a mix of modesty and amusement. The Elysian lord shook his head and raised a cloven hand. "Oh…no!" Pan laughed. "Do rise, Pheidippides!"

The satyrs and nymphs all giggled lightly, while Keres rolled her eyes in silent amusement.

Pheidippides nodded humbly and rose on unsteady legs. But he kept his head bowed, reluctant yet to meet the Elysian god's eyes.

"Oh, for the love of all that is truly worthy of respect, do *not* avert the eyes from any who dwell here in Elysia, as though you were some pathetic Persian underling kneeling before loathsome Darius!" snapped Keres. Her golden eyes flared with annoyance.

Pheidippides wriggled in embarrassment at the unexpected rebuke. "I…uh, yes," he stammered. "Forgive me, please. I did not—"

"Enough, Athenian," she said quietly. "Enough." Keres settled back smoothly into her flowery throne again, eying the scene before her with an air of impatience.

Pan shot her the kind of look a father might turn on a sassy daughter, then regarded Pheidippides once more. "Now, good Pheidippides, you must realize that abandoning your quest to save Athens may very well doom that fair city and—"

"But do keep in mind, brave courier, that Athens is also capable of surviving without your…heroics," broke in Keres. "That mighty army you left behind marches for the city even now, and…"

Her words trailed off as Pan produced, with a casual wave of one hand, a foggy portal that materialized before them, so that everyone standing in the glade could see within it a swirling mass of figures taking shape. They formed into a smoldering image of the Greek army marching briskly toward the very Pallini Hills that Pheidippides himself had crossed over some time ago.

"They, eh, do not appear en route in time to arrive before the Persian fleet—which in all likelihood did catch a fair wind in setting forth from the Bay of Marathon," said Pan. The smirk on the Elysian lord's face was unmistakable, and Keres scowled defiantly.

Pheidippides, however, was mesmerized by the vivid image of the Athenian army and the men with whom he had fought side by side earlier that day. He squinted, sure that he caught a glimpse of the noble General Milteades leading and hastening everyone onward. And, for a fleeting moment, the young courier was sure he also saw his father, Captain Boros, and—

The globular window into the earthly realm roiled abruptly and reformed itself. Pheidippides blinked and shook his head, then turned to face the two Elysian lords. He noticed Keres flaunting a smile of satisfaction as, with a simple pass of her hands, she muddled the image of the army Pan had produced, invoking one of her own design instead. The boy took a fearful step back as two husky figures on horseback appeared.

"But *others* also await your return to the Realm of Earth…brave courier," she quipped.

And indeed, there was the stark sight of Jamjon and Rojese, mounted and scouring the narrow woodland path in search of their suddenly missing prey. Pheidippides trembled and stepped back again, raising his arms in a motion of warding off an attack, as though the two riders might spot him through the portal's haze and urge their mounts through it and right at him.

Seeing the brewing panic in the lad, Pan waved both of his cloven-shaped hands in one swift pass and dispelled the image of the two assassins. Pheidippides shook his head, unable to hold pace with all this magical shifting in imagery created by the two Elysians. He lowered his arms in relief that this menacing one had at least been dismissed.

Another took its place: this time, the glossy portal showed the Persian fleet under a solid wind and sailing swiftly toward Athens. The smirk of satisfaction on the face of the horned god made it clear whose work was reflected in this latest image. Pheidippides stared in dismay. "By all gods, dear Athens may yet fall!"

Keres frowned in anger and leaned in close to one of Pan's narrow-tipped ears: "Might I be permitted to tempt *alone* as we agreed?" she fairly hissed.

The proud Lord of Elysia recoiled meekly under her rebuke. He turned to Pheidippides, an air of imposed humility in his tone. "Eh…good Pheidippides, it is your own choice, of course, whether you remain here in fair Elysia or return to your mission on behalf of Athens. But, as time here is but a blink of an eye in the realm of Earth, do give my sweet Keres a bit more of it, if you will." A mischievous smile curled over Pan's face. "It, eh, appears she has…taken to you."

Pheidippides' eyes widened in surprise, feeling greatly flattered. Unseen by him, the saucy nymph queen sidled up closer to Pan and delivered a sharp elbow to his ribs, eliciting a muffled grunt from the Lord of Elysia. He smiled somewhat crookedly in an attempt to make light of her well-placed jab to a tender spot. With an attempt at mock gallantry, Pan bowed in a grand manner and vanished with a breezy puff.

Keres waited a moment more, her bright golden eyes darting about—assuring herself he was not still lurking nearby and ready to interrupt again. Satisfied that she and the Athenian courier were indeed alone now, she took the boy by the wrist and guided him effortlessly up into the soft Elysian air. Pheidippides marveled at finding himself floating suddenly alongside the beautiful dryad queen over a grove of bountiful trees...until finally they alighted near a dust gray little cove, banked by a light blue pool.

An overhang of dreamy willows drooped over the stony curl of rock that seemed carved out deliberately for comfortable seating, while the pool beneath them absorbed the sparkling rush of silver-and-blue foam that rained down from a glistening little waterfall overhead. Keres faced him, her features smooth and perfect in the comforting light of a sun far more temperate than the blaze that had tormented him earlier. How had he come to suddenly be in the presence of this bronze-skinned goddess...and by what right had he been granted salvation here in fair Elysia?

"You know, Pheidippides," she said with a deliberate innocence in her tone, "your gallant run to save Athens does threaten your well-being—your very life, for that matter. Your weary body strains beyond its limits."

Pheidippides trembled involuntarily, a knot tying inside his stomach. His mouth moved as if to reply but did not utter a sound. The Elysian goddess tilted her head, the shoulder-length golden hair flipping to one side with the motion. "And such efforts—though noble indeed—might prove the death of you," she added firmly. She peered deep into his eyes as though probing his thoughts. A long moment passed between them.

"But...is it not the way of a true Greek to die for his state?" he asked, unsure of his own belief.

The response contained in the cool fire of her gaze, so penetrating and calm, gave him cause to shiver inwardly. She edged closer to him, each melodious word reflected by the sensuality of her body's sleek movements. Pheidippides found her hypnotic, alluring...

"Oh, but it is indeed the way of a 'true Greek,' " she retorted with unmistakable disdain. "And it seems you are indeed set on dying for this noble state that has treated *you* so nobly."

"But Athens is my home," he protested meekly, not wanting to draw the ire of this godly creature. "And...and what of my mother? I must see my quest to its end."

"And surrender what Pan offers you here?" she coaxed.

From behind a bush of bright lavender lilacs, a feminine face of vixen charm popped forth, wearing a wisp of a smile as it said, "Would your soul not be more comforted to rest here in peaceful Elysia?"

Pheidippides turned in response to the chirping voice, still awed to be in the presence of mythical Elysian dryads.

"What matter the fate of Athens?" insisted another of the dryads from her perch inside the lilacs.

"Do you wish instead the fate of Zagorus?" asked another dryad from behind a cypress tree.

Pheidippides started at mention of Zagorus. He turned to Keres, who shrugged coyly in response.

"A feebleminded man with visions of strange

woodland gods…and now deemed mad? Mmm?" the nymph in the lilac bush piped.

"So noble, those fair Athenians," the nymph behind the cypress quipped.

Keres smirked in approval of her two dryads, then dismissed them with a wave of one hand. She placed an arm around the young courier's shoulder, her voice more seductive. "Oh, and we did offer dear Zagorus the very same as he ran back from Sparta," she cooed softly. "But he, too, chose to run on to Athens instead…where they might have gained my Lord Pan's aid had they honored him with a temple—as they have always done for their favored Olympus gods."

Pheidippides dropped his eyes, recalling all too well that moment when Zagorus had returned. Keres reached down and placed a hand under his chin, easing his head back up so their eyes met once more. "Zagorus did speak to them of the Elysian Fields, did he not?"

Pheidippides nodded a shameful yes in response.

"Stay here with us, dear courier," she implored. "Your mother is of such a heart, she too would be welcome here…"

The boy pursed his lips, confusion reigning on his face. "Queen Keres, how is it that *I* should know such eternal joys? The stoics of Athens have always said the Elysian Fields is a place only for those most favored…"

"Mmm…Your stoics say a lot, don't they," she mused, her golden brows knitting with a hint of agitation. "Well, Lord Pan has *different* feelings on who should be favored."

"Perhaps you do not understand, good Queen, because you are an immortal Elysian and I am—"

"It is *you* who does not understand, wretched

Athenian!" she hissed abruptly, her friendly eyes changing to a fiery red—the fair sunlight of the beautiful grove faded in a flash, and even the pale blue waters darkened.

Pheidippides shrank back from her unexpected rebuke. She did not relent. "Listen well as Keres the immortal Elysian tells you the story of a young girl born to a Spartan woman…and a man of the lowly Helot tribes!" she said, hovering over him like a flushed bird of prey. "Have your learned stoics spoken to you of the poor Helot people the Spartans conquered and enslaved long ago?"

Pheidippides nodded solemnly. "I listened in once when Stoic Rolios spoke to a group of his students of how the people known as Helots were treated most cruelly by the Spartans," he said, trying to measure his words carefully. "The stoic said they did so to remind all Helots they were nothing more than slaves to Sparta. And these slaves were sometimes made to understand it by having to crawl on all fours like beasts of burden and…and that they were even used as—"

"—*living targets* for young Spartan boys of the war training schools, the *Agog*, to practice on while learning the arts of battle," she said coldly.

Yes, he knew this too and had often wondered if these were all merely queer tales told by those who were known to twist stories trying to make others believe them, or if Athenian adults told younger people such things to frighten them into fearing and loathing rival Sparta all the more. But he dared not say such a thing now, or even think it here in the presence of this Elysian goddess who had spoken of it with such passion. So Pheidippides nodded, acknowledging having heard such tales.

Keres eyed him wryly, as though questioning whether he was being truthful or just placating her. She paused, and finally sat down next to him again, both hands gripping the boy gently by the shoulders and turning him so he stared straight into her piercing amber eyes. "What would you say, dear Pheidippides, of a Spartan woman who foolishly fell in love with a Helot man and then died giving birth to his daughter? What of that young girl…knowing her own father had been executed because his love caused the death of a Spartan woman!"

A cold hand squeezed the young courier's heart. He wanted her to stop, but dared not even speak, so fierce was her fervor.

"And do you want to know the means of his execution?" A sardonic little smile formed on her otherwise perfect lips. "Why, this foolish Helot man who'd dared share a bed with a true Spartan woman was forced into service as a human shield in battle. Thus was his death deemed a service to any Spartan warriors his body shielded from harm—an exchange for the Spartan woman he 'slew.' "

Pheidippides felt sick. He wanted to retch at the thought of such cruelty. These same Spartan cousins who had told Zagorus they *might* come aid Athens once due homage to their religious rites had been met. He drew a long breath and finally put forth the question burning in his mind and in his heart.

"What of their child?"

Keres released her grip on his thin shoulders and seemed to struggle with her own emotions. "Oh, come now, loyal courier of Athens," she said with quiet cynicism. "It should be of no surprise the fate of that child—the spawn of a Spartan lady so derelict of her people's ways to have had union with one seen as barely more than a beast crawling on all fours? Why, once the infant girl was able to walk on her own and fend for herself, she was 'trained for battle'...as any who bore Helot blood would be."

Her entire frame trembled now, as if gripped in seizure. And for a brief instant, there was no sign at all of an Elysian immortal, only a bewildered and lost young girl. "That girl was made to serve the 'pleasures' of Spartan warriors...and then served in the same way as did her Helot father."

Keres paused, shutting her eyes briefly before she said, "Come down now to the pool...where we might see it all."

With an uncomfortable reluctance, he followed her down a mossy bank to a small cluster of odd-shaped boulders that seemed magically to shift into shapes that suggested seating. Keres gestured Pheidippides to settle back amongst the boulders, which appeared to shift once more, as though accommodating him for comfort and fit. An arched waterfall, not fully visible from where they had been perched earlier, now presented itself in all its translucent silvers and blues. The dryad queen gestured toward the smoothly pouring falls that fairly whispered rather than roared. Within the shimmering curtain of rolling water, abstract shapes took on momentary tangible forms, then broke up again only to reform, once more, into a swirl of new figures set against other backdrops. "Now, dear courier, behold *this* shell of what once was," Keres proclaimed with cynical melody, "and speak never again to me of 'service to a blessed city!' "

The images within the archway of falling water slowly reflected a steadier flowing, more corporeal array of figures and physical structures. Pheidippides gasped as he watched in astonishment, a column of marching hoplites—Spartan, based on their red battle garb and stern regimentation—while out in front, a far less regimented group, scantily armored and wielding weapons of poor craft, stumbled along under the prodding of the hoplites. These could only be the onetime tribal Helots, conquered and suppressed long ago by their Spartan masters and now pressed into a denigrating service—both socially and militarily—to Greece's most militant state.

Their service here as human shields was clear.

And there he saw, within the archway images, bunched among the plodding gaggle of dispirited Helots…a young teenage version of…*Keres*.

Pheidippides swallowed hard, a ball of choking air coursing down his throat. Unable to speak right away, he steadied himself with one hand, resting it on an adjacent rock, and rose shakily to his feet. He slipped his other hand onto Keres' arm, hoping to offer comfort…and apology. "Queen Keres, I am sorry. I…did not know."

The Elysian queen merely stared straight ahead at the ethereal image she had resurrected that now appeared so vivid. Pheidippides thought he perceived, on her part, an attempt to control an urge to cry. "It no longer matters," she said softly and with effort. "It is all long past."

She started to turn back to face him, then halted, eying the image that still lingered inside the mysterious waterfall. "My dear Lord Pan often chides me for remembering too clearly," she added, her golden eyes no longer aglow but faded now, less piercing.

Pheidippides trembled at the depth of her sorrow and, before he might rein in his own abrupt urge, he tugged gently on her shoulder in an attempt to turn her gaze so she faced him. His heart skipped a pair of beats as, slowly, they stared at one another a long moment.

"I see now, Queen Keres, that our stoics understand nothing of immortals."

Keres regarded him with an air of silent surprise. She smiled softly. Then, on seeming impulse, she lifted his hand to her lips and kissed it gently, then let it slide back down to his side. They continued staring at one another.

"How did you come to be…?"

"An Elysian?" she said almost matter-of-factly. "I wish the tale were a prettier one."

"Would you…share it with me?" he asked ever so delicately, mindful of her volatile nature. Her former life as a dweller of the Peloponnesian territories was stained enough with tragedy as it was. His request that she relive any more of it might well provoke another outburst.

The Elysian maiden's eyes swirled like a pair of small suns, and Pheidippides braced himself for the anticipated rebuke. But none came. Instead, she raised a hand to his face and ran her fingers gently over one cheek. Keres shut her eyes and nodded. Pheidippides breathed a sigh of relief as she slid her fingers away, turned, and with both hands made open-palmed passes that caused the images within the waterfall to become mottled again…until clear shapes formed once more.

From above the tiny waterfall gully, Pan materialized within the boughs of swooping willows that overlooked the mystic falls and the stony shore, where Keres stood next to Pheidippides, raising image after image of her past. The Elysian god folded his furry arms, watching with a growing interest.

The Athenian courier stared fixedly into the watery screen as he now beheld moving picture images of weaponless Helots huddled round nightly campfires where armed Spartan hoplites were also gathered. "We need only go back to when another Athenian dictator, after Hippias, sought to regain his hold on the city that had ousted him," Keres said solemnly. "Only this one sought the aid of Athens' rival city, Sparta—knowing a debt would be owed to the Spartans for helping him." She gestured with one arm at the image in the falls: "Like King Darius, this sly Athenian did not care for the rising new 'Rule of the People'—the democratia. All tyrants despise it. And this one, like Hippias before him, was also willing to betray his home city for his own ends."

She pointed at the misty images inside the falling curtain of water, which now showed a bearded, short rotund man, middle-aged, and garbed in the green-and-white robes of the Athenian Elite. He stood in an austere hall of gray-and-white columns and stairs and was speaking with several men of obvious important bearing. "Sparta, of course, was oh-so-eager to see Athens return to its days of single rulers. How well it would serve the purpose of a state that had always believed in the rule of kings," she added coldly, her features again darkening to a stormy gray. One more image of the Spartan Council meeting showed the portly Athenian dictator embracing both Spartan kings.

The image inside the falls crumbled once again into a pouring rain of glittering liquid, then formed into yet another mosaic of human figures and rolling, twisting shapes. This time the foggy images took on the shape of a Spartan war encampment with Helot slaves hustling about, waiting hand and foot on the hoplites who were gathered round fires in the wooded glades. Men were seated on rocks and sharpening their swords, while their shining armor and blood-red cloaks and red-plumed helmets lay nearby. Many were bedding down for the night.

Among the Helots hustling about the nightly encampment—all of them dressed in simple muslin tunics and sandals—was the young teen version of Keres, less the splendor and enchantment of her Elysian self, yet a budding beauty harboring an inner dignity even in so undignified a state.

From above, as the roiling, living picture inside the pouring falls altered and shifted...Lord Pan also watched, a tear seeping from one eye. He wiped it away with a cloven hand and continued watching solemnly.

Pheidippides, meanwhile, was still utterly mesmerized as shapes continued whirling within the foggy mass that reformed once again—this time showing the younger Keres with a gleaming dagger concealed inside her white sleeveless chiton as she sneaked out from the Spartan camp under the cover of the night and the trees. Pheidippides sat up straight as he watched incredulously.

Squeezed in close to the young foot courier, Keres caught his sharp reaction and turned to him as the grim saga taking place within the haze of the waterfall continued to play out. "You see, I thought it *wrong* that Athenian traitors should use Spartans and Helots to go off and slay innocent people," she said, choking back an uncontrollable sob. "I only wanted to warn Athens so her army would be ready enough to discourage the attack!"

Keres wrung her head sorrowfully as the next image revealed her younger self confronted by Athenian guards outside the city walls as she pleaded with them. The Elysian queen's tone of sorrow changed abruptly to one of bitter frost: "Oh, and 'sweet Athens' was most grateful for my warning."

Pheidippides watched in dark dismay as the very next image showed the young Helot Keres being seized roughly by the Athenian guards.

"So grateful, they decided it best that they hold me there and deal with me later," she said hollowly. The image changed once again, showing her with a single Athenian guard looking her over amorously—then attacking her sexually.

Pheidippides gaped. Were these truly Athenian men behaving thus?

The image shifted once more, and he was snapped from his dark reverie by a sardonic laugh from Keres. "Oh, but Sparta trains its women—even its lowly Helots," she said coolly. For there now stood the young Helot Keres, brandishing a dagger that had been concealed inside her chiton, as she loomed triumphantly over her attacker, who lay dead on the ground.

Pheidippides stared wide-eyed at the Elysian standing next to him; but she barely noticed. Keres' eyes were fixed firmly on the next image materializing within the watery curtain. "Do you want to know how foolish I was then?" she said darkly. Her face tightened and her lips pursed with pain as she gestured him to pay heed to the phantom drama that churned on relentlessly.

Still perched above them in the boughs of the willow, Pan shook his head sadly, tears spilling freely now down both sides of his coarse face. He knew the tale well, and it pained him to see his beloved young nymph reliving it.

"Instead of running away, as I should have, I stole my way back to the Spartan camp, thinking I would tell them how I had 'gone off to spy' and learned that Athens knew of our planned attack."

Pheidippides turned to her, puzzled.

"I hoped if the Spartans knew their plans for a secret ambush were already known to the Athenians, then they might not go through with the attack. But I was too late."

The misty figures inside the falls this time showed the Spartans and the Athenian traitors slipping like woodland ghosts through the trees and toward the city walls of Athens. And, as the young Helot Keres had feared, the attack indeed took place—only more brutally than she had ever feared, for the Athenians were primed and readied due to her earlier warnings.

The Elysian queen trembled as she relived the gruesome outcome. "I just wanted to stop them all from killing each other...but all I did was make it worse for everyone!" As she hung her head and turned her eyes from the ghostly past scene, Keres dropped suddenly to one knee and sobbed, more overwrought by the past than she had expected. Pheidippides made to comfort her, but she shook her head at him, the golden locks brushing over her face and obscuring it. She recomposed herself and rose again, pointing to the falls where the sight of the Spartans and the Athenian traitors being repelled and killed by the city's militia played out.

"And oh, did I pay dearly for my own noble efforts to have them avoid such bloodshed," she said glumly, hanging her head. The sorrow in her tone yielded to her cold cynicism of earlier.

Now it was Pheidippides' turn to slink down onto the rocky ground as he beheld the disturbing image of the younger Keres being pursued by a party of Spartans and Athenian renegades. He choked back a cry as he watched the ephemeral figures inside the curtain of water changing once more. One of the hoplites pursuing the fleeing girl was hurling a spear that pierced her in the shoulder blade and cut deep into her flesh. Her soundless cry of agony may just as well have been audible as Pheidippides watched in horror, his own face pain-wracked in seeing the teenage Keres falling to all fours and crawling desperately into the shelter of a rocky alcove.

Above, in the leafy boughs of the overhanging willow, Pan turned his head, unable to watch any further a memory he knew that neither he nor his young queen would ever forget.

"They never found me where I lay bleeding to death." Her voice drifted up to Pan as the image of her bleeding younger self, crammed between two lumpy boulders, was too much for him to watch. He did not care to see Keres reliving the trauma of booted feet stomping by her hideaway, swords and spears scraping the hard ground within mere steps of where she crouched—the memory of it even now bringing quiet whimpers from the Elysian queen…and gasps from the young courier clutching her in angst. Perched above them, the Lord of Elysia wished dearly that he had foregone what he had merely intended as playful eavesdropping.

"My Lady Keres," Pheidippides finally eked out, "how did you—"

"Oh, foolish Athenian," she said sternly as she rose and shrugged him off. "Why must you learn so harshly this day!" Pheidippides stepped back under her rebuke, and Keres saw instantly the impact of her words. Her tone softened. She reached a hand over and touched him gently on the arm. "I do not mean it in so bitter a way, oh, courier. But you see, my enemies—both Spartan and Athenian—who I'd failed to save from themselves, never discovered where I hid from them." She grimaced and drew a long breath. "But someone else did."

Pheidippides swallowed hard, and his eyes widened as large as walnuts in watching yet another chilling scene emerge inside the glossy Elysian falls: this time a black-clad warrior, close-helmed and on horseback, materialized within a ghostly portal…mere feet from the mortally wounded girl. The figure extended a gauntleted hand toward her…

"For it was there, in the hills where I lay dying from that spear wound, did Charon of Erebus, Lord of the Eternal Dark, come for me."

Pheidippides felt his bones rattle inside him. If he had wanted to speak, his lips would have failed to move, let alone utter a sound. The spectre of Charon reaching forth to grip the young Keres and haul her out from the rocky cleft seemed all-powerful…until another figure burst through the very air! It was tall and bestial-looking, with sharp, curled horns upon its head...lowered in battle gesture. Its gray eyes flared with a godly fire as it glared reproachfully at the gruesome underworld lord.

"It was my Lord Pan who appeared and warned Charon that the Pure of Heart were not for him."

The spectre of Charon vanished in the face of the Elysian god's wrath, and the images inside the falls also dissolved...the last one showing Pan scooping up the dying teenager and bearing her off. Keres turned to face Pheidippides again, once more her usual saucy self. "And now I am no longer a foolish Helot-Spartan mortal doomed to serve those who thought they were my betters."

High in the branches, Pan beamed down solemnly, proudly at his beautiful young queen. The Elysian lord nodded to himself, a smile on his wooly face, then vanished from the tree.

Pheidippides wanted to rise and face Keres, but could not. He managed himself onto a single knee and remained that way, head bowed to her in reverence. "By all Olympus, Queen Keres—"

"No!" she snapped reproachfully, the golden-hued eyes once more ablaze, only this time with unmistakable resentment. "Your petty Olympus gods had *nothing* to do with it!" She gazed about the mystical realm in which they basked, safe from all harm...and from her grim ordeals of the past. "'Tis the kind and generous Lord Pan who aids those who are lost...those in need of a god they can believe in! Olympus favors only those who pay earthly homage to them. We of Elysia understand what it is to be outcast…to be ostraka."

Her words struck deep into the breast of the perioki lower-caste Athenian lad, who had never in his life known the praise or respect of those deemed his betters.

"And those who turn to Lord Pan of these Elysian Fields need not grovel for his help," she added, "the way Zeus and his fellow Olympians demand of them."

Pheidippides kept his head bowed, ashamed that it was he who had provoked this outburst. But Keres composed herself again, as though remembering now the very Elysian realm that had transformed her into a splendid, lustrous queen—no longer a badly treated Helot girl. She reached a hand down tenderly to the kneeling lad and slipped it gently under his chin, urging him to meet her eyes. With her other hand she gestured him to rise.

"Why run back to that other world and all its sorrow, Pheidippides?" she cooed. Before he could answer, she caressed him lightly round the shoulders…and kissed him on the lips. Soft little waves rolled inside his chest during the next few beats of his heart. She drew him in closer. "Your heart is Elysian," she said. "It belongs here where the cruelties of that earthly realm may not follow." She kissed him tenderly once more.

Pheidippides shut his eyes solemnly and summoned his will to its fullest.

"I cannot, Queen Keres."

She regarded him incredulously.

"I am yet an Athenian, and all the promise of what our city might become is why I must run on." He tried wrenching his eyes away from hers, but knew he could not. He was lost in her golden gaze, so he spoke his truth as best he could muster: "It is true that those such as my mother and I—and those ostraka who befriended me with kindness—are not among the favored in Athens; but perhaps one day that fair city may grow into a better world, such as this one: a world unlike Sparta and so many others...a world where dread empires ruled by cruel lords like Darius will not make miserable the lives of people who are born with less. It is why one such as I must struggle in that hope...not just for myself."

Keres could not believe what she was hearing from this awkward young courier committed to his own doom.

"Call me a fool, but I cannot stay here. I am still an Athenian and must see my quest to its end or die trying. Else my soul shall live on in eternal shame—even here in fair Elysia."

She shook her head, wondering if he had truly comprehended all she had shown him of her own tragic past. Keres sighed deeply. "Very well," she said curtly. "Go...run on. Serve those who serve only themselves!" And with a few intricate passes of her beautiful supple arms, the entire world of the Elysian Fields began to dissipate. Pheidippides' eyes darted side to side and up and down as he beheld the impossible happening once more in the form of a world gone suddenly ephemeral. He made one last appeal to the now phantom and rapidly disappearing image of Queen Keres.

"I am sorry...but upon my word, if I succeed, I will beg that Athens build the grandest of temples to Lord Pan!" He was still talking to her as the Pallini woodland hills again surrounded him. "Truly I will," he gasped, his throat parched once more.

It took a fluttering few moments more before Pheidippides fully realized he was no longer in the dazzling realm of the legendary Elysian Fields or in the presence of Queen Keres, but once again on a narrow woodland path, suffering heat exhaustion, fatigue, and pursuit by dread Persian assassins. Pain wracked his entire body once more, and sweat rolled down from his head and shoulders in great round beads. He gazed around in disbelief, then crouched over as one side of his abdomen muscles ripped with a vicious side stitch.

"Oh, wretched gods...all an illusion!" he cried, oblivious to the danger that cry could bring him.

For, lurking farther back on the path, Jamjon and Rojese had joined up again and both heard the boy's cry. "What creature makes such a sound, Jamjon?" said the bearded Macedonian. "Might our courier have met with—"

"Perhaps," said Jamjon. "This wood is as queer a one as any I've seen." They mounted and galloped off in the direction of the piercing cry.

Farther up on that very trail, Pheidippides forced his failing body onward. "Oh, dear Athens, have I not served you well enough by now? And why do the gods all tease me with such tempting visions of eternal comfort and peace?" He tried urging his aching legs on faster, but the incessant throbbing of his muscles caused him to stagger and collapse. One sandaled foot caught on a gnarly root that seemed to have wriggled up from the ground itself and snagged his ankle with sentient deliberation. He lurched forward, and his weary arms reached down to break his fall.

Pheidippides splattered down face first onto the steaming woodland turf that was hot and moist despite the shade of the trees overhead. With temperatures in the afternoon glare a good hundred degrees, and humidity just as high, there was no escaping the omnipresent sapping of his energy and strength. The ground greeted him savagely and the boy felt the wind being knocked out of his lungs by the unyielding turf. He fought to breathe as he coughed, the heaving of his own diaphragm increasing the pain in his battered chest. Pheidippides pounded the ground with one fist, dismayed and disgusted with his own weakened state.

'Noble courier' indeed, he thought to himself. How foolish of his father to have put such faith and hope in one so frail as himself to carry the fate of Athens. To have run more than six leagues—nearly twenty miles—only to endure the hallucinations of a madman, then to see failure of both muscle and bone in trying to withstand the rigors only the true hemeredrome were capable of undergoing... No, thought Pheidippides. He was indeed as his own father had told his mother that day when he had overheard them talking: weak... incapable.

A horse neighed from somewhere on the path behind him, reminding him of the grim reality that he was indeed in the Earthly Realm again, where no illusion of mythical Elysian gods would save him. Pheidippides forced himself up painfully onto both knees, his eyes darting about for some place—any place—he might find refuge on either side of the trail.

The sound of galloping hooves increased. Panic seized the boy. He squirmed and wriggled toward the trailside brush, scraping his stomach and legs on the stony turf that was riddled with gnarly roots. The hoof beats seemed nearly upon him as he worked his elbows through the weedy overgrowth and toward the bole of a thin fir, knowing already it did not have the mass to effectively conceal him. He groaned inwardly and could not contain a burning urge to risk a single glance back in the direction of the approaching riders.

And there they were—not thirty feet away. Pheidippides could not tell if they had spotted him or not, but in that brief instant he knew there was no mistaking these were the two who had been after him while outside the strange woodland. Still crawling, he used both elbows and forearms to fairly launch himself off the trail entirely and into a skimpy thicket that promised only scant cover.

A shout from out on the trail gave cause to dread the worst, knowing he had not eluded them.

"There!" rasped Rojese, pointing a thick finger toward the spot where the boy had wriggled off the path.

"I saw," said Jamjon. The two exchanged a nod of agreement, accentuated by a grin on the Macedonian's face. They urged their steeds into a more earnest gallop, the bizarre pursuit about to end. What tales they would tell afterward upon rendezvousing with the warships awaiting them at one of the southern coastal inlets of the Hellespont! Then, finally off to Athens itself...

They would have to hasten, as riding down this particular courier had proven more troublesome already than either assassin had imagined. Though the wretch had squirmed off into the thick of the trees and brush, he would not scurry far, given the absence of any visible paths. They had him now.

****

From another woodland—one more temperate and

bright with flowery splendor—the pair of Elysians with whom young Pheidippides had earlier shared audience peered through a glossy portal, watching the boy's predicament. Both observed the skimpy amount of leafy cover along the slim path where he had ducked away in a futile attempt to conceal himself. Fallen limbs from the thin fir trees and bits of juniper shrubs would not suffice in hiding him; nor did he dare rise and try making a dash farther into the woods. The snarl of thorny stems poking out inside the bushy thickets there would slow his progress and announce his presence with each crackle and snap brought on by his flight. There was no hope of escape for the young courier, and he knew it.

So did the two Elysian lords observing his plight.

****

The horsemen thundered down onto the very spot where their quarry had slipped off the trail. They dismounted, drawing their weapons, victory at hand now.

Barely ten feet away, Pheidippides flattened himself to the hot turf, pebbly and moist as it was. His eyes were fixed on what seemed a pair of armored behemoths advancing on his flimsy hideaway. He would surely be spotted in the next instant. Flight would prove absolutely futile; he could barely rise, let alone run, at this point. They would seize him and likely slay him for good measure.

His mind drifted suddenly back to the battlefield earlier in the day—which now seemed the distant past—to when he and his brave Plataian comrade had engaged the great Persian warrior. Would that his friend Kretus were here with him now, he thought. But Kretus had been slain, while he, Pheidippides, had lived and...

His right hand slid suddenly to the sash wrapped round his waist, and he gripped the dagger sheathed there. If he was to die here in this spot, then it would not be without a fight, he vowed to himself. Pheidippides waited, poised—but no attack came.

Jamjon and Rojese both stared, mystified by the heavy foliage and overgrowth of brush that had greeted them no sooner than they had dismounted and sought to forge their way inside the thicket. What they beheld, though, was an impenetrable tangle of briars that only small rodents might have penetrated. Where had that stumbling, fatigued lad gone? Certainly not here...for there was no sign of man or beast having wrangled a way into this twisted crunch of wild growth.

"Perhaps 'twas farther up," Rojese growled, frustrated.

"Or perhaps..." said Jamjon, his handsome ebon features clouded with an air of contemplation. His deep brown eyes roamed, then stared fixedly into the thick of the overgrowth. He shook his head, suspicion creeping over his face now.

"Come, my friend, we are mistaken here," Rojese urged. He beckoned they should mount and try farther up the trail. Jamjon hesitated, his eyes still roving the area. His gaze halted not more than five feet from where Pheidippides still lay flattened to the turf, one hand on the dagger handle and trying not to breathe while wondering why neither assassin appeared to see him.

The Nubian nodded, disquieted by this dilemma. He finally turned and followed after his comrade.

****

Not until the Persian henchmen had mounted and ridden down the trail—far enough so the pathside thicket was well behind them—did the snarl of bushes, low-hanging branches and unnaturally thick leaves shimmer and systematically vanish. Only then, from the other side of the murky portal—a realm apart from where young Pheidippides still lay hidden—did Pan turn to Keres and offer a matter-of-fact shrug of his furry shoulders in regard to the oddly shifting nature of the thicket. Queen Keres offered nothing more than a shrug of her own, while concealing a tiny smile of approval.

"The lad is deserving of *some* aid at least," the Lord of Elysia uttered wistfully.

His dryad queen nodded in silent agreement.

"Of course you realize there is no more we can do—now that he has left Elysia," said Pan.

"I know," Keres replied softly, shutting her eyes.

Pan put a hand to one of her sleek shoulders, curious of her subdued air. "What is it, dear Keres? Something troubles you?"

She stared soulfully at him, the golden-hued eyes again harboring the look of someone seeking answers of one older and more learned. "He goes on," she said with a slow shake of her head, "even though…"

"Yes…" Pan responded, inquisitive of her lead.

The dryad queen shut her eyes and shook her head again, dismissing the troublesome thought.

"A true Greek…eh?" Pan mused quietly. Keres eyed him sharply, then fell back into her own thoughts.

Chapter Forty-Three

Pride and Dissension in Athens

Kallimachos, High Archon of Athens, stood grandly at the dais atop the stone steps of the agora's Bouleuterion, where the bulk of those within the city walls had now gathered. He was flanked by his usual entourage of hoplite guards and other council dignitaries. The tall Athenian leader regarded the throng of citizens and noncitizens alike: men, women, youths, servants, slaves—even a few curious ostraka who had remained inside the city—had all gathered in the large public square. Kallimachos also knew that a number of political dissidents were present in this crowd too, ready to create discord that might severely disrupt the fabled city-state in its most vulnerable hour.

No word had yet come from Marathon, where the destiny of perhaps the entire Hellespont lands—of all Greece—had by now been determined. What indeed had transpired on those scorching plains in the morning hours? Did the Persians now march on the city...even as its proud people awaited word of their fate? Kallimachos knew well what would become of them if the hordes of Darius appeared on the horizon to strike down what little resistance Athens might hope to offer in a last-gasp defense. And he thought bitterly of their rival Spartan kin of the Peloponnese, who had not come to their aid.

So he had to hold the loyal people of his city together, sustain their hopes…whether they were recognized citizens or not. He had but a scant number of hoplites left behind for this last stand, should it come to that. If the people gathered here before him were to lose heart, they might easily fall prey to Hippias' fervent loyalists…men like the sniveling Hahnitos, whom the Archon knew had covertly been poisoning the minds of those Athenians most gullible and most fearful of Persian conquest.

"Even if Darius were not to march on Athens," Hahnitos had hissed from the shadows, "what of those Eretrians who sought to flee him by making their way here in such numbers? Why, the Persian King would then surely storm down through the Attica and punish us for giving asylum to conquered foes!"

That had filled many of them with fear. "And remember," Hahnitos had crowed even in public— where it was his democratic right to do so—"it was good Hippias who did send the Tribute of Water and Earth to King Darius that we, as a land, recognized Persia's Lord as the rightful ruler of Earth. And it was Kallimachos and his ilk who *violated* that pact by joining with our foolish Eretrian kin and sending aid to the Greek Ionians in their revolt against the Great King! That is why Persia destroyed Eretria and will do the same to us!" Hahnitos had squealed angrily to any Athenians who bothered listening to him.

The Archon was fully aware of the divide that especially faced Athenians here and now—and that men like Hahnitos who fawned over such tyrants to gain their favor lurked here within this very crowd. But on this same day, one had come forth with perhaps the answer to men who behaved in such ways.

Kallimachos turned his gaze toward a simply dressed woman, whose tender beauty radiated far beyond the peasant status suggested by her garb…a woman he himself might have yearned for as a companion had he met her under different circumstances. She stood between two hoplites, assigned now to guard her as they would a city dignitary. The Archon smiled as he held up the clay tablet she had presented him earlier.

"Fellow Athenians!" he called out, raising his free hand to the crowd. "In this time when our brothers fight to defend us at Marathon, and we wait here to learn our fate…I offer you words of hope written by one of our own warriors…a true *Marathonomachoi!*"

Symethra's eyes swelled with tears at the High Archon's words of honor and praise for her boy as a Marathon warrior. And if nothing else this day, her son's own heartfelt words would reach into the hearts and minds of the people living in the city he loved most dearly.

The Archon lowered the tablet, gripping it firmly in both hands. He exchanged one more glance with Symethra, smiling subtly at her, then read aloud to the gathering:

"To all of you who dwell here in our beloved Athens—whether you are deemed citizens or not—I have learned for myself this day how loyalty and love of one's home lies not in your position or in your wealth, but in your hearts! And may those who serve on our Prytany Council embrace these words written by one young Pheidippides Deglos, who is not among those recognized as an Athenian citizen, yet marched off bravely to help defend all he has expressed on this tablet!"

The Archon's deep-set eyes scanned the vast gathering, as though daring any dissenter to decry his proclamation, then began majestically to read: " 'My Athens, my home. She stands here before me, sparkling in the sun. Glorious city, place of my birth, still standing unharmed...' " The Archon paused, again peering out over a throng that had only moments earlier been grim and grumbling. Now the entire assembly area of the fabled agora had fallen into an eerie silence.

****

Pheidippides waited until the clop of horse hooves had faded away before daring to finally part the sparse overlay of leafy brambles which he simply could not believe had concealed his presence from the pair of Persian assassins. Surely they should have been able to detect the contours of his shape crouched there. But no. Just as he had thought he might have to make a futile attempt at fending them off with the dagger sheathed at his side, the two had given up searching and galloped off.

Or were they merely toying with him...feigning to have ridden off, but then backtracked on foot and now waited for him to emerge from the brush so they might seize him as a prize for Darius—or perhaps worse. The boy had heard gruesome tales of the way Persian enemies, whether living or dead, were displayed and humiliated as symbols of those conquered by the legions of His Imperial Lord. Pheidippides shivered at the thought of how brutally his own body might be mutilated and then savagely displayed by his captors.

Yet he could not remain here in this thicket, cowering like a worm fearful of squirming out from its cover for fear of discovery.

No.

His mind flashed back to that moment between the boulders when he was climbing the ever-rising Pallini Hills and had beheld the plucky gnat's escape from a seemingly overpowering spider web and the eight-legged monster the tiny insect had cheated of its prey. And with that thought, the fatigued young boy reached for the knife sheathed at his side, drew it forth, and all but sprang out from his brambly hideaway onto the narrow trail. He scrambled painfully onto his feet, forcing himself into as best a fighting stance as he could assume. Had either assassin been there in waiting, they might have laughed, so sad in martial appearance he was. But the weary young courier was quite alone on the slim woodland trail, his legs barely able to hold him up in all his delirium and thirst.

Pheidippides eyed the path ahead, glanced side to side, and finally craned his aching neck as he shot another glance behind him, seeing nothing there either. He gazed up the pathway that veered off to one side. He half expected to see a pair of mounted riders thundering down on him—or springing forth from the trailside trees. But no such attack happened. He breathed deeply, knowing—for at least that moment—a slice of relief.

Pheidippides urged his ailing legs into a stumbling forward motion that barely resembled a walk; he blinked, trying to rid his vision of the haze that now clouded the way before him. His throat was raw and wrung out like a dried rag, and he reached to the sash at his hip, tugging forth the leather waterskin. He paused in his painful progress and raised it to his lips, managing to squeeze out the last few scant drops. It only tantalized his thirst all the more. Pheidippides coughed bitterly, then crumpled the waterskin and tossed it aside. He forced himself another step forward, nearly toppling over…then blinked incredulously.

Another path—one that had not appeared visible to him an instant ago—now loomed to his left. How could it be? Or was this yet another illusion his overwrought mind suffered? After all, it was but a short time ago he had imagined himself to be in the legendary Elysian Fields. How long indeed had his mind roamed so recklessly while his nearly spent body had run on? Was this some other cruel illusion beckoning him and luring him into another dangerous dream state? Perhaps it was just his own tired mind tempting him to surrender his grueling trek to Athens.

Pheidippides resolved now to dismiss further acknowledgment of alternative paths that offered refuge from the Persian assassins who might well reappear again at any moment to seize him. But as he made to press onward and down the main path, he caught, from the corner of one eye, a flicker of red and green amongst the trees on the side path. He peered into the fissure that had seemingly opened within the cluster of trees. He could ill afford any more distractions or allow himself to be teased by more visions. But the trees along the trail seemed almost to beckon now, their branches as supple as arms, twigs like long fingers stretching deliberately in his direction, tips round and soft, like so many grapes.

Grapes.

Pheidippides blinked, then rubbed at his eyes,

wanting to be certain that what he saw along this spit of a path was no illusion—no cruel trick of the mind. For there, drooping down from a number of the branches were actual grapes: red ones, green ones, some a deep purple, and seemingly enough to constitute a vineyard! How could this be? Had he missed sighting them earlier? Perhaps the steaming fog that had gripped his mind earlier had prevented him from this blessed discovery?

Pheidippides righted himself and staggered his way inside the narrow archway of fruit trees. He reached eagerly for a batch of grapes he prayed was not a mirage. The soft cool feel of them in his hands certainly did not give reason for doubt, nor did the sugary taste on his tongue give cause for him to question his own senses. The cool juice from the grapes seeping down his parched throat fulfilled his ailing thirst, affording him clearer thought than he had known in some time. Again and again, Pheidippides reached into the low-hanging branches, plucking forth the succulent fruit—then took a moment to sit down against the bole of a thick cypress and bask in a brief respite of relief.

****

Pan stood by the grotto falls, arms folded across his chest as he eyed, with an air of feigned reproach, his dear Keres. The golden-haired beauty was unaware of his presence behind her, for she sat cross-legged on the rocky ledge, staring fixedly at the ephemeral images shifting constantly inside the watery mist. The current one now showed the young Greek foot courier rising from the turf inside the narrow grape grove and marshaling his newly recovered strength of body and spirit.

Absorbed in the drama being played out inside the misty curtain of rolling water, the dryad queen failed to sense her lord's presence.

"There can be no more than six miles left," both Elysians heard the boy utter resolutely as he rose to his feet. Keres clenched both fists in a gesture of support as she watched Pheidippides departing the tiny grove, his renewed determination evident in his stride. With a wave of her hands she dissolved the images within the falls and smiled to herself. But her smile faded, as abruptly as the images had faded, at the sound of a gravelly voice behind her.

"Did I not make it clear we can interfere no more?"

Keres shut her eyes in annoyance and pursed her lips. Whether it was what Pan had said or his undetected emergence behind her, she was displeased nonetheless. "It was only a small batch of grapes," she said with a dour innocence as she turned to face him. She did not bother to rise but held his seemingly stern gaze, failing to note the Elysian lord's attempt to suppress any trace of a smile.

"I seem to recall that particular vineyard growing *elsewhere* in these woods," Pan quipped.

Keres shrugged innocently and rose to her feet.

"Was it not you who wagered *against* the lad's run to Athens?" he added.

"And was it not Lord Pan of Elysia who once saved a young Spartan-Helot not far from this very wood?" she responded pointedly.

Pan cleared his throat. "Eh…there was no wager for precious nectar or ambrosia that day."

"There are things more precious," she said quietly.

"Oh, indeed?" said Pan.

Keres looked away stubbornly, unwilling to answer. In doing so, she failed to see the warm smile of undisguised pride that crossed his face.

Chapter Forty-Four

A Ghostly Chase

Rojese and Jamjon once again searched in vain for their remarkably elusive quarry, who apparently possessed some vast knowledge of woodland nooks and crannies...or did indeed benefit from supernatural means, for there had been no trace at all of this courier whose initial appearance had suggested one they should have ensnared immediately. Now even Rojese bore the look of a man concerned that forces unexplained might truly be present here...forces favoring the youth they pursued.

A glance over at Jamjon and a brief exchange with his Nubian comrade made it clear such notions were no longer to be flippantly dismissed, especially after the assault by the giant eagle that had burst out from the trees and startled them earlier. And the boy's vanishing made it all the more clear that relieving Lord Darius' dread of a messenger bearing word of their sneak assault had grown more urgent. Before them lay another pair of deer paths veering off from the banked one they had already searched with little sign anyone had passed recently.

"If our courier now hides along either of these trails, his progress to Athens will be greatly slowed," mused Jamjon.

"Even so, Darius demands a body be delivered, either living or dead," said Rojese.

"Aye," said Jamjon, indicating with a tilt of his head that he would explore the side trail to their left. Rojese nodded and urged his mount down the short bank to the right. Had either waited but a few more moments, they'd have heard the soft stomp of footsteps coming in their direction—those of a solitary runner barely able to hold himself upright.

****

Pheidippides slogged his way wearily again along the path, the heat and humidity of the over-one-hundred-degree afternoon sapping his strength and parching his throat again, his aching arms dangling at his sides instead of raised and pumping his upper body into a solid rhythm with his legs. The grapes had refreshed him while off on the mysterious side trail, but once out and back onto the main path, the strain of heat and exhaustion had soon returned. He no longer resembled the eager young lad who had departed the battlefield, filled with martial vigor from the army's victory and his father's encouraging words. Pheidippides now appeared more a singed zombie struggling through each painful stride. Thoughts of his pursuers faded from his tired mind like a fleeting dream, all caution slipping away…

He soon approached the same banked path the two assassins had passed over earlier, unaware they had already been there. It sloped down sharply on either side and he trudged over it, staggering by the very spot where Rojese and Jamjon had split up. He recognized the sharp dirt ridges where the Athenian army marched through a day earlier, and it lifted his spirits a little. Perhaps, he thought.

A dirty brown stream, still and uninviting, lay at the foot of the slope, leading off into some thin ash trees. The path atop the loose bank was choppy, and Pheidippides stumbled as he glanced down at the tiny stream, causing him to drop to one knee. Blood spurted from the wound as he staggered back to his feet.

"*And he can run, Boros,*" He heard in his head the voice of his mother...only now her tone was mocking.

"*Aye, he can run...as he did today when he chased the discus: much like a dog.*" He heard the answering voice of his father—the sound of it crueler than when a younger Pheidippides had actually heard those words come from Boros' mouth. He shook his head in feeble protest.

"*They called the broken pieces with the names on them...the ostraka!*" Garathi's voice mocked.

"No!" Pheidippides gasped, lurching to his right and again losing his footing. He tried avoiding the edge of the embankment, but his right foot caught just where the loose soil rolled downward. His arms flailed in a vain attempt to keep his balance, but to no avail. With half his body weight tottering on the brink of the embankment, the rest followed. Over he tumbled, down the mossy slope, and fell sprawling, face first, next to the strip of a stream where what little water it held was literally mud brown.

Pheidippides choked, his throat raw and hot, his chest, stomach, and knees bruised and bleeding. He lay there gasping, then suddenly recalled his pursuers and wondered how long it might be before they came galloping along the trail above him while he lay there in plain sight.

"What sort of courier do you see now, Father?" he muttered in quiet bitterness.

As though in response, a hoarse rasp beckoned him from across the spit of still brown water. Pheidippides peered up slowly and found himself staring straight into the sharp amber eyes of a small, fierce-looking wildcat. No more than twenty-five pounds and black-footed, the feisty little felines were not shy of taking on animals many times their own size, and did so often enough to assure their survival and ongoing presence in the hilly Attica woodlands. This one, a mix of gray-black, white, and brown, bore many scratches and bloodstains across its whiskered face, shoulders, and chest.

The cat crouched perhaps four feet from the prone young boy and was casually lapping up water from the muddy stream, though never letting its sallow gaze shift from the boy's widened eyes.

"And what is one of your ilk doing here, *human*?" the wildcat's primal stare seemed to say to the sprawled lad. "Are you so weak and weary you must die here—though water even such as this might revive you?" The scarred feline face all but taunted him. The cat lifted its chin from the stream and rasped again. "Come now, boy. Be strong and fight on, as those of us who dwell here have long done," the snarling voice inside the lad's head seemed to declare. The cat's eyes closed for an instant, then slowly opened back up, the shine of their yellowish hue warmer now: friendlier, more assuring. And then the wildcat turned and was gone.

Still resting while propped up on his bleeding elbows and knees, Pheidippides squinted and peered out at the thorny brush and tree trunks within his scope of vision. By now he no longer trusted his own senses and did not even try determining if his encounter with a wild forest cat had truly taken place. And he did not know whether it was shame or survival that drove him to his next action. Taking the cat's lead, he squirmed over to the edge of the dirty stream...and drank of the brown water. Incredibly, it coursed through him, not only quenching his thirst but filling him with renewed resolve. In a surge of energy he rose, first into a kneel, then to his feet, and he heard his father's words from the battlefield in his head once more: "*There is no Zagorus now, no Ginakos, no courier in sight whom I might choose instead.*"

Pheidippides paused, drew a breath, and threw back his head. "Let all the gods of Olympus turn their backs on me, if they so choose, and let all Elysians tempt me if they will! I run for my city!"

He turned his head back in the direction where the wildcat had disappeared, smiled triumphantly, then scrambled his way back up the muddy embankment and onto the narrow path again. Pheidippides stared ahead resolutely and resumed his run...unaware that his proud boast up to the heavens had also been heard by someone other than any gods who might be listening.

For, within the sliver of a side path he explored, Jamjon caught the lad's cry, harkened, and veered his horse back toward the main trail.

Knowing less than two leagues remained, Pheidippides ignored the heavy weight of his own legs and the grinding protest of his lungs as he pushed valiantly through the stifling heat. His thirst would rise again soon, and his muscles would again begin to throb and ache...but it was not so far now, not so hard. Perhaps the Persian riders had grown frustrated or even lost their way trying to find him. He ran on more forcibly than he should, not noticing that the sun now seemed dimmer in its glow, while the overhead canopy of trees was thinning. It grew foggy and gray. But how could that be? Still the fog thickened.

And Pheidippides sensed he no longer ran alone.

He bristled nervously and stared straight ahead. The woods seemed about to break into an open tundra...if he reached it. He gritted his teeth and churned ahead, feeling, incredibly, an abrupt chill falling over the narrow path with the foggy mist. His heartbeat increased, and his breathing fell into choking gasps. How long had he been running in this blistering heat and with so little water? Hours at least...and nearly four times as far as he had ever gone in his life!

The clammy chill that had draped over him so suddenly and seeped inside the pores of his skin confused and alarmed him. It felt alien...unnatural. Pheidippides heard what sounded like the faint beat of horse hooves off in the distance somewhere, but then lost all sense of it as a low *hiss* lashed out at him from close by. A snake perhaps...one of those venomous adders curled dangerously at his feet this very moment and readied to strike? Pheidippides risked a glance to his right...and choked back a cry that gurgled up from the pit of his stomach.

"Run with me...to Erebus!" a dark figure croaked.

Pheidippides' throat heaved, and a hoarse shriek belted out into the August air. He knew from old Athenian lore precisely who it was that had burst out of the fog at him and now accompanied him on his journey: the very decrepit creature that had plagued Zagorus—and the young Spartan-Helot Keres, too—

when both had skirted the slim borders of Death itself. Now Charon, Lord of the Eternal Dark, materializing here in yet another of his frightful incarnations, had come for *him*.

And from farther back on the trail, no more than fifty yards away, rode the source of horse hooves Pheidippides had heard only moments earlier. The stunned Nubian warrior stared, just as wide-eyed as the boy who was within mere feet of Lord Charon's deathly grasp.

"By Mithra...it is the Soul Thief!" Jamjon cried hoarsely, the horror contained in his tone so unnatural to him. Terror gripped the Nubian as no earthly entity might grip him. He reined in his huge black steed, the horse wanting no part of the ghastly creature ahead of them.

Pheidippides was unable to resist a glance into the dark folds of the spectre's hood, his eyes locking onto a pale gleam he caught in the cowl's recesses—and a bony face staring back out at him. He stumbled as Charon closed on him.

"Run, Pheidippides...for your life!" a feminine voice cried out defiantly.

Pheidippides knew the voice, recognized it as that of Queen Keres. He glanced round, not seeing her anywhere in the blackened fog—but seeing, from the corner of one eye, the grisly shape of Charon. He stared ahead again toward the end of the tunnel of trees, now a virtual gantlet of drooping black willows he would have to pass under. The thin branches dangled down over the path like gnarly fingers ready to snatch him up as he passed beneath them. But thirty yards more at the most and he would be out from the dread woodland—once again on the hot open plain, but safe at least from this unholy pursuit; safe in the light of day, where he sensed the Lord of Darkness chasing him could *not* follow.

"Run—for Athens!" the voice cried to him.

And then Pheidippides beheld a beautiful white gull soaring alongside him, keeping pace and urging him on with its graceful flight. Encouraged, he pushed ahead harder, his chest bursting as he shouted out in desperation, "Yes, for my city, my Athens…" And the words came to him again, the very words he had written: "…my home. She stands here before me, sparkling in the sun!"

Charon hissed as though slapped.

"Glorious city…" gasped Pheidippides, "place of my birth…still standing unharmed!"

Farther back on the trail, Jamjon steadied his great steed, watching in astonished awe the bizarre spectacle of the young foot courier being pursued by one of the most terrifying spiritual beings in the lore of his own people—and in the lore of so many others. The Nubian marveled at the boy's resolve to elude the dread Soul Thief. The lad's words—though foreign to Jamjon—drifted back through the steaming woodland air, one phrase at least recognized by the assassin:

"My Athens, my home!" the boy shouted out again as he ran on valiantly.

Jamjon shook his head in amazement, and a soft smile crossed his lips. He nodded as though already certain of the outcome, then turned his horse and cantered back in the opposite direction.

****

The crowd that had gathered at the Bouleuterion remained attentive as High Archon Kallimachos continued with his vivid public reading of Pheidippides' poem. Some held hands, while others wept openly, but a number of them—dissidents and lingering partisans of Hippias—glowered at the Archon's growing command of the people. Such words, though written by a mere lad, were dangerous, thought Hahnitos, the most prominent of all the dissidents present. The chubby partisan leader took note of how the Archon's impassioned delivery of this poem had even started to impact his own band of zealots, and a dark frown crossed his wrinkled brow.

"Her streets, her groves and vineyards, full of the sounds of the passions of life!" the Archon's strong, clear voice read proudly from the clay tablet. More of the crowd found themselves being caught up in this lyrical tribute to their home city—all of it written by a boy most of them had never even met. And so regally did it ring out through the voice of the respected High Archon that many nodded and smiled at the simple dignity of the words. So Kallimachos continued with his reading…and the angst that had previously filled the faces of a number of them earlier now faded.

Hahnitos glanced round the square, then up the great council steps where the Archon loomed majestically, appearing now as if some god out of the revered accounts written by Homer himself. How dare he stand there so, Hahnitos thought sourly, reading words written by a mere whelp who had likely already been slain at Marathon. Had Hippias been here at this moment—or had the Great King Darius suddenly come bursting through the city gates—how enraged they both would have been in hearing these lies, these deceitful promises of a glorious life in a state soon to be destroyed. Why, these very people here would be annihilated if they dared continue resisting inevitable conquest by the mighty Persian Empire. No, far better to survive and live as healthy vassals to someone more powerful than to be crushed by his fearsome legions.

Hahnitos could take no more. He hollered out from the shadows where he lurked, hunched down behind some other dissidents and unseen by the Archon or his hoplite guards. "Athens' streets, groves, and vineyards will not be here much longer if we try standing against King Darius! His mighty army comes to demand our surrender…and we'd best do so!"

The Archon halted in his recitation and gazed round sharply, seeking the source of the voice that had so brazenly interrupted him. But Hahnitos kept his portly body hidden from the scope of the Athenian leader's probing eyes. The other dissidents, however, knew from where and whom the dark words of protest had burst forth. The spell of the High Archon's poetic reading was broken and murmurs of malcontent rose abruptly like a dark tidal surge, rippling through the crowd of Hippias' supporters.

Discomfort spread instantly throughout the entire agora.

Made bolder by the angst he had stirred, Hahnitos pressed his advantage. Still concealed behind a veritable column of fellow dissidents, he cried out again in his grainy voice: "These streets will not be filled with the 'passion of life' but with the anguish of death!" The words were echoed by his band of cohorts, and now even by some in the crowd who, only moments earlier, had been enraptured by the Archon's moving oratory.

Atop the Bouleuterion stairs, some of the hoplite

guards took note of a sector near one of the colonnades and recognized it as the core area of the protest that was now sweeping the entire public gathering. One of the more prominent officers nudged others of his company and started in the direction of where the strongest negative chants filled the air—but was surprised to feel a hand grip his arm, discouraging the action. The guard was startled to see it was Archon Kallimachos who had stayed him and his men from taking action. The Athenian leader shook his head no, allowing a smile of reassurance to cross his lips.

He held up the clay tablet once more and proclaimed loudly the next words of Pheidippides' poem, his voice rising above the crowd's as an eagle's cry might rise over the din of a storm: "I can see her now in all her glory…Her graceful buildings rising so golden in the sun!"

The Archon's voice was strong, commanding… reassuring. Those in the crowd who had begun falling under the sway of the protesting dissidents fell silent and harkened, once more, to the Archon's recitation of the poignant verse.

Hahnitos scowled from behind the barrier of men that still shielded him from the Archon's view. He yelled out again cynically: "There will be no more Athens after—"

"Glorious city, place of my birth, will stand here tomorrow…unharmed!"

It was *not* the Archon who had cut off Hahnitos; rather, it was a pleasant feminine voice that had broken into the chubby cynic's rant. It was Symethra.

The entire gathering fell into a stunned silence. Kallimachos himself was caught off guard by the haetera woman's bold action in reciting so vivid a stanza written by her own son. He regarded her through his deepset eyes, then smiled and raised an arm in a gesture of salutation before turning back to the crowd and repeating the very same verse: "Glorious city...place of my birth...will stand here tomorrow unharmed!"

The crowd repeated after him, again...and again.

"My Athens, my home!" the Archon proclaimed once more, concluding the poem that everyone in the agora echoed...all but Hahnitos, who skulked off, a lone, defeated figure.

****

Pheidippides ran as the voice of Queen Keres had urged, straining with all that his muscles, legs, and lungs could muster—the soaring gull on one side of him, Charon the Lord of Erebus on the other.

"Run with *me*...to Erebus!" The crackling old voice ripped through the sweltering breeze at him, the smell of Charon's rotted flesh tainting the air. Pheidippides choked as he gasped for another breath, his lungs rejecting the foul intake. And Charon cackled in triumph as the youth's knees buckled and nearly gave way.

The gull sang out again, its avian chirps emitting the melodic chime of the Elysian queen's voice: "By all Elysia, I wish to help you more, but I may not do so!" she exclaimed, fluttering right by his ear. "For *what* do you run, dear Pheidippides?"

The young Athenian inhaled one last painful breath, then forced his knees to hold up his legs as he churned harder, faster through a final stretch of cavernous old willows that drooped down over the trail like weedy fingernails. "I can see her now in all her glory…her graceful buildings rising so golden!" he gasped out defiantly. The snarl of branches and twigs snaked down closer, stroking his shoulders and back, their tips like sharpened nails—the air around him boiling, stinking of rot—as though Charon and a gaggle of moldy corpses joined together in a final effort to seize him. The woody portal at the path's end narrowed all the more. Could he still squeeze through if he managed to reach it?

"*My Athens…My home!*" Pheidippides hollered triumphantly…and burst through the portal of twisted willows. An angry *hiss* ripped the air behind him, followed by a violent thrashing of branches and brambles. A mournful moan of defeat rose from inside the tunnel. Then all was silent.

Pheidippides collapsed to his hands and knees, down onto the rough turf of an open plain.

When finally he was able to crane his neck and gaze behind him, he saw nothing more than a skimpy woodland of soft willows and fir trees, the very ones through which he had marched with the Athenian army barely more than a day ago. He shook his head incredulously, then turned back—and gaped. Standing before him was the ethereal form of Queen Keres, shifting from that of the white gull. She smiled pleasantly at him. "'Twas not me that dispelled cruel Charon of Erebus, Pheidippides. 'Twas *you*. You and your Athens. Now…finish your journey!"

Pheidippides reached out to touch her, but she was gone. "More illusions?" he asked himself aloud, blinking in disbelief. The young courier stared long and thoughtfully at the sparse little woodland, which only moments ago seemed the inner belly of the Hellworlds. He blinked again, dismissing so disturbing a notion, then gritted his teeth in resolve. "I must hasten."

He rose painfully to one knee, using both arms to push strenuously against the dirt-and-stone-riddled turf, till finally steadying himself into a crouch. He stared through the sweltering haze, his throat raw and parched. His eyes widened suddenly.

"I know these rocks!" he exclaimed in recognition of his immediate surroundings. A parody of a laugh coughed up from his throat. "Less than two leagues remain and I shall be at Athens' gates!" Pheidippides forced himself upright, wondering if indeed he could still run a distance he had done so often in the past, then pushed onward in what barely resembled a run.

****

Jamjon veered his horse round a sharp bend of oaks and saw his comrade Rojese cantering his big Persian war steed toward him. The tall Macedonian wore a frown borne of frustration. He eyed the Nubian expectantly.

"This day is not for Persia," Jamjon said flatly as he approached.

"What, by all gods, does that mean?" said Rojese, his frown deepening. The heat and the fruitless search for their remarkably elusive young foot courier had worn greatly on him, and he was in no mood for riddles.

Jamjon simply shook his head.

"Come, Jamjon, I must know more," Rojese insisted, long accustomed to his fellow assassin's occasional strange ways.

"We are best to leave this place," the Nubian

replied mysteriously.

Rojese tugged at his reins and laughed, then saw that his comrade was quite serious. "And just where should we go, then? Our Lord Darius will soon rule here, and—"

"Not this day," said Jamjon.

Rojese sat back in his saddle, running a hand through his beard. The Nubian was serious. "Jamjon, we've still a battle to fight!"

"It has already been fought," the grand black warrior answered. He guided his horse over to his Macedonian comrade, placed a hand to the big man's shoulder, and gestured silently for him to follow. The two men locked eyes for a long moment. With another nod of his head, Jamjon urged his longtime compadre to follow him back up the trail.

Rojese eyed him in utter confusion...then shook his head.

Jamjon smiled a soft farewell and guided his horse off into the thick of the woods.

"Come follow me when you feel right," Rojese called out, then turned and rode off in the direction of Athens.

Jamjon rode on through the mysterious little woodland...then caught sight of a spit of a side path that seemed to have materialized before his eyes where none had been before. Cypress and olive trees and firs leaned over it like an arched leafy gateway. A vibrant but welcoming glow of soft green and red and yellow sprinkled forth from the queer path, and Jamjon could not resist the urge to explore it. No sooner had he directed his great stallion under the overhang of colorful boughs than he heard a queer *thump* behind him, like something sealing up. Before he could turn back and look, the Nubian warrior beheld a sight the likes of which he had never before seen: a tall, smug-looking cross between man and beast, surrounded by several wood nymphs…all of them smiling.

"Greetings, Jamjon!" said Pan merrily.

Chapter Forty-Five

On to Athens

Pheidippides tottered wearily atop a sandy knoll strewn with huge boulders. His throat was parched with thirst and his legs were wobbly; choking breaths came to him at choppy intervals. Through the haze of the late afternoon August heat, and his own sweat-clogged vision, his eyes fell upon a distant sight—one he recognized eagerly: the far-reaching high walls of Athens.

"By all gods—" Pheidippides caught himself in his own oft-spoken proclamation "—Nay...by all Elysia!" he cried hoarsely in as much a voice as he could manage. "I am not too late!"

He was perhaps a half mile from the walled city and did not bear the swagger of one who had endured several trysts with life and death; nor did he flaunt the look of one who had bested his deepest fears in the most daunting odyssey of his short life. Now, a sweat-drenched, bruised husk of a youth tottered along on a pair of unsteady legs as he forced himself across a range of rolling hillocks. But the sight of his beloved Athens—the city walls apparently still intact and with no indication of battle or strife—gave him cause for hope. It lent him a strain of renewed vigor as he drew another long painful breath, threw back the mop of wet hair from his face, and started down the knoll.

He did not get far.

A shape sprang out from behind the thick boulders and tackled him roughly to the ground. Pheidippides went tumbling down in a heap, landing face first on the rocky turf and feeling the wind knocked soundly out of him. A bony knee slammed into the small of his back as he lay there helpless; he heard a coarse laugh and the tramp of more footsteps approaching.

****

Farther back and marching with furious haste— over two leagues behind the struggling courier—the Athenian army crested the steep Pallini Hills. General Milteades, at the fore of the double column of hoplites, called back encouragement for them to hasten all the more, while Captain Boros roamed up and down the ranks, doing the same. The men were clearly exhausted and sweating profusely as they pushed onward. Boros bore that same worry and strain on his rugged face— with the worry of a father compounding his angst all the more.

****

Pheidippides lay flat on his stomach, arms and legs splayed out, his face pressed down onto the stony turf. He could not rise, for the assailant that had sprung upon him from behind still had a hard knee driven into his lower back, arms gripping Pheidippides from the rear by his elbows and holding him virtually immobilized. Fatigue alone made resistance impossible. Any will to try and fight his way back to his feet fizzled away.

"And what have we here?" an older male voice barked out hoarsely with an air of dark delight. Pheidippides thought that voice sounded vaguely familiar, but through the haze and pain of his rattled mind and battered body, he could not place it.

"A little lamb, it seems to me," snickered a younger male voice, one that also rang of familiarity to the stricken courier. These men did not sound like Persians.

"Speak up, then, lamb! Have you money?" demanded the older voice.

Where had he heard this voice before?

"No money," Pheidippides croaked. The weight on his back lessened as the first assailant rose. Rough hands gripped him firmly and twirled him over onto his back. Pheidippides heard gasps of recognition suddenly from both assailants.

"Pheidippides!" cried the younger voice in surprise, now sounding more familiar. Through the fog of his clouded vision, he recognized, hovering directly over him, Barthus, the young Kaboni rogue. And standing next to him was the gaunt elder who led that clan of Athenian outliers: Garathi. A thread of a smile formed instinctively on the young courier's sunburnt face.

"What happened, lad?" asked Garathi, kneeling down and placing a gnarly hand gently on the boy's chest.

"Aye...You look like death itself," quipped Barthus, also kneeling. They helped the exhausted courier into a sitting position.

"Nearly death," Pheidippides forced out from his lips.

"I see you are doing much better since you left us," Barthus added mischievously.

A sharp glance from Garathi wiped the glib grin

from Barthus' tanned face—though Pheidippides himself could not repress a tiny smile at hearing something, anything, from a familiar and friendly voice.

"Water…" he gasped pleadingly. Nodding, Garathi tugged loose a waterskin from the sash at his waist and put it gently to Pheidippides' parched lips. Barthus' own expression grew instantly grim at the pale look of suffering on his friend's sweat-drenched face.

Pheidippides tried speaking again, but choked on his own breath.

"Easy lad, easy. Take your time," said Garathi.

"There is no time," Pheidippides gasped again, trying vainly to rise, but held in place by the rogue leader's strong hands. Barthus placed both his hands on Pheidippides' thin shoulders as Garathi slipped a hand under the courier's chin. The elder's gray eyes peered into the soft brown of the boy's.

"Are you being chased?" he asked, nodding to Barthus to check the pathway behind them.

Barthus glanced down the slope Pheidippides had just climbed, seeing nothing there. Another glance toward the crest of a rocky rise that overlooked the summit of the knoll revealed two figures atop it who peered down at the three of them. Startled for a moment, Barthus rose back to his feet, but then, through the sun's steaming glare, he recognized both figures.

Azelina, the free-spirited girl from the Kaboni ostraka, stood there like a wild sentinel, her dog Atlas at her side. Barthus relaxed at the sight of her and raised a hand in a wave of assurance, then gestured for her to watch, from her vantage point, the trace of a path where Pheidippides had emerged. She nodded solemnly in response. Barthus turned back to Pheidippides.

"How is it you are here?" he asked of the exhausted boy he had come to know as a friend.

"I...come from the great battle at Marathon," Pheidippides eked out. "We are victorious."

Garathi and Barthus both gaped and eyed each other in amazement.

"But the Persians now sail for Athens...I have run here to warn—"

"You say you have *run* here, all the way from Marathon?" exclaimed Barthus. "In heat such as this? Impossible!"

"I do not lie, Barthus!" Pheidippides snapped back, trying again to rise. But Garathi held him back and calmed him with a gesture of one hand.

"No one thinks you are lying to us, lad," the bandit leader assured him. "But small wonder you look so deathly now." Garathi and Barthus exchanged looks of incredulity.

Pheidippides squirmed in their grasp. "Please, I can wait here no longer," he implored. "Assassins chase me, and...and I must go...must warn the Archon."

Garathi helped Pheidippides to his knees, holding him with both arms as though he were his own child. "Fear not, my boy. No assassins shall find you."

"But I must be on my way," Pheidippides pleaded, straining to break free. "The Persians will soon be in Athens!"

"Pah! Why should ostraka care whether it is Darius or the Archon ruling in Athens?" Barthus spat, his hatred of being lower caste to the Athenian elite boiling up from deep inside him.

"*Because we are still Greeks,*" Garathi declared, his tone of indignation and pride unlike any they had heard from the man in the past.

A good dozen or so feet above them, still perched on the huge boulder, Atlas at her side, young Azelina also heard the very words she herself had uttered so passionately that evening in the glen—now spoken with such conviction by Garathi. She marveled as the bandit leader put a hand to Barthus' shoulder and proclaimed: "This brave courier here puts us all to shame." He helped Pheidippides the rest of the way to his feet, then handed him the waterskin. "It is *our* city too, good Pheidippides," he said. "Now go and finish your quest."

"Garathi!" cried Azelina from above them. She had turned her gaze away from the three below for but an instant and spotted something coming up the hillock trail that froze her blood. "A rider comes...in battle armor!"

She squinted and made out the tall, burly form of Rojese guiding his huge roan slowly over the rock-strewn ground. The Macedonian horseman was perhaps a mere stade away and unaware he had been spied approaching from the quarter-mile distance.

Garathi nodded and gestured her to come down as he prepped Pheidippides to press on.

Atlas scurried down in advance of the lithe young woman, both dashing over to Pheidippides as he took another long draught from the waterskin. His entire face smiled warmly as Azelina and her loyal dog rushed over to him, the girl shedding tears as she hustled up and hugged him tightly.

"Oh...Pheidippides," she choked as she beheld, up close, his frail condition.

"You must go on now, my boy," said Garathi. He turned and eyed savagely the direction from which he knew the rider Azelina had sighted would soon appear. "No Persian henchman shall pass this mount...be it Darius himself," he added with a cold assurance.

Barthus' eyes danced with a dark delight at his mentor's words. "Yes, run on, my friend," the young rogue added assuringly. "And we shall do our part as Greeks...here."

Pheidippides stared at the small group of Kaboni ostraka, wondering if there were any in all of Athens who might dare question the loyalty and will of those not even recognized as citizens.

"You are more than Athenian...all of you," he said quietly.

Azelina leaned forward and kissed him, then called to her dog. "Let Atlas run with you the rest of your way and sound your coming," she said, eying the exhausted courier with pride.

Pheidippides nodded warmly, then turned and started down the knoll, Atlas in tow.

Garathi motioned to the other two. "Come, we have work."

Chapter Forty-Six

The Persian Advance

From the prow of the Persian flagship, Captain
Kazek peered out at the nearing shores of southern
Greece. The massive war fleet had already rounded the
Hellespont's southern tip, passing the tiny islets north
of Naxos, and now veered northerly again toward the
bay of Phaleron—little more than a march of four
stades—barely a mile from Athens. The grand city-state
would be unaware of its peril—an assault from a
Persian horde marching down from Marathon more
anticipated. Sentries would likely be posted on the
city's high walls or on the hillocks not far from the
gates, Hippias had assured them all. The eyes of Athens
would be peering in the wrong direction, Kazek thought
as the flagship plowed on through the warm Aegean
waters—unless by some miracle, or through some quirk
of fate (or favor) granted them by the gods, the courier
from Marathon had eluded Darius' two prized assassins
and managed to alert the city.

Even so, with the bulk of the Athenian army
having had to engage the trapped soldiers the Persian
king had so callously abandoned, then having to march
over eight leagues back to Athens in time to intercept a
force that still greatly outnumbered them, a Greek
victory was beyond what anyone of sound military

sense might conceive.

The fleet commander could already imagine the Persian Lord basking in the praise of General Mardonius and his two groveling satraps as they all assured themselves the Athenian courier had either been captured or slain by the assassins. And, as with the loyal warriors Darius had left stranded at Marathon to slow down the Greek forces, the Persian king had also left both assassins to their own fate after they were not sighted on the coastal jetty for re-boarding.

"The Macedonian and the Nubian are capable enough of finding their own way to Athens—with that hapless courier as their prisoner or with his corpse lashed to one of their horses," Darius had quipped. "If not, they can suffer their own incompetence by roaming these soon-to-be Persian lands till they do surface again. Neither is a true-blood of our homeland anyway," he had added callously.

The Great King had been even less gracious when speaking of the men he left stranded on the shores of Marathon: "I prefer warriors of a more heroic sort," Darius had retorted when Fleet Commander Kazek had expressed concern over leaving them to be slaughtered by the Greeks as the Persian ships set course for Athens. "It is a sign of blundering cowardice to wander into ambush and then retreat in the face of an enemy that is so outnumbered," the flustered king had proclaimed, his dark eyes flashing with an anger also directed at General Mardonius. The general had bristled under the rebuke, but said nothing, nor had the two squeamish satraps, Datis and Artaphernes, nor had the onetime Athenian tyrant Hippias spoken up—knowing the grand city would soon be his to govern again.

Kazek's hawklike face grimaced as the flagship now veered starboard and toward the distant coastal landing of Phaleron. He heard the Lord Darius again proclaiming triumph in spite of the debacle at Marathon: "'Twas our divine god, Mithra himself, whose will it surely was that we conquer and suppress these treacherous Athenians in this coy manner instead. That mishap at Marathon occurred merely so we might employ a more cunning maneuver—one that I have deemed better suited for demonstrating our right to lands destined to be part of the Persian Empire!"

Kazek shook his head in bitter angst, thinking back on the men sacrificed so coldly this day—and on past campaigns too. And he shivered at the notion of any ruler daring to equate himself with the gods, while also denigrating those who disagreed with or failed to fully flatter him. The tall captain bit down on his lip as he considered how there was no sign yet that the two assassins had indeed captured or killed the Athenian courier; nor could he dismiss how valiantly those intrepid Greeks had fought at Marathon, and under such crafty leadership.

For here in this land of dreadfully rough country, the terrain itself seemed a living enemy—while its people apparently found war to be a way of life. After all, he had heard from Hippias himself how the Greeks had been at it for hundreds of years in these forsaken Hellespont lands. The onetime tyrant had presented to Darius a weakness here to be exploited...a people so lacking in unity that conquest was inevitable. But even Hippias failed to recognize what the Greeks themselves regarded as their agonistic spirit—their competitive ferocity. For indeed, those Athenian devils at Marathon had seemed far more committed to the defense of their home than Great King Darius' invading army of countless more had seemed committed to conquering it. Captain Kazek continued peering out at the coastline, still distant, and wishing it could stay that way.

****

On foot, Rojese guided his roan carefully through the rock-riddled turf of the jagged slopes. Having finally crested the summit of the sandy knoll, the big Macedonian gazed down over a much flatter plain that led to the majestic walled city-state of Athens looming in the distance. And sure enough, there was the staggering figure of the slender courier he and Jamjon had trailed for leagues. He squinted, as it appeared that a large dog or perhaps a wolf trotted alongside the youth now. Odd, the Persian henchman thought, as so much in this strange land had been. How had this fleeing lad—

His musings were rudely interrupted by a hard sting he felt through his helm! Rojese thought he had been struck by an arrow or a spear, so sound an impact it had made upon the steel casing that covered his head. Instinctively he reached a hand up to feel for a wound, his brain fairly ringing from it. He grunted loudly and craned his neck back and forth to see where the missile had come from. And as he did, another blow of the same sort struck him alongside his head, clanging again into his helm. "By all devils, what—"

He was cut off by a taunt. "Ho, Persian scum! I bear word of your filthy fleet sailing for Athens!"

Rojese glimpsed another rock being thrown expertly at him. He barely avoided it and glanced up, seeing none other than Barthus perched above on a high boulder, gesturing obscenely at him and readying himself for another throw. The Kaboni teen's sneering voice in itself grated on the assassin's already worn nerves. Rojese cursed aloud and measured the distance between him and the swaggering youth goading him from atop the overlooking boulder.

"I, too, bear a message from the Archon of Athens…Persian coward!" cried a defiant young female voice—just as another large stone came sizzling through the air at him from a rocky alcove farther down the slope that led toward the city. He failed to dodge it, and it caught him squarely in the chest, only his thick metal breastplate dulling the stone's savage impact.

"Which of us do you chase, scum?" Azelina shouted. "One of us will live to warn our city!" She waved her arms in a deliberate taunt, beckoning Rojese to mount his horse and give chase.

The hefty assassin did indeed start to mount, but then a hail of rocks rained down on him from nearly every direction. One large stone caught him square on the cheekbone as he hung there with a single foot in the stirrup and woefully out of balance. It threw his equilibrium off enough to make him topple back over and land with a hard smack on the ground. Rojese bellowed like an enraged water buffalo, his fury powering his lungs more than the pain of the fall. What new strange allies aided this elusive lad that he and Jamjon had first thought to be so simple a catch for them? And exactly what had his bold longtime comrade encountered earlier that had caused him to abandon the chase?

A loud snort interrupted his thoughts as his steed reared onto its hind legs, then neighed furiously. The roan settled back onto all fours, dropped its head down, and nudged its sprawled rider anxiously, twisting its head back toward the direction from where they had come. "Time to leave this place," the horse's glossy eyes seemed to say.

Rojese grunted and raised his head, his vision blurred from the impact of the rocks that had battered his helm and from the force of the impact when he had pitched backward onto the hard turf. He glimpsed what appeared to be a fair number of figures scattered along the crests of the jagged row of high nearby boulders and knolls. One, in particular—a tall, gaunt fellow with a rascally sort of grace—gave him a mock salute, then hurled another rock his way. A veritable fusillade of stones followed, and Rojese scrambled backward in crab fashion toward the cover of some brambles and the other large rocks his horse had indicated earlier with a heave of its snout.

"Aye!" he acknowledged, and followed the loyal beast to the safety of a stony outcrop. He would not chase this accursed courier any longer. "Darius be damned," he muttered grimly as he scrambled his way out of range of the sizzling barrage of rocks, while enduring the cackles that followed his forced retreat.

****

Rounding the Cape of Sounier, the Persian flagship led its massive fleet of war galleys down swiftly through the bay of Phaleron, where rolling mounds loomed over an open sandy beach that would soon host the horde of invaders. How similar it seemed to Marathon, thought Captain Kazek...and a tinge of unwelcome dread seeped through him as he stared out at what appeared would be a clear and smooth beaching on the nearing shores.

The breeze in the bay was softer than the potent winds that had powered the fleet swiftly down the Hellespont coast. The disembarking and coordination of their forces would be slowed a bit, but the Persian commander felt confident the army from Marathon would not be among the city's forthcoming defense. Kazek knew that in itself would offer some comfort to King Darius.

As if on cue, he heard the Persian lord chortling: "Now…if our two worthy assassins have done their deed properly with that nuisance of a courier, we will lose few men here. And in spite of vile untruths spread by the likes of couriers and bards and other messengers of malice, we will rule in Athens this very day, and then eliminate all leaders of their dangerous 'Rule of the People' forever! Heh! Let their army from Marathon die outside Athens' walls trying to take their precious city back from our legions…This entire Hellespont land shall be a prize for all Persia to flaunt!"

****

Pheidippides stumbled along, less than a half-mile from the city's walls. He was spent from an abrupt burst of speed he had put on in all his eagerness to finally complete the grueling ordeal he had undergone since late morning. Now, deep into the waning afternoon, the sun still blazing down on his scorched skin, and with nothing left in Garathi's waterskin which he had wrung dry, his arms flailed and his knees buckled uncontrollably.

He reached down toward Atlas running at his side and steadied himself by gripping the thick fur round the dog's strong neck. More than once that had saved him from pitching forward and going down. But this time his knees finally gave way and down he went, losing his grip and landing face first on the ground. A ghost of a cry belched up from his throat, audible only to his canine companion.

"No..." he barely eked out. "*Not now*. Not so close!" He could utter nothing more, able only to lift his chin mere inches so he might glimpse the city walls and somehow gauge the distance left.

Atlas had been trying to tug him along, associating the walls looming ahead of them with home. But the young human struggling alongside him had finally lost all strength and gone down. The dog whined in dismay, then trotted back to where the prone boy lay on the ground, eyes raised and staring desperately toward the nearby walls.

Chapter Forty-Seven

A Battle to the Finish

The walls of Athens loomed in the near distance like glossy sea waves as they seemed to shimmer under the sun's glow. Did the gods of Olympus—or Elysia—truly care whether Athens would stand or give way to the devils of Persia? In the mind of the stricken young foot courier, armored demons rampaged through the city. He envisioned them slaying all in their path, mercilessly hacking people to death; he saw them tumbling sacred temples to the ground, and putting to flames the stalls of vendors and artisans; and he saw them pillaging the dwellings of the wealthy, while also ruining simple homes like the one that housed his mother and him.

Pheidippides thought of cherished places like the dreamy little pond where he had sat and etched out his poem about his love for Athens in all her soulful dignity and all that she might become. But no longer…for the Persian tyrant Darius would ruin their grand city, just as he had ruined the island home of the Eretrians.

"*No…*" his heart cried out. No! He, Pheidippides, *would not permit it*. He did not come this far only to collapse when strength mattered most. He would crawl, if need be, to those gates…or his ghost would do so and give warning to everyone if he himself could not!

He strained to rise, then felt his face was soaking wet. Something rough ran incessantly over his cheek. A soft but firm whine, one of urgency, found his ears. Pheidippides forced his eyes open wider—and knew it was Azelina's dog Atlas licking him round the face and barking at him. With one last surge of failing energy, the exhausted young courier gripped the dog by its powerful shoulders and neck and hauled himself painfully to his feet.

"Thank you, my loyal friend," the boy gasped. "Now we run to Athens…together." Refusing to fall again, Pheidippides pushed on with all that his weary legs could deliver and made for the city walls in the near distance, Atlas at his side barking in encouragement.

****

Sergeant Ambrus Kellos stood at his post on the platform that jutted out from the fifteen-foot-high wooden wall that encircled Athens. His keen eyes scanned the plain that stretched out before the city. The vigilant hoplite almost wished he would catch sight of the outlandishly garbed Persian legions nearly everyone had anticipated here in the waning hours of the sweltering summer afternoon. Few had truly held any hope of even a master tactician like General Milteades defeating the Persian King's mass of invaders. Only those who chose to delude themselves knew the most they might expect was a valiant effort at Marathon to perhaps impair the Persians—enough to at least weaken them for their long march through the day's brutal heat. It might then result in a less spirited attack on a city fortified by towering walls.

Kellos had lamented how he and other hoplites had

been ordered to remain behind with the remnants of a citizens' militia for Athens' final defense. They would much rather have marched off with the others and met these dread invaders spear for spear, sword to sword, club against club on the plains of Marathon. But some were needed for a likely final stand at the city itself. So they would now make this "Great King Darius" pay dearly for his coveted conquest here...even without Athens having drawn aid from their Spartan kin, whose presence would indeed have troubled the enemy.

Now Kellos recalled the touching words of the young poet—words that had been read aloud in the agora by High Archon Kallimachos. They had not been lost on anyone in the city who still believed in the promise of something beyond a world that favored only the few. His bark-brown eyes roamed the plain with a never-ending scrutiny—and then stopped abruptly.

There!

Approaching the city gates was a lean figure, tottering from side to side and seemingly on the verge of collapse. It was...a boy, in his late teens, it appeared, and he was no more than a mere stade away. He wore no armor and certainly did not seem to pose any martial threat.

Alongside the struggling lad trotted what looked to be either a large dog, or perhaps a *wolf?* Whichever, the animal held close to the swaying boy and seemed to stay in step with him deliberately. And no sooner than this spent young runner lost his balance and stumbled, he reached a hand down to the canine at his side to prevent himself from toppling to the ground. Righting himself once more, while clutching the animal's thick fur, the boy raised an arm and waved feebly yet frantically in the direction of the watchtower, and the canine at his side barked excitedly.

Ambrus Kellos felt a surge of fire in his blood. "A courier...a *courier* approaches!" The hoplite turned and scrambled down the wooden steps leading from the sentry post and to the street path below. "Part the gates!" he hollered vigorously. "A courier finally!"

****

Pheidippides saw only hazy images of the pebble-and-dirt streetpath he had run so many times past when returning home from his treks to regional villages and back during his delivery routes. A stretch of stony dwellings loomed on either side like ghostly sentinels. He gasped and heaved, nearly doubling over, but would not allow the hoplite jogging alongside him to assist him—other than serving as a means of steadying himself, as with Atlas trotting in step on his other side.

He would finish this quest on his own.

Choking on his own breath, the boy fought the pain that tightened every muscle of his body into a blistering knot; he imposed his will over his aching legs as he staggered finally out into the wider pathway that led toward the agora and the Bouleuterion Council area. Ambrus Kellos had already belted out commands to summon the Archon and his Council, while people had gathered and were cheering themselves hoarse at the sight of this daring young hero: one who had raced all the way from Marathon—through the day's scorching heat—with word of their fate!

Pheidippides heard the cheers...heard the praise...heard the hoplite guardsman running along beside him and assuring him with, "That's a good, brave lad!" Tears rolled down the young courier's cheek. With Atlas hugging one side of him and Ambrus Kellos on the other—both supporting him and keeping the battered youth from tumbling over—they finally reached the lower stairs of the Bouleuterion, where Archon Kallimachos and his personal hoplite guard had arrived.

Seeing only glossy images now of columns, temples, stoas—and Athenian citizens everywhere—young Pheidippides knew he had finally prevailed! No Persian foe had yet to assail Athens. Not yet. With one last surge of his failing strength, he freed himself from his hold on Atlas and from the noble hoplite who had first sighted him out on the plain, took two more wobbly steps toward the Archon, and collapsed at the stately city leader's feet.

"Rejoice Athenians...*We conquer at Marathon!*" he gasped out hoarsely. "But beware, Archon, *the Persian fleet sails this way...to Phaleron!*"

With that, Pheidippides lost all sense of time and place, all awareness fading as his mind passed into oblivion...even as a woman he would have recognized cried out from among the hoplite guards at her son's collapse.

Chapter Forty-Eight

Phaleron

Darius smirked as the flagship of the vast Persian fleet, guided by Captain Kazek, coasted through the bay of Phaleron. "This man is indeed a master of seamanship," the Great King mused wryly to himself. For, in spite of fickle winds that had often failed and threatened to impair their progress, Kazek had engineered the war fleet with greater speed than the elements should have allowed. For that accomplishment alone, Darius admired his surly captain. But the man's incessant questioning—perhaps even doubting his King's choices—would need to be addressed once their campaign in these strange Hellespont lands was over. All underlings, be they slave, subject, satrap, or of military status, needed to know their responsibilities… and their place. The greatness and glory of the Persian Empire was always foremost. And that began with everyone understanding fealty to their King.

The ships beached and moored near the rolling shoreline hills, not a single Athenian visible. Standing on the flagship deck, both satraps—Datis and Artaphernes—along with General Mardonius and Hippias, all chortled their congratulations to one another…and to Lord Darius. The impending victory was, of course, due to this cunning scheme conceived by the Great King himself.

Fleet Commander Kazek, however, eyed the sloping shoreline uncomfortably. "Not unlike Marathon," he thought, disquieted. He watched warily as gangplanks were lowered and warriors began disembarking. The entire beach area was deserted. Other than the steady lap and crash of waves—the clink of armor, weapons and shields, and the creaking of ships gliding into the shallows, mixed with the groan of gangplanks—no sound other than the screech of gulls wheeling overhead was heard.

General Mardonius had dispatched a squadron of officers and commanders onto the shore to coordinate the disembarking soldiers, and to assemble them into marching formation while the rest of the ships beached and moored. A number of soldiers were sent on ahead for reconnaissance of the surrounding hillocks.

They did not get far.

From behind those hills…and from just beyond their summits…from passageways leading out from higher mounds farther up the beach—*warriors charged!* Most were civilian militia wearing the olive-green colors of Athens—men and even some women, all armed with spears, axes, clubs, rocks, roared down upon the Persian invaders, while directing this charging mass was a smaller group of armored hoplites wielding swords and shields. How many charged the beach could not be determined.

"By Mithra…Are these the same demons that sprang from the hills and ground at Marathon?" boomed Darius, wide-eyed and instantly disheartened. He watched in horror as they swooped down upon his own legions that had barely begun gathering on the beach—men who had not even had time to assemble into battle formation. Precious few were able to muster together a proper defense.

"The courier!" General Mardonius snarled. "These cannot be the same devils from Marathon. Impossible!"

"And what of your two fine assassins?" Darius roared.

Both satraps avoided their king's sweeping, accusing eyes. Mardonius muttered something under his breath, and it was fortunate for him that the Persian lord did not hear it. Hippias, meanwhile, tried placating Darius: "Great King, I—"

"Be still!" Darius hissed. "It was from your knowledge of these coasts, these moorings, *of this very site*, that we entrusted our way to you!"

Horrified, the wretched Greek elder skulked away. Hippias feared he might well be better off leaping overboard and trying to swim ashore than staying to face his Persian Lord's wrath.

The invaders on shore were in disarray, but what happened next would turn doubt into panic.

From the deck of the flagship, a silent Captain Kazek gaped as he beheld a squadron of advancing apparitions...as did a lone, mounted figure from high on the summit of a nearby knoll.

Rojese, having finally evaded the vicious rock assault by Garathi's thirty-some Kaboni rogues, now stared down at the spectacle of the same ambush that had routed the Persian force at Marathon. His mind refused to acknowledge what his own eyes verified: this land itself—its very trees and rocks and brush—seemed *ally* to its people. How foolish a war Persia's "Great King" had sought to wage here, the big Macedonian thought as he watched. Hah! Waged upon a people for whom war itself seemed *welcome*. The mightiest of empires could not overcome people of such resolve. "How could you have known, friend Jamjon?" he heard himself murmur.

As if in answer, Rojese found his grim musings interrupted by what seemed a veritable chorus of discordant voices. His jaw dropped at the fearsome sight he beheld on the rocky plain below. Was it some dread illusion caused by the stifling heat he had endured all day? For he felt sure he now saw, rising from the ground itself—even emerging out of the moist air—a ghostly legion of red-cloaked, armored warriors—bestial in appearance! The big man blinked, wondering in a rare shiver of horror if this might indeed be but a fearful vision brought on by the day's strife. For there they were—merging into the fray of the battle and attacking only the Persian soldiers.

Panic filled the ranks of Darius' warriors, who were already stunned by a second unexpected Greek ambush this day. *And now this?* The slaughter that followed was dreadful to behold.

Watching from the prow of his flagship, Great King Darius appeared suddenly all too human to his equally terrified underlings. Perspiration poured down his ruddy face, while his large hands trembled. He stuffed them quickly into the folds of his leopard skin robes, not wanting another soul to witness the abject terror seeping over him. But every one of his underlings had already seen.

"What manner of beast-men do these Greeks command?" the Persian king gasped, the fear in his voice palpable.

"Perhaps they are the fierce Spartans we have heard of, Great King?" Datis the satrap uttered in a shaky whisper. The man's knees shook as he spoke.

"Aye, it is said the Spartans bring terrible sounding horns into battle with them that frighten their enemies into submission," Artaphernes added nervously.

"Then Spartans are more beast than man...for look at them!" grunted General Mardonius, his dark eyes filled with fear at the appearance alone of a warrior legion that did seem more animal than human. The discordant moans and cacophony of sour music—if music it could be called—was enough to drive any enemy away. Yet the Athenians themselves did not seem aware of these strange allies.

"Devils cannot be defeated when the gods too have turned against us," Darius moaned.

No one heard Captain Kazek snicker to himself at that. He repressed a sardonic little smile before speaking. "If devils they are," Kazek said mysteriously, "then all on board our ships might fall prey to them too."

Darius paled, his eyes shifting superstitiously back to the battle on the shore where his men-of-arms were being brutally slaughtered by the fierce Athenians, who now sensed a dispirited foe, seemingly stricken all the more by some terror that could not be explained.

The Persian king did not hesitate. "If Lord Mithra desired that we conquer this land today, then why did the plans of my own governors and commanders—and a sniveling Greek traitor—fail so miserably?" he proclaimed accusingly. "Next time, I myself will lay the plans for conquest." His eyes roamed everywhere. "Prepare to make sail...We return to Persia!"

Everyone on deck but for Captain Kazek stared at their King, agape.

"But sire," urged Mardonius, "those men of ours ashore—"

"They failed once more to prevail. I dare not anger the gods further by tarrying here so cowards among us may turn and flee to safety. We sail!"

"Aye…Great King," said Kazek, knowing in his heart that once back in their homeland he himself would not remain a single day longer in a land ruled by a madman.

"And bring that bumbling fool Hippias to me," said Darius. "He and I have much to discuss."

****

From atop the knoll, and still mounted, Rojese continued to watch, wiping his craggy, sweat-drenched brow. His huge hands shook, and he finally wrenched his gaze from the gruesome massacre taking place below on the sands of Phaleron. He urged his steed round…then blinked. Yet another improbable sight greeted his eyes. Barely a half stade away, and on a grinding force-march, was the Athenian army of hoplites and militia that had fought at Marathon—supported by the Plataian legion—rushing to join the battle on this very shore!

Rojese drew in a deep breath, then guided his roan down the knoll and north toward the wild Greek inland. Perhaps he might stay north instead and seek his way back to his homeland of Macedonia… Yes, he was sure of it.

Chapter Forty-Nine

Athens…and Beyond

Pheidippides ran through a beautiful forest of towering pines and sturdy oaks and other rich trees. It was lovely. The grove he passed through was an absolute splendor, reminding him of nearly every cozy wood that had ever blessed him with comfort and grace. Grapes hung low from swooping boughs, while cypress trees spread their curling branches wide enough overhead to allow in sunlight—providing him with soothing warmth, as well as a welcoming soft breeze.

The young courier's body felt strong and potent, no longer the aching frame that had barely eked out his words of victory and the dire warning of impending menace. All around were magnificent animals and birds, even colorful insects flying by—and so he ran on blissfully, viewing his surroundings as he would the fleeting images of a painting too vibrant to be contained in a frame.

And always there was light—a fair golden light. Pheidippides threw back his head to let loose a shout that would proclaim his sensation of bliss…but only a choking gasp escaped his throat. Abruptly, the trees and wildlife and tantalizing sunlight were gone as he coughed painfully and stared straight up into the face of…Captain Boros.

"Rejoice…we conquer," his father said softly, his ruggedly handsome face wearing an even softer smile. Pheidippides blinked, and his eyes shifted from side to side as the ethereal woodland in which he had left all pain and angst behind had faded, and his memory of the day's grueling trial returned in the same roiling rush as when he had departed the dreamy world of Elysia.

"Where…?" he croaked hoarsely.

"You are in Athens' honored Hall of Healing, my boy—where only those permitted by the Archon himself may be treated," said Boros.

Pheidippides shut his eyes in quiet astonishment, and when he opened them again, he saw that Boros was flanked by Archon Kallimachos…and by Symethra. His mother's tanned, gentle face gazed down at him in loving pride, but with a contained sorrow too. He felt her hand holding his own.

"How…" he whispered. His other hand dangled down over the side of the soft bed. It was resting on something living, something furry: Atlas. Pheidippides smiled.

Boros put a thick finger gently to his son's lips. "Your warning came in time, and so there was little for us to do once we arrived, other than capture the few Persians that wretch Darius left behind."

Another tiny smile formed on Pheidippides' face. He did not see the elder physician glance over to the Archon, then to Boros and Symethra. The man sadly shook his head. But the boy himself could feel the strength of life ebbing from his own body.

General Milteades also stood to one side of the dying youth, his helmet in one hand. The husky commander leaned over the bed, his face a mix of sorrow and pride. Two other robed figures, meanwhile, lurked in the shadows of an alcove, watching silently.

"It seems the Great King Darius thought all of Greece had united at Phaleron, awaiting him," the general proclaimed. "And all because you, young Pheidippides, arrived in Athens with time enough for those in the city to surprise those Persian swine as we did at Marathon…where I'm told you proved yourself a warrior on the battlefield too."

A chorus of "ayes" and "praise Pheidippides" erupted throughout the sparkling marble hall.

Another tall figure, garbed in a long samite himation and sandals, sidled up behind Boros. Pheidippides could not see who it was through the haze of his failing vision. But he squeezed his mother's hand tightly as he realized the most important dignitaries in all of Athens were all gathering round him.

"There is more," said Boros, leaning down closer to his son. "The bold hoplite, Ambrus Kellos, who first spotted you and later helped lead the ambush at Phaleron, said the Persians saw…something else that appeared to have alarmed them."

"A legion of *beast-warriors*, so some of our prisoners claimed," said a voice that Pheidippides recognized as belonging to Kellos. "At first a number of Persians believed it was our Spartan kin come to aid us, for the fierce-looking helms and red-cloaked armor our cousins wear have alarmed many a past foe."

"And though Sparta did indeed finally come, it was much later, as dark began to fall," added Milteades, looking as puzzled as the rest. "No, 'twas not the Spartans they saw coming to assist us."

"One Pheidippides is worth a hundred Spartans," a

quiet voice said solemnly. The tall, slender figure dressed in the samite himation stooped down at the side of the bed and stared fondly at the young courier. It was none other than Zagorus, the hemeredrome who had run to Sparta and back seeking the aid of those who had come too late to the battle. "We both know who the Persians saw at Phaleron," Zagorus added quietly.

"Lord Pan...and his legions," said the dying boy. "I saw him...in Elysia."

Zagorus nodded gently, placing a hand on the boy's chest, then turned to the others, expectation in his eyes. This time there was no sign of skepticism or doubt on the face of anyone.

"A great figure with a horned head is what our prisoners spoke of," agreed General Milteades.

Zagorus gazed down once more into the eyes of the dying young courier, and they exchanged a solemn look of understanding. The famed elite courier raised a hand to his own forehead and followed with a touch to the head of Pheidippides in gentle farewell. Zagorus then rose and stepped back.

Pheidippides' eyes glittered with a quiet light. He started to speak, but Symethra, still kneeling, nudged closer to him. "Do not try to speak more, my boy," she urged softly. "We will—"

"*Our* boy," Boros said, putting a hand over hers. He turned his head, the intelligent hazel eyes roaming the room and meeting with those of everyone gathered round the boy. "*Our* son. Let all of Athens know my shame for denying, for so long, a son that any man would be proud of..." He turned his gaze tenderly on Symethra, adding, "And a woman the most fortunate of men could ever hope for in a wife."

A silence fell over the room, and Captain Boros of the Elite Hoplite Guard knew well the significance of what he had just proclaimed. His words, in essence, defied accepted Athenian mores. Pheidippides summoned all the strength he could from his quivering innards and reached an arm up from where it rested on the dog Atlas' shoulders, to place it gently on Boros' arm; he followed by taking the hand that still held his mother's and joined it with his father's.

The silence in the room still reigned and might have remained unbroken but for a commotion erupting at the arched entry to the Healing Hall. General Milteades and Kellus both turned to the entryway, instantly on the alert. A fiery teenage girl, bronze-skinned and slim, burst through the archway and straight through a pair of acolytes trying to restrain her. Just as abruptly, Atlas rose and turned, growling at the two frustrated acolytes. Two raggedly dressed men followed after the girl.

"Pardon, sires," said one of them. "These ostraka are quite slippery and—"

"Lay your hands off them!" a woman's voice commanded.

Everyone in the hall—including Pheidippides lying weakened on the bed—stared in astonishment to see it was Symethra who had uttered the sharp command. "These are my son's *friends*," she added in a quieter but equally assertive tone.

Archon Kallimachos raised a hand to quell the commotion. He eyed the scamp of a girl, Azelina, then regarded the rangy Garathi and cocky Barthus behind her. "These are the...outliers who saved our Pheidippides from the assassin who pursued him?"

Symethra nodded solemnly.

Kallimachos turned back to face the three Kaboni rogues. "The lad spoke of you while in his stricken slumber, and of how you aided him. You are welcome here…Athenians."

The Archon gestured them over to the bedside. Barthus hustled over first and squeezed through, kneeling at Pheidippides' side. "All the Kaboni welcomes you, good friend—in this world or the next."

Azelina was already in tears. "I will not forget you…ever," she said through her sobs, then leaned over and kissed him tenderly.

Pheidippides forced out a hoarse whisper: "Met someone like you this day…" He reached up and touched her cheek, then brought his hand back to cover his heart. Azelina stayed a moment more with him, Symethra reaching over to hug her. Finally the teenager rose, she and Barthus stepping back with Garathi— though the ever-protective Atlas remained by the dying boy's side.

The Archon leaned in closer to Pheidippides, bearing a beautiful wreath of gold-tinted leaves. He knelt by the boy. Eyes widened in amazement at the sight of the most elevated and dignified of figures in Athens kneeling so reverently at the side of a teenage boy—one who had never been recognized as a citizen. Kallimachos placed the beautiful wreath over the brow of the dying courier.

"A grand temple shall be erected to honor Lord Pan of Elysia," the Archon declared firmly. Heads nodded in agreement. Pheidippides caught sight of Zagorus smiling at him knowingly. The Archon rose. "And great odes shall be written of Pheidippides, beloved son to

Symethra and Boros…and of his gallant run to save Athens!"

"Aye!" a chorus of voices sounded once more in respectful agreement.

Pheidippides squeezed the hands of both his parents, ran a hand affectionately over the neck of the wolfish dog cuddling closer to him now, then smiled a strained but peaceful smile…and died.

The physician tugged the sheet over the boy's head.

"Never has there lived a braver warrior," said Milteades.

"Or one so favored by the gods," proclaimed a coarse, gentle voice from the alcove shadows.

No one in the entire hall seemed to have heard the voice…for no one had budged. But the limp form of Pheidippides stirred slightly at the sound of it.

The two robed figures previously concealed in the shadows of the marble alcove stepped out now—though none of those gathered round the body of Pheidippides noticed them.

None but Atlas, who sensed a presence. He stirred and wriggled his way out from the bed where the body of the boy lay. The huge dog was suddenly aware of something rising from the bed—a shape he recognized as familiar.

"It is time now, Pheidippides."

The commanding voice of Pan, Lord of Elysia, reverberated throughout the elegant temple hall…heard only by Atlas, who had glimpsed the shadowy image of Pheidippides' spirit drifting over the bed while everyone else continued kneeling there. And now Pheidippides saw clearly the Lord of Elysia looming before him—with Queen Keres hovering beside Pan.

"The temple they will build to me is much appreciated, of course, but it takes a good deal more to allow one into the Realm of Elysia." With a single swipe of one arm, Pan caused a large portal to materialize out of the room's very air—revealing the lovely, serene realm Pheidippides had romped through before opening his eyes to the Hall of Healing. The boy stared, flabbergasted.

"A much greater promise was kept by you this day," Pan said with pride.

"A promise some might have scorned at first, but a promise *someone* has finally come to understand," Keres said, smiling tenderly. "It is said that Elysians live on…so others may live better."

Pheidippides glanced back one more time at those gathered around his earthly body. "Behold my shell," he said knowingly. And Keres led him by the hand and through the portal…into Elysia.

But not before the antics of Atlas caused Boros and Symethra…and Azelina, to glance up and behold the ethereal form of Pheidippides stepping into the beautiful world of the Elysians.

Author's Note

Though I did blend into this fable a mix of history, mythology, and ancient Greek legend, I hold true to its essence—the origins of democracy and how this event did indeed determine its fate. Many historians stated clearly that had the Athenians not held at Marathon (and later at Phaleron), the Persians would have swept through the entire country, and the ancient Greek culture we know would have been aborted. More than the origins of the marathon race began with this telling moment in history; the notion of "Rule of the People" would have been lost in the ashes of a visionary old culture, but for the courage displayed that day.

I also found it prudent to emphasize the proverbial *voice of youth*...one well worth heeding.

You may find similarities in this saga to contemporary national and world events. Coincidence?

A word about the author...

Nicholas Checker is a published author of two novels, *Scratch* and *Druids*, and a number of short stories that have appeared in the literary market.

He has written several independent short films that have been featured in cinemas and in film festivals across the country—including *The Curse of Micah Rood*, which featured former sitcom star Ron Palillo of the old *Welcome Back, Kotter* TV series.

In addition, he has also written stage plays that have been produced, including performances at the prestigious Eugene O'Neill Theater Center in Waterford, Connecticut.

This current novel is an adaptation of a musical stage play he wrote, which has seen several successful productions: *Run to Elysia* (music and lyrics by Rick Spencer).

Nicholas Checker also writes freelance news features and teaches creative writing to adult and teenage students, many of whom have been published and produced.

He is also proud of his Greek heritage from both parents, Lillian and Peter Checker, and of having run two marathons—Marine Corps and New York—among many other races of varying distances.